Indigo

To Betty

Indigo

Latrell E. Mickler

Latrell S. Mickler

Contents

THIS BOOK IS DEDICATED TO
MY WONDERFUL HUSBAND YULEE.

PROLOGUE

"A boy brought this for you while you and Ana were at church, Mis' Caty," Mandy said, holding out a small package.

Puzzled, Caterina took the package and removed the wrapping to find a small, black book that tugged on some long buried memory. The pages were ragged and dirty, and half the book had been torn away.

"What is it, Mama?" asked Ana.

Shaken, Caterina answered, "I don't know, Ana. I'm going to my room, and I don't want to be disturbed."

Entering her room, she closed the door and sat in the chair by the window where the light was good. With trembling hands she opened the book and began to read.

March 10, 1768. Dr. Turnbull agreed to let us go to Florida to work on his plantation with Rafael and all the others. We sail soon on the ship HOPE. I think that's a good sign, because we all have lots of hope about going to live in Florida where the land is fertile and green, and there are no droughts. We will be indentured to Dr. Turnbull for six years, at the end of which we will be given land.

Rafael wants to marry me and take me with him as his bride. Mama and Papa think I am too young to marry. They decided to

come to Florida with us, so we will not be separated. We have been
promised to each other for so long.

Minorca has suffered a severe drought for three years, and things
have not been good for any of us. We have lost many animals, and the
crops will not grow.

March 31, 1786. We are on board the Hope. Minorca looks like
a pile of gray rocks jutting out of an emerald sea behind us. Mama is
already seasick.

May 17, 1768. Mama died yesterday. She had been sick since we
left Minorca. Many older people and babies have died. Many more are
sick, including Papa. Father Camps holds a Mass for them. They
wrap the bodies and slide them overboard.

I hurt so bad. I'll never see Mama again on this earth. I'm scared
Papa will just give up. Conditions are worse here than they were at
home. But there is nothing we can do now except go on and hope and
pray.

April 12, 1768. Papa passed away a week ago. He just didn't
want to get well without Mama. It would have been better if I had come
without them. If it wasn't for Rafael, I'd want to die, too.

Water and food are rationed. What there is, is wretched. Every-
one is thin and lacks energy.

June 3, 1768. Today is my wedding day. Rafael and Father
Camps think it is best for us to marry now. I'm still mourning for
Mama and Papa, but Father says a sixteen-year-old girl must have
someone to take care of her. "You love each other. You wanted to marry
before you left Minorca. Your parents wanted you to wait, but many of
your friends and cousins marry at thirteen or fourteen. In these diffi-
cult times, who knows what awaits us in British Florida? Under the
circumstances, you must marry now."

I must admit I feel some happiness for the first time since Mama
died. I love Rafael so much. He is good and handsome, twenty-one
and sure of himself. When the bell rings, it will be time to go on deck for
my wedding. God, I promise you I'll be a good wife to Rafael.

July 8, 1768. Today we go ashore to our new home. From our first
sighting, Florida has been beautiful and green. My home in Minorca

used to be like that before the rains stopped. Florida is flat and low, and the ocean is as clear as it is around Minorca. Already Rafael wants to cast his net over the fish that jump out of the water all around the ship.

PART ONE

I

Tears stung Caterina's eyes. In her mind she could see Rafael now, as she had seen him that day. He stood tall and happy on the ship's deck, looking at the land where their dreams would come true. His dark, wavy hair blew across a tan forehead in the balmy sea breeze. Dark eyes fringed with black lashes smiled into her own. The cleft in his chin accented the strength of his determined jaw. Only the fact that Mama and Papa were not there had marred the happiness of the moment.

The book slipped from Caterina's hands as memories flooded over her. She remembered when they had finally left the ship. Her legs had felt like sponge. Four months at sea had caused her body to feel its rhythm although she stood on firm ground. She swayed, and Rafael put a steadying arm around her waist.

She slipped deeper into her reverie and found herself again being led down a narrow path through thick undergrowth. The ground was wet and swampy in places, palmetto thickets in others. Neither had ever seen anything like it. "It's a jungle, Rafael," Caterina said, as she slapped at hordes of hungry, black mosquitoes.

They walked for over an hour, their belongings in sacks over their shoulders. Finally the overseers told them this was where they would build their palm-thatched huts. Then they would start clearing land to grow indigo.

All these bewildered people, once so hopeful, stood in the middle of a jungle after four miserable months at sea. They were hungry, had lost family members and friends already. They were tired, sick and grieving. They had at least expected to find shelter. Indeed, it was promised in their contracts. But they were told the five hundred Negro slaves who were to build their huts had been lost when their ship went down at sea. In their present state, they didn't realize what food there was available would have had to be shared with those slaves, had they arrived.

When some of the men protested their harsh treatment, one was taken before them and beaten to remind them they were indentured to Dr. Andrew Turnbull, owner of the plantation New Smyrna.

Just before dark the hungry and weary settlers were called to supper. Rafael found Caterina staring at hands that were cut and swollen from clearing palmettoes.

Supper was no more and no better than that served on board the *Hope*. A cup of hominy was ladled out to each of them.

New Smyrna was to be built on the east coast of Florida at Mosquito Inlet. It was also called Mosquito by many because of the tormenting, biting, black insects the inlet was so aptly named for.

It seemed the overseers were chosen for their cruelty. Beatings became frequent, as the people became sicker from starvation, malaria, and exposure. Mosquitoes plagued them while they worked, prevented sleep at night, and were responsible for sores, especially on the children. The indigo they cleared the land for, planted, and cultivated grew close to their shacks and drew flies. The stench of it was with them constantly. Caterina felt their dreams of a better life shrivel up and die.

In all, about one thousand four-hundred Italians, Greeks, and Minorcans had come to Mosquito in eight ships. Dr. Turnbull had gathered the others on Minorca to prepare for the journey. Minorcans began asking to join the venture when they heard the glowing promises held out by Turnbull. In the end, there were more Minorcans than Greeks and Italians combined.

In July of 1769, about a year after their arrival in New Smyrna, Caterina discovered she was pregnant. Although she wanted a baby, she was afraid for a child to be born into conditions of near slavery, starvation and mistreatment. She put off telling Rafael. Then one of the overseers began making crude advances toward her. She tried to stay away from him, but he always found her. She wouldn't tell Rafael, because she was afraid for him if he tried to stop the overseer, Pedro Ponti.

One day when she was working in the field, she fainted. When she came to, she was in her hut on her bed. Ponti was squatting beside her.

"You're very beautiful, you know," he said. She saw that her blouse had been opened and fumbled to close it. His hand shot out and grabbed her wrist. "No!" he said. "I can make things easier for you and your husband if you'll let me." He bent to kiss her. The foul odor of his breath nauseated her. She clawed his face with her free hand. He grabbed it, too, and easily held both wrists in one big hand. With his other, he slapped her face.

"It would be better for you and Rafael if you'd cooperate. I don't want to hurt you." He tried to kiss her again, as one hand reached into her blouse.

Caterina bit his lip and screamed. At that moment Rafael burst in. Someone had told him Caterina had fainted. He had run all the way from the other side of the field. He stood in the doorway in shock, as Caterina, blouse open and skirt to her waist, struggled on their bed with Ponti. She had gotten one had free and was hitting and scratching Ponti's face. He was cursing her, raising his fist to deliver a blow to Caterina's already bruised face.

Rafael leapt across the room and caught Ponti's wrist. They fought, knocking the wall out on one side of the flimsy hut. Ponti pulled a wicked-looking knife from somewhere and poised it to slash Rafael.

Caterina was up and across the room with a piece of firewood. She hit Ponti across his back. The knife went flying. Ponti fell forward, the breath knocked out of him.

Rafael was insane from the sight he had seen when he burst in the door. He grabbed the firewood from Caterina. He hit Ponti over the head with it, and then again. Caterina yelled, "No! You'll kill him!"

Rafael seemed not to hear. She tried to stop him. He shook her off. She fell against the corner post, stunned.

Only when Rafael saw her lying on the dirt floor, her face bruised and blood running down it from a cut in her scalp, her clothes nearly torn off, did he return to reality.

Dropping the firewood, he ran to her, kneeling beside her. "Caty, oh Caty, what have we done to you?" he lifted her gently. The next thing she remembered, she was back on the bed. Rafael was washing her face tenderly, tears in his once again gentle eyes.

"He didn't . . .?" Rafael began.

"No," she said. " Oh, Rafael, I was so scared. But you got here in time. Is he dead?"

"I think so. I can't say I'm sorry. When I saw him on the bed with you, I wanted to kill him. He hurt you! He would have . . . Oh my God, Caty! And that scum has killed others. He's starved, beaten, and locked our friends in solitary confinement. Why? Just because they were too weak or sick to work? We won't miss him."

"There will be others to take his place. What are we going to do? They'll kill you when they find out. We've got to get away from here."

"There's no place to go but St. Augustine. It's too risky. It's about eighty miles away, they say. There are Indians out there who hate us because we look Spanish. We'd have to go through swamps. There are wild animals. Panthers, alligators, snakes, bears. We'd probably never make it. They'd send someone after us. We'd have a better chance if we could stow away on a ship, but we aren't allowed near the dock, and the captains are warned not to even talk to us. If we stay, they might kill me, but they might not punish you."

"Stay for what, Rafael? So another overseer can do what Pedro tried? What kind of life would that be for me? Anyway, we're going to have a baby. Do you want your child to have no father? To be a starving slave like we have become"

"A baby? We're going to have a baby? I didn't know. You didn't tell me." The surge of joy he felt at the news quickly changed to despair when he remembered their present circumstances.

"I want children so much. But not here. Not to live in misery or die like so many others. Oh, Caty, what have I gotten us into? I only wanted to have a better life for us. What Turnbull promised us was so good. But we don't have anything he promised. I don't think he ever meant to keep those promises. He just wanted slaves, but instead of paying money for us, he bought us with false promises." He held her and stroked her back, feeling warm tears on his neck.

"Things were bad in Minorca, but not horrible like here. We were free. No one mistreated us. And now we're going to bring a baby into this new world without hope," he said.

"I didn't tell you, because I knew you'd worry," she sobbed. "Besides, I've only known for a month or so. Please, Rafael, we've got to get away from here."

He held her a moment longer, then gently released her.

"No one will be in from the fields until dark. We've got about four hours. I'll make a litter to drag Ponti to the creek. The tide is going out, and the creek is deep and narrow. Maybe the swift current will take him out to sea, and no one will know what happened to him. You can sweep the tracks away behind me, and turn under that bloody dirt. Maybe he won't be missed for a while. I guess eventually they'll connect our disappearance with Ponti's. Maybe we can get to the governor to tell our story first. If he believes us, we may have a chance," he said.

They left New Smyrna taking a small sack of belongings, including Caterina's diary, Ponti's knife, their few ragged pieces of clothing, and a blanket.

The road to St. Augustine was only a set of rarely used wagon ruts. They had no choice but to follow it or be hopelessly lost. They hoped to cover the distance to St. Augustine in four days. There was no food to take, since meals were communal. They had learned to catch gopher tortoises, turtles, snakes, frogs, and anything else they could capture to supplement their hominy. They knew they would have more freedom on their trek to catch and gather food than in the colony.

The saddest part was that they had spent their lives near the sea. Rafael and the other men were fishermen. The ocean and creeks were teeming with fish. However, they were neither given time to fish, nor allowed near the ocean.

When dark caught them, they were about eight miles from their hut. They didn't know whether they were still on Turnbull's property or not. They had seen no one, but were aware that Indians roamed the area. Following a deer path, they left the road. In a little while they came upon a blackjack ridge. Rafael selected a tiny clearing surrounded by huge palmettos to spend the night. It was August, and hot. A fire wasn't necessary. They hadn't eaten, so they foraged among the leaves for acorns which they cracked and ate. They pulled the palmetto buds to eat the tender, white lower portions. The colonists had learned to eat these and the heart of the sable palm which they called swamp cabbage.

Exhausted, they slept on a bed of leaves covered by the blanket to keep some of the hungry bugs off.

In the morning they ate more acorns. Rafael stuffed his pockets with them before they returned to the wagon trail. Around ten, they came to a place where the ruts forded a sandy bottomed creek. They drank their fill, removed their clothes, and bathed in the cool clear water.

Rafael stood transfixed by his wife's beauty. Like other Minorcan women, her hair and eyes were black, her skin fair. And she had dimples and large, wide-set eyes that were trusting and gentle. Her mouth was small, nearly heart shaped, her chin firm, showing the determination she possessed. He had never seen her, or any other woman, without clothes in good light, although they had been married over a year. There had been no privacy when they were first married and aboard the *Hope*. They had not been alone except after dark since reaching the plantation. Even the dark, swollen bruise on her face did not prevent his thinking her the most beautiful vision in the world.

Caterina was embarrassed by his staring, and, blushing, stooped to splash him. Their water play soon turned to tumbling in the shallow water like a pair of frisky otters. The sweetness and naturalness of the passion that followed was something they'd always remember.

A little later Rafael caught some small fish. They left the trail and made a little fire over which to cook them. Their stomachs were fuller after eating them than they could remember.

That night they found an oak hammock with a large, hollow tree big enough to sleep in. This had been the best day of their married life. Both were beginning to feel optimistic about leaving Mosquito.

During the night the rain came. They were awakened to startling bright flashes of lightening and immediate thunder. The wind brought down oak limbs festooned with gray Spanish moss that resembled the beards of old men. Their hollow tree afforded some protection from the wind and rain, but soon both were soaked and shivering. Neither remembered returning to sleep, but woke huddled together in the wet blanket to a sunrise devoid of clouds, and vegetation that was shiny and fresh after the deluge of the night.

Rafael opened his mouth to speak, and Caterina put her hand over it. She pointed to a trail that led into the hammock. Three Indians walked single file straight toward them. Rafael pushed Caterina's head down and covered both their heads with the blanket. He was thankful it was the gray color of the oak bark, and they were in the deep shade of the hollow tree. The Indians took a few steps more. The one in the lead quickly fit an arrow to his bow and aimed straight at them. Caterina nearly screamed before he adjusted his aim higher and to their left. The arrow flew, and there was an angry roar. A large black bear reared up on its hind legs not far from their tree. All three Indians were now side by side, down on their knees, arrows aimed at the bear which was heading toward them. It was followed by two cubs.

Suddenly other Indians stepped into the clearing. They had the bears surrounded. Some shot arrows, others threw spears at the animals. The cubs were killed first, but the mama bear steadfastly tried to protect them. Finally some brave Indians attacked the bear with tomahawks. In the melee the bear was killed, but she left three wounded Indians, one seriously so.

An arrow had entered the interior of their tree, barely missing their heads before it lodged in the back of the trunk. Indians began scouring the area near them to recover arrows and spears. Caterina and Rafael held their breaths as an

Indian walked within five feet of them. He stooped to recover an arrow on the ground. Caterina closed her eyes for
fear they would meet the Indian's. She felt the hair on her
neck rise. But the Indian picked up his arrow and walked
away.

They peeked from under the blanket as the bears were
skinned and butchered. The meat was divided into portions
and wrapped in skins. One Indian attended the wounded
while others made litters, and still others laughed and appeared to be acting out the hunt. Then the seriously
wounded man and the bear meat were carried off in litters in
the direction from which they had come. The rest of the
party went toward the wagon trail.

The Indians wore loincloths woven of fibers with tomahawks tucked in their belts. Their feet were encased in deerskin moccasins. Each wore his arrows on his back and carried
a bow. Some also carried spears. They were tattooed, some
heavily. Their skins were bronze. They had eyes as dark as
Rafael and Caty, and their hair was shaved away from the
right side of their faces, apparently to prevent it from
being caught in the bowstring when it was released to
propel the arrow.

"Do you think the bear was after us?" asked Caterina.

"No, I don't think it could have smelled us, because our
trail was washed away by the rain. I've been told a bear is more
ferocious when she has young. The Indians just happened
to meet up with the bear here," he answered. "The rain also
covered out tracks, or the Indians would surely have found
us," he added.

"I wish they had left a little piece of bear meat, but they
took every bit of it with them. It's been so long since I had red
meat, I almost forget what it tastes like," she said wistfully.

"I know, Caty. I kept thinking the same thing when I
wasn't thinking about our scalps hanging from their belts."

"Oh! I was so scared they'd find us, but I didn't think

about what they might do if they did. Now I'm really shaking," she said as she touched her lovely hair.

"I'll see if I can find you some breakfast. You stay here."

In a few minutes he was back. "Look what one of them left behind." He held up a tomahawk with edges as sharp as a razor. "It must have belonged to the seriously wounded Indian, because the owner would never have left without it if he had been able to search for it. I saw the handle sticking out from under some moss."

After eating more acorns and palmetto buds they followed the same trail the Indians had taken to the wagon ruts. There Rafael looked at the Indians' tracks and told Caterina they had gone toward New Smyrna and had probably entered the swamp.

Several hours later they entered a different swamp. The cool shade felt good, and Caterina suggested they sit on a fallen log to rest a few minutes. She took Rafael's hand and led him to the log. As she started to sit, he jerked her hand so hard, she was thrown to the ground behind him. Before she could protest, he pulled the Indian tomahawk from his belt. She sat where she had fallen, her mouth open to protest his harsh treatment of her, as he poised the tomahawk to hurl at the log. Then she saw the coiled cottonmouth moccasin, its mouth open, revealing the white interior and huge curved fangs. It was waiting silently where she had planned to sit.

The tomahawk severed the snake's head from its body and was buried an inch deep in the log. Caterina jumped up, ran to Rafael, and threw her arms around him. He hugged her to him, smoothed her hair and said, "Well, Caty, there's lunch."

They had long ago passed the stage where eating snake made them squeamish. Besides, having eaten it before, they knew its taste to be delicate and delicious.

That evening they camped on the bank of a spring-fed lake a little distance from the trail. They bathed in the cool, clear water and slept on the sweet-smelling pine straw, hidden by the spread and drooping branches of a large tree.

Rafael awoke just before sunrise. There was just enough light to see a herd of deer drinking from the edge of the lake about fifty feet away. He shook Caterina gently, so she could see them, too. They watched the deer drink and feed along the water's edge for fifteen or twenty minutes. Then a doe raised her head, ears large and upright. It sniffed the air, turned its head, snorted, and flipped its tail. All the deer ran toward them. Just as they got between the lake and them, Caterina and Rafael saw the big cat running behind the frightened animals. A small yearling in the rear had gone perhaps twenty-five feet past them when the panther leaped and landed on its back, taking it down immediately. The huge cat sank its teeth into the deer's neck and shook its huge head. The yearling went limp, its neck broken.

As the sun rose, the cat began to drag its kill toward a huge oak. They watched in fascination as the panther pulled the deer up into the tree and draped its limp body over the limb. Then it began to feast on the tender young venison.

Caterina shuddered, thinking the cat might have one of them on that limb if the deer had not been there. She envied the cat the venison, but had no thoughts of challenging him for it.

While the cat was busy with its meal, Rafael and Caterina, being sure to keep bushes between them and the animal, sneaked quietly toward the wagon trail.

About noon as they rounded a curve, they saw a wagon coming toward them in the distance. Rafael pulled Caterina into the bushes. "We can't let anyone see us. They might try to take us back to Mosquito." He led her away from the trail and then took a course parallel to it. The palmettos were thick and, if they stooped, would hide them from view, if necessary.

They walked awhile and heard voices. He squatted, and

motioned for her to do likewise. "Stay here," he whispered. He crawled toward the voices. When he came back he said, "There are two men, a woman and two children. They are eating lunch in a clearing up ahead. They are heading toward Mosquito. We'll have to circle around them."

They had nearly sneaked past the group when a loud bark caused Rafael to groan, "No! A dog!"

As the dog came into view, a child's voice yelled, "Here, boy. Come back here."

Rafael said, "Get down, and don't ask questions. I'm going to be an Indian." He stripped off his shoes and clothes to the bare skin, grabbed Caty's well-worn veil, using it as a loin cloth. Then he took the tomahawk he had found after they witnessed the bears being killed, and crawled away from her. The dog followed him, barking and growling. Looking over the bushes he could see the boy now. He was about ten and was asking the dog, "What's the matter with you, Brownie? You after a rabbit or something?"

Rafael jumped up, gave a bloodcurdling yell, and waved the tomahawk. As soon as the boy saw him, Rafael ducked back into the bushes only to come up yelling in another place.

"Indians! Pa, Indians!" the boy yelled as he ran back to the clearing.

Everyone there had heard Rafael. All were on their feet.

"Get to the wagon! How many were there, Johnny?" the man asked the boy.

"Two, Pa! I saw two! They were big and almost naked as the day they were born! They waved big hatchets at me!"

Just then, Rafael, closer to the clearing now, raised up again. He was careful to keep the arm waving the tomahawk in front of his face, because he didn't think he looked at all like the Indians he had seen. Waving the tomahawk, he yelled again. He hoped the tomahawk, the yelling, and his nakedness was convincing proof that he was indeed an Indian.

"Yep, it's Indians all right. Damned naked heathens," the other man said, swinging a musket up to his shoulder. But Rafael had already moved to another place to repeat his performance.

Swinging the musket around in that direction, the man said, "Woods is full of 'em! Can't go back to St. Augustine, 'cause they're between us and it. Get in! Get in, I say! Our only chance is to out run 'em."

Once in the wagon the woman threw a protective arm around each child. She began praying aloud. The girl, smaller than the boy, was yelling, "We can't leave Brownie!"

Paying her no attention, her Pa grabbed the reins and urged the horses on with a whip. The last Rafael and Caterina saw of them was a cloud of dust with a little brown dog following it.

Caterina doubled over with laughter. "I didn't think they'd believe you were an Indian, even with the loin cloth; Your body is whiter and your hair style so different, you sure don't look like the ones we saw, but they sure thought you were."

Removing her veil, he gave it back to her. "I didn't let them get a good look at me, especially my face. I was hoping a naked, yelling person waving a tomahawk would cause enough panic they wouldn't be able to think very clearly, and their fear of Indians would take over. Looks like it worked," he said as he stepped back into his pants.

Miles later Caterina would still break into occasional giggles at the thought of what had happened.

That evening Rafael spotted a rabbit hiding in a briar patch near the edge of the trail. He threw the tomahawk at it, thanking the Indians for leaving such a helpful tool for him. That night they finally had red meat.

Rafael felt this would be their last night before reaching

St. Augustine. They made their bed in the pine forest. Rafael held Caterina tenderly. "Caty, you know how much I love you and our baby. No, don't interrupt. I have to say this. We don't know what's going to happen when we get to St. Augustine. We may be sent back to Mosquito. Or I may be put in prison. But this was a chance we had to take. You made me see that, and I'm glad we did it. We have been free for four days. We've faced danger together, we've laughed together. We've seen Indians, wildlife, and we've eaten better than we did at Mosquito. We've shared adventure and fun. It's been good no matter what happens. At least we've had this time to ourselves. I'll never forget it. If I can never tell our child about it, you will, won't you?"

Tears shone in Caterina's eyes when she raised her head from Rafael's chest to look at him. "Rafael, you're scaring me. They *can't* send us back. And I couldn't bear your being in prison. Please, don't even think that way. You don't really believe that will happen, do you?"

"I don't *know* what's going to happen. It's certainly possible we could be sent back. We *are* indentured. And I could go to jail. I did kill a man. Of course, I hope and pray the governor is a kind and sensitive man, and that he will give us protection. But I've heard he's from Scotland like Turnbull, and that they're good friends. It could go either way, and I want you to understand that." Privately, he felt he, at least, would have to pay, but he had agreed to come to St. Augustine because he thought it was the only chance he had of getting protection for Caterina and their unborn child.

"Let's don't talk anymore. We'll know soon enough. Tonight we're still free, and we're together. I love you so much. Just hold me and kiss me," she said.

Neither of them slept much that night, unable to stop thinking about what tomorrow might bring. When the first light of dawn brightened the eastern sky, Rafael raised up on an elbow to look at Caty. He was surprised to see her eyes wide open. "You're awake early," he said.

"So are you. I've prayed most of the night. Oh, Rafael, let's not go to St. Augustine. Can't we just live like we have the last few days? I couldn't bear to lose you, and I'd rather be anywhere than Mosquito."

"Caty, Caty, aren't you forgetting someone? What about our baby? We've got to take a chance on St. Augustine for the baby. Besides, what about the Indians? What happens when winter comes in a few months? We have no warm clothing and only one blanket. We have nothing to hunt with or for protection except the tomahawk and Ponti's knife. We aren't Indians. We couldn't survive in the woods for much longer than we have. St. Augustine is our only chance," he said.

They came into town about nine in the morning. The road led to the Spanish-built plaza, and they could see people milling around from several blocks away. They met a man and asked him where they might find the governor.

"I'm on my way there now. Joseph Adams is the name," he said, extending his hand. He couldn't believe their emaciation nor the ragged condition of their clothing. He thought they were comely individuals otherwise, but he was puzzled by the large bruise on the girl's face.

Rafael took his hand and replied, "I am Rafael Reyes, and this is my wife Caterina. We've just come from New Smyrna."

"My God, man. You'd better come with me," said Joseph, hurrying them away. He led them to an iron gate in a coquina wall. They entered the gate and found themselves in a little garden where Joseph invited them to sit on benches also made of coquina. "You're the couple who ran away from Turnbull's colony. They're looking for you, you know. A ship came up here from New Smyrna yesterday and the crew spread the news all over town. You'll have to go back, you know.

Do you want to tell me why you left?" From the looks of them he thought he already knew at least part of the answer to that.

"No, Mr. Adams! You can't let them send us back! It's terrible there! Turnbull's starving us! So many are sick and dying, but they beat them and make them work anyway! They put so many in solitary confinement and some even die there! And this overseer, Pedro Ponti, he . . . he . . ." Caty began to cry.

"He tried to rape her," finished Rafael. "She fainted in the field. He carried her back to our hut. When I got there, he had her on the bed with her clothes half torn off. Her face was bleeding, and his fist was raised to hit her again. He pulled a knife on me when I tried to stop him. I killed him with a piece of firewood."

Shocked, but trying to appear calm, Joseph looked at this beautiful young woman and her protective husband. Being the good man that he was, he knew he would have to do what he could to help them.

"I'd have done the same. But Turnbull says you have to go back. Nothing was mentioned about a dead overseer, though. If they don't know the circumstances we may have a bargaining point. I have a little influence with Governor Grant, although not as much as Turnbull has. Still, if you like, I'll go with you to be of what assistance I can."

"Would you, Mr. Adams? We don't know anyone here, and Caty's going to have a baby. She can't go back there," Rafael said.

"Please call me Joseph. Let's have tea first. I'll bet you're hungry. This is my home. I'd like you to meet my wife. You'll like her, Caty," he said, as he led the way into the two story house.

"Sarah, we have guests," he called.

Into the room came one of the prettiest ladies Caty had ever seen. She was blond, about twenty-five, and her eyes were blue as the sky on a cold day. She was taller than Caty, slim with pale skin. Her face was kind and her smile wide. She came to her husband, and he put an arm around her. "Caty and Rafael, this is my wife, Sarah."

Just looking at the two of them, Caterina knew they loved each other as much as she and Rafael did.

A slave girl brought tea and biscuits. Joseph explained their situation to Sarah as they ate. She was horrified that they might be sent back to such a terrible place. "Can't you do something, Joseph?" she asked.

"I'm going to try. That's all I can promise." Joseph said.

After they finished their tea, he said, "Come on, you two. We might as well face the music and get it over with."

They walked the few blocks back to the governor's place which was on St. George Street facing the plaza. They had only been a couple of blocks from it when they met Joseph.

The governor's secretary greeted Joseph, looking at Rafael and Caty in amazement. She told Joseph he had been expected an hour ago. He ushered them in, and Joseph introduced Rafael and Caterina. "Our business can wait. I want you to hear what these young folks have to say," he told Governor Grant.

After they repeated their story to the Governor, Joseph asked him not to send them back to New Smyrna.

Visibly upset with Joseph for complicating a matter that had already been decided, Governor Grant's corpulent face became livid. But since the government of East Florida owed Joseph's shipping company a lot of money and depended on it to extend even more credit, he could not afford to offend the man. He promised to send a message to Turnbull explaining what had happened to cause the Reyeses to leave and asking Turnbull to come to St. Augustine to discuss the matter. Joseph also sent a note offering to pay off the couple's indentures.

It would be a couple of days before the ship returned from New Smyrna, hopefully with Turnbull. They understood he might refuse to come, or might not be able to leave at the present time . Joseph invited the Reyeses to stay at his home while they waited.

Caterina and Sarah liked each other immediately. Rafael and Joseph also got along well together.

Joseph owned a fleet of ships that carried merchandise between Florida, the upper colonies of the new world and England, including indigo from Turnbull's plantation at New Smyrna. He offered Rafael a job on one of his ships if they were allowed to remain. He confided in Rafael that Sarah was not well, and he hoped they would stay on with them, because Caterina was obviously good for Sarah. Besides, Sarah's condition made it impossible for them to have a child. A baby was Sarah's fondest wish.

Their stay in St. Augustine was pleasant and their hopes high. They were given the spare bedroom and slept in a real bed for the first time in their married life. The Adamses outfitted Rafael and Caterina from their own wardrobes. Caterina had to shorten her dresses, but Sarah insisted she shouldn't take the waist in on hers or Rafael's, because she intended to fatten them up.

They were summoned by the governor on the evening of the third day. Joseph accompanied them. Turnbull himself declined to come, saying he could not leave the plantation. Under the circumstances, he would agree to sell Caterina's contract, but Rafael would have to be returned. Men were too badly needed for him to let even one go. Besides, if the other men knew Rafael had been released from his contract or had been given asylum in St. Augustine, more would leave. It would set a bad precedent. He did promise no punitive action would be taken against Rafael, and conceded the overseer had been wrong. It was presumed he, too, had fled, because he had not been seen since Rafael and Caty's disappearance.

Turnbull requested Rafael be returned to New Smyrna on Joseph's next supply ship which was due to leave.

Caterina's heart sank when she found that Rafael had to go back. She wondered if God even heard her prayers anymore. Alone in their room that night she cried bitter tears as she hugged him to her. "You're all I've got, Rafael. They can't separate us. Let's run away again. We can go to Georgia, or maybe West Florida or anywhere else," she begged.

"Caty, I hurt as bad as you do. I don't want to go back. I don't want to be separated from you. But the reason we left Mosquito was the baby. And that's the reason you're going to stay here. I only have five years of my indenture left. Joseph says he and Sarah want you to stay with them. Sarah needs a companion. She's not well, and she's been so happy to have you here. She wants you to have the baby in this house. She's looking forward to it. Joseph says you'll be doing them a favor if you stay here. You like and trust them, don't you?"

"Sarah is one of the nicest ladies I ever met, and Joseph is wonderful, too. But they can't take your place. Maybe after they go to sleep we could sneak out and leave East Florida."

"Caty, we've been through this. We can't run forever. I have to go back. There is nowhere else to go. I know you and our baby will be safe here. I can accept going back if I know that. You'll wait for me here, won't you Caty?"

"Oh, Rafael, you know I'd wait forever if I had to. But I don't want to wait. I want you now and forever."

"Caty, please stop crying. It's not good for you or the baby. We're stronger than we think. We can do what we have to do. I'll be all right. I'll be back before you know it. I'll try to send messages to you, if I can find a way. I don't want you to come to the ship with me tomorrow, either. We'll say good-bye here."

Rafael left at dawn the next morning. The weather was clear and calm as the ship sailed away. As can happen in the tropics, within a few hours ferocious winds and driving rain were whipping the coast. The hurricane held the East Florida coast in its grip for three days while it dallied, unable to decide which course to take.

A few days after the storm was over, word came that the ship carrying Rafael had not arrived and was presumed lost. Other ships were sent to search for it, but eventually the search was called off. Some of the cargo and debris had been found floating far south of New Smyrna where it had broken up on the reef.

Caterina steadfastly refused to believe Rafael was dead. When Joseph told Caterina the ship had been broken up by the storm, that there was no hope Rafael or anyone else had survived, he was prepared for a weeping, even a hysterical Caterina. However, she had looked him in the eye and with calmness he could not believe was real, she had said, "Rafael is not dead. I would know if he was dead. I don't know where he is, or if he is hurt, but I know he's alive. He'll send word to me as soon as he can. You'll see."

It was during this time she learned there had been an uprising in Turnbull's colony. A trial was being held in St. Augustine for Carlo Forni who had declared himself commander and chief of the Italian and Greek settlers of the colony. They had seized a ship which had brought provisions to New Smyrna. Turnbull's manager had been kidnapped and wounded, then left on the beach. Forni and his men had planned to escape to Havana. At first only twenty men joined Forni. But after they became intoxicated on stolen rum, he was able to recruit two or three hundred more. They broke into Turnbull's storehouses, stole firearms, rum, and other goods. What they didn't take, they destroyed. They were accused of attacking some of the Minorcans who wouldn't join them. Caterina knew how much her people abhorred violence, only using it in dire cases, as when Rafael had been forced to kill Ponti to save her.

Three days after Forni and about three hundred followers

seized the ship, it was retaken by the British military. Only thirty-five escaped and were later captured in the keys.

Caterina remembered Turnbull's manager, Mr. Cutter, as being particularly cruel. She followed the proceedings with much interest.

Mr. Cutter had tried to resist and had been wounded. Besides stealing provisions from Turnbull's stores, a cow had been killed for meat, a capital offense. A grand jury decided Elia Medici, the cow killer; Guiseppi Massiodoli, the man who injured Cutter; and Forni, as leader, would be punished.

'Caterina, against Joseph's better judgment, insisted on being present when the sentence was carried out in the plaza. She felt she owed it to her fellow colonists to witness what she considered to be a gross miscarriage of justice, considering there was nowhere the colonists could turn for help.

Following a barbaric British custom that was meant to be a fate worse than death for Elia Medici, his life was spared and he was pardoned for killing the cow, but he would have to execute his friends Forni and Massiodoli.

When Caterina found out what was to take place, she became sick. By then the crowd of British onlookers was so large, she couldn't get through it to leave. She and Joseph were in front of the crowd near the execution stand. She saw and heard Elia Medici, whom she had known well, cry out, "I'd rather die than kill my friends. Please, don't make me do this! I can't do it!" as tears streamed down his face, and he fell to his knees at the feet of his friends.

Knowing they were doomed at any rate, they begged Medici to do it, one saying, "I'd rather die at the hands of my friend. Please, get it over with." And the other, "Remember your wife and children who need you. And do what you can for our families, too."

In the end, Medici begged for the forgiveness of his friends, prayed the "Hail, Mary" with them, kissed them and released the trap door from beneath them.

Mercifully, Caterina had fainted before the ropes tightened.

Never would she forget the attitude of that crowd of British onlookers. She had never seen an execution and was only there to lend support to her fellow colonists. They had come for amusement! They had bellowed, "On with it! We came to see them swing!" and they had cheered when Medici mounted the steps and again when he released the rope.

II

The days passed, then weeks, and finally a month with no word from Rafael. Caterina's faith that he was still alive began to falter, but still she clung to the hope that he was. Then something happened that made her face what Joseph termed the reality of the situation. A ship bound for St. Augustine had come upon a dinghy from the ship Rafael had been on. It was beached at the southern tip of East Florida. In it were three men whose bodies were beyond recognition. A metal box in the dinghy contained the ship's log. This was brought to Joseph.

The captain of the downed ship had meticulously listed the names of those aboard, and by each name had listed that person's fate. Beside Rafael's name he had written, "When the main mast broke, it fell on Reyes, hitting him on the head and breaking his leg. His head was cut badly. He was unconscious. Before we could get him below deck, a gigantic wave swept him overboard and drowned him." Similar notes were beside each name except the captain's and two others. These three, according to the log, had spent days lost at sea with severe injuries and no food or water. They were presumed to be the bodies found in the small boat and buried at sea by the crew of the vessel that found them.

Finally convinced that Rafael would not return, Caterina wailed, "I want to die, too."

Sarah sat on the edge of Caterina's bed, tears running down her cheeks in sympathy for the young girl who was alone, except for herself and Joseph, and in a strange land. Tenderly she smoothed the hair from Caterina's forlorn and tear-stained face. "You can't give up, Caty. You told me how Rafael loved you and your unborn baby so much that he risked death to get you here, so you and your child would have a chance to live, a chance to be free. Now that he's gone, you can't let his death be in vain. You have to live not only for yourself, but most of all for the child. Yours and Rafael's child. Rafael can only live in his baby now. Don't let his death be for naught."

A week passed since she had been told of the finding of the ship's log. She had been in a state of shock, and until today the doctor had kept her drugged. Although the concoction he gave her kept her quiet and asleep most of the time, she had still been in agony. Her drug-induced sleep had been full of terrifying dreams. She had relived her parents' deaths, the misery of life in New Smyrna, the attack by Pedro Ponti, the trek to St. Augustine, and the final goodbye when Rafael left to board the ship that would return him to the colony. She had also relived the awful executions in the plaza. In between she saw Rafael standing on the deck of the *Hope*, the wind blowing his hair, his face tanned and handsome, dark-fringed black eyes smiling into her own. And her heart would lurch, a horrible feeling would begin in her chest, painful and terrible. It would spread its fiery pain throughout her body, culminating in pin-prick sensations on her forearms. Her mind would deny his death. He had been too alive; she loved and needed him too much. She couldn't live without him. Didn't want to. He couldn't be dead.

Now the drug was wearing off. She heard what Sarah said, but it really didn't register at the time. She was still deeply in shock. Her mind was numbed to all but the terrible reality that she had lost the most important part of her life.

Sarah and Joseph had been wonderful to her. Dimly she realized they had tried to be family to her. Then, suddenly one day, she remembered her indenture had been bought by Joseph. She owed him and Sarah five years. She was supposed to be a companion to Sarah, but here Sarah was taking care of her.

She got up, dressed, and after putting her own room in order, she found Sarah in the kitchen and asked what she could do to help.

From then until the birth of the child, Caterina only concentrated on keeping busy. She often worked zombie-like, her thoughts unknown to any but herself, her face an expressionless mask. Frequently tears crept down her cheeks as she sewed or cooked or tidied a room. Usually she wasn't even aware of them. At night Sarah and Joseph could sometimes hear piteous sounds coming from her as she cried in her bed.

Sarah was dismayed at the change in the once spunky girl she considered her dearest friend. She was afraid Caty was overdoing it and would harm her unborn child. There was Mandy, the young slave girl, to do much of the work. She only wanted Caty's company, but a companion Caty was not. Sarah ached for her, but couldn't communicate with her. She stayed locked in her own miserable thoughts, speaking little and usually not hearing what was said to her. She didn't look pregnant yet, although she was five months. Her appetite was poor, and she had to be urged to eat at all. She took little interest in anything except work. Even the coming birth of her baby seemed not to interest her.

Rafael had said good-bye on August 23, 1769. Caterina

went into labor on February 21 of the following year. Small to begin with, she had gained practically no weight during her pregnancy. She seemed not to care whether she and her baby died.

Her labor lasted two days. The doctor offered little hope that she or the baby would live. Caterina drifted in and out of consciousness. On the second day she had a dream. In it she relived Rafael's and her life together. Her dream emphasized Rafael's love for her and the baby, his desire that they live safely and in freedom. She heard Rafael telling her to tell their child about their escape from New Smyrna and the experiences they had in those few days of freedom. She realized Rafael wanted her and his child to live. She also realized her grief had been killing them both. She felt she had reneged on a promise to Rafael, had made the sacrifice of his life in vain.

When she regained consciousness that time, she prayed as she had never prayed before that she and her child would live. She promised God if he would allow them to live, she would do her best to make Rafael's dreams for their child come true.

She didn't lose consciousness again. She began to fight for her life and that of the baby. Within a few hours she delivered her daughter, a thin but beautiful baby with dark eyes and thick, dark hair.

She named her daughter Ana Marie after her mother. She promised little Ana she would always be free and that she would lack nothing. She wouldn't allow herself to think how she, who was indentured to Joseph, would keep that promise, but she intended to just the same.

Sarah and Joseph were enchanted with Ana from the start. They lavished gifts on both Ana and her mother. Caterina protested the gifts they gave her, but accepted those for Ana with heartfelt thanks.

The Adamses could not help noticing the changes in

Caterina. She had returned to the land of the living. It was as
if she had been reborn with the birth of her baby. She was
responsive and attentive. She was eating correctly and filling
out. She found joy in Ana. In nearly all ways she was the
Caterina they had first met. Only now it appeared she just
lived for Ana. The only impulsiveness and gaiety she allowed
herself involved the child. She seemed mature beyond her
years and had but one purpose in life: to be Ana's mother.

She was a much better companion for Sarah, and they
both doted on Ana. The baby gained weight and flourished
under their care and attention.

Caterina wanted to do everything for Ana, but forced
herself to let Sarah share the baby. It meant so much to this
gentle woman, only eight years older than Caty, who had
mothered her all those months between the death of Rafael
and the birth of Ana. She still cried over Rafael some nights,
but during the day when thoughts of him caused her heart to
contract and that awful, helpless feeling threatened her composure, she would tell herself, *Stop! I can't think of that now,*
and she would shove it to the back of her mind. At first this
didn't always work, but as time went by she became more
adept at it.

The friendship between Caterina and the Adamses blos-
somed. Joseph made frequent trips involving his business.
Sometimes he would be gone only a week. But every few years
he had to go home to England. Then he would be gone
seven months to a year. He had not been to England since
the Reyeses' arrival in St. Augustine and was due a trip soon.
It was because he was away so much, and Sarah was in ill
health, that she needed a companion.

While Joseph was on a business trip to ports in several of
England's colonies to the north of East Florida, Sarah had
her first bad spell since Caty had been with them. Little Ana
was seven months old that September, and Joseph had been
away for one month of a planned three-month trip.

The day had started like so many before it. They had just finished lunch and were playing with Ana when suddenly Sarah's hand went to her chest. She slumped into her chair, nearly dropping Ana, who was on her lap.

Caty jumped up and ran to catch the baby. "What is it, Sarah?" she said in alarm.

After a few seconds Sarah smiled weakly. "Just give me a few minutes," she said in a strained tone.

A little later the color began to return to her face. She seemed to feel better. She had refused to allow Caty to have Mandy get the doctor. "It was just a pain. I get them occasionally. Sometimes they go away immediately, but once in a while, they don't. Then we have to send for Dr. Johnson. I know Joseph told you my health isn't good, but did he tell you I have a weak heart? Don't look so scared, Caty. I'm all right now."

Indeed, she did seem all right for an hour or so. It was after they had put Ana down for her afternoon nap and were embroidering that Sarah suddenly gasped.

Caty looked up in time to see Sarah slide from her chair and crumple unconscious on the floor.

"Mandy!" she screamed, summoning the startled girl from the kitchen.

"Oh, my Lord! Mis' Sarah is having one of her spells! We got to get her to bed, and I'll fetch Doc' Johnson."

They managed to get her up the stairs and into bed.

Sarah had regained consciousness, but her skin was pale and clammy. There was an odd blue color around her mouth and nose. As Mandy ran out the door to get the doctor, Caty began to loosen Sarah's clothing. She found that Sarah did not have even the strength to lift an arm.

She opened her mouth to say something, but Caterina was too alarmed to even allow her to talk. "Save your strength. Don't try to talk. The doctor will be here soon."

Mandy returned with Dr. Johnson in a short time. After

spending a half-hour or so with Sarah, he asked Caty, waiting outside Sarah's door, to come in. "Sarah says Joseph won't be back for two more months. She is in worse shape than I had thought. If she spends most of that time in bed, she may be able to be up and about a few hours at a time when Joseph returns," he said.

Dr. Johnson returned to check on Sarah daily at first, then several times weekly, then once a week until Joseph's return. He told Joseph it was unlikely Sarah would live more than six months. It was November of 1770. Sarah was only twenty-six years old.

The doctor said she had suffered a heart attack from which it was unlikely she would completely recover. There was no way to prevent another, and Sarah's heart was so badly damaged she couldn't possible survive another. He advised Joseph to delay any further trips and spend Sarah's last days with her.

Sarah was not to exert herself and was to be kept as calm as possible. Since the end was inevitably near, she could do as she liked within reason. Sarah had insisted he tell her the truth, so she knew and had accepted it.

Joseph had known of Sarah's weak heart since shortly after their marriage when she had suffered her first attack. Still, it was impossible to stop the tears that clouded his vision. "Please tell Caterina, Doctor. I have to be alone. Tell her I'll be back as soon as I can," he said, nearly colliding with the doctor in his haste to leave. Tears streamed down his face as he walked the few blocks to the docks. If he passed anyone along the way, he was unaware of it. *Poor Sarah. So sweet and gentle. She wanted children so badly. Now when she has Caty and little Ana to love . . . How can she be so accepting. She's only twenty-six. God, I'm only thirty-nine, and here I am about to be a widower,* he thought.

It was dark before Joseph got his emotions under control.

Mandy was putting supper on the table when he opened the door. Sarah and Caty had just put the baby to bed.

Sarah smiled her sweet smile. He crossed the few steps between them to kiss her forehead and encircled her with his arms. Holding her close, he moaned, "Sarah, Sarah."

Caterina, fighting back tears, turned to help Mandy.

Leading Joseph to the sofa, Sarah pulled him down beside her and cradled his head to her breast. Joseph never remembered the words she used to comfort him. He only knew her words and her strength gave him such a feeling of peace. She had made him aware she was ready for whatever God had planned for her. From that moment to the end, Joseph determined to devote all his efforts to making Sarah as comfortable and happy as possible.

Such was the climate here that even in winter there were many days warm enough for Sarah, Caterina, and Ana to spend outdoors. Sarah loved carriage rides along the bay and into the countryside, boat rides across the Matanzas River, and picnics on the beach. Joseph took them on these outings. On cold days Sarah and Joseph would curl up in front of the fireplace and read to each other from the many books Joseph collected.

On occasion, weather permitting, they would attend concerts in the plaza provided by local talent.

They were frequently invited to the governor's house for quiet suppers or fancy balls. Sarah enjoyed it all, and even managed to dance a waltz occasionally.

As a matter of fact, Sarah seemed to blossom. She even added a few pounds. She looked more radiant that ever. Except for tiring quickly and being short of breath, it was hard to believe that Dr. Johnson had been correct.

Ana's first birthday was February 22, 1771. Sarah insisted on having a supper to celebrate the occasion. Many of their friends had been invited, including a few British officers stationed at the St. Augustine garrison. The house was full of laughing people and the smell of good food from Mandy's kitchen.

One of the soldiers, Captain Thomas Andrew, was an avid hunter. He had insisted on supplying wild turkey to be served for supper which Mandy stuffed, baked, and served with all the trimmings. After supper Ana was led by Sarah holding one hand and Caterina the other, to the huge birthday cake. Pulling her hands free and clapping in delight, she said, "Ana's cake! Ana's cake! Ana's one year old!" And she held up one finger momentarily before it darted to the cake and captured a pink icing flower which she promptly ate and pronounced, "Good!"

Everyone laughed, sang happy birthday, and applauded as Ana blew the candle out.

When Caterina returned to the gathering after putting a sleepy, happy Ana to bed, Captain Andrews was waiting at the foot of the stairs. He knew her story from Joseph. He had long admired her beauty.

Caterina found herself looking into a pair of pale blue eyes under which a well-shaped nose topped a blond mustache. He was tall and broad shouldered, a strikingly handsome man.

"Mrs. Reyes, please don't think me too forward. I've known you some months now, and I would be honored if you would attend the governor's ball with me."

Caterina blushed. She had not thought of seeing another man since she had accepted the fact that Rafael was not coming back. It had been well over a year. Still, she wasn't sure she was ready, or that she would ever be. Besides, when she thought of the governor, the terrible scenes of the execution in the plaza flashed before her, not to mention her belief that he could have overridden Turnbull's objection and prevented Rafael from being torn away from her. Then, too, the governor was Turnbull's friend.

She hadn't noticed Joseph standing there. Having heard

Captain Andrews' invitation, he said, "It will be fun and good for you. Sarah and I will be there. I think you should go, and I can vouch for Captain Andrews. He's a gentleman."

"Good. That's settled," said the captain. Caty opened her mouth to say no, she didn't want to go anywhere near Governor Grant, and she was sure he felt the same about her. In fact she believed he would be enraged that one of his officers had brought an indentured servant, especially an escapee from Turnbull's colony, to his ball. Undoubtedly, Andrew Turnbull himself would be there, which would bring further embarrassment and discomfort. But before she could say anything, the piano struck up a merry tune, and everyone began to sing along. She didn't have the opportunity to decline the invitation.

After everyone said good night, Caterina thanked the Adamses for the wonderful party for Ana, asked Joseph to take Sarah to bed, and helped Mandy tidy up.

The next morning before six, Caterina was awakened by the most mournful wailing she had ever heard. Jumping out of bed, she hastily dressed. When she got into the hall, she realized the sound came from Joseph and Sarah's room. Joseph was making the most heart-wrenching sounds she had ever heard. She knocked on their door. Only Joseph's painful sounds came back.

"I'm coming in," she said. Opening the door, she saw Joseph kneeling by the bed, holding Sarah's hand. Sarah's face had a peaceful expression, her eyes closed as in sleep.

"Joseph, she's not . . . dear God, no!"

"Mandy! Mandy!" she ran from the room to find Mandy in the kitchen starting breakfast. "Get Dr. Johnson! Hurry! It's Sarah!" and ran back to the bedroom.

Joseph was making a pitiful sound and holding Sarah's limp hand. Caterina knelt by him and put her arm around him. She forgot everything except her understanding of the pain he felt as she rocked him like a baby.

After a while she said, "Joseph, it's over. I've sent for Dr. Johnson."

Turning unseeing eyes toward her, he said, "She was so happy last night. She enjoyed the party so much. She went right to sleep. She never woke up." Then remembering Caty had suffered a similar loss, he put his arms around her. "Oh, Caty, you'll have to help me. You know how I hurt. I never realized until now how much it can hurt. But you've been there. Help me, Caty."

Caty knew about the pain, but was powerless to help him. She had heard all the cliches about time healing all wounds. She knew better. She knew from experience that in time you learned to better live with your loss, but the wound was still there. She thought it always would be, and there would always be times, no matter how many years after, that the pain would return in a blinding rush. All it took was something as simple as a glimpse of someone with a resemblance ever so slight to the lost loved one, or some little word, or place, or sight or sound. Even a smell could trigger the memories. It would take faith in God, the support of loved ones and friends, and keeping busy. Eventually, he'd desire to resume life in order to busy his mind elsewhere, to push his grief and pain back into his subconscious where it would always reside. He would have to learn to be stronger than it. But he wasn't ready to hear this yet. Incoherent as he was, all she could do was to cry with him, hold him, and rock him like a child.

When Mandy and Dr. Johnson came, they found Caterina and Joseph huddled together by the bed, arms around each other, tears flowing freely.

After Sarah's funeral, Caterina began to pack Ana's and her belongings. She didn't know where to go, but she knew she couldn't stay in the house with Joseph. A widow and a widower couldn't live together, no matter how innocently, without scandal.

When Joseph realized she intended to take Ana and

leave, he couldn't believe it. "Where would you go? Back to Mosquito?"

"I realize I'm still indentured to you, Joseph. But you can't expect me to stay now. Don't worry. I'll pay you for the remainder of my contract some way. Surely you realize people will talk if I stay with you."

"Caty, I didn't mean I'd send you back there if you didn't honor that contract. Didn't you know you aren't indentured to me? I only bought your contract to free you from Turnbull, not to buy your services. You and Ana are family to me. She's like a daughter—the daughter I never had. You can't take her away from her home. Sarah and I discussed this. She said I must make you stay.

"I'm leaving for England in two days. I've been neglecting my business. I have to throw myself into it now for my sanity's sake. I may be gone a year. No one can talk if you're here and I'm in England. Please stay, Caty."

So Caterina Reyes had become the mistress of Joseph's house for at least the time this trip to England and back would take. Joseph had promised to help her make other arrangements after his return is she wanted to leave then.

About a week after his departure Caterina answered the door to find Captain Andrews there. "Mr. Adams isn't here, Captain. He's gone to England," she said.

"I came to see you, Mrs. Reyes. The governor's ball is next weekend. I came to remind you of our date."

"Oh, no, Captain. I can't go to the ball when this house is in mourning."

"But surely you aren't still mourning your husband. He's been gone well over a year."

"No, Captain. Didn't you know Sarah died the night of the party? Joseph woke to find her dead beside him. It was awful. He really took it hard. We all did."

"I'm so sorry. I didn't know. I've been gone since a few hours after the party. I just returned to St. Augustine, Mrs.

Reyes. I had no idea," he said, raising his hands to take her arm and lead her to a chair.

Caterina backed away. The Englishman obviously didn't know Minorcan custom forbade a man to touch a woman who was a casual acquaintance, or even to hug or kiss a spouse in public.

Still standing in the doorway, Captain Andrews said, "May I come in, Mrs. Reyes?"

"Or course, Captain," she stammered, knowing Joseph would want his friend treated with the utmost courtesy.

"When I returned to the barracks after Ana's party," he started as he crossed the floor to the sofa, "I was told to saddle up immediately. There was Indian trouble in Picolata. We only got back last night. Surely you realize I would have been at the funeral if I had known. I'm so sorry. She was a lady of great kindness. I liked her very much.

"You said Joseph has gone to England?" he asked.

"Yes. He left right away. He said he'd neglected his business too long. But, I think he left so soon so I would stay here." She found herself talking to this man like he was a long lost friend. She told him about packing to leave and Joseph's response. Then she told him about the morning Joseph woke to find Sarah dead. But when he would extend a hand in sympathy, even though tears flowed down her cheeks, she'd pull away.

Mandy came in with tea which Captain Andrews eagerly accepted. She served it with biscuits and honey. The honey reminded Caty of home. Her countrymen had brought beehives to New Smyrna from Minorca.

Then, to her own amazement, Caty found herself talking about the execution of the colonists. "I didn't say I'd go to the ball with you, Captain. Because Joseph said he thought it was a good idea, you assumed I would go. I didn't get a chance to decline. You see, Captain, I could never go to a ball Governor Grant held. He is cruel to my people and a friend of Dr.

Turnbull's. They're killing the colonists. Just last week I learned almost seven hundred have died since we left Minorca. That's about half of us. And they are dying of starvation; they're beaten when they're too sick or hungry to work, sometimes until they die. They live in miserable conditions in palm-thatched huts on dirt floors with no protection from mosquitoes which carry diseases that kill old folks and babies. Men have been made to beat their own wives. And I won't even tell you what an overseer tried to do to me. I'm lucky, because they have succeeded with other women.

"Captain Andrews, we aren't used to being treated this way. We were promised plenty to eat, good land to grow our gardens, decent living quarters and conditions, and a share in what we produced. We brought vegetable and datil pepper seeds, honey bees and cast nets for fishing. We could take care of ourselves if allowed.

"Colonists are supposed to be given land and freed at the end of their indentures. After all the other broken promises, I don't believe he'll honor that part, either.

"I don't know why I've told you all this. I've not talked so much to anyone but Sarah since Rafael. But even if I weren't in mourning, I wouldn't go to the governor's ball, because I think he's an awful man. Besides, Mr. Turnbull will probably be there, and you might be embarrassed or even reprimanded for bringing me."

The captain was shocked at the things he'd just heard. The governor had always been stern with the troops, but he had never known him to be cruel or unfair. But he knew what Caterina told him was true.

Evidently, to the governor and to Turnbull, the colonists were not people, but property to be used and abused as they saw fit. He felt great compassion for them and especially for Caterina, the only one he knew. Joseph had told him why she and Rafael had left New Smyrna.

He thought, *How I'd love to see her smile again as she did at little Ana's party. Her dark eyes had been alight, dimples playing at the corners of her pretty mouth. A woman this young and beautiful should be happy and gay, but except for her daughter, there's little that makes her happy. I'd like to change that.*

Caterina suddenly remembered it was past time to get Ana up from her nap. When had she ever forgotten the child for a single minute before?

"It's time for Ana to wake up. I'm sorry for unburdening myself to you. I think I feel better than I have in a very long while, though, and I thank you for listening," she said.

"I'm sorry to have brought it all back to you, but if talking about it has helped, I'm glad. Joseph would want me to check on you and Ana while he is gone, I am sure. And if you need me, I'll be at the barracks. If I have to leave town again, I'll get a message to you. I'll see you soon. Good afternoon, Mrs. Reyes. Thanks for tea." And he was out the door, thinking how much he liked her. He planned to get to know her very well, indeed.

The captain came frequently to visit Caty and Ana. He usually brought some wild game—turkey, venison, duck, rabbit, or quail. Sometimes it would be mullet, flounder, or redfish instead. He was an excellent hunter and fisherman, and he always cleaned and prepared whatever he killed so it was ready for Mandy to cook.

Within a couple of months they were calling each other Caterina and Thomas.

Spring came, and the three of them enjoyed picnics on the Matanzas or San Sebastian River. Then it was summer, and they took Ana to the beach. The fresh air and sun were good for the baby, Caterina told herself. She loved to frolic in the little sloughs that filled as the tide came in or were left as it receded.

Caty had returned to wearing her native dress soon after Ana's birth, as she could get material to make clothes. (Joseph had left her with money to run the household, as well as a small account for her personal use in exchange for running his household.) She would remove her stockings and white leather shoes, hike up her full petticoats, which were shorter than the English version, reaching only mid-leg, and with her hair braided, remove the veil that had been pinned under her chin. Holding one of Ana's hands while Thomas held the other, they walked in the surf or on the beach in search of pretty shells.

Both Caty and Ana enjoyed it. By May, Thomas could no longer deny to himself that he was in love with Caterina. They were never alone together. She had explained the taboo about being touched in public to him. He had never even held her hand. Although he enjoyed these times with the two of them, he longed for some time alone with Caterina. He hadn't asked for fear of scaring her off.

As for Caterina, she was beginning to be more like the girl who had left Minorca. She smiled frequently. She was more content than she had been since Rafael and she had spent those few days together between New Smyrna and St. Augustine. She still had nights when the thought of her loss was unbearable. She still missed Sarah, and even Joseph. But she like Thomas, enjoyed his company, and adored Ana. Having been born and raised in the country, she loved eating wild game and fish. Picnics, the smell of the salt air, and the endless, glimmering ocean reminded her of her home in Minorca. And one day she realized with surprise that she was happy. She had never thought she would ever experience happiness again, but she had to admit she had been wrong.

One warm June day Thomas asked if she would have Mandy cook a redfish he had just caught for their supper. He had never been invited to stay for supper by Caterina. She agreed, and after supper, Ana insisted he help tuck her in bed and hear her prayers. Then he asked Caterina to walk along the bay with him.

The night was clear with a full orange moon. A warm breeze swayed Caterina's veil and rippled the surface of the Matanzas River. Caterina marveled at the tiny, bright phosphorescent organisms that sparkled in the ripples. No one was about, and Thomas slipped Caterina's hand in his. She automatically started to pull her hand back, but Thomas tightened his grip, turning her around to face him.

"Caterina, there's no one here but you and me. We've been friends for a long time. We've been seeing each other since March. We always have Ana with us, but that's all right. But how do Minorcans do things if a guy can't hold a girl's hand? My dearest Caterina, I love you."

At that she broke away. Gathering her petticoats in her hands, she turned and ran as fast as she cold all the way to St. Marks Fort, confused and alarmed.

Thomas caught her in the shadow of the fort, stopping her flight. He turned her around to face him and pulled back the veil which had blown over her face. In the light of the moon he could see her eyes, wide with fright. "I won't hurt you, Caty," he said, putting his arms around her to hold her to him. "I want to kiss you, but not until you're ready, too. So when you stop shaking, I'll let you go. We'll just hold hands till I get you home. Is that all right with you?"

The shaking subsided. Caterina began to feel such comfort in those strong arms. How long had it been since Rafael had held her this way? She leaned against him, thinking of Rafael, and put her arms around his waist. They stood there for a while. She was no longer afraid. She had never kissed a man besides Rafael. She wondered how it would feel to be kissed by Thomas. At that moment Thomas took her head between his hands and held it so he could see into her face. Tears were in her eyes when the words came unbidden, "Kiss me, Thomas."

The kiss was long and tender. To Caterina it was warm and comforting, holding such promises . . . of what she did not know. To Thomas it was lightning and falling stars. It was all he could do to keep it tender, such was the passion that welled up within him. Instinctively he knew she wasn't ready for the intensity of his passion.

After the kiss he took his arms away reluctantly. She lingered against him for a moment, not wanting it to end. Nor did she realize how hard it was for him to end it. "Race you back to the bay," he said, breaking the romantic spell.

In bed that night, Caterina went over the evening's events. She was torn between the enjoyment of remembering how much she had liked being held and kissed, how alive she'd felt after all that time of feeling dead inside, and the guilty feeling that she had betrayed Rafael.

But Rafael is dead, she thought. *I'm alive and I've felt dead too long. I have to think about myself as well as Ana from now on. Rafael loved me. He'd want me to be happy.*

As for being in love with Thomas, she didn't think so. He was a wonderful friend that she had come to depend on, the only one she had except for Joseph, now that Sarah was gone. And she was alone and lonely and had been for too long. She needed warmth, comfort, companionship, and caressing. Nothing she did now could hurt Rafael.

Things were different from that night on. She allowed Thomas to hold her hand and even to kiss her cheek in greeting in front of Ana. They still enjoyed their outings with the child, but afterward he stayed for supper and helped tuck Ana in. Sometimes they'd walk along the bay. Sometimes they'd sit in Joseph's garden talking, holding hands, and kissing.

By October Thomas wanted to know whether she loved him. He had first told her he loved her back in June. He wanted more than hugs and kisses. He wanted love—and a wife. So he decided he'd ask her to marry him.

The evening was stormy. Caterina invited him to sit by the fire in the living room after Ana was settled in bed. They talked for a while. The held and kissed each other. His kisses became hungrier and more passionate. Caterina, comfortable and trusting with him, didn't pull away. Suddenly she realized she was being pushed down on the sofa.

Thomas's mouth was trailing kisses down her neck.

"Thomas, stop," she said, returning to reality.

"Caty, I love you. You're driving me crazy. I won't hurt you. Please don't stop me."

Caty was bewildered. She knew they mustn't. But his mouth continued its search. His hands tugged at her blouse.

"We can't, Thomas. It's not right. Don't! Please!" She began to sob.

"Caty, Caty, I'm sorry. I love you and want you so much. Say you'll marry me," he said as he released her and helped her to straighten her clothes.

Caterina was truly shocked. She had never thought of marrying Thomas. Realizing her responsibility for what had nearly happened, she said, "Oh, Thomas, I'm so sorry. This is my fault. I haven't meant to lead you on. It's just that I've been so lonely until you came into my life. It felt so good to be cuddled and kissed after all that time of having no one but Ana to hold. I didn't realize what I was doing to you; I've only been thinking of myself. How could I have been so selfish? I just wanted it to go on like it has. Can you forgive me Thomas?"

"Caty, are you saying you don't love me? Won't marry me?"

Caty thought for a minute. Then she looked into his eyes, tears in her own. "I don't know, Thomas. I mean, I know I love you, but I don't know if it's the kind of love a woman should feel for her husband. It's different from what I felt for Rafael. I'm so confused. I can't say I'll marry you unless I sort it all out. It wouldn't be fair to either of us. You're my best friend. You've been so good for me. I don't want to lose you, but I just don't know."

"Caty, I don't want to be just your friend. We can't go on like this. My outfit is leaving St. Augustine tomorrow morning early. There's trouble over on the St. Johns with Indians. There's a place called New Switzerland owned by a Swiss fellow named Fatio. We have to clear the Indians out so he can continue building his plantation. I had hoped to leave knowing you'll become my wife when I return. But maybe, as you say, you'll have it sorted out by then," he said, rising from the sofa and moving to the door, obviously angry.

Jumping up from the sofa, Caterina followed him. She threw her arms around him from behind. "Don't leave like this. I can't bear that I've hurt you. I do love you, but I'm not sure it's the right kind of love. I know I need you, but . . ."

Turning, he cut her words off abruptly with a kiss more passionate than any he had ever given her. When he lifted his face, they were both shaken. "Caty, if you don't let me go now, I'm going to do something we may both regret. I love you. I want you. If you don't back away from me this second, I'll finish what we started on the sofa. God knows, I want to, and I think you do, too. You've given me every indication that you do. Caty, you've been a married woman. You should know a man can take just so much. But, I don't want to force you or cause you to do anything you believe isn't right," he said with just a hint of sarcasm.

She backed away in stunned silence. Thomas opened the door and went out, closing it firmly and, she thought, with finality.

Confused and lonely again, Caterina turned inward. Except when she was with Ana, she thought about Thomas. She tried to sort out her true feelings. She missed his company and the comfort of his strong arms. But she couldn't imagine herself as his wife. Where was the adoration she had felt for Rafael? The tingling at his touch? Comfortable was the best word she could find for their relationship. He was a comfortable companion—kind, tender, and gentle until that night. Where had things gone wrong? How could she have allowed things to progress to that point? She had not heard from Thomas and it had been two months. She missed him. But she only wanted to be his friend.

III

One December evening Caterina answered a knock at the door, and there stood Joseph.

"Hello, Caty. My ship got in an hour ago. Am I too late for supper?" he asked.

After he had eaten, he went up to peek at Ana. He exclaimed over how big she had grown and bent to kiss her sleeping face. He had gifts on the ship for them and he told Caty he just couldn't wait until tomorrow to see "his family" again. He surprised her as he started to leave by turning back, hugging her to him, and lifting her chin to kiss her on her forehead.

After spending the night aboard the ship, he returned early the next morning to his home. When Caterina and Ana came down to breakfast, he was sitting at the kitchen table talking to Mandy.

When Ana saw him, she exclaimed, "Papa Joe!" She ran to him with her chubby little arms outstretched. Caterina had never heard her refer to him that way before. After thinking about it, she realized it shouldn't have surprised her, since he was the only papa she'd ever known.

Joseph was obviously delighted, both with Ana's name for him and her happiness at his return. He held out his arms to her and lifted her on his lap, hugging her to him. She covered his face with little wet kisses. Then she asked, "Is Aunt Sarie with you?"

She still had trouble understanding that if Sarah and her daddy were in heaven, and Joseph was in England, Joseph could come back, but her daddy and Sarah could not.

Joseph explained again, as Caty had done countless times, that Aunt Sarah had gone to heaven to live with God. She would not be coming back.

Putting her head on his shoulder, the little girl said, "I love you, Papa Joe. I sorry Aunt Sarie gone. My daddy in heaven, too. You stay with us now. You live in my house with me and Mama."

Joseph looked at Caterina, who stood blushing and speechless. "You know, I think you're right. I've been thinking along those lines myself. I plan to discuss that with your mama."

Caterina was still nervous and wondering what Joseph was proposing when, after breakfast, he gave Ana one of the gifts he had brought from England. It was a beautiful doll. Its body was stuffed and soft, the head, arms, and legs beautifully carved of wood and painted in lifelike colors. It had a little wig of real hair the color of Caterina's. The hair was bound with a blue ribbon, and a blue, silk veil covered the head and was pinned under the chin. The veil reached the doll's waist as Caty's reached hers. It also wore a wide, gathered, blue skirt that reached mid-leg, blue stockings and a white blouse. Its shoes were white leather decorated with tiny pinholes. It held a silver rosary in one hand and a white lace fan in the other.

Ana bounced in delight, while clapping her hands excitedly. Then she reached out for the doll, saying, "Pretty baby! Thank you! Thank you, Papa Joe!"

Caty said, "Joseph, it's beautiful. It's dressed in the clothes of my people. Wherever did you find such a doll? I've never seen one like it."

"I had it specially made for Ana. I sketched the clothing and chose the material. The miniature rosary was made for me by a silversmith. I chose the hair to match yours. I'm glad you both like it."

They watched as Ana hugged the doll to her, than laid it down gently on a cushion and examined its clothing, the features on its face, and each tiny finger. "Dolly looks like Mama. She is pretty like Mama," the child said.

Joseph said, "I believe you're right, Ana."

Blushing, Caty replied, "I'm not so pretty as that. But thank you both, anyway. Joseph, I can't thank you enough for being as thoughtful as you always are."

Then Joseph handed her a package. When she protested, he laughed and said, "Just open it, Caty."

He had given her a beautiful black silk and lace veil, a fan, and a rosary with clear crystal beads and a golden crucifix.

She couldn't hide her pleasure. "They're so beautiful! I've never had such fine things. But you've already done too much for me, Joseph. I can't accept this."

"What will I do with them, then? I don't know any other Minorcan women."

Caterina could think of no response to that.

Then Joseph said he had business at the ship. Ana played with her doll. Caty went about her daily tasks, thinking of Ana's simple solution to their dilemma and Joseph's response. She had been embarrassed and didn't want Joseph to think she had anything to do with Ana's idea or her calling him Papa Joe. She decided she'd have to tell Joseph so at the first opportunity.

Then there was Captain Andrews. She guessed he was still fighting Indians. She hadn't heard from him since the night she had almost driven him to the point of no return.

He had proposed to her, but she had decided she didn't love him as she should a man she was to marry. She wasn't really sure he wanted to marry her. Maybe he just wanted a wife. Maybe he just needed a woman in the physical sense. Here in St. Augustine men outnumbered women by a large majority. The British government had sent families, military men, and political appointees to East Florida. Except for a couple of Spanish families who had elected to stay when Britain acquired the Floridas, and the local Indians who had been baptized by the Spanish priests, there was no one else in the area. Caterina didn't want to be anyone's wife just because she was the only woman available.

When it was time to put Ana to bed that night, she insisted Papa Joe hear her prayers and tuck her in. When he came back downstairs, Caterina was in the rocker embroidering by lamplight.

"Caty, would you mind putting that down for a while? I want to talk to you," he said.

"Of course, Joseph. I have to talk to you, too."

"Come sit by me," he said, patting the sofa next to him.

Hesitating, Caterina said, "I'd rather sit here, Joseph, if you don't mind. I have to tell you I was stunned when Ana called you Papa Joe."

"Does it bother you for her to call me that?"

"It's not that. I just don't want you to think it was my idea. It was the first time she ever said it. I guess I shouldn't have been surprised, since you're the closest to a father she's known.

"I was also embarrassed by her suggestion we all live here together. She doesn't know what she's saying. We know that's impossible. Now that you're back, will you help us find another place? Maybe somewhere there are other Catholics? People with a similar culture to mine? Maybe you could help us find a place in Havana? I miss the Church, my people, and my language."

A look of alarm crossed his face. Rising from the sofa he came to her and knelt by her chair, "Caty, you don't want to leave me. Not now. I've been thinking of you for months. What Ana said made me so happy, because I know she'll accept my plans. I've loved Ana since before her birth. In fact, I awaited her birth like a father awaits the birth of his own child. You have been part of my family since the first day you came to St. Augustine. I've loved you, too. But my love for you has changed. I want you to marry me. No. Don't say anything now. Think about it. I'll be staying in my cabin aboard ship. I'll talk to you again after Christmas. At least I know there will be no problem with Ana accepting me as her father and your husband," he said, taking Caterina's hand and kissing it. Rising, he put his hat and coat on, said, "Good night," and left.

Caterina tossed and turned most of the night. Sleep eluded her. Her mind toiled with what she should do. She thought, *I'd like to marry again. I want a good father for Ana. I want security for her. But for me, I want what I had with Rafael. Joseph could certainly make Ana's life and future secure. She already loves him and thinks of him as a father. But does he—could he—love me like Rafael did? Could I love him like I loved Rafael?*

On the other had, even if I was sure Thomas truly loved me, that he didn't just want me because there were no other choices available for a good-looking, healthy man, could he even provide for Ana and me? He is in the British army. He lives in a barracks. Could he afford a wife and child? Could he afford a home and to provide the best for Ana? I want more than the bare necessities of life for her. Thomas couldn't give her the best, but Joseph would stop at nothing short of it.

When she finally fell into a troubled sleep, she dreamed of Rafael and of their childhood together on Minorca. She dreamed of their great love for each other and their gentle passion. In her dream she asked Rafael what she should do, but she woke before he could answer.

When she returned to sleep, she dreamed of being married to Thomas and living in a shack much as she and Rafael had shared in Mosquito. She dreamed of Thomas being sent off for months to fight Indians. She dreamed of Ana in rags and hungry; that Thomas had been killed in an Indian raid; of being widowed and destitute again; of Ana being orphaned a second time. When she awoke, she was sure her decision not to marry Thomas had been right, no matter how good he had been to Ana and her.

On Christmas Eve, Joseph was having tea with Caty while Ana napped. He answered a knock at the door to find Captain Andrews there. "Welcome, friend," he said, shaking the captain's hand.

Caty nearly panicked. Both men who wanted to marry her were here together, neither knowing of the other's interest in her. At least she hoped they didn't. She wondered what would happen if one told the other he had proposed to her. Would Joseph bow out if he knew his good friend had been courting her?

Thomas joined them for tea, and she did her part to keep the conversation away from herself. For the most part, the two men discussed Joseph's trip and the Indian situation along the St. Johns River. But Caty didn't leave them alone for a second. As the captain prepared to leave, Joseph invited him to Christmas dinner.

Caterina knew she must make a decision or risk the possibility of the situation being taken out of her hands. Seeing the two together had left her no doubt it was Joseph she truly wanted. After Ana had been tucked in bed, Caty said, "Joseph, may we talk before you leave?"

"Don't we talk after supper every evening, Caty? What's bothering you? You've acted strangely since tea."

"I've been thinking of your proposal. I have to ask you something, and I'm embarrassed."

"Caty, you can talk to me about anything. What is it, dear?"

This was the first time he'd used a term of endearment

to her. "Joseph, do you just want to marry me because it's convenient, and you love Ana? No, wait. I'm not through. Or do you want to marry me because no other women are available, and you need a woman?" she stammered. "I mean, why do you want to marry me?"

Crossing the room to sit by her, he took both her hands in his. "Caty, when I got to England, and my family and friends learned of Sarah's death, everyone had a 'friend' for me who would, naturally, make the 'perfect' wife. I didn't want to think of another wife, but they nearly drove me crazy, forcing women on me. Now, I don't want to sound conceited, because I'm not, but more than one of these ladies was more than willing to become my wife. But as they kept putting me in these situations, I was forced to think of marrying again. And every time I thought of marriage, I thought of you. I had plenty of opportunities to choose another woman. You were the only one I could imagine as my wife.

"Of course I love Ana. I won't deny it's convenient. Yes, it solves your problems, too. But that would never be enough for me. Caty, I've come to love you more every day. I want you for my wife in every way. I think you'll learn to love me as I love you. But, I'm not rushing you. Take all the time you need. Consider all the aspects of it."

Moved tremendously by his speech, without even thinking further about it, she said, "Joseph, I'll marry you."

He swept her into his arms and buried his face in her hair. "You won't regret it, Caty. I'll be a good husband and father." He tilted her head back so he could look into her eyes. "Caty, I'm not going to ask if you are marrying me for any of those reasons you spoke about. It doesn't matter to me. Some of them should be important considerations for you. But, I want you to love me, too. I think I can teach you to." He kissed her then, trying desperately to control his passion, to keep it gentle so he wouldn't frighten her with the intensity of his feelings for her.

When Joseph finally lifted his lips from hers, she felt abandoned. In his arms she had somehow felt home. She put her arms around his neck and kissed him again. In those kisses she found what had been missing with Thomas. She knew she wanted him—not only for Ana, but for herself. She knew that with Joseph she'd have it all.

On Christmas morning Joseph gave her the most beautiful ring she had ever seen. It had been made in England and was inscribed, *Caty, love forever, Joseph, 1771.*

At Christmas dinner, Joseph proposed a toast to Caty and announced that she had agreed to become his bride.

Thomas's face paled, and he hoped Joseph didn't notice him looking at Caterina as if she had betrayed him. Regaining his composure, he congratulated Joseph and offered another toast, this one to both of them.

Little Ana offered, "Papa Joe is going to really be my daddy."

Shortly after dinner, Thomas left. Caty was relieved. Now that he knew of her engagement, he wasn't apt to tell Joseph that he, too, had proposed to her. She had told Joseph how kind the captain had been to her and Ana and of the outings they had shared. She was ashamed of her behavior and hoped she hadn't hurt Thomas. She was glad he was a gentleman and hadn't taken advantage of her loneliness, as she now realized some other man might have. She was very fond of him, as was Joseph, and she hoped he'd still be their friend.

She and Joseph discussed and planned their wedding in the evenings after supper. Caty wanted to be married by Father Camps. Joseph wanted to share her religion. But when he asked the governor's permission to go to New Smyrna to be married by the priest, the governor adamantly refused.

He said Caty could not go to the colony. The presence of a former colonist, now free and living in St. Augustine, would incite even more "malcontents" to run away. It was out of the question.

When Joseph asked if he could bring the priest to St. Augustine to perform the ceremony, he was told, "Absolutely not. Britain allows no papist priests in East Florida. It is only with special permission that Dr. Turnbull was allowed to bring two priests from Minorca to minister to the colonists. The Minorcans would not have come without their priests. Reverend Forbes, our Anglican minister, will perform your wedding, or you may have a civil ceremony." He wanted to dissuade Joseph form marrying the Minorcan woman, but couldn't take a chance on losing the crown's credit with Joseph's shipping firm.

Joseph had brought bolts of material from England. Among them were white satin and lace, from which Caty styled a lovely wedding dress and veil in Minorcan style.

Ana celebrated her second birthday on February 22, 1772. The next day was the anniversary of Sarah's death. Joseph and Caty visited her grave. They took a wreath Caty had woven of wild azalea and other local plants. It was at Sarah's grave that Caty learned Sarah had been the first to suggest that after her death, Joseph should marry her. It was a great comfort to them both to know they had the blessings of Sarah, whom they had both loved.

The year of mourning over, it was now proper for the widowed Joseph to remarry. Caterina had been bitterly disappointed that permission had not been granted for Father Camps to marry them. She had met the Reverend Forbes on several occasions, and liked him, but he was not a Catholic priest. She was devout in her religious beliefs, even though she was living in a place where there was no Catholic church and she could not receive the sacraments. A civil ceremony was also out of the question.

She had not been to confession since before leaving New Smyrna, and she felt the burden of her sins. Little Ana was two years old and had not been baptized. She wanted to rectify all this and start her new marriage to Joseph with the blessings of her church.

So on March 15, 1772, Joseph, Ana, and Caty sailed for Cuba on Joseph's newest vessel which he had named *Ana*. On March 20, Joseph and Ana had both been baptized into the Catholic faith. The next day, Caterina, age twenty, and Joseph, age forty, entered their second marriages. Caterina, looking into Joseph's face as he said, "I do," saw an extremely handsome man with brown hair beginning to gray at the temples, a neat mustache, thick brown brows over blue eyes with golden glints. His face held such a look of love and appreciation for her that her eyes filled with tears. She said a silent prayer that she would always be worthy of his love and trust.

Before they left Havana, the bishop asked Joseph to deliver some religious materials to Father Camps in New Smyrna for use in St. Peter's Church. Joseph knew Governor Grant would disapprove, but he decided to do it anyway. He had allowed the governor to prevent Father Camps from performing the marriage, but his patience was growing thin with Britain's treatment of the colonists and the lack of religious freedom allowed in East Florida. Besides, Governor Grant needed him more than he needed the governor.

Upon reaching New Smyrna, Joseph asked permission to make a delivery of religious supplies to St. Peter's. A plantation manager verified the contents of the shipment and told him to leave it on the docks, and he would have it delivered.

"I can't do that," said Joseph. "I must have Father Camps' signature that he received shipment. Besides, I have a Cuban crewman on board who suffered a serious injury since we left Cuba. He's begging for a priest," he lied.

That didn't sway the manager, but finally Joseph offered a substantial bribe, and the priest was sent for.

When he arrived, Joseph sent the priest to his cabin to 'tend the sick crewman', while he plied the manager with expensive liquor.

Father entered the cabin to be greeted by a beautiful young Minorcan woman and her little girl. "Father, it's me, Caterina Reyes. And this is my daughter, Ana," the young woman said.

"My child, what are you doing here? No one knew what happened to you. You just disappeared. And where is Rafael?"

"It's a long story, Father. Briefly, the overseer, Pedro Ponti, tried to force himself on me. Rafael stopped him and killed him in self defense. We escaped to St. Augustine where we met Joseph Adams. He went with us to the governor and tried to arrange to buy our indentures. Turnbull would only sell mine. The ship returning Rafael to Mosquito was lost in a hurricane. Rafael was killed. He never even saw his daughter.

"I became Sarah Adams's companion. She died a year ago last month. After her death Joseph went to England on business, and Ana and I stayed in his home. When Joseph returned, he asked me to marry him. We wanted to be married by you, but Governor Grant forbade it.

"We went to Havana where Joseph and Ana were baptized, and we were married. Then the bishop asked us to deliver supplies to you. Joseph bribed the manager to get you on board so I could talk to you. He doesn't know Ana and I are here," she finished.

"I'm so sorry to hear about Rafael, child. I shall say a Mass for him. But I'm glad you escaped the hell we are in. The news of your escape will give our people new hope and courage. Rest assured, I shall tell them. Of course, I won't reveal my source.

"Caterina, Dr. Turnbull has not kept one promise he made to any colonist. We are all in rags. We don't get enough to eat. We are abused, and denied any freedom. In short, we are but ill-treated slaves. Some indentures have been completely served, but by threatening other family members, confinement and other forceful means, Turnbull has caused those colonists to sign new indentures. He doesn't plan to free any of us. And Governor Grant is his friend and co-conspirator. We have no one but God to turn to. Pray for us, Caterina," Father Camps said.

Then, blessing both Caterina and Ana, he said, "I'd better go before the manager discovers he has been tricked. Besides the consequences to me, you might be forcibly taken back to the colony, and your new husband might suffer political or financial consequences. Good-bye, dear Caterina and Ana. May God be with you."

"Wait, Father, I haven't asked about Josefina or my relatives and friends. I don't know who is alive or dead . . ." Caty started, but was interrupted by a knock on the door.

A crewman said, "Father Camps, the manager says if you don't come on, he's coming after you. He says he don't trust you no way, and you've had long enough to hear a dozen confessions and give as many of them other papist sacraments."

After Father Camps left, Caterina wept at the plight of her people. She wanted to help them but was powerless to do so. She thanked God that Ana didn't have to live, and possibly die, in such conditions. She remembered with rushes of love and gratitude that she owed this to Rafael, who had gotten her safely to St. Augustine, and to Joseph, who had been able to keep her there. Rafael had given his life for them. She wouldn't forget that, nor would she let Ana. Joseph had seen that she and Ana had been taken care of and would continue to do so. In fact, he would see they had the very best.

On their return they learned Governor Grant had left East Florida on a leave of absence. In 1773, he resigned as governor of Florida. That same year the British began building the King's Road to the St. Marys River on the north and to New Smyrna on the south end. It was to make it easier for goods to reach the main British port of St. Augustine for shipping. Sixteen feet wide, it was of coquina rock from the King's quarries on Anastasia Island. Governor Grant had conceived the idea; it was his biggest accomplishment in East Florida.

The year 1774 saw the arrival of a new governor, Patrick Tonyn, in St. Augustine. From the beginning he and Andrew Turnbull didn't see eye to eye.

Ana, now four, was a little replica of Caty. Joseph adored both of them to the point of overindulging their every whim. Except for Caty's concern for the plight of the colonists, they were happy in every way. She had recently learned that Turnbull had deported Father Casanova, assistant to Father Camps and fellow Minorcan. He had stood up for the rights of the colonists, rightly so, and was branded a troublemaker. He was accused of insubordination, no matter that he felt accountable to God, and not to Turnbull. Caterina had hopes the new governor, Tonyn, would treat her countrymen with fairness.

Nicholas Turnbull, son of Andrew, lived on St. Francis Street in St. Augustine. Joseph had to deal with him frequently concerning the shipping of indigo and other produce from New Smyrna, since he was the government commissar. He had let it be known he wasn't all that happy Joseph harbored and then married a former indentured colonist. Easygoing Joseph would fold his arms across his chest, plant his feet apart, tilt his head back and look down at Nicholas through half-closed eyes as though amused. This infuriated Nicholas, but he knew Joseph was a powerful man in the business world. He also suspected if he pushed too far, mild-tempered Joseph could be powerful in the physical sense.

Former Governor Grant had ordered a detail of soldiers

to keep order at the plantation almost from the start. Now, Caterina learned their friend Captain Andrews was being sent to replace the former captain in charge of the detachment. She urged Joseph to invite him to dinner before his departure.

Thomas was happy to be invited. Caty and Joseph rarely entertained guests for dinner, except for business or holidays. Many of Joseph's former friends didn't like Joseph's having become Catholic or his marriage to Caty. Independent as he was, he didn't care. It only hurt him for Caty's and Ana's sakes. He had little patience for the snobbery of such people. He declared they had never been friends to begin with and called them ignorant, intolerant busy bodies.

Caty was so wrapped up in her family and the plight of the colonists at Mosquito, Thomas supposed she didn't mind their semi-isolation. He also sensed Caty felt awkward in his presence because of their former relationship. Maybe she hadn't told Joseph and was afraid he would. He had plenty of chances to do so, because he and Joseph frequently saw each other outside their home. She needn't have worried. He still felt a strong attraction and affection for her. But Joseph would always be his friend, and he would never do anything to harm either of them.

Dinner was delicious. He was surprised to find he was the only guest. The conversation was lively, and after the first few minutes, Caty took her cue from Thomas, joining in the conversation freely.

It was after dinner when the three of them were visiting in the living room that she said, "Joseph tells me you are being sent to join the so-called peacekeeping force at New Smyrna. May I ask you a favor?"

Thomas thought, *Ah, so this is the reason for the dinner invitation,* but he said, "Of course. What can I do for you, Caterina?" He always wondered whether he should be calling her Mrs.

Adams, but couldn't break the habit of calling her by her first name.

"Would you carry a message to Father Camps for me and send me news of the colonists? I have relatives and friends there. I don't know if they're alive or dead. In particular, I would like to know about my little cousin, Josefina Pons. She was twelve when I left. She'd be seventeen now. I used to babysit her in Minorca. I wish I could send clothes and food with you, but I know you wouldn't be allowed to take them. I know I'm asking a lot. You could get into trouble, and I don't want you to endanger yourself. If you think it's too risky, I'll understand."

Thomas didn't even have to think about it. He hated the fact that he was being sent to New Smyrna. He had heard rumors of the ill treatment of the Minorcans, as the group of Italians, Greeks and Minorcans had all become called. He remembered the things Caterina had told him about conditions there. He also knew Joseph had tried and been denied permission to send food and clothing to his wife's former fellow colonists. He had determined no matter what the consequences, he would be fair and kind to them.

"I'll take your message, Caterina. And I'll check on Miss Pons. I don't know how often I'll be able to contact you, or even how, but I'll find a way. I, too, am upset about the way those people are mistreated, and you can be sure I'll be fair to them," he said.

It was then that Caterina realized that, like Joseph, Captain Thomas Andrews was truly a good man, and that he harbored no ill feelings toward her. She felt as though a great weight had been lifted from her. She knew he was probably their only true friend in East Florida. She wished he could find a girl to marry and be happy with, but there was little chance of that here.

Thomas had been in New Smyrna three weeks when a

British soldier brought a letter to Joseph from him. Ana could hardly wait for Joseph to come home to read it.

When Joseph broke the wax seal and opened the envelope, he found a letter to both of them from Thomas and one to Caty from Father Camps.

Father Camps's letter began with a cross in the upper left corner. Then:

> *My Dear Caterina,*
>
> *Captain Andrews bought your letter to me today, February 26, 1775. Things are no better here than when I last saw you. People are still mistreated and dying. The food is awful, sometimes full of weevils, or sour, or even rotten, and there is never enough. Those poor souls who have been ordered confined are not allowed meat or fish. Dr. Turnbull himself sometimes picks through their hominy to see if there are any pieces of meat or fish in it!*
>
> *I am sorry to tell you your Uncle Luigi died last year. He was too sick to work, so he was put on half rations and beaten. Several hours after one of the beatings he died, God rest his soul. I gave him the last sacrament.*
>
> *Two years ago your Uncle Gaspar and Aunt Juana finished their indentures but were not allowed to leave. Your Uncle was isolated in chains because he insisted on the conditions of his indenture being fulfilled. They nearly starved him. Later he was beaten and put in stocks for a week. Juana and the children were threatened and also beaten. In the end, he signed to extend his indenture. Shortly after, your Aunt Juana died, as did the two youngest children. Their eldest daughter, Josefina, is now seventeen. One of the overseers won't leave her alone. I am powerless to protect her. She only has her father left, and I believe she is of*

a mind that she will do whatever she has to in order to protect him.

I cannot write you often for fear of retribution against my poor, miserable people. I hope and pray your husband's position will keep you and Ana safe and unharmed, but I beg you to remember he cannot help us. Please be careful. Pray for us, please. Only contact me if you must so as not to cause further harm to your fellow countrymen.

Yours in Christ,
Reverend Pedro camps

Caterina wept while reading the letter, great tears making splotches on the ink. Without speaking, she handed the letter to Joseph. He gave her the one he had just read from Thomas.

Dear Joseph and Caterina,
I found Father Camps and gave him your letter as soon as I safely could. I am absolutely sick at the conditions in which these poor people are forced to live. Everything is filthy. Their clothes are little more than rags. Little children are covered with flies and mosquitoes. Mothers can't keep flies out of the eyes, mouths, and noses of their babies.

There is very little flesh on anyone except the overseers, some of whom are quite portly. If anyone sneaks away to collect oysters or to fish, it is confiscated. A snake or lizard doesn't stand a chance. I am told they even boil any scraps of leather they can get and try to eat it.

I have witnessed beatings and even stopped several. Once I even saw Dr. Turnbull beat and kick a man. None of these beatings seem necessary or deserved.
Caterina, I have found your cousin, Josefina.

She is a beautiful girl, even though she is much too thin. She and her father are all that is left of her family. Her father is very ill. An overseer is trying to convince her to have a liaison with him in exchange for food and medical treatment. I have intervened and even gone to Dr. Turnbull. For the present the overseer is staying away from her, but I don't know how long it will last.

Already the overseers hate me. Evidently this peace-keeping force I am part of has only been supporting the colony's leaders. You know how biased the crown is against Catholics and toward anything that will help to colonize East Florida, not to mention turn profit for the crown.

Please do not write me. It is too dangerous for these poor people and my position. I cannot help them if I am relieved of my command. I'll do what I can to get information to you when it's possible.

Your friend always,
Thomas

Thomas was amazed at what went into making the blue dye, indigo. He was also amazed that men in power could believe the dye and the money it generated was a fair trade for the miserable conditions the colonists endured and the lives of so many of them. He noticed Dr. Andrew Turnbull had built his coquina mansion some four miles from the fields. The colonists lived in palm-thatched huts bordering them and near the stinking curing sheds.

First the colonists cleared the ground, which had to be made flat. They loosened the soil and sowed four bushels of seed to an acre. They planted all through the spring. Indigo took ten weeks to blossom and the colonists harvested from spring through fall. The indigo was cut and tied into bundles to be steeped in vats. It was weighted down with heavy timber and allowed to ferment in water. The purplish blue liquid took eight to twenty hours to ferment. Holes were then un-plugged in the bottom of the vats so the liquid could seep into the beating vats.

The strongest men churned this brew by drawing two bottomless buckets on the ends of a pole, up and down into the liquid. The residue was drained off into another vat, allowed to settle for eight to ten hours, and strained. The pure indigo was put in bags and hung to drain, then put in boxes to dry. It was cut into small blocks and dried some more before shipping. Indigo was extracted and cured in sheds to prevent the sun from fading the color. The drying blocks of dye had to be turned several times a day.

The stench of the fermenting indigo was overpowering. Colonists were constantly employed to keep the flies drawn by the foul odor off, so they wouldn't damage the indigo. But the flies and the stench plagued the Minorcans at work and in their nearby miserable shacks; they made it almost impossible to raise chickens and livestock.

Indigo must have water, so Turnbull had his laborers dig canals for irrigation. The canals increased the mosquito population. The mosquitoes carried malaria and other maladies.

Every stage of the indigo process was backbreaking hard labor, done by people virtually enslaved, starved, and mis-treated in the middle of a jungle far from their homes. No one cared whether they lived or died, only that they pro-duce a large quantity of good indigo so Turnbull could turn a profit. Never mind that the crown also wanted to people East Florida, and these colonists were supposedly also here to do that. It seemed that was not high on Turnbull's list of priorities, as the colonists were killed in large numbers by the conditions they were forced to live in, lack of food and medical care, unending hard labor, and the cruelty of Turnbull and his overseers.

At Thomas's first meeting with Josefina, he had felt

strangely drawn to this skinny, ragged girl with the haunt-ingly beautiful, suntanned face and big brown eyes made even larger by the hollowness of her cheeks. He guessed it was because she had such spunk. Except for her father, she had lost her whole family. Her father was ill but had been beaten and forced to work anyway. And the overseer, Guiseppi, offered medical care for him and better food and conditions for both if she would be "nice" to him. In order to save her father, she had been willing to give in to the overseer when Thomas had first met her and become aware of the situation.

After Thomas's intervention, he though she would be grateful. Instead, she was angry. "What business is this of yours? I could have gotten help for my father. Sure, you help us. But, where will you be next week, next month, or even next year? I've seen you soldiers come and go. Conditions here only go from bad to worse. Guiseppi will be back. If not, someone worse will replace him. And when that happens, he will just take what he wants, and he won't help Papa, either," she said.

Only when she was with her father did he see her face soften with tenderness. At those times he also saw fear on her face. Thomas knew that fear was that her father would die, too.

But after a couple of months when Thomas was still there, still their protector, she began to soften toward him. Her father was healing but would never be well enough to work in the fields again, and Thomas would not allow the overseers to force him.

Josefina worked from daylight to dark. This time of year the fields were being tilled for the new crop of indigo to be planted. She no longer had the fair skin of her cousin, Caterina. The sun had bronzed hers so it was as dark as the Minorcan men who were accustomed to making their living outdoors, fishing, hunting, and farming before coming to

New Smyrna. Her veils had long ago been used to patch the tears in her skirts and blouses.

There were no new clothes for the colonists. When someone died, his or her clothes were passed on to someone else. When clothes were outgrown, they were handed down or made over in the feeble light of candles or lamps in the late hours of evening. Eight years had taken their toll on clothing as well as colonists. Curtains and bed clothing brought from Minorca had been turned into skirts, blouses, shirts, and pants. Josefina's waist was no larger than it had been at ten, so she still wore what was left of a couple of skirts she had brought with her, only now they were above her knee, stained and patched. Her blouses were tight around her bosom. Underwear was scarce to nonexistent. And she worked barefoot from April through October to save her mother's worn-out shoes to wear in the cold months.

Still, she managed to keep herself, her hut, and her clothing clean. And although her hair had lost most of its gloss due to poor nutrition and the relentless sun, it was always neatly braided.

Thomas thought that neither her ragged, ill-fitting clothes, nor her much too evident bones, could hide the beauty nor the spirit of this young girl. Her dark eyes still sparkled at times, and her sense of humor remained. He knew, as she did, that no matter what, she was a survivor. But he wanted so badly for her to be more than a mere survivor.

Somehow word of the American Revolution to the north had reached the colonists, and Josefina frequently questioned Thomas about it. Plainly she wanted her fellow colonists to follow the example of their northern counterparts and rise up against the tyranny of the English.

Thomas had always thought of himself as a loyal English-man, but the things he was witnessing here were showing him the cruel harshness and bitter reality of English coloni-zation, at least on this plantation. Still, Governor Tonyn had made it clear that he was alert to disloyalty to the crown. Thomas could not take a chance on being tried for treason. At any rate, he knew very little of what went on outside of St. Augustine, although rumors of a revolution against British rule had been around for several years and had been more prevalent as of late.

Josefina knew Thomas had a soft spot for her. She felt a warm glow when she thought of him at night alone in her bed, the only time she had to think of anything outside of work and survival. But this didn't stop her from using him to find out all she could and to get whatever help he could give her father and her people. She hated the British for what was happening here in Mosquito, and he was, after all, the enemy.

One evening when she knew Thomas was coming over to check on them, she urged her father to visit and comfort a friend whose wife had also died. When Thomas arrived, bringing some of his rations to share with her and her father, she was alone. The lamp had been placed where it shone on her cot in the one room shack. Sitting on the edge of it, head thrown back, she brushed her freshly washed hair. Her pretty legs, crossed and bare to her upper thigh under one of her outgrown skirts, were posed to excite him.

As she hoped he would be, Thomas was overcome by her beauty and thought her too innocent to realize how provocative she looked.

Right away she told him, "Papa is spending the evening with a friend. Come and sit by me, Thomas."

Seeing her like that, in the glow of the lamp with her long hair loose and her bare legs showing to best advantage, Thomas could not help himself. Going to her, he knelt by the bed, lay his head on her Lap, and put his arms around her waist. His heart was pounding fast as he said, "Josefina, do you know what you are doing?"

She leaned forward, her long black hair covering him,

her breasts touching his head. "Yes, Thomas, yes," she said in a soft voice, lifting his head between both hands so their lips could meet.

"I love you, Josefina. I think I have since the first moment I saw you," he said, shocked by the realization of it and by his desire. They kissed hungrily for a while, and when his lips and hands became more insistent, she didn't protest. It was only after that he realized she had not only known exactly what she was doing, but she had planned it. But it wasn't for love of him. Her love for her people and desire for their freedom had caused her to use him and his love for her, as she had been about to let the overseer use her.

After he had loved her as gently as a man in such a passion can, she had asked, "Now, Thomas, will you tell me all you know about the revolt in the upper colonies? Will you help me to help my people join in that revolt before we are all dead?"

Saddened more than angry at her misuse of his feelings, he said, "I've told you all I know. I'm helping in every way I possibly can. And I wasn't doing it so I could have my way with you. That never crossed my mind until you set this little charade up. I love you. I thought you loved me. But now I know you wouldn't blink an eye if I was hung for treason, which I may well be committing, if you could trade my life for just one of the lives of your people.

"Josefina, are you incapable of any personal feeling because of your great love and pain for your fellow colonists and your hate for your captors? Are you driven to do anything you imagine will help them?

"For me, this is madness. I have risked everything tonight in my blind passion for you, even my ability to help you. I'm little better than the overseer I sought to save you from, except it can't be said I used you or took you against your will. Nor can you say it was my idea. I won't be seeing you alone again," he said.

As he turned to leave, he added sarcastically, "It's a shame your people will never know the sacrifice you made for them tonight, and for what I would have done anyway—my best to help you all."

He didn't see the tears in Josefina's eyes. She did love Thomas, but she had purposely tried to use him. She was sorry it had backfired, and she was sorry she had hurt this good man and probably her chances of a life with him if that would have some day been possible. But just as she'd survived the death of loved ones and all the other miseries of this stinking place, she'd survive without Thomas, too, if she had to. But she didn't plan to give him up just yet.

She also knew what Thomas was suffering was slight in comparison to the suffering her people were enduring, and which she wanted to find a way to stop. She could put death, that of her friends and relatives which had already occurred, even that which she and the remaining colonists faced daily, from her mind. Surely she, and Thomas as well, could push this from their minds. At least, she thought they could.

Father Camps wrote to Spain asking to be relieved as priest of St. Peter's Parish. Sick at heart and in failing health, the good and holy priest could no longer bear the suffering of his people. But when permission was granted, he found he couldn't bear to abandon them. He stayed to give them what spiritual strength he could, and so they would not be without Mass and the sacraments.

From the time of his arrival in East Florida, Governor Tonyn had suspected Dr. Turnbull's loyalty to the British crown. Turnbull decided to go to London to complain about the governor's treatment of him and his colony. Rumors reached the colonists that persuaded them there were problems between Turnbull and Tonyn, so they decided in his absence to send several people to St. Augustine to tell their story and appeal to the governor, whom they hoped would be sympathetic to their cause. Two months later, in May 1777, while Turnbull was still away, ninety colonists walked to St. Augustine to tell the governor of their treatment. Among them was Josefina.

Of the ninety, eighteen were chosen by Attorney General Yonge, on Tonyn's instructions, to give depositions. The others, including Josefina, were sent back to the colony to help harvest the crops.

The depositions charged six or seven murders. Everyone complained of starvation, withholding of wages and provisions, contracts not being honored, cruel overseers, beatings and imprisonments, and not being released at the end of their indentures. There were charges of rape and attempted rape. One starving woman had been beaten for roasting an ear of corn in the field. A man working in the field ten miles away was caught, beaten and made to return when he tried to get to his dying wife. She died without his having seen her. Others were beaten when they refused to work on holy days, which was against their religion.

A young, sick, and starving child was beaten and made to work anyway. When he could no longer stand, an overseer put him on a stump where he ordered the other boys to stone him to death.

Turnbull himself was reported to have committed some of these atrocities, including whipping some men who were too weak and sick to cut grass for the horses, and picking through the hominy of others who were in chains and isolation because they asked to be discharged at the end of their contracts. Turnbull was checking to be sure his order that further punishment forbidding meat and fish for his prisoners was being carried out.

Governor Tonyn sent the depositions to Lord George Germain along with a letter denouncing the tyranny and oppression of Turnbull. He was afraid the rebellious Georgians would invade East Florida to free the Minorcans. He advocated their release and said he had advised the attorney general to "settle the matter with justice."

Joseph had learned of the Minorcan's arrival and had brought Josefina to stay overnight with Caty. They had been overjoyed to see each other. Josefina had eaten her fill for the first time since leaving Minorca. Caty had fitted her with clean and practically new clothing and shoes. Josefina gave her news of family and friends and told her of complaints they had brought to the governor. For the first time since their arrival in New Smyrna, Caty had real hope for her people. She felt the end of their enslavement must surely be near.

So much was there for Josefina to tell her, and so short was the time, that she never had a chance to discuss Thomas with Caty.

Caty knew her people had finally found a sympathetic ear when Governor Tonyn ordered the release of the colonists, and in May of 1777 they were led to St. Augustine over Governor Grant's King's Road by Francisco Pellicer, a Minorcan carpenter who had helped build Turnbull's mansion. The journey took three days for the six hundred men, women, and children.

The sick and dying were unable to make the march. Father Camps stayed with them, as did Josefina, whose father was too sick to march. She aided the priest in caring for these people. Captain Andrews also stayed, as he was ordered to. When they were shipped to St. Augustine, Father Camps was not allowed to go with them. Turnbull's men blamed him for the spirit his people showed in finally standing up for themselves.

A military ship was sent from St. Augustine to transport those who had been unable to walk. Thomas and Josefina were the only able-bodied aboard except for the military crew. They helped care for the needs of the sick, but they still found some time to be together. Standing at the rail, Josefina glowed with happiness. She was a Josefina Thomas had never seen before, and he thought he had never seen her more beautiful. Turning to him, she said, "Can you forgive me for hurting you? I can't say I'm sorry for trying everything to help my father and the others. But, I didn't set out to deliberately hurt you. It's just that you, me, us—we weren't important compared to a whole colony of starving, sick and mistreated people," she said.

"Josefina, I understand what you're saying. And I know how much of your life has been spent in hell. But, I've never known a *lady* to use her womanly charms like that. You may call it unselfish, courageous, and maybe it was. But to my way of thinking, it was immoral and wrong. I loved you. I thought you loved me. You used and abused my love. I can forgive you, but I don't know if I'll ever be able to forget," he said.

Lifting her chin to smile at him through her tears, she said, "I swear there has never been anyone else. And I promise you this: you'll never find anyone else to love you like I do. I was meant for you. And now that my people are free, I'll turn all my energy and attention, and use any means I can, to become Mrs. Andrews—including your desire for me and the memory of our shared passion. You'll forget. I'll make you forget."

He opened his mouth to speak, but she put her finger to his lips to stop him. "Don't deny you desire me. I've seen enough in that wretched place we just left to recognize that you do." She looked around to see if anyone else was about. Seeing no one, she lifted a foot to the rail, slid her skirt up to her thigh, and, through the tears that were sliding unbidden down her face, she forced herself to laugh at him.

Shocked at first, he, too, looked around to convince himself no one else had seen her shocking behavior. But, he had seen past the laughter to the pleading in her eyes. It cut him to his soul. And she was right; he couldn't deny it. So, playing her game, he pulled her to him roughly, pressing her body to his in an embrace meant only for the marriage chamber.

He grabbed her braid with the other hand, pulling it gently down to lift her face to his. Looking boldly into her eyes, he kissed her, not trying to hold back the passion he felt. The kiss was long and hard, and neither closed their eyes. After, their lips still searing from the kiss, he released her and said, half jesting and half seriously, "I may learn to like this game." Turning, he strode away, barely able to suppress his surprise and delight in the knowledge it was going to be all right between them after all.

Caty was happier than she could remember. She was reunited with relatives and friends she hadn't seen in years. But there was sadness, too, because of those who hadn't lived to see this day, especially, Rafael. How they had looked forward to the day when they could be together, and free with their child. But that would never be. And now she was married to Joseph, a good man who would fight the world for her and Ana.

Then, when the ship arrived bringing the sick and old, Josefina and Captain Andrews, she and the other colonists were at the dock to welcome them. All were dismayed when they learned Father Camps had been detained and was not among them. They determined then and there to petition the governor for his release, also.

Joseph and Caty insisted her Uncle Gaspar and her cousin Josefina stay in their home. How good it felt to have friends and relatives again! How good to be among Minorcans once more!

In the whole of St. Augustine in 1777, there were only about three hundred houses, and these were occupied by about fifteen hundred residents and their slaves. Another hundred or so families lived in East Florida, mostly scattered on plantations such as Lieutenant Governor John Moultrie's lovely Bella Vista on the Matanzas River and his Rosetta on the Tomoka, and Governor Tonyn's Broclair Bluff on the St. Johns.

And so, once more, six hundred plus settlers from New

Smyrna found no accommodations for themselves. The fall
and winter they spent huddled in the shelter of the coquina
walls of the city they had looked to for salvation.

Father Camps arrived November ninth. With him the
beloved church of Saint Peter was transferred, to the delight
of the new community. To them, the church, through good
times and bad times, was the center of their lives. It was relo-
cated to a dilapidated building on the northern end of St.
George Street. The former Catholic church that had served
the Spanish in previously Spanish St. Augustine had been
turned into a British military hospital.

The rain and cold inflicted its toll on the remaining
Minorcans that first winter. By January, their numbers had
diminished to 419. Then Governor Tonyn granted them small
plots outside the city gates in northern St. Augustine.

But in St. Augustine there was no one to prevent them
from fishing and hunting. And there was time to do it. There
was freedom to come and go. There were no beatings, solitary confinements, or other cruelties inflicted purposely by
man. Their hope had returned.

The Catholic Church became the center of their cul-
tural and social life as it had been on the other side of the
ocean. The streets rang with the melodic languages of the
Minorcan, Greek, and Italian immigrants.

Shortly after Father Camps arrived, Josefina and Thomas
told Caty and Joseph of their plan to marry. Hugging her
cousin, Caty said, "I'm so happy for you both. We'll have a real
wedding, the kind none of us has seen since we left home.
St. Peter's may be dilapidated and small, but Father Camps
and our folks are here. Now that you're eating better, you'll
fit my wedding dress if you'd like to wear it. Oh, honey, I'm so
glad for you," she said.

Then she turned to Thomas and hugged him. "Welcome into our family, Thomas. I know she'll be happy with
you, and I wish you both the very best."

Joseph likewise congratulated them both. Then, winking at Thomas, he said, "We're two Britons who decided if we couldn't beat the Minorcans, we'd best join them."

Later, Joseph asked Thomas what his plans were concerning the military. Thomas replied, "I'll have ten years in come January tenth. I'm not going to reenlist. Josefina wants to live here among her people. Naturally, her father will live with us. I'm a good hunter and fisherman. I've saved a little. I've already put in for a grant of land from the crown. We won't have a plantation, but I think we can manage a small place outside of town and live off the land. Gaspar will teach me how to farm."

"If I can help you in any way, friend, let me know. If you need a loan, I'll take care of that. And seeing as your bride is my kin, I'll be giving her a wedding and a dowry. Since you want to farm, the dowry will be livestock of your choosing."

On May 7, 1778, in the little church on St. George Street, Father Camps united Caty's cousin and Joseph's best friend in holy matrimony. At twenty-one, Josefina was no longer the skinny kid she had been when Thomas first met her. Her black hair was now lustrous and fell below her waist. Her eyes sparkled under the same thick lashes as Caty's. But her personality was completely her own. She was bold, and her sense of humor was well developed. When she laughed, she threw back her head and let it come from deep within her. When she set her mind to something, she persisted. She did whatever was necessary to make it happen. She held her head high, and her smile mirrored her happiness as she walked down the short aisle of St. Peter's church on her father's arm to become Mrs. Thomas Andrews.

Thomas, in a new black suit and white shirt, waited at the altar. *He's more handsome now at twenty-nine than when he thought he was in love with me,* Caty thought. *He's happier than I've ever seen him. It's good to know he's gotten over me and that I made the right decision for him as well as for me when I turned him down. And Joseph standing beside him as his best man looks almost the same as when we married eight years ago. His hair has more gray. Why, Joseph is forty-six and, and I'm twenty-six. Sometimes it seems we've been together forever. At other times I wake in the middle of the night to see him beside me, and I'm shocked because he isn't Rafael. But I mustn't think of us now. This is Josefina's day.*

Joseph, giving Caty a look of infinite love during the wedding vows, thought, *I'm really lucky Caty is mine. She's as pretty as the day she became my bride. Lately she seems happier. When she told me a few years ago about Thomas courting her while I was in England after Sarah's death, I didn't like it a bit. In fact, I was mad as hell. The green eyed monster nearly made me act like a jealous fool until I remembered she chose me. And she's as happy for Thomas and Josefina as I am. I only have one regret: as much as I love Ana, I'd still like us to have a baby.*

Only family and very close friends could attend the wedding because of the small size of St. Peter's. But the whole Minorcan community, Thomas's military friends, and a handful of Joseph's English friends attended the outdoor reception given by Mr. and Mrs. Joseph Adams. It was held in the plaza. Besides food and drink, there was music and dancing. St. Augustine had not seen anything like it since the British came to town.

Joseph and Caty felt as if they'd renewed their wedding vows. That night at home he said, "Caty, I wish I could find the words to tell you how much you mean to me. It's hard to believe we've been married eight years. I still think of you as my bride. The better I know you, the more I love you."

"Darling Joseph, I've been thinking the same about you. When I saw you standing beside Thomas at the altar, my heart jumped in my chest. It did that on our wedding day. Our marriage has been more than I ever dreamed a marriage could be. After Rafael died, I thought my life was over, too. You've given me a new life. I've never been able to discuss Rafael's death with anyone before, but after Sarah died, I knew you understood. I knew no one would ever take Rafael's place, just as you must have known no one could take Sarah's. But, if we allow it, the human heart never stops growing. There's always room for more love in it. You've made a place of your very own in my heart, my darling Joseph, that is only yours."

That night would always stand out in Joseph's mind because of Caty's words and because for the first time he knew she truly abandoned herself to their lovemaking.

A week later, Joseph regretfully had to leave for England.

Life in St. Augustine took on an entirely new character. Caty saw her impoverished countrymen once more able to display their spiritual richness. Social life became centered on religious celebrations. Holy days and Sundays became holidays as they had in the old country. St. Augustine celebrated with food, music, dancing, and sometimes even horse races. How Caty and Ana enjoyed it all.

St. Augustine had no school, but Caty taught Ana, now eight, to read and write, in both the Minorcan dialect and English, and to sew, cook, make candles and soap and to perform other domestic duties.

One morning in July when she was helping Ana with her lessons, she suddenly felt weak. Ana saw her face go white. Touching her, she felt her face was covered in a cold, thin sweat. "Mama, what's wrong?" she asked as Caty leaned her head back on the chair. Then Caty slid from her chair onto the floor. The frightened child eased her down as best she could.

When she came to, her daughter was rubbing her hands with tears running down her cheeks. Things were whirling around her, and she felt weak and drained. In a minute or two she said, "I must have fainted. Just let me lie here and get a wet cloth for my head. I'll be all right in a minute."

When Ana returned with Mandy and the wet cloth, Caty

said, "Ana, I'm sorry I scared you. Don't fret so. I'm all right now. It's probably the heat."

The next morning, when she came to breakfast, the smell of cooking food nauseated her. She began thinking back to when Joseph had left in May. Suddenly it dawned on her, *I'm going to have a baby! Finally I'm going to give Joseph a child! He'll be so happy! He's such a wonderful father to Ana, and I wanted so much for us to have a baby. Oh, thank God! At last you're giving us the one thing our marriage has lacked,* she thought.

She waited another month to be sure, then she invited Josefina to have tea with Ana and her. "I've got the best surprise. Ana, you're going to have a baby brother or sister in February."

Ana's face lit up with excitement. She ran to her mother to hug her. "Oh, Mama, won't Papa Joe be happy! Does he know? When did you find out?"

"Whoa, Ana. One question at a time. And, no he doesn't know. I've written him, but it will be months before the letter catches up with him. I first suspected last month when I fainted that morning at breakfast and was nauseous the next morning. I haven't been able to eat breakfast since, and that's why I asked Mandy to fix your breakfast before I came down, Ana."

"You fainted, Caty? Why didn't you tell me? Never mind. You didn't want me to worry. That's so like you. And I suppose you didn't want to tell anyone anything until you were sure. You are sure, aren't you? I'm so happy for you all, Caty, and I want to be Godmother," said Josefina.

"Yes, I'm sure. Of course you will be Godmother, and since Thomas became Catholic, I'm sure Joseph will want him to be Godfather. I planned to ask you, but you beat me to it. Now, let's go to St. Peter's and say a prayer of thanks."

Returning to the present, Caterina thought, *I must have sat here for hours, while most of my life passed before me.* When she stirred, the little black book, the catalyst that had prompted her journey through the past, fell to the floor. Picking it up she read her parting love letter to Rafael. The facing page held an entry, also, but it wasn't in her handwriting.

It read: Please meet me tomorrow morning at ten at the abandoned Spanish mission called Nombre de Dios north of town. Come alone.

Caterina couldn't imagine who had found the diary or where. Nor could she imagine who wrote that note. She didn't care to have all those old memories brought to the surface to mar her newfound happiness in the release of her people, the renewed vigor of her love for Joseph, and the coming birth of their baby. But she knew she would have to meet with whomever had returned the diary with that intriguing note. She couldn't help herself. She had to know what it was all about. Her curiosity had the better of her.

At ten sharp she stood outside the old mission. It had been allowed to fall into a terrible state of disrepair when the British got St. Augustine from the Spanish. The walls were crumbling in places, and the roof was falling in. She saw no one about. Struck by fear and indecision, she was about to change her mind when a bolt of lightening preceded a sudden shower. Stepping inside, she waited for her eyes to adjust. After a moment she could see a man coming toward her. He appeared to be an Indian. As he closed the gap between them, she could see he didn't look like a local Indian. His black hair was long on the left side and short on the right. Around his head was a yellow, red, and black band. She recognized it as the dried skin of the deadly coral snake. The Indian walked toward her with a slight limp, his feet shod in doeskin moccasins. He was tan, and as he came closer she noticed a thin, jagged scar rose from his right eyebrow and ran into his hair.

She wanted to turn and run out into the rain, but she was immobilized by fear. But even at the time she knew it wasn't fear for her personal safety. It was a feeling she could not have described and one she'd never had before.

Then he spoke her name, and she looked into his black eyes. As he reached out to touch her, she fainted and would have fallen into the water that had been rushing through a hole in the roof to form a puddle at her feet, had he not caught her up in his arms.

PART TWO

I

In my nightmare I was being pulled apart by a demon and an angel. The demon's face I could not see. He pulled me down until angry, cold water covered my head and filled my mouth and nostrils. He offered an end to my struggles. He promised me sleep forever.

The angel was beautiful. Her skin was fair, her hair black. She had sparkling dark, wide-set eyes, and each cheek had a deep dimple. Every time the demon pulled me under, she reached out her hand and pulled me above the swirling water. I don't know what she promised, but her face was enough to make me desire it, whatever it was.

The dream went on and on. I don't know how long the demon and the angel struggled for my body, or was it my soul? I was so cold and tired. And then, finally, blessed oblivion, a time when I neither knew nor felt anything.

When I opened my eyes my first thought was, "The angel won," for I was looking into a beautiful face with a pair of wide-set, dark eyes framed with glorious, silky black hair. But then I realized this was not the same face I had dreamed of. This face did not have fair skin, but skin the color of pale bronze. There were no dimples in her cheeks, and the cheek-bones were high and finely chiseled. Her eyes were slightly tilted, and her mouth broke into a wide and pleasing smile.

She stood and turned to leave me. I noticed she was tall and slim, and she wore a short deerskin skirt and a necklace of sea shells. On one thigh a flamingo was tattooed in red. So finely drawn was it that the muscles of her thigh when she walked made the flamingo appear to walk, also.

I was lying on the hide of a black bear and covered with another. The roof above me was of thatched palm fronds. Clay pots and woven baskets of palmetto and pine needles were stacked neatly or hung from the corner posts and roof frames. There were no walls, but skins were rolled on poles to be dropped in cold or wet weather. The floor was raised three feet or so off the ground. I could hear waves breaking and smell the familiar, fresh scent of sea water in the wind.

As I surveyed my surroundings, wondering where I was and how I had come to be here, a shadow fell over me. Turning toward it, I saw a tall, handsome man whose bronze skin was slightly darker than the girl's. His eyes and hair were also black, and his eyes slanted slightly at the corners as did the girls. He wore a breech cloth of deer hide, and around his neck on a rawhide thong were the claws and teeth of a panther. The panther's tail circled his head, and he, too, was tattooed. Across his chest leaped the magnificent animal whose parts he wore.

Kneeling beside me, he smiled and began to speak. But I didn't know his language, nor he mine. With signs he made me understand that my head was hurt and my leg badly broken. He handed me twelve pieces of twigs to show me how many days I had lain unconscious since his people had found me on the beach after a terrible storm. He asked my name, but I couldn't remember it. I couldn't remember anything.

The man seemed pleased that I could not. It was a good

omen, he believed. I would be called Water Gift, because I had been sent to him by the Water Spirit to be his son. I was to learn all this later, when I began to learn their language.

When he left, the girl returned. She fed me clam broth from a pottery bowl, and a strange bread, fresh and hot. Then she changed the bandages on my head and leg. I was puzzled as to what the bandages were made of, as they were a cloth unlike any I had ever seen. Then, I slept again.

I don't know how long I was confined to the chickee, unable to walk. At first things happened as if in a daze. When I became more lucid, the girl began to teach me their language, and she learned some of mine. She was called Flamingo like the pink, long-legged water bird that adorned her thigh.

She told me the man who called me his son was the chief of this small tribe. His name was Leaping Cat. His band of thirty-five was all that was left of the original inhabitants of this peninsula. They called themselves the First People. The others of his tribe who had once dominated the region had died of white man's diseases or had been captured by both white men and other tribes from far north in slave-gathering raids. Some had left for Hispaniola and other islands on their own. The last of them had gone with the Spanish when they left six winters past. Leaping Cat and his people would not leave the land of their ancestors and the place they knew had plenty of all they needed to survive and live happily, including a favorable climate. They thought their continued existence here unknown to white men, who believed all the People were now gone from the area.

Soon after I learned enough of their language to understand, Flamingo told me, "Twelve moons ago Leaping Cat's only son, Little Fox, was fishing in his canoe out past the reef. A huge shark attacked, overturning the canoe and killing Little Fox. Leaping Cat offered many sacrifices to the Water Spirit to cool his anger against the People. He also sacrificed

and prayed to the Sun Spirit who is the great enemy of the
Water Spirit, asking the Sun Spirit to fight the Water Spirit
on behalf of the People. We believe the Water Spirit took
Little Fox to punish us for something.

"When you were found washed up on the beach after
the big storm, Leaping Cat ordered feasts of thanksgiving,
because our prayers have been answered. The Sun Spirit
sent a great storm to disturb the water, causing the Water
Spirit to give forth a new son for Leaping Cat. The Spirit is
no longer angry with us. The Sun Spirit has been our ally.
Leaping Cat has adopted you to replace the son he lost.

"Little Fox and I were to be married. Now my uncle says
I am to be your bride."

Since I could not remember anything that happened
before I opened my eyes in Flamingo's chickee except the
dream of the demon and the angel, Leaping Cat and his
tribe were even more sure I had been sent to replace Little
Fox. Flamingo told me, "Can't you see? The demon was the
Water Spirit. The angel was the Sun Spirit."

When I was able, Flamingo helped me out of the hut. I
leaned on her shoulder to take limping steps on the beach.
She brought me string and bone hooks with which to fish.
She cooked the fish I caught for us to eat.

Flaming made my breech cloths. She wove baskets of
palmetto leaves and pine needles and fashioned clay pots
for me. When she determined the time was right, she removed the splints from my leg. She decided when my head
was healed, and she asked Leaping Cat to teach me to use
the spear and the bow and arrow.

Flamingo caught crabs and lobsters and other delica-
cies, she gathered coontie root for bread and sofkee gruel,
swamp cabbage, palmetto berries, nuts, wild grapes, and other
foods to prepare for me.

I began to realize Flamingo was falling in love with me. I
was grateful that she was. She had saved my life. At times I

even fancied myself in love with her. She was fun to be with, and her touch caused a strange excitement in me. But sometimes when we were together, that other face would flash before me—the fair, dimpled face. Who was she? Her appearance always disturbed me. The Sun Spirit she was not. This much I knew. But I could remember nothing.

Flamingo was getting impatient with me. She wanted to do her Uncle's bidding and marry. She was already seventeen winters old. She would have been married two winters already had Little Fox lived. But I wanted to know what that other face meant first.

I had been with the tribe for more than a year. Flaming became tired of waiting and took matters into her own hands. I was asleep in my bear skins one cool night. There was no moon to shed even a little light. I dreamed of the beautiful angel with fair skin and deep dimples. She had come to me in the night and told me she would always love me. She pressed her warm body to mine. She made love to me. I awoke in the morning to find Flamingo in the skins with me.

"Now you have planted your seed in me, Water Gift. You must talk to my uncle about our marriage. It's no secret that I love you. During the night you said you love me, too. You have shown that you can provide for me by the fish you catch. I have shown I can care for you and gather and prepare fruit, coontie, and shell fish. There's no need to wait any longer," she said.

I couldn't tell her I had not made love to her, but to a dream. She was so kind and good to me. How could I not love her? Why should I let a face that appeared momentarily to me, a face to which I could attach no name, no memory whatsoever, come between me and reality? So we were married by the laws of her people.

Still, I wondered about my past. Where did I come from?

Who was I? And who was the fair-skinned beauty with dimples whose face appeared before me at the strangest times?

My leg no longer bothered me, and my limp was barely noticeable. Occasionally I still suffered severe headaches, and I could feel with my finger the thin, jagged scar that ran from my eyebrow into my hair. I suspected a concussion had caused my loss of memory.

In a few moons it became evident that Flamingo had been right. I had planted my seed in her. When she told me we were going to have a baby, I had a feeling I had heard these words before, and that something unpleasant was associated with that knowledge. But I was too happy at the thought of becoming a father to give it a second thought.

"I'll give you a fine, strong son," said Flamingo. "He will be beautiful like his father and love you as much as his mother does."

"What if 'he' is a 'she'?" I asked, teasing.

"No, no, Water Gift. He will be a son. I'm sure of it. A spirit came to me in and dream and told me I would bear a son."

I knew her too well by now to dispute the word of a spirit. Besides, among her people, Flamingo was a shaman, mystic, medicine woman, witch doctor. Call it what you may. She communicated with the spirits, they believed. And the people put much faith in dreams which were interpreted as messages from the spirits. It was Flamingo who told them what their dreams meant.

I had often wondered how Flamingo would interpret all the apparitions I had of that fair and dimpled face still; I had never been able to share those continuing appearances of the angel she had explained as the Sun Spirit. Maybe someday I could.

I became nearly as good with the bow and arrow and the spear as the men of the tribe under the tutelage of Leaping Cat. No one could out fish me or handle a canoe better. I had an instinctive affinity for anything to do with the sea.

I often thought that in my other life (for that is what I called the time before memory) I must have lived near the sea.

I liked being an Indian. I liked this place that was a myriad of small Islands off the end of Florida. I liked the fellow members of the tribe, and I grew to love Leaping Cat, my father, and Flamingo, my wife. But more than all of these, I loved my freedom. I didn't know why it meant so much to be free, but it did. I was almost completely happy. Only the appearance of the face with the dimples marred the contentment I felt. Why? Why should that face cause such pangs of guilt? Would I ever know the answer, or was I forever doomed to be tortured by that vision?

Some of these islands had herds of tiny deer. Many types of fish were abundant around each island, as were lobster, sea cows, turtles, conchs, clams, crabs, shrimp and oysters. Wild grapes, palmetto berries, cabbage palms, prickly pear cactus, coontie and other edible roots and fruits abounded. There was more food than we could ever eat. I thought Leaping Cat very wise not to leave such a place.

In the cooler moons the People would journey to the mainland to hunt the big swamp called Grassy Water. Alligators, crocodiles, bears and larger deer were there in great numbers, as well as swamp rabbits, possums, raccoons, and cotton mouth moccasins. All but the very old, the sick, young children and a few of the women to tend to them, went on these extended hunts. The year of Flamingo's pregnancy she could not go, and something would not allow me to leave her.

The people went to the swamp in a dugout canoe. We made these by hollowing out large cypress trees with fire and scraping with stone and shell tools. Some were made for one person, but we had longboats large enough to transport our whole small tribe.

After a hunt, what meat that wasn't used fresh we dried into pemmican. We wasted nothing. Bones became needles, tools and hooks. Skins became blankets, rugs, and clothing. Feathers made ornaments, capes, and ceremonial implements. The sinews of some animals we used for thread and string. We made glue from hooves. Bear fat became grease to season and fry with, and to keep insects off us. Parts of the insides of large animals made water holders and waterproof containers. These hunts were important to the whole village.

Men of the tribe and a few women hunted and fished. Men made bows, arrows, tools, canoes, and did other heavy work. Women caught crabs, lobsters, conchs, dug clams, gathered roots, berries, turtle eggs, and other foods. They made pottery, wove baskets, tanned hides, sewed, cared for the children, and tended the garden. But with so much abundance, there was time for swimming, games, exploring, canoeing, and anything else we might want to do. At the time, I felt this place and this society was as close to paradise as this earth was likely to provide.

In the spring of 1771, Flamingo's labor began. Her abdomen had gotten much larger than normal, considering the child was not expected for another moon. I was truly terrified that I might lose her and the child. Flamingo herself was calm. Her face wore a mysterious look which seemed to say she had a secret which only time would reveal. She assured me the spirits had given only favorable signs.

She went to the birthing hut, as was the custom among her tribe, when the labor began. The First People believed the birth process was contaminating, therefore had to be carried out away from men. I was very nervous and wanted to go with her, but this was taboo. About noon the next day, Flamingo came back to our chickee. I had finally managed to fall into a light sleep. I was startled awake when she called my name.

Flamingo was pale, but her smile was radiant. I jumped to the ground, and she handed me a small bundle. "Your son," she said.

I folded back the wrap and looked into the tiniest face I had ever seen. "He's too small. Is he all right?" I looked at Flamingo. Then I saw she held another bundle.

"Your daughter," she said and pulled the wrap away from another tiny face.

I couldn't believe it! Flamingo had given me twins! I was concerned about their size, but they were beautiful and perfectly formed.

Among Flamingo's people the birth of twins was a mystical event. It was believed the youngest was meant to become a shaman. Our daughter was the youngest. It was then that Flamingo told me she had been a youngest twin. Her twin, another girl, had died as a baby. She hastened to assure me our twins were healthy and would not die.

Somehow I remembered Christianity, and I wanted to give our children Christian names. Flamingo told me that was taboo. She explained that among the First People, inheritance was through the mother. This was why Flamingo's uncle, Leaping Cat, and she had so much influence on each other. He was her mother's brother. And as the niece of the chief, she was considered a beloved woman by her people. This gave her special privileges not enjoyed by other women.

"Our children belong to their mothers. They are part of the mother's clan. My clan is the Wind Clan. A child is named by its mother and is not related to the father by blood. The closest male relative to my twins is Leaping Cat, since I have no brother. He will teach and guide them in Indian ways, especially our son. You are of the clan of Little Wren, your adoptive mother. That is the Fox Clan."

I found this alien and didn't like it at all, but like a true Indian I had learned to keep all emotion off my face. I could not buck the tribe. But, how could I not be a father to my own children?

The children would be named by Flamingo. She would name them for something they did or reminded her of.

When the boy came of age, he would be renamed. Still, I determined they would have Christian names. They would be Juan and Margarita to me.

I was beginning to learn a little about myself. I decided I must have been religious in that other life.

Flamingo named our daughter first. She was about a week old. She was strapped to the board that Flamingo's people attach their babies to. She opened one eye and appeared to smile. Flamingo said, "She is as adorable as a baby deer. We shall call her Fawn."

"You don't mind if I call her Margarita?" I asked.

"Margarita," Flamingo tested the name. "I like it. It has a pretty sound. But be warned. You cannot give my children Christian names. Your God does not like my people. For many winters past, white men have come in the name of your God. They have killed our people, stolen our land and belongings, and taken us slaves, all in the name of the Christian God. The Christian God is powerful. He has reduced our numbers by many. But He does not want us to be His followers. Now you are one of us. You must forget this Christian God. Do not mention Him among the People for fear of your life. And do not let them hear you call Fawn 'Margarita'."

This really disturbed me. It was true the Indians had fared badly at the hands of white men. It was true white men had used God as a reason for the things they did to these natives of the New World. It had always been so. Man had always made conquests in the name of whatever god they believed in. Maybe by doing so they hoped to appease their gods, or maybe they lied to themselves in hopes of covering up their wrongdoing and guilt. I suspected it would always be this way. Perhaps the young and naive who were enlisted to carry out such deeds really believed they did it for God. But those in command, those who planned conquests and the acquisition of riches and land, surely they knew better. They knew they did it for power and riches. If a few good priests and many fervent and naive young men died for their dreams of glory, they considered them well used. Nor would they let the sacrilege of using the name of God, a god of mercy and love, to rob, kill, and enslave, bother them if it got them what they wanted. But I knew God had no hand in it. He had never used men to do evil. Instead, men had attempted to use Him to justify their greed for what others had and what some "Christians" did and were still doing to take whatever they wanted. I could not blame the First People for the way they felt. I was thoroughly ashamed of what some men do in the name of God. I wanted Flamingo to understand His goodness versus the evil in some men.

A few days later when Flamingo was bathing our son, he began to scream and kick. Flamingo said, "Look, he is fighting in the water like a little conch. He shall be called Little Conch."

"To me, he is Juan," I said.

Flamingo said nothing, but the look she gave me said plenty.

When the twins were two weeks old, Leaping Cat sent for me. I went to his chickee. He was sitting on the floor with his ankles crossed. His pipe was lit, and he offered it to me. I hated the vile taste of that powerful tobacco and the strange feeling I got after I smoked it. But I had learned you dare not refuse an offered smoke of the weed the People believed to be sacred.

Taking the pipe, I drew one long pull of the smoke into my lungs before handing it back.

"Water Gift, I have something of yours. Our Shaman Flamingo does not know what it is, but she believes it possesses a power of some kind over you. She and I thought it best not to return it to you at first. But now we feel we hold a power at least equal to it. Now you are truly one of the People, a husband and a father. Your wife and children are the power that will overcome any magic in this object." He turned and pulled something in a waterproof pouch from a small woven box.

Gravely, he handed it to me, explaining it had been fastened to my belt when I had been found on the beach.

I reached for the package, a strange feeling coming over me. I could not tell if it was the smoke or the thing I held in my hand. Suddenly that face appeared again, smiling and dimpled. I had not seen it as much since some moons before the birth of my babies. Somehow, I knew the peace I had felt recently was about to shatter. I felt a sudden urge to hand it back to him, to tell him to destroy it, but I could not. No matter the consequences, I had to know what was in the pouch.

I opened it and held in my hands a small black book. It was hard to keep my hands from trembling. I was strangely afraid to open it, yet I felt an urgency to do so. A voice within me said, "Wait. Don't open it in front of Leaping Cat. Wait until you are alone. Be like the People. Do not allow your face to betray your emotions. Pretend it is unimportant. Thank him. Talk of something else."

So with great effort, I turned the book over in my hand, while I tried to rid my face of any show of emotion. I returned the book to the pouch and attached it to my belt. Then I looked into Leaping Cat's eyes with a coolness I did not feel. "Thank you. It is only a book. No magic. No power. I don't even remember it." Then I said, "Will Flamingo and I go on the big hunt to the Grassy Water this time? I know it is several moons away, but we could not go last time because of Flamingo's condition. It's been on my mind, and I really want to go this time."

"We look forward to your first big hunt and to the return of Flamingo to our hunting party.

"The thing I have returned to you—it is not what the Christians call a Bible—a book of their faith and beliefs?" he asked.

Suddenly I realized why he thought the book held power—why they had kept it so long from me. They thought it was a Bible, the book of the hated and feared Christians.

Was this, then, a test? Laughing heartily, I assured Leaping Cat the book was not the Bible. I told him there was no need to fear the book. It held no power over me or his people. But somewhere deep inside me, I knew that when I read that book, it would reveal something of my past. The thought both excited and scared me. I wanted to hurry away and discover whatever secret it held, but I knew things would not be the same after I read it. Perhaps I *was* being untruthful. Perhaps the book did hold a power over me—a power I was, as yet, unaware of. I couldn't wait to sneak away alone with the book. I told Flamingo I was going fishing.

The Indians fished differently from my people. They used a line with many hooks strung across the water. I liked to use a single hook and line on a pole. Flaming brought my pole to me. Neither of us mentioned Leaping Cat or the book. I knew she was aware it had been returned to me, that she had shared in the decision to give it back.

I went to a secluded place along the western shore of the island where I had often fished successfully alone. Along the shore and into the edge of the water were a tangled mass of mangrove trees. Their roots formed the shapes of twisted tent frames above the ground and water. A large coral head shaped like a chair sprung out of the edge of the water at low tide as now, making an ideal place to sit and fish. I could not be seen from our village. Here I sat and pulled the package from the pouch at my waist. I lay it in my lap, baited the bone hook with a clam, and dropped it into the water. I unwrapped the book and held it. My skin tingled, and the hair at the nape of my neck raised. Was it fear of what the book contained, or excitement at maybe finding out who I had been?

Opening the book, I began to read:

March 10, 1786. Today Mr. Turnbull agreed to let us go to Florida to work on his plantation with Rafael and all the others . . .

At the name *Turnbull* I experienced a feeling I can only

describe as apprehensive. Then there was the name, *Rafael*. It seemed very familiar to me.

As I read further, I began to see in my mind the things I read in the book. Minorca actually appeared, the island surrounded by an emerald sea. I had a comforting feeling of home. I saw the ship *Hope* and the people on board, and I knew them! I remembered the kindly face of Father Camps. I saw Rafael's young bride. She had black hair and eyes, fair skin, and deep dimples. Hers was the face that haunted me! The angel who had saved me! And suddenly I knew her name! It was Caterina—Caty. Then it all came back in a flood. "I *am* Rafael! All this happened to Caty and me!"

I sat there for a long time as memories of the past washed over me like the tide. Suddenly, I was brought back to the present when the fishing pole I had jammed into a crevice in the coral bent nearly double, and the water thrashed wildly. I had hooked a fish large enough for Flamingo and me to have for supper.

Then it finally hit me, and I thought, *Flamingo! Oh, my God! I have two wives. I am married to Caty by Christian law. She is in St. Augustine, expecting our baby. At least, she was when I saw her last. We must be parents by now! And here I am, married to an Indian witch doctor in an Indian ceremony. We have twins. I love Caty. I love Flamingo. What am I going to do? What can I do?*

The last entry in the diary said Caty's indenture was bought by Joseph Adams, and she would wait for me there until my indenture was up. That was to be five years after that entry, which was made in 1774. About a year and a half had passed since then! The rest was a love letter from Caty to Rafael, to me. She had written it before I boarded a ship to return to New Smyrna. She had given me the diary in a waterproof pouch as a small comfort and a remembrance of our lives together. I remember her telling me not to read the letter until the ship left St. Augustine.

I must think this out logically and coolly, I thought. *Caty must think me dead. She must have been informed of the shipwreck. She may no longer even be in St. Augustine. If I go back, I will be sent to New Smyrna to finish my indenture. I still owe Turnbull five years of my life. But after the freedom of the past year and a half, I couldn't be a virtual slave again. Not ever.*

Flamingo is my wife, too. She is not to blame for any of this. We have two babies. I love my Indian family. I can't abandon them to return to an uncertain future. Nor would it help Caty for me to go back to New Smyrna. She's probably past mourning for me. She may even be married to someone else.

At the thought my heart lurched in a pang of anguish. But no one, not even Caty, would believe I had lost my memory, and that's why my life was now so complicated.

Then her face appeared before me again. This time I knew who she was. And I knew I loved her still—that I always would. I realized her apparitions had kept me from giving up, from drowning after the terrible injuries I had suffered in the shipwreck, and the unknown hours, maybe days, when I had been tossed, beaten, and otherwise abused by the cold and angry sea. I wondered if our child was a boy or a girl—if it was healthy. And I absolutely didn't know what to do—what was right and what was wrong.

I prayed. I thought. I planned. I replanned. Then I heard Flamingo's voice calling, "Water Gift! Water Gift! It is dark. When are you coming?"

I saw the tide had come up, nearly covering the coral I sat on. I hadn't noticed. "I'm coming. I must have fallen asleep," I lied. I returned the diary to the pouch and carried my fish to Flamingo.

She didn't ask me about the book, but I could tell by the way she looked at me that she was hurt, because I didn't tell her about it. I wasn't ready yet to talk about it. I wished, in a way, that I had not been given it back. Things were simpler when I did not remember. Yet, I had longed to know who I was. Does the grass always look greener?

From Minorca, a new world, New Smyrna seemed a better idea. When I didn't know who I was, I wanted to know. I became very despondent. I felt I had surely made a mess of my life. Of Caty's. But I couldn't undo what had been done. And I didn't have to ruin Flamingo's, Juan's and Margarita's lives, too. I resolved I would stay here with them and try to forget once more who I had been. But, a voice in my heart would not let me get rid of the diary.

It had been returned to me in the moon of the blackberry. The nearest I could figure, it was May 1771. The First People counted not months, but moons. There were thirteen in a year, each named for something that had to do with that time of year. Now the luscious blackberries were ripe and juicy. The women and children picked them daily until there were no more. The teeth of the People were stained purple from the juice of the delicious fruit.

The People divided the year into two seasons. The cold season was the time of the eagle. The warm was the time of the snake. Years were counted in winters past. I had been among them for two winters past, but two years would not be complete until the end of the time of the snake.

I didn't know Flamingo and the People thought the magic they believed the book possessed had control of my spirit, and that had caused my depression. But it is true, my newfound knowledge of my past affected me greatly.

One night after the children were asleep, Flamingo asked, "Where is the book?" She had not mentioned it since the day it had been returned to me. It had been as though she pretended not to know of it.

"It's in my pouch."

"You must get rid of it. It has a power over you. Its magic is making you ill. Maybe your God does not like you anymore, because you are now one of the First People now," she said.

I realized she still believed the book was a Bible. I knew I'd have to tell her what the book was, even though I wasn't ready to explain it. I didn't know if I'd ever be ready. It wasn't that I didn't want her to know I had a wife before her. It was accepted practice for a man to have more than one wife among the People. I just didn't want to discuss Caty with her or with any of the People.

"Flamingo," I said, putting my arms around her, "the book is not a Bible. It has nothing to do with Christianity. It is a diary. That means it is a record of someone's thoughts and feelings and the things that happened to them."

"Is it your diary? Does it tell these things about you?"

"Well, no. It's not my diary, but it was written by someone I used to know. It tells some things about me. Flamingo, there's no magic or power in the book, only memories. Memories that are painful. I love you, Flamingo. Someday I'll read the book to you and explain it all. But not yet. Please trust me."

"Do you know who you were, now, and where you came from?" she persisted.

"Yes, my name was Rafael Reyes. I came from an island far across the sea. It is called Minorca. That's all I want to say for now, Flamingo."

Having made up my mind to stay with Flamingo and the twins, I tried to forget my past again. I knew that to stay with the tribe meant I must *be* Water Gift. I carefully wrapped the diary in waterproof skin and put it in the bottom of a chest Flamingo had woven for me. My personal belongings were stored there—breechcloths, capes, fishing hooks, and such. I put the diary under it all, and it stayed there untouched for a long time.

But Caty's face still appeared from time to time, making it impossible to forget. I knew I still loved her, but I loved Flamingo and our children, too. This was here. This was reality. I tried to live in the present and to put forward as contented a face as I could, despite the turmoil and guilt I felt to my very soul.

Otherwise, the time of the snake, 1771, was pleasant.

Seafood, roots, and berries were plentiful. There was no need for anyone to rush. I learned that the society of the First People had been more structured before white men came and destroyed much of their culture and most of their people.

During the last of the season the worst of the rainy moons began. We could see rain coming miles out over the ocean. The gray clouds rolled in across the sky, bringing continuous and cold rain. Sometimes it seemed a foot of water would fall in a day. For the worst two moons of the storm season, not a day passed without the rain. Lightening crackled, searing the sky with blinding light. It was after one of these horrendous storms and during a spectacular sunset of violet, gray, rose and blue that Flamingo and I walked along the beach hand in hand. We searched for treasures swept ashore by the wind and waves. We had gathered a basket of crabs, some live conchs, shark teeth, and pretty shells from among the seaweed, timber and debris.

"Another ship has broken apart on the coral reef. I don't know why the white man doesn't figure out that this time is the stormy season and use the seas in calmer moons," she said.

Then we spotted some large shapes appearing in the surf as the waves ebbed back to sea. "Go get help. We will bring in things from the shipwreck to see what we can use'" she said.

I ran back to the village to tell Leaping Cat we needed help to salvage some things from a wreck. He and half the village returned to the beach with me.

After dragging the large objects and floating debris ashore, we went through it all. There were three large wood and metal chests, so heavy, it took four men to carry each. When we broke them open, we found Spanish coins of gold and silver, jewelry set with rubies, sapphires, emeralds and pearls. One chest contained altar ornaments, jeweled goblets, chalices, crucifixes and bowls. There was also a crate of steel knives. Between the high and low tide lines we had found shiny bars of silver and gold half buried in the sand. For weeks thereafter, these bars and other objects continued to come ashore and litter the eastern beach. A large fortune had obviously been aboard the sunken ship.

The People highly prized the coins and medallions to wear around their neck, on their belts and hung from their ears. Some of the gold and silver bars they melted and fashioned into jewelry, belts, and other ornaments. I had seen a few coins around the necks of some of the elders, no doubt from an earlier wreck. But never had any of us seen so much wealth. Nor had the people ever owned such knives.

Each of us was given a portion of the treasure. My share was a sizable fortune. Having no use of it at present, I put it away in one of the chests it had arrived in. I sensed without consciously thinking about it that someday I might have need of it.

Flamingo took some of the gold and silver and long strings of pearls to the metalworker to be made into ornaments of her own design. Thereafter, her ears were adorned with various ear bobs, and handsome gorget dangled from her neck. But the most fascinating was the tiara she had created to wear during ceremonies in her official rolls as shaman and beloved woman.

Everyone was excited about having a supply of knives that were far superior to any the People had ever used. They looked forward to using them during the deer-hunting trip to the Grassy Water, which was about to occur.

II

The hunting dance began early in the morning. One of our beloved old men placed a curiously shaped staff in the ground. Another sang a ceremonial song and proclaimed the dance had begun. He prayed for blessings of various spirits that our hunting trip would be successful.

We painted our faces and bodies with red and black designs, donned quivers laden with arrows, and carried our bows. Flamingo, as shaman, approached the staff in the ground, shaking her rattles. Leaping Cat and five elders joined in with their rattles. The rest of us gathered around while they rattled and danced around the staff for some time. I followed the lead of the others, because I didn't know what came next. We acted out the hunt with some of the men wearing the heads and antlers of deer take on previous hunts. The rest of us pretended to be hunters and acted out the hunt.

We did this over and over until supper. I felt like a child playing a game with other children. Some of the People who swooned were said to have been overcome by the spirit whom they were honoring and beseeching. Personally, I thought they fainted from hunger and exhaustion.

Then all of us men went into the gathering house to drink the white drink. Although the liquid is black, Flamingo told me it was called "white drink" because it purified those who partook of it. When I drank it, I found out what she meant. I was totally unprepared for the severe cramps and violent vomiting it caused. I was mortified, but afterward, I noticed all the other men who drank the potion were running out and vomiting, also.

Then it was time to go on my first hunt to the mainland. This was to be a deer hunt in the big swamp called Grassy Water. The old people, children, sick, and some of the women would stay. Flamingo would be with me. I was excited about hunting again. I had enjoyed hunting in that previous life which seemed so long ago, back in Minorca.

Flamingo presented me with a decoy she had made a previous year. It was the head and neck of a deer stuffed and stretched on a frame. The antlers had been hollowed to make them lighter. She said, "You will put it over your neck and shoulders, moving it with one hand and holding your bow with the other. When the deer is near enough to kill, you will drop the decoy and shoot the deer. Then you will wait awhile for the deer to lose enough blood to lie down, where it will bleed and die. Then you will track it down." While she was telling me, she was going through the motions to show me how it all was done.

Then she gave me a bladder filled with bear grease, instructing me to rub it all over to prevent the mosquitoes and other bugs from biting me.

The hunt was to take a moon, and we would count our days with the bundle of sticks Flamingo would carry. She would throw away a stick each day until all were gone. Then we would return. There were twenty-eight sticks in the bundle.

We all settled into a big dugout. The men all rowed. We went out the west side of our island into the calmer, smaller sea and paddled our dugout through many islands, being careful not to upset the canoe on any of the many coral heads that dotted the water, some below the surface. The water was mostly shallow. Some of the islands we skirted were tiny, but some were large enough to have white sandy beaches. Occasionally we would pass one of the larger keys. By evening we had reached the mainland. We followed a small channel not visible to me through mangroves—those strange trees that completely cover some of the small islands and grow profusely where fresh and salt water meet. Their roots form arches that join above the water to make the trunk of the tree. Coon oysters and small shells attach themselves to these roots.

Farther up the channel we passed through custard apple trees and met the saw grass over which the shallow water flowed. It was this that gave the place its name.

It stretched endless before us, broken only by small hammocks. It was on one of these larger hammocks we stopped to roast little coon oysters for supper and spend the night.

As Flamingo and I lay snuggled in our bearskins that night, I felt really happy. I reveled in the freedom of this life. It felt so good to be surrounded by the vastness of nature, to hear the bellows of bull frogs, the chirps of crickets, and all the other small sounds that broke the silence of a starry night. I was excited by the sheer joy of it all, when Flamingo turned over and put her arms around my neck. "Water gift, I'm so glad you washed up on our island. The spirits were good to us. Lately, you seem happier, too. Are you glad that other life is over?" she asked.

Then I felt the most terrible pang, and the sweet face of Caty appeared before me. I was reminded of the time about two years ago when she and I lay wrapped in a gray blanket in the hollow of a huge oak. I pulled Flamingo to me and loved her with a passion she had never before experienced. After, the thought came to me unbidden, "Tonight I made love to

Caty again." It had been Flamingo I held in my arms, but it was Caty in my heart and mind. And I knew I must be very careful, lest I call that name from the past while I held the present in my arms.

In the morning the women made sofkee by boiling some of the coontie flour we had brought with us. This gruel was a main staple in our diet. Then we all got back into the dugout to resume our journey to the deer-hunting grounds. That day I lost count of the alligators, some as much as fourteen feet long, we saw. On many pieces of floating wood or debris lying in the sun was at least one cottonmouth moccasin. When we saw these snakes, whether swimming, crawling, lying full length, or coiled, they always held their heads raised at an arrogant angle. When disturbed, they opened their mouths to show white interiors and sometimes their deadly fangs, while emitting an offensive, pungent odor.

Turtles shared their rests, sometimes ten or fifteen on the same log.

"On our return we will get some of those moccasins. We can use some new skins and fangs, as well as feast on the tender meat. We may get some for supper tonight."

I asked Flamingo, "What do we do with the fangs?"

"The fangs and their poison sacs I use to make potions and other things. The poison can also be used on the tips of arrows and darts to poison prey. Our elders remember using such weapons against enemies, also."

"The People have a use for everything," I said.

"The spirits told our ancient ancestors how every plant and every animal could be used for our benefit. This knowledge has been handed down over the generations from one shaman to the next," she said.

That afternoon we left the saw grass for another channel through the mangroves. Then we were in a creek that took us to an oak hammock.

"Acorns cover the ground. We'll stay here tonight.

This hammock stretches along both sides of the creek for a long way. The deer will come to eat the acorns," Leaping Cat said.

During the night I awoke to hear the sound of deer pawing among the oak leaves on the ground for the abundant acorns.

Next morning we separated into twos to hunt. Flamingo and I were together. She was an excellent hunter. She taught me tracks and sounds of the different animals that lived here. We saw a lot of sign, but no deer that morning. The People eat no breakfast on the morning of a hunt. By noon we were hungry. As we sat under the limbs of a large, spreading oak, our backs to its trunk, eating coontie cakes and pemmican, I heard a familiar sound, as two goats ramming each other. Goats roamed the island of Minorca, but I knew of none here. "What's that?" I asked.

Flamingo whispered, "Stand up and look on the other side of the tree. Be quiet and ready your bow and arrow."

I did as she said, just in time to see two deer run at each other. As their heads hit, their large racks entangled, and they fell to their knees in the struggle. They were well in range, and broadside to us. One buck turned his head sharply, rolling the other over. The impetus of the others body turning caused the first deer to also roll. Then their antlers unlocked. The stood up and surveyed each other intently. Then they lowered their heads to charge again. "Now! Take the one on your side, I'll take the other," she said.

We both let our arrows fly. Flamingo's arrow entered the neck of her buck, severing its spine and causing it to drop to the ground immediately. My arrow went into its target in the chest.

Flamingo said, "Watch carefully where he goes." She ran to her deer with one of the steel knives ready in her hand.

She slit her deer's throat expertly. We hung it in a nearby tree.

"After we trail yours and find it, we'll bring it back and get mine," she said.

Going to the place where I had last seen the deer, we picked up the trail. At first there was a lot of blood. Then there was just a drop here and there. Flamingo told me to get on all fours and search for crushed plants, disturbed leaves, tracks, or splatters of blood. We followed the trail like this for about twenty minutes, and came upon part of an arrow near a small oak. Flamingo pointed to blood and hair where the deer had rubbed against the tree as it passed, breaking off part of the arrow. From there to the deer, which lay in a palmetto patch about two hundred feet away, sign showed the deer had staggered, fallen, bled, got up, and stumbled again, before finally dropping in the palmettos.

"Don't forget to ask the deer to pardon you, or its spirit will come back and make you sick," she reminded me.

Instead, I said a prayer of thanks to God, and we dragged the deer back to the other, where we made a litter to drag them both back to camp.

I was bursting with pride at the knowledge and skill Flamingo possessed, and that we had both killed deer. It turned out five have been taken that day.

Flamingo was the only woman who hunted on this trip. The other seven women who had come stayed in camp to cook, and after the deer had been gutted, skinned and quartered by the men, they took care of the meat, skins and other usable parts. The meat had been washed in the creek by the men, and a piece of each deer had been thrown in the fire as offerings to the spirits. The women would make soups and stews of the bony parts, dry some into pemmican, roast the hearts and livers, make waterproof containers of kidneys and bladders, save bones for needles and hooks, sinews for thread, hooves for glue, and use every part of the deer possible.

A few days later we came upon a herd of deer feeding on the abundant acorns. They were too far to shoot from where we stood. I donned my decoy and bent in a crouching position as Flamingo had instructed, walked to within forty feet of them before a doe began to snort and paw the ground. Knowing she smelled something she wasn't sure of, and that she would soon bolt taking the herd with her, I chose a yearling near her that offered an easy broadside shot. Throwing off my decoy, I let my arrow fly. The yearling fell to its knees, staggered back to its feet, and fled after the rest of the herd. We tracked the deer and found it.

By the end of the moon, we had hardly enough room in the boat for us, so full was it with pemmican, hides, antlers, sinews, bones, and other parts selected by the women. And we had eaten fresh venison daily.

We started the two day journey home. On this trip we speared moccasins, begging the pardon of each as we dropped it into a covered basket. The snakes did not die immediately, as we avoided spearing them in the head in order to save the fangs and poison sacs. Being cold blooded, most would still be alive when we reached home. One youth, being trained by Flamingo to be a shaman, was the tribe's snake handler. He took care of the basket of snakes. I stayed as far away as I could.

Each time the basket was opened from behind, the lid held as a shield in front of the handler, the open side to the water. As the basket filled, the writhing, striking snakes were visible over the top of the basket. Those near the basket held their spears ready should a snake get lose in the boat, as several did. Occasionally one would fall back into the water. This part of the hunting trip was the least enjoyable to me. Any minute I expected someone to be bitten. Such was the skill of the First People that no one was.

We returned to our island to be honored with feasts, singing and dancing. It had been a successful trip, and we would have venison, skins and many other useful things for a long while.

The snake meat was broiled the day after we returned. It was served with cooked swamp cabbage and coontie bread. We stuffed ourselves until we were all miserable and spent the afternoon lying in the shade, while the cool ocean breezes lulled us to sleep.

Just before dark one of the young boys who had fish hooks strung in the water between our island and the next, came running into the village. "There's a ship coming into the bay across the channel!" he said.

Flamingo and the other women gathered all the children into the meeting house, while the men went to see what was going on. The ship bore a flag like none I had ever seen. It had a skull and crossbones. The thought that I might leave with them ran fleetingly across my mind, to be quickly replaced by thoughts of my Indian family and friends; the life I had come to love in so many ways; and of being returned to Turnbull's colony.

Leaping Cat took one look and said, "Pirates! They probably want only drinking water. Or maybe they're hiding from other white men who hate them, also. We must go back to the village and prepare to defend ourselves, in case they discover us and decide to attack. A lookout will stay to watch them. They capture our people and others, also, to sell as slaves."

I saw the ship wasn't too large, but figured it held as many of them as there were of us. I also had seen the cannon on board. I knew their weapons were far superior to ours. I had never seen the pirate flag before, but I knew about pirates. I said, "If we stay in the village and they find us, they will kill many with their guns and the big cannon they have. If we hide on shore to attack them if they come, some of them will escape. They will know we are here. They will come back until they get us all, or we will be forced to leave this place we love. I have an idea.

"It's nearly dark, so they won't come to this island before morning. We could wait until they're all asleep, then attack them. We could surround the ship with canoes, and shoot flaming arrows into it. It will be a moonless night. We will stay far enough away that we won't be targets in the firelight. Some of us will be waiting on shore, so that when they jump over or lower their landing boats, those that we don't get from the water can be captured as they come ashore. No one must be allowed to escape to tell others we are here."

I thought of my Christian beliefs. I was making plans to kill people. How could I have become so savage? Then I thought again of Flamingo and my children. I could not stand idly by while I knew their lives and the lives of us all were threatened. God forgive me. I could see no other way.

Leaping Cat said he must confer with the council. It seemed they agreed with me, because the meeting was over quickly, and we prepared for the night's events. Flamingo shook her rattles over us and said some words I didn't understand. We painted our bodies in bold red and black designs and put our tomahawks and knives into our belts, our filled quivers on our backs. When the lookout came to tell us all had been quiet on board for a while, we gathered our bows and spears, shoved our canoes into the water, and paddled them to preplanned positions.

The ship had anchored just outside the reef. It would be nearly impossible in the pitch black night for anyone who didn't know the channels to cross that reef. But just in case, three men waited on shore to use their keen ears for voices, paddles in the water or any other sound that would alert them to escaping pirates.

Leaping Cat was to give the call of a certain night bird as the signal for everyone to light their arrows from the carefully shielded fire pots on board each canoe. The arrows would be sent into the ship's hull and onto the deck. But first my canoe had been sent to the anchor rope, so that when the signal was given, I could sever it, thus allowing the ship to drift onto the coral reef. After this was accomplished, we waited as the flames spread, looking for people running on deck and trying to escape by launching landing boats, or simply jumping overboard to escape the fire.

Undoubtedly some of the pirates were trapped below deck by the fire or overcome by smoke. Of those who jumped over, only five were picked out of the water. A small boat was launched, but overturned on the reef, and one of its occupants made it to shore. These became our captives.

One of the survivors, a big brute of a man with a full black beard and long, drooping mustache, couldn't keep his eyes off the young women who were very scantily clad according to European customs. I tried to tell him to leave the women alone, that to do otherwise would be taking his life in his hands. But he wouldn't listen.

One afternoon the men came into the village after a day of fishing to find the mustachioed man tied to a stake, a wicked gash in his scalp. He had tried to run away and take one of the young women with him. One of the other women who was digging coontie roots nearby saw the scuffle and hit him in the head with her hoe. While he was unconscious, the women bound and brought him into the center of the village, where they tied him to a stake. Since then, when one of them passed him, she spit on him, pinched, scratched, or slapped him. Now his fate was up to Leaping Cat and his council.

About a week later, Flamingo told me what his fate was to be. Her village had not made any human sacrifices since the last of the other members had left many winters past. There were not enough of the People left to do so. But they had decided to sacrifice the pirate, who was named Jacques, at the green corn festival which was held in the harvest moon when the corn was ripe.

I was horrified at the thought of human sacrifice. I tried

to keep any expression off my face. I had learned a lot about how the People thought. One thing I was sure of: they were unpredictable. Just as I enjoyed their approval now, I could be their sacrifice tomorrow, especially if I tried to interfere with their beliefs or the rulings of the council.

That night and many nights after, I dreamed of the coming green corn festival. I dreamed there was dancing, chanting, games, and feasting. But Jacques and I weren't doing any of it. We were both tied to stakes in the middle of the village while the sacred fire was lit around our feet. I would wake in a cold sweat and lie there, unable to return to sleep.

And then it was the eve of the full moon, the time of the green corn festival. I wasn't looking forward to the ceremonies as the rest of the People were. Two of Jacques' friends had tried to release him a moon ago. When they were hunted and found, one had resisted to the death. The other was to be sacrificed with Jacques.

When we emerged from our chickee, we were greeted with all the splendors the People were capable of providing. Vivid pictures of creatures from the upper and lower worlds had been painted on wood. The People wore their finest attire, Spanish gold and jewelry, and other ornaments. Bodies were painted in garish designs. Leaping Cat wore a full eagle-feather headdress. Others wore the feathers of eagles, turkeys, egrets, herons, and other birds on their heads, attached to bands around their ankles and on their belts.

As chief shaman, Flamingo must wear white. She was resplendent in a white doeskin skirt embellished with pearls from the Spanish galleon. She wore a short cape of egret plumes that went over her left shoulder and under her right arm. Around her waist was a belt of gold doubloons. Her ears, wrists, ankles, neck, and fingers were adorned with creamy white pearls. White doeskin sandals decorated with pearls cuddled her feet. And on her head sat the magnificent tiara she had designed for the village metalworker to create for her.

I wore a breechcloth of tan doeskin with moccasins to match. At Flamingo's insistence, I wore the headband she had made for me of the red, yellow, and black skin of a coral snake I had killed. She had braided the hair on the left side of my head (the right was shaved) and woven the red tail feathers of the cardinal into the braid. Around my neck she placed a silver gorget studded with rubies, and around my waist a belt with a matching buckle. Then she kissed me, saying, "You will be the most handsome brave here."

We had fasted since noon yesterday, and I was feeling hunger pangs. All the men and boys who had reached puberty, and Flamingo as shaman, went to the center of the village ground which had been prepared for the festival. Each of us was given a gold or silver goblet, chalice, or bowl from the ship wreck. Then each container was ceremoniously filled with the white drink by the boys we were going to be initiated into manhood. We drank it to purify our minds and bodies. It made us run to the edge of the square and vomit, thus cleansing our bodies. It was supposed to also stimulate our minds and cause us to think clearer.

Then the puberty rites were held. New warriors were given their names. Those who had committed offenses were forgiven, or punishments were decided and carried out.

A married man had committed adultery with a married woman; both were sentenced to the long scratch. It was then I discovered one use for the moccasin fangs. The wife of the guilty man slashed him deeply with the snake fangs from his hairline to his heels. The husband of the guilty woman did the same to her.

During the puberty rites the young men had splinters stuck under their skin and lighted. To prove their manhood, they weren't to flinch. Then we, the men, got in line so

Flamingo could scratch our arms with gar teeth to allow the evil to flow from our blood.

Those who wanted to divorce their spouses could now do so. The man whose wife had committed adultery divorced her, but the woman whose husband was the other woman's lover did not seek divorce.

Next, Jacques and the runaway pirate who were tied to stakes near the fire became the center of attention. All the old fires except this one had been extinguished. It was put out and a new fire was started. This fire ceremony honored He Who Gives Breath, the supreme spirit of the People. After a while smoke appeared, then fire. Four logs had been laid to form a cross. The fire was in the center. The logs were pushed toward the fire and four ears of ripe corn were burned in thanksgiving. Then Flamingo carried a torch from the new sacred fire to each home, relighting these fires.

Briefly I wondered if He Who Gives Breath was somehow the Indian name for the God of the old testament, the logs in the form of the cross a before Christ promise or prediction of His coming, and the sacrifice of corn the same sacrifice as that in the Old Testament, a knowledge handed down by mouth to these people from the time of Adam that had somehow been tainted by the worship of nature and other false gods. I saw more than a couple of seeming parallels with my own beliefs. But things were moving too fast for me to think long of anything but that which surrounded me.

Then the People, led by Leaping Cat and Flamingo, danced around the men tied to the stakes. They chanted, shaking turtle shell rattles and those of the rattlesnake, blowing wooden pipes and beating drums as they piled sticks under the feet of the men.

Shortly after the dance around the men started, I slipped out of the crowd, knowing that in their ecstasy they wouldn't miss me. I had no stomach for what I knew was going to happen. I knew I was powerless to stop it, but I wanted no part of it. Besides, I was afraid Flamingo would be the one to bring a torch from the sacred fire to ignite the sticks under the feet of the pirates. I didn't know how I could live with her if I saw her do that. So I crept behind the gathering house, and there found the other three pirates.

Their faces were ashen. They now spoke haltingly the language of the People. One of them looked at me accusingly and said, partly in French, partly in the People's language, "How can you be one of them? You're white. You're a Christian. Yet you're married to a heathen Indian, a witch doctor. They're barbarians"

Just then we heard the screams of the men at the stakes above the din of the chanting, rattles, pipes, and drums.

"They're burning them! My God! Can't you get your squaw to stop them?" the other said.

I found myself in the strange position of defending the People. "Are they any more barbaric than pirates? Do you not attack Indians and whites alike, steal everything they have that you want, burn what's left, and sell into slavery those you don't kill? You can't even condone what you do by saying those you kill or sell are guilty of offending you in any way. The People at least held a council to decide the fate of Jacques and the other after they had committed their offenses. Don't talk to me of barbarism."

Then the stench of burning flesh assaulted our nostrils. We all became violently ill.

When the chanting subsided, I knew I had to get back to the ceremonies. I surely didn't want to be caught with these three and accused of some plot.

A huge feast was served that night. There was new corn, boiled and roasted, roasted sea turtle, oysters, fish shrimp, sea cow, lobster, and the ever present coontie bread. Unfortunately, as hungry and weak as I was, the thought of eating was out of the question while the smell of burning human flesh still filled my nostrils caused my stomach to turn over. Flamingo brought a large dinner to me, but I could eat nothing.

The People danced late into the night. Then for two more days we played games. The men used rackets of looped wooden sticks covered with strips of rawhide to hit stuffed deer hide balls at a mat attached to poles. At night there was more feasting and dancing.

The young bucks often ended up in the cornfields with the young maidens where they were initiated into the pleasures of the flesh during this festival which also revered the Green Corn Goddess, the goddess of fertility. Among them sex between unmarried adolescents was acceptable behavior, but I felt it particularly offensive to my Christian moral code, and I carried my own guilt for my behavior with Flamingo the night our twins were conceived. However, I knew if I wanted to go on living, and I did—if I didn't want to be a sacrifice at the next green corn festival, that I had to be a part of the festivities. I couldn't show my dislike or uneasiness with any of it. And above all, I couldn't mention my Christian beliefs or moral codes, much less try to Christianize the People.

Flamingo was obviously enjoying it all. She was in the spotlight, a leader, looked up to and admired for her wisdom, her powers, and her beauty. On the one hand I loathed what she stood for, the anti Christian practices and beliefs she espoused. On the other, it strangely attracted me. A leader she most surely was. A healer she was, too. She was wise, good, kind, and gentle with her people and her family. She was no hypocrite. What she believed, she practiced. And as to her beauty, there was no question about that.

Her legs were long and slim. I could span her waist with my hands. Her long, slender neck supported a well-shaped head. Black hair glistened above eyes as black and shiny. When she spun and danced, her cape of plumes lifted to show her shapely bosom. And she was mine. At least she was mine until the next green corn festival. At that time a person could divorce his or her spouse for no reason but that he or she was tired of the other.

The ceremony ended when a beloved elder reminded us we must abide by the ancient customs in the coming year. "We are bound together in unity by this sacred fire," he finished.

Finally it was over. I was glad for it to end. But it was all the People spoke of for days.

The twins were one now—fat, bronze, black eyes and hair. Fawn and Little Conch were inseparable. Where one toddled the other followed. I adored them. But it was their uncle, Leaping Cat, who, according to the ancient laws of his people, would have the most influence on them. It was he whose job it would be to instruct Little Conch in the ways of his tribe, to teach him to hunt and fish. For in this matriarchal society I had no rights concerning my children. They would even call him "Father" and he would call them "Son and Daughter."

And Flamingo had already decided Fawn would be a medicine woman. She was the youngest twin, as was Flamingo. This was enough to assure Flamingo that Fawn was born to be a witch doctor. The ways of the People were full of immorality by Christian standards, and I wanted my children to be Christian. But how? Although I was sure by now that I could get back to civilization, I knew I could not do it with two babies. Neither could I take the children from their mother who loved them as much as any Christian mother could. In spite of all the freedoms I now enjoyed, I was trapped—trapped by my love for my Indian family and in a culture alien to my own. And I was torn in my conscience as to which was the more moral—for these children to be with the mother who loved them and raised in the ways of her people which were both good and bad, or to be taken from their mother to be raised in the ways of Christianity whose *teachings* were everything that was good and holy, but whose followers *practices* were no less good and bad.

I knew as long as I acted like one of them, they would treat me as one of them. I was loved by Flamingo, and I loved her. Leaping Cat had been as my father. The People had always been good to me, treated me fairly. But I could not help remembering my faith—and Caty.

Always when I played with the twins, I thought of our child, Caty's and mine. Was the child a boy or girl? Was it healthy? Did it look like Caty? Did Caty tell the child about me? Did he or she have a stepfather? I would be overwhelmed by sadness at times. According to the People's customs, I was not a father to the twins, and neither could I be a father to Caty's and my child. I couldn't be a father to any of my children, and I wanted to so very much.

In the summer, called the time of the snake by the People, there was a lot to do and see. Leaping Cat introduced me to the bellow of alligators announcing their readiness to mate. He showed me how to catch them. He stood over an alligator hole and grunted as the alligator does. When it poked its nose out of the hole near his feet, he grabbed it by its snout, straddled the animal, and sat on its back. "You can hold its mouth shut with two fingers, he said, demonstrating by re-leasing all but a finger on top of its nose and a thumb under its chin. "But when its mouth is open, it can close it with enough force to break bones," he cautioned. He pulled the 'gator from its hole. "Watch out for its tail. It can slap with it and break bones, too." He flipped it on its back, and it lay there unmoving while he tied it up. "Alligator meat is good as you already know, and the hide tans well."

He showed me their nests. "The female makes water weeds and grass into a mound in the edge of the water. This rots and shrinks and she adds to it. When it's just right, rot-ting vegetation causes the nest to be hot and steamy. The 'gator makes a hole in the top into which she lays many eggs and covers them. The heat and moisture incubate the eggs in about two moons. The young will all be the same sex.

"When they begin to squeak, she uncovers them. She will ferociously defend her nest," he said.

He told me a crocodile nest, instead of being on inland water as the alligator's, was on the beach. The crocodile, like the sea turtle, lays its eggs in a hole it makes in dry sand. If the nest gets wet, the eggs die.

It was Flamingo who showed me the sea turtles coming ashore to nest. Through most of the time of the snake they came. Many nights we walked the white, sandy beaches of our island to see them come ashore by the dozens. The turtles, all female, struggle up the sandy beach past the high tide line. With their back flippers they dig and lift the sand, throwing it out to make a hole. The weight of their massive bodies pack the sand as they turn and make it impossible to tell exactly where the eggs have been laid. The turtle returns to the water, huffing and sighing. The process takes more than an hour.

We would catch the eggs in our hands as the turtle dropped them. The animals were gentle, and we sometimes pried barnacles off their shells as they laid their eggs. The eggs were delicious boiled or roasted. Their shells were thin and leathery, with a dimple in each. After cooking, we would pinch a hole in the shell and suck out the egg, which wouldn't harden no matter how long the egg was cooked.

The turtles usually came at night on high tide to lay. But any day during the nesting period the women could go to the beach, find fresh nests, and dig eggs. Flamingo showed me how to find them. "Look for the crawl, the tracks leading from the water to the nest and back," she said as we walked the beach one morning.

"There's one," I said.

"Now, poke a stick into the sand here," she pointed to the area a little higher up the beach between the coming and going tracks. "Keep poking the stick into the ground until you find a place where the stick suddenly goes in easy and comes out wet and sticky on the end. That shows you have punctured an egg."

I did as she instructed. When I found the eggs, we dug down until we uncovered them. We took what we needed and recovered the nest.

In the time of the eagle, when the weather was cold farther north, the sea cows would come. We hunted them in canoes. This winter was the first time I was allowed to make a kill. We had been searching on the west side of the island for maybe an hour when several of the huge animals were spotted. They were in fairly shallow water grazing on grass. We could see their backs come out of the water, and occasionally one would roll over. We brought the canoes up to one. I fastened a knife to my belt and looped the rope onto my arm. When we had the animal where we wanted it, I roped it and jumped on its back. As it carried me for the ride of my life, I pulled out my knife and began to stab it. The sea cow has to breathe, but not as often as I. It swam to deeper water, and I held my breath until I thought my lungs would burst. I couldn't let go, because I would be the laughing stock of the People. Finally, when I could hold my breath no longer, it brought me to the surface. I gulped the air hungrily. Down we went again. It struggled. I stabbed. It carried me under.

When it seemed I would die for want of air, it carried me to the surface. It turned over two of the canoes, and in the instant I was above water I saw men frantically swimming toward the other canoes, hoping to avoid the thrashing manatee for fear it would land on them. It seemed the struggle went on for hours. Finally, I won. We drug his body to shore behind our remaining canoes. That night we ate broiled manatee steaks. It tasted as good as any meat I have ever eaten.

The hunting, the fishing, the vast panoramas of nature,

and the freedom—most of all the freedom—were the things I loved about this life. And there were the pleasant times of an evening when Flamingo, the children and I did the things together that families do: walk on the beach; sit around a fire on a winter's eve while Flamingo sang softly or told the children the fables of her people, while I carved little animals of wood for them. And after they were asleep, there were the tender moments shared by a man and his wife.

Like it or not, there was never any monotony. There was always something to do, and most of it I liked doing.

When Little Conch was three, his great-uncle, Leaping Cat, gave him a little bow and arrows and taught him to use it. He and the other little boys learned to hunt by shooting lizards, mice, and other small animals.

Fawn put up such a fuss that she, too, was allowed to have a bow and arrows. She helped Flamingo gather roots, berries, or other foods, and with planting corn, beans, and squash. She was learning traditional women's work. She was also being introduced to herbs, potions, healing, and witchcraft. But, Flamingo allowed her time with her brother and Leaping Cat to master the bow, perhaps remembering when she, also, insisted upon learning to shoot.

Flamingo sometimes had dreams which she and the People believed to be communications with various spirits. She interpreted these dreams, and she and the People took whatever action she determined necessary based on what these visions meant.

One morning she said, "I had a dream last night. A spirit came to me and told me we must hide the treasure you have in your trunk. We are not to tell anyone about this. Tonight, after everyone is asleep, we will bury it under out chickee."

"Why did the spirit say we must do this?" I asked.

"I do not question the spirits. It will be revealed when the time is right," she said. So late that night under a moonless sky when the village was asleep, Flamingo and I removed the treasure trunk from our chickee. I had removed a set of matching rings, one a man's and one a woman's. I meant to give them to the twins someday.

I dug a hole about four feet deep under our home. We placed the trunk containing sacks of coins, jewelry and other pieces, as well as Caty's diary, in the hole. I had decided to bury it along with the treasure, as that part of my life was undoubtedly buried.

In the early time of the snake in 1776, I accompanied the able-bodied men and a half-dozen women, including Flamingo, on a turkey hunt. During this part of the year the turkeys mate. The male turkey gobbles to call the hens to him. Their feathers are more colorful and shiny than at other times, and they fan their tails in a display to attract hens. Gobblers normally gobble only during the mating season, but sometimes the young males will gobble at other times.

We went in our dugout through the Grassy Water to a place west of the big lake called Mayaimi. There among the oak hammocks and cypress swamps many of the magnificent creatures could be found. We could see the three-toed tracks and sandy little craters where the turkeys had dusted. Here and there lay a breast or a tail feather. Droppings littered the ground

Flamingo pointed at the ground. "That's a gobbler's dropping. See, it is straight with a hook at the end," and, pointing to another, "This is from a hen. It is round.

"The turkeys will roost in trees like that, maybe even in these very trees," she said, pointing to some large cypress trees in the swamp. "They like to sleep over water. This is a very large flock. We should be successful in the morning."

The next morning we strung out along the edge of the swamp with about two hundred yards between each of us. I squatted with my back against a large cypress stump. I had cut a half dozen palmetto fans which I stuck in the ground to form a semicircle before me, being sure to leave clearance for my bow and arrow. When the whippoorwills and other birds began their calling, I took from my pouch the caller Flamingo had helped me make from the wing bone of turkey killed on a previous hunt. With this I made the soft tree yelp of a turkey waking and telling the other turkeys where she is.

Turkeys are very social, I had learned. They like the company of other turkeys. This time of year the hens usually travel together. Young males flock together, too. But old gobblers stay separated except to mate. What I, and other members of our hunt, hoped to do was fool the gobblers into coming to our calls in the belief we were hens.

Immediately when I gave my tree yelp, I heard a gobble from the swamp in front of me. The turkey was still on his roosting limb. Before he finished his eerie-sounding gobble-oble-oble-oble-oble, turkeys on either side started to gobble, also. Then I heard the answering tree yelps of other turkeys around me. The flock was waking up.

I could not hear the sound of a turkey gobble without my heart pounding so wildly that I had trouble hearing over the sound of it. To me, hunting the wild gobbler in spring was the ultimate in game hunting. I had to fool the gobbler into believing he was hearing a lovesick hen. I had to make him so certain of it that he would come to me. This goes against his nature, because usually the hen goes to him. And I had plenty of competition from the real hens.

As it became light enough to see what was around me, I yelped a little louder. Several gobblers responded. Then I slapped my hands repeatedly on my thighs, hoping to make the sound of a turkey's wings as it left the roost. Immediately, I gave a louder series of yelps. When I heard the gobbles that time, I saw the dark form of a turkey on the limb of a huge cypress, his neck and head stretched straight out in front of him as he gobbled. I watched him strut on the limb as we talked to one another. The sun came over the horizon. Its light caused the feathers of the magnificent old bird to sparkle in iridescent bronze, blue, green, and red. He was out of range of my bow and arrows. Had I tried to get up and sneak toward him, his keen eyes would have seen me. He would have spooked and flown in the other direction. I sat and watched his display, my heart jumping in my chest, a wild stinging in my veins.

Then, with a great flap of wings, he left his roosting tree, landing about halfway between it and me in grass and white sand. I was pinned. I could not move until he passed behind one of the huge cypress trees between us. He took a jagged course toward me as I continued to yelp. His tail fanned, his breast feathers fluffed, making him appear much larger than he was. The wrinkled skin of his head and neck was red, white, and blue. The beard (that's what the hair that hung down in long strands from his neck was called) was thick, black, and so long he nearly walked on it with each step. Surely he was king of the swamp.

Avoiding the trees, he kept his beady black eyes on the spot from which he was hearing the insistent hen yelp. Closer and closer he came. I began to despair of his putting a tree between us, so I would have an opportunity to raise my bow which I had fitted with an arrow before he left the limb. Then, when he was no more than twenty-five feet from me, he turned broadside. He strutted a few feet to the right, stuck his brightly colored head in front of him, and gobbled. Then he turned his back to me as he circled in the other direction. When his back was to me, his fanned tail blocking his eyes, which being on the sides of his head, could have seen me otherwise, I raised my bow.

I was fascinated by the display of these noble birds during their courtship ritual. I should have loosed my arrow immediately, because out of the corner of my eye I saw a quick movement. Then I saw another bird, quite like a twin to the first. He made a sound I cannot describe and had never before heard, as he ran toward the first bird, who by now had turned to face him. The two birds jumped at each other, attempting to stab each other with the long, sharp spurs that grew from the backs of their legs a couple of inches above their feet. They sent each other rolling on the ground as they slapped with their powerful wings. Then one pecked the neck skin of the other. The other twisted in an attempt to get away, but the first kept a hold on it. They struggled in this manner until the lengths of their necks were twisted together, the one still keeping a strong grip on the other with his beak. Several hens had gathered around the clearing, scratching and pecking, pretending not to be impressed by these magnificent males as they fought for the position of dominance among them.

I was fascinated, watching down the length of my arrow. Then, remembering why I was here, as the two birds turned at an angle where I thought I could get both with one arrow, I let it fly. It pierced both birds and stopped in a cypress trunk, pinning the birds to the tree. I jumped up, knife in hand. Then Flamingo said, "No!" as the other birds scattered.

"What are you doing here? You were supposed to be hunting over there." I pointed.

"When I heard all the action over here, I lay on my stomach and wriggled over to watch the fun. Don't approach those turkeys now. They will stop their flapping and die in a few minutes. If you try to finish them with your knife, they will spur you. Their spurs have sharp tips and can go through a hand or into an arm or leg. Be patient. They are yours. And both with one shot! I never knew another do that. Are you sure you were not born one of the People? I would never have believed one not born of us could truly be one of us. But you are. The spirits really transformed you when you were drowning in that storm."

I glowed under her praise. That night as we snuggled in our skins, she asked if she could make capes for the twins, now five, from the feathers of the two turkeys I had killed. I could think of nothing I would rather have done with them. The beards she would weave into a necklace for me. From it the four spurs would hang.

At times I did feel I was one of the First People. I was even proud to be one of them. But at other times . . .

III

In late summer I was among several braves fishing on the mainland. We had rowed our canoe through the marsh and were stretching a gill net across the mouth of a small feeder creek. We planned to catch fish as the outgoing tide brought them into the net. As I returned to our canoe to get baskets to put the fish in, I saw another canoe across the marsh. A half-dozen braves not of our tribe were in it. They obviously had not seen us. I bent down below the grass tops and returned to the others, pointing toward the braves in the canoe. My companions squatted so they could just see over the grass.

It was not unusual to see the larger ships of pirates, traders, and even the Spanish and English military out past the reef at sea. But in all my winters among the First People, I had never seen a single Indian vessel except those belonging to us. Indeed Leaping Cat and Flamingo believed our tribe was the last of their kind on the peninsula.

The other canoe was at a distance, so it was impossible to tell what its inhabitants looked like, only that they were Indians.

When we returned to the village with our catch, we went straight to Leaping Cat to tell him of the other canoe. While the women prepared the fish, a council was called to discuss the other canoe and what it might mean to us. To my amazement, I was invited to join the council in this meeting. When Leaping Cat, our chief, invited me, even Flamingo was surprised. Only the chief, the beloved men, and Flamingo usually attended.

We entered the gathering lodge. Chief Leaping Cat, my adoptive father, sat first on a bench that circled the walls. Then the rest of us sat. Leaping Cat ceremoniously lit his pipe, took a long puff, and passed it to his right, to Flamingo, who also took a long drag. It was passed thus until it reached me, the last to smoke it. I, too, took a long puff of the heady tobacco the pipe held. It left me, as always, feeling dizzy.

Then Leaping Cat asked me to tell the others what I had seen. After I told them, Leaping Cat said, "Who can these people be? Many winters before Water Gift came to be one of us, the white men who called us Calusa took or killed all of the First People out of this area except us. They don't know we are here. When we discovered they would send or take us away, we hid from them. The others either left with the white men, free or as slaves, or left in their longboats for other islands far from here. I've heard names like Havana and Bahama and Hispaniola. We have seen no sign of others of our kind since that time."

One old man, He Who Thinks, said, "We must send out a scouting party to find where their village is, how many they are, and if they are peaceable."

Another said, "We must know why they have come and from where. Are more to follow? Will they be our friends or our enemies?"

I said, "I saw Indians in the moon that I came to be found in the water. I had escaped from a place called New Smyrna in the area known as the Mosquitoes. Do you know it?"

Leaping Cat nodded that he did.

"In St. Augustine I saw Indians in the market trading hides and game for English goods. These Indians looked different. The men wore their hair long and free or drawn back and tied. Some wore bright cloth wound about their heads. Some of the women wore clothes that covered them in the European manner. Many of these were the Indians that had become Christians and lived in the villages around the town. They were not feared by the townspeople. However, the St. Augustinians did not hunt or fish far from town, because they recognized that unfriendly Indians frequented the forests and swamps. Occasionally Indians raided farms and plantations in outlying areas, stealing cattle, killing and kidnapping whites and slaves, and burning farms to the ground. Some of those Indians have guns and ride horses. The whites call them Seminoles and said they had come into Florida from Georgia, the Carolinas, and other areas east of the Mississippi River. They had been driven south by the white colonists.

"I learned that most of these Seminoles live in the interior of Florida, west of the big river called St. Johns. I was in New Smyrna for fourteen (I counted out fourteen sticks from the basket kept for this purpose) moons. I only spent a few days in St. Augustine. On market day some of the Seminoles from across the St. Johns came in to trade, also.

"In New Smyrna we rarely saw an Indian. But they did attempt to raid us when we first arrived. And they were said to raid the area from north and west of us. My people feared them more than the English, who had a sort of peace with them. But we were told they hated us, because we looked like the Spanish and shared the Catholic religion," I said.

Leaping Cat and the others discussed what I had said among them. Then, to my surprise, Leaping Cat suggested that as his son it was time I joined the council. He said I had proved myself to be brave, a good hunter and fisherman, and in every way as much one of the People as any of them. After a vote, in which all but one of the beloved old men were in favor, I was admitted to the council.

Then we decided that I was to lead a party that would scout the lower part of Florida up to the top of Lake Mayaimi to see if there were other inhabitants, who they were, and how many. I was to choose two other braves to accompany me. No more could be spared, since our village now held nine old people, eight under the ages of fourteen, thirteen men and ten women, plus the three pirate slaves. We were to leave on the morning after the full moon, which was three days away.

I chose as my companions Little Bear and Squint Eyes. Little Bear was about seventeen, short in stature with the slightly tilted eyes and high cheekbones of all his tribe. His face was round, his nose long and hooked. He had large, intelligent eyes, a keen sense of humor, and had proved his ability, loyalty, and bravery on other occasions as had the other scout, Squint Eyes.

Squint Eyes, as you can imagine, avoided the light by squinting his eyes. His face was weathered, with many tiny wrinkles around his eyes. His mouth was a thin, grim line. He was humorless. His age, I thought, was somewhere between forty and forty-five, much older than my twenty-seven years. He had been over the territory we were to search many times before most of his people left or were taken away.

The next two days were spent preparing for the trip, the evenings playing with the twins, and the nights in tender lovemaking and farewell to Flamingo. We didn't know how long we would be apart, but we knew it would be measured not in days, but moons.

And so on the morning after a full moon in August or September 1776, we departed our village in a light canoe made of skins that we could easily carry overland between waterways. We had coontie cakes and meal, dried deer, turkey, bear and manatee meat, and smoked fish. We also had spears, bows, and arrows. In our belts were our knives and toma- hawks. We wore only breech cloths and moccasins and our bodies were smeared with bear grease. Packed in the canoe were capes and leggings of deerskin and fur blankets, for we knew we would not return before the cold of winter.

Having seen no traffic in the bay that afternoon, we de- parted for the island next morning. I felt very vulnerable in our little canoe in the open water of the bay in broad day- light. Squint Eyes explained that had we seen any traffic in the bay we would have waited till night for our trip to the island. We found the place deserted. Here and there was evidence of previous inhabitation, but no one lived here now. There was, however, a rude camp that showed signs of intermittent visits by white men, probably pirates who used this as a base when in the area.

We visited other islands briefly, searching the bay be- tween the coast and outer islands for canoes. Then we re- turned to the Grassy Water having found no trace of Indians. We searched the various hammocks scattered throughout the Grassy Water for more than two moons, so large was it.

The Grassy Water is what it sounds like. It is miles and miles of saw grass dotted with hammocks. Shallow water runs south through the saw grass. Under the vegetation the decay- ing grass and debris form a muck that is like quick sand. Squint Eyes said that in dry times when this muck is above water, lightening sometimes sets it afire, and it will burn for many moons. Deeper channels ran through this vast plain of grassy water. Around the edges of it there was jungle. To the south were the custard apple trees, nearly impenetrable, and the ferns and vines. To the southeast the jungle consisted of scrub willow and elderberry and scattered sand ridges jutted in from the coast. Moonvines covered all the trees. Around the outer edges pine and palmettos grew on the high ground, with live oaks in the hammocks and on the little islands.

Around the oaks grew the strangler figs. And everywhere
there were cabbage palms.

We spent the rainy season in the Grassy Water, searching
for the village of the other Indians. The only villages we had
found so far had been deserted many winters past. Jungle
growth had reclaimed them.

Many times we startled great colonies of egrets, storks,
and other water birds, so that they covered and darkened the
sky with their sudden flight, sometimes to light in our path
only to be disturbed again, as we continued on our way.

The large blue herons and their smaller cousins of
brighter blue, the great white and others were ever present,
standing silently, often on one leg, to spear fish with their
sharp beaks. The Indians told me they wiggle a toe to re-
semble a worm to attract fish. Pink flamingoes dotted the
shallows, and the brown speckled limpet stood on muck
banks eating apple snails from the water around them.

Raccoons could be seen everywhere eating crawfish, snails,
wild fruit, and small oysters from the roots of mangroves.

We emerged from the Grassy Water into an area of water
oaks, bare branched in the winter cold. By now we saw fewer
of the cold-blooded snakes, alligators, and turtles we had
seen at the beginning of our search. Only on the warmest
and sunniest of days did we see a few sunning at midday on
debris, muck heaps, or in the case of snakes, looped around
the branches of trees.

We searched the creek banks on our journey toward the
big lake for Indian villages or signs that Indians used the
area, ever watchful for canoes or longboats on the water. We
searched the area between Lake Mayaimi and the east coast.
Still we found no other Indians, nor anyone.

It was now January or February, the coldest time of the
year. Even then we had been having unseasonably cold
weather for this area. Squint Eyes had remarked on the
harshness of the weather the past few days, as we had been

plagued with a light snow three days ago which had not as yet melted. It was about four inches deep. Squint Eyes had heard the old men and women speak of a time in the ancient past when this had happened, but this was the only time it had happened in his life.

This night we built our fire and roasted a raccoon over it for supper. Afterward, we rolled up in bear skins on top of palmettos as close to the fire as was comfortable and safe for a cold winter night's sleep.

Sometime in the early hours before dawn, Squint Eyes and I were awakened by the frightened scream of Little Bear. In the light of the fire we could see him standing. In his hand he held a coral snake, its neck between his thumb and forefinger, its body encircling his wrist like a bright bracelet of yellow, red, and black.

"I have been bitten! I awoke and this coral snake was chewing on my little finger! I am a dead man!" said Little Bear.

I couldn't believe what I was seeing. In the coldest part of winter he had been bitten by a coral snake. Though they usually don't hibernate in such a warm climate, they had to have in the freezing weather we had been having the past few days.

We jumped from our fireside beds as Little Bear flung the snake into the fire, begging its pardon for taking its life. Then we saw dozens of the bright little wriggling snakes on the ground around the fire where the warmth of the flames had warmed the earth.

"We have built our fire over the place they were hibernating," I said, as I began to sweep them into the fire with a palmetto fan from my bed.

Little Bear and Squint Eyes likewise began sweeping the creatures into the fire, begging the pardon of each. Then we carefully shook out our skin blankets and searched through the palmetto fans we had placed beneath them and our belongings for more snakes, which we also swept into the fire. After being sure we had burned all the pretty and deadly snakes that had so far emerged from the heated earth, we turned our attention to Little Bear.

"I will die. There is no cure for the bite of the coral snake. Our shaman is not here to evoke magic for me. It will be a death of agony," said Little Bear in the fatalistic tone which did not betray the terror he must have been feeling.

Squint Eyes described the memory of another coral snake bite, the only he had ever seen. "She was a child of only a few winters. I, myself, had not yet become a man. She picked up the beautiful snake to drape around her neck. It bit her several times on her little hand. All the adults were in a terrible state of panic, but at first the little girl hardly noticed the bites. She was more concerned that her 'pretty' had been taken from her.

"I began to think the adults were making much fuss over nothing. But in a little while, in spite of all the witch doctor's prayers, potions, and administering, she began to show the fatal symptoms. Spittle began to run from her mouth. Then she seemed to be in a kind of ecstasy. She lost control of her arms and legs. She became paralyzed, was lost in the sleep from which she could not awaken, and then she ceased to breathe. By nightfall she was dead."

"We can't stand by and do nothing. We all agree you will die of the snake's bite. If there is no hope, will you let me try something? Let's cut the little finger off. Maybe the poison has not yet left the finger. What do we have to lose? Little Bear, would you trade your finger for your life?" I asked.

I saw hope flicker in his eyes. Then the brave young man's face was again expressionless. He tried to hide his hope, his only hope, when he said, "It might work. I barely feel that I have been bitten. It's only beginning to swell. You may take it off," he said, extending his hand.

"Squint Eyes, get some ice from the edge of the stream,

please. We will freeze his finger first, so he won't feel it so much. While he is holding his finger in the ice, I will get my knife blade hot in the fire to sear the blood vessels so he won't lose so much blood," I said. Some medicine I had learned from Flamingo, but some I remembered from my former life.

When this was done, I had Little Bear sit and place his extended little finger on the stump of a tree we had cut for firewood. "Squint Eyes, you hold him. Little Bear, look the other way. I am going to remove the finger one joint past the hand." I touched the joint with the knife to help my aim, lifted the knife and brought it down with all my strength so as to sever the finger with one chop.

Little Bear gasped. He turned to see his finger lying on the stump. Then he slumped to the ground, unconscious.

I bandaged the slump with a strip of material from a loin cloth Flamingo had woven for me.

"Squint Eyes, we will have to camp here until Little Bear heals or dies. We must build a chickee away from this snake den. One of us must stay with Little Bear while the other chooses a place and builds another fire. Then we will move him and cut palmettos and trees for the chickee."

"You stay. I'll find a place and make a fire," he said.

By now Little Bear was conscious and embarrassed at having fainted. He insisted he could help us. I insisted he must be still and stay calm and warm.

After the fire was ready, Little Bear was able to walk to it. I had him lie wrapped in his bear skin by the fire while we erected a chickee. Then we cooked sofkee and insisted Little Bear eat, although he said he wasn't hungry. We stayed camped for three days. Little Bear's appetite returned on the second day. By the third day we had trouble keeping him in the chickee. Although it was still cold, it was no longer freezing. We were feeling certain the snake bite was not going to kill Little Bear. He sang praises to the spirits for saving his life. I had been praying to the Almighty Father since I had removed his finger.

On the fourth day we resumed our search.

We reached the northernmost part of Lake Mayaimi in March or April. In this area we saw signs of recent Indian occupation. Squint Eyes believed some tribe had spent the summer here catching and eating the fish, frogs, alligators, and other life that teamed in the lake.

We discussed going farther north to see if we could find the winter grounds of these Indians. But, finally, we decided to continue around to the western edge of the lake. From there we would search to the west coast of the peninsula.

We traveled the western edge of Lake Mayaimi, always watchful for other traffic on the water and signs of Indians on shore. About two days from the summer camp we took a creek to the west. It meandered through huge cypress trees whose roots formed knees above the ground in their quest for air. The water was clear but tinted red-brown over a white sandy bottom. We quickly saw that this swamp was home to many of the beautiful wild turkeys. Squint Eyes said he had hunted here as a boy before the tribe had been virtually destroyed by the white man. It was not a long way north of where we had hunted last spring. We were continuously treated to the court-ship ritual of the gobblers, as it was again the spring mating season.

The area also abounded in deer, bear, wildcat, otter, sand-hill cranes, and other animals. We saw a panther with a cub drinking from the creek in the early morning.

On the edges of the swamp stood sandy ridges with huge, moss-draped live oaks. It was an enchanting place. As we walked through one such hammock, Squint Eyes froze. He pointed to the ground, which was covered with cow tracks. But, the track to which he pointed was that of an Indian moccasin.

Our senses quickened. We became more alert to sights,

and sounds. Farther along the hammock, we came to a small village of seven chickees. We climbed into an ancient oak, perching in the huge limbs to observe. We saw only women and children going about their daily chores. To one side of the village lay a garden, which was being seeded by five women and twice as many children. Three women were making meal from coontie roots. These women had babies still strapped to boards. Beyond this small village we could see the smoke of many fires. We decided this must be an outpost of the main village, which was probably large.

A sudden bolt of lightening and an afternoon thunderstorm sent everyone running to the shelter of the chickees.

We scampered down from our tree to continue around the little village toward the larger one beyond.

As we neared it, we came upon a huge corral containing many horses. Little Bear didn't know what animal this was, having never before seen a horse.

Squint Eyes said, "Men ride the backs of those animals. I, myself, have never ridden one, but as a child I visited a village on Lake Mayaimi where there were other villages of the First People. The chief of that village had three of the splendid animals. He had gotten them in trade with a white man who used to come once a year to buy furs and skins from the People. All the different villages of our tribe would come together at this village yearly to trade with the white man and with one another. The white trader brought firewater which our men drank until they were useless. And he brought beads and looking glasses. But he would not sell the fire sticks of the white man to us.

"Once the white trader told the chief about these animals which carried men about. The chief had never seen one, but he had carvings of them done by his ancestors and remembered the stories of the Spanish riding such animals.

"He told the white trader he wanted some of the animals the man called horses.

"The trader had seen a few gold and silver gorgets and coins worn by the chief and some members of the tribe. He would only trade horses for these. The chief wanted the horses so badly that he gave a small basketful of the shiny metal coins he had gotten from a shipwreck to the trader for three horses that were brought on the trader's next trip.

"I was there when the horses arrived. They were splendid. One was a big male, black with white feet. Another male was red-brown with a white blaze on its forehead. The third was a gold-colored mare.

"A little later, after the trading was over and all the other villagers had gone home, many white men came. They had guns. They wanted all the silver and gold. They killed many braves. They stole women and children. Some villagers escaped to tell about what happened. The First People never traded with the white man again."

We followed the edges of the corral to the village. The rain was pelting us with huge drops. The sky had darkened with clouds. We were at the edge of the village before we realized it. No one was about, all seeking the shelter of the chickees or gathering house. We circled the village, counting the chickees. There were sixty-two. Milk cows were tied near some chickees, and cows roamed free in the woods around the village. Here and there a dog barked. Chickens scampered to find dry places. Little Bear had never seen dogs or chickens, either. There were none in our village. These Indians were farmers and cattlemen. They had cleared fields on the outskirts of the village.

As the rain began to abate, we found hiding places in the palmettos at the downwind end of the village. It was nearing nightfall, and we needed to learn all we could about these people.

Soon the men began to return from their day's tasks.

Some were on foot, some rode bareback on horses. Some of the men were black. I assumed they were runaway or captured slaves. But the biggest surprise to Squint Eyes was that some of the men carried the white man's fire sticks. In fact, about half of them had guns. Most of them were English made, but I recognized two Kentucky long rifles like the one Joseph Adams had shown me in St. Augustine. These were American-made flintlock guns known for their deadly accuracy.

Squint Eyes determined these Indians were of no tribe he had ever seen before. He had heard of Indians north of the Peninsula, as his people called Florida, but had never seen them.

I said, "I have seen similar Indians on market day in St. Augustine. The English call them Seminole and say they are renegades or runaways. The Georgians claim they raid their farms and plantations, burning, killing, and stealing livestock, slaves, and sometimes their wives and children. They cross the border into Florida. Runaway slaves sometimes join them.

We watched from our hiding place until the only light was that of the village fires and torches. Then we sneaked closer to see better and to hear, but we could not understand the language of these Indians.

They had among them many garments of white society, as well as brightly colored cotton loin clothes, skirts, and capes. Whether these had been stolen in raids or gotten in trade I did not know. They also had pots and pans and other white man's utensils, and there was definitely liquor. A half-dozen men sat about a fire drinking firewater from tin cups.

Children chased each other, giggling and wrestling, through the village. Women served the men their suppers of some sort of stew and bread. The smell of it made me remember we had not eaten since breakfast.

Dogs sat by their masters, wagging their tails and waiting for the bones tossed their way when every morsel of meat had been sucked from them. After supper a couple strolled through the village, gaining the attention and respect of all. The man was tall and his shoulders were broader than any I had ever seen. His hair was fairly short, black tendrils curling from beneath a scarlet cloth wound turban like around his head. His shirt was of white silk, open halfway down the front to show a magnificent, large, silver gorget on a rawhide thong threaded through tubular beads of silver and scarlet. His breeches were black and fitted, molding to the muscles of his buttocks, thighs, and calves. Around his waist he wore a scarlet sash, and his feet were shod in the most handsome pair of beaded moccasins I had ever seen.

The man's skin was bronze, definitely Indian, but I thought I detected something else, too. His face bore the high cheekbones and slightly slanted eyes of his race. His nose was long with a beak-like curve. Above his mouth he wore a thick mustache that left only his lower lip visible. I had never seen a mustachioed Indian before. He walked among the other Indians, smiling down at them as though they were his subjects.

At his side, her arm hooked through his, strode the most strikingly beautiful woman any of us had ever seen. She was of average height, but nothing else about her was average. Her hair was black and had been pulled back to the nape of her neck, then twisted and piled high on her head. It was held in place by pearl-encrusted combs. Her gown of white satin and lace covered her feet, but revealed a creamy bosom. It could have been a wedding dress meant for some high-cast Spanish bride in Havana. For all I knew, it well might have been.

Her neck, wrists, and fingers wore more pearls. Thin, black brows arched over perfect, large blue eyes. She had a well-shaped nose, and scarlet lips smiled regally from a face of creamy white.

My first thought when I saw her was, "What is a woman like that doing in a place like this?"

Squint Eyes whispered, "They have to be the chief and his woman."

"They act more like the king and queen indulging their subjects with a royal display. See how regally they carry themselves? They even hold their heads at an angle where they appear to look down their noses at their people. She is definitely not an Indian. She looks like a Spanish woman of gentle, if not royal, birth," I said.

Little Bear said nothing, but the look on his face in the flickering light told me he was hypnotized by the woman's beauty.

Then from behind the woman's skirt appeared a child of five or six. He was a miniature of his mother, even to the blue eyes. His hair reached his shoulders, glossy black and wavy. He wore a scarlet cape that stopped just short of the bottom of pants that fell just below his knees. The moccasins on his feet were high top, laced to the bottom of his pants. On his face was a pout, as he addressed the woman in Spanish, "Mama, why must you dress me like this? I like better to run naked with the other boys."

She answered, "Because Brave Eagle is chief. In the world from which we came he would be king and you would be a prince. I, myself, am of royal blood. A royal family must look and act royal. Brave Eagle insists upon it."

"But, Mama, I do not want to be different from the other boys. We are Indians. I do not remember anything else. I feel silly when you dress me up like this and parade me through the village."

Brave Eagle tightened his grip on her arm, and a look of annoyance briefly crossed his face. He said something to her in the language of the Seminoles. Then she turned to the boy and said, "Esteban, your adopted father says we must stop speaking in Spanish when we are among the people. He says it is rude. He wants that pout off your face."

Tears of frustration sprang to little Esteban's eyes as he, once again, tried to hide behind his mother's voluminous skirt.

Then I realized Brave Eagle and his family were headed toward a chickee from which a man was just emerging. He was young, of medium height, with short, sandy hair. His clothes were in the English style. He walked toward the chief with a friendly smile and an outstretched hand. He spoke haltingly in the Indian's dialect, using signs and English for words he could not translate. I understood he was a trader named Jim Stokes representing a trading company. It seemed he was seeking permission to set up a permanent trading post within the village.

Trader Jim joined the chief's family as they continued their evening stroll through the village, stopping here and there to gesture toward a cleared field or in the direction of a horse corral. Once they stopped before a chickee where the chief spoke to a man. He went into his chickee and returned with a Kentucky long rifle which Trader Jim handled, aimed, and admired. Perhaps Brave Eagle wanted to know if the trader could supply more of the long arms for his men. We observed the goings-on in the village until everyone, except four of the men who had been drinking, retired to their chickees. These four lay on the wet ground between a fire and a chickee in a state between drunken stupor and sleep. A dog licked the face of one and then another, then the tin cups that had fallen to the ground near them.

Creeping away, we found a safe place to sleep until just before dawn, when we would cross the creek and scout the other bank.

We were awakened by the cock-a-doodle-dos of roosters and the mooing of cows. We dared not build a fire to make sofkee. Instead we ate dried venison from our packs as we headed through the cypress swamp to the creek.

We saw the tracks of a large panther in the white sand. We followed the tracks a little way and came upon the cat with a freshly killed calf. Lifting his tawny head, he opened his mouth, baring long, wicked-looking fangs. Carefully we retreated, making a wide semicircle around the feeding panther.

We approached the creek and followed it to a place not too wide, partially bridged by a fallen cypress. There was an Indian trail here that evidently began at the village we had just left. Squint Eyes beckoned us to squat behind some grass while he carefully checked to see if anyone was around before we crossed the creek. In a few minutes he gave us an all clear sign and we walked the log as far as it went, jumping the last couple of feet to the other bank. We followed the trail until midday, coming upon another small village of ten chickees. The two outposts and the large village held a total of seventy-nine chickees.

There may have been other small outposts, but I decided we had seen enough here. We had now been away from home for eight moons. We were still many miles from home. I did not want to take unnecessary chances. If we were caught, we might not be able to explain our spying to the satisfaction of Brave Eagle. It was imperative we return to our village with the information we had.

We headed our canoe back toward Lake Mayaimi and south along the western edge. The next day we came to another river that we followed all the way to the western shore of Florida. We saw signs that Indians hunted and camped the area, but found no villages nor saw anyone. Within ten days of leaving Brave Eagle's village we were back on the lake.

We spent another moon searching the rest of the shore of Lake Mayaimi and the area southwest of it where we had turkey hunted and the area between the lake and the Grassy

River. Then we headed home along the western part of the
big swamp. We arrived in our village just a few days before the
Green Corn Festival of 1777.

We were greeted with much happiness by our families
and the whole village. Flamingo had never looked better to
me, and I could not believe how much the twins had grown
in the ten moons since I had last seen them. They were now
six years old, or as Flamingo put it, they had been with us for
six winters past. They were most beautiful children and
extremely intelligent.

I wanted nothing more than to spend the afternoon and
evening with my family, but Leaping Cat could not wait to
hear of our discoveries. A council was called, and Little Bear,
Squint Eyes, and I told the assembly what we had seen and
heard. After much discussion, Leaping Cat instructed everyone to think about what we had told them. We would decide
what to do when the council was assembled for the Green
Corn Festival that would begin in three days. We would feast
tonight in honor of our safe return. It was so good to have
a whole, fresh meal again. We were just in time, because
the fast would begin tomorrow.

When we were finally able to sneak away from the festivities and go to our chickee, it was too late to visit with the
twins. They had been asleep for hours. Flamingo came to
me, her long denied desire for me as fervent as mine for her.
In my exhaustion I fell asleep immediately after. During the
night my dreams were jumbled. I dreamed of Flamingo and
Caterina and the Spanish wife of Brave Eagle. They all wore
white wedding dresses. They all had dark hair. They were all
my wives. And then they all became one, but I didn't know
which one. As the face of Caterina with her dimpled cheeks
became the bronze face of Flamingo with her high cheekbones, and then the creamy face with blue eyes, each in turn
laughed at my torment.

During the next two days we prepared for the Corn

Festival. On the morning of its beginning, the council con-
vened. Leaping Cat said, "We will have to send a delegation
to the village of the tribe that now lives on the west of Lake
Mayaimi. We must try to join with them in peace. For if they
do not feel peaceful toward us, we are doomed. They are too
many, and they have the fire sticks of the white man. Does
anyone else have any thoughts on this?"

So it was decided we would leave for the Seminole village
two days after the Green Corn Festival.

Little Bear had grown taller and more manly during our
mission. Suddenly he was much in favor with the young
women in our village. Even more handsome than when we
left, he had faced death by coral snake bite and had lost a
finger. He told of places they had never been, animals they
had never seen. There was some jealousy on the part of the
other young men, rightfully so. He was seen going into the
cornfield at least once with each of the young girls who had
reached puberty during the corn festival. Each returned with
lips bruised from kissing, starry eyed, and begging Flamingo
for potions to win him permanently. Little Bear ate it all up
and seemed to show no particular preference, happy to go
into the cornfield with each and every one. I could not help
but realize that somehow I must get my children away from
here before they reached the age where they would engage
in this promiscuous practice. But how, I agonized?

I enjoyed this corn ceremony more than any since I had
been among the People. There had not been a human sacrifice since the pirates. And after the initial fasting, the feasting was wonderful. Ten moons away from the village eating
mostly dried meat, sofkee, and coontie cakes, with only an
occasional fish or roasted small animal made me appreciate
all the good food and the variety of it heaped before us during the feasting. And I could enjoy it all with my beloved
twins.

My son had become quite a hunter in the moons I had

been gone. He had killed numerous raccoons, 'possums, rabbits, squirrels, and even a wildcat in my absence. Flamingo had cured the wildcat hide and made a cape of it, which he insisted on wearing during the ceremony, although the weather was much too hot.

Fawn could now identify all the herbs that grew in the vicinity and knew their uses. I was so proud of them and happy to be with them again. After the corn festival I decided the children were responsible enough to have the rings I had chosen for them from among the Spanish treasure. I knew their fingers would not be large enough, yet, but they could wear them on thongs around their necks.

I had not buried them with the treasure, but had placed them in a drawstring purse in my trunk.

The gold rings were unique, a matching set. One had been made for a man, the other for a woman. Each ring bore a peacock on its face and was set with chips of rubies, emeralds, sapphires, and diamonds, adding a sparkling blaze of color to the beautifully molded and set birds. I had meant for them to belong to the twins since the first moment I saw them, but I had not planned to give them to the children until they reached puberty.

Perhaps I had been around Flamingo for too long, because a voice inside me had been urging me to give them to the twins ever since I had returned to the village. I could not deny that voice.

So on the eve before we left, Flamingo, Little Conch, Fawn (I rarely called them Juan and Margarita anymore, because Flamingo didn't like it, and I was feeling more Indian all the time) and I went for a walk along the beach. We watched the great turtles struggle ashore to lay their eggs and gathered a few for Flamingo. The twins each rode the back of a turtle as it returned to the ocean. They were excited and happy, but the time had come to tell them their mother and I were leaving on another mission.

Having been raised among the First People, they were true Indians. They did not beg us to stay, or even to take them with us. Although tears welled in the corners of their eyes, they brushed them away quickly.

"You will stay with Little Wren," Flamingo said. "Leaping Cat is going, too. You will be the man while we are gone, Little Conch. You must take care of Little Wren and your sister, Fawn."

"I can take care of myself," Fawn said. "I shall help take care of Little Wren."

I knelt and hugged my children to me. "I love you so much. I hate having to leave you again so soon. But your mother and I must go for the good of all in the village. I know you will be good and take care of Little Wren and each other.

"I have something for each of you," I opened my pouch, withdrew the thongs with the rings attached, and placed one around the neck of each child. "Wear this around your neck until your fingers are large enough to fit them. I have saved these for you since you were babies. I think you are responsible enough to have them now."

"It's so pretty. What is it? A bird of some kind? I have never seen one like it," said Fawn.

"It's a peacock. They are not found here. The rings each have the same bird. You might say they are twins, like you," I said.

"I will always wear it," said Little Conch.

"And I," said his sister.

Little Conch put his finger through the ring to admire the way it looked on his hand.

The next morning early we began our trip back to the village of the Seminoles. This time it was I, not Flamingo, who had premonitions.

We took two skin canoes. Squint Eyes and Leaping Cat were in the lead canoe; Flamingo and I followed. We traveled through the Grassy River, then through creeks and overland to the shores of Lake Mayaimi. Then we took the western edge of the big lake until we reached the creek that would take us to the Seminole village.

It rained on us during the whole trip, sometimes sprinkling, other times in great deluges. The Lightening was frightful, crackling and crisscrossing the sky in blinding displays. Several times we felt the hair stand up on the backs of our necks just before we saw trees split from top to bottom by its mighty impact. At night, though it was summer, we shivered, wrapped in our hides. Our skins, which never dried, were shriveled and wrinkled. Many nights it was not possible to start a fire. We ate pemmican and coontie cakes, even for breakfast, as it was to wet to build a fire over which to make sofkee gruel. Mosquitoes were thick and ferocious. Bear grease did not spread well on our wet skins and washed off more quickly. Finally, on the ninth day of our sodden journey, we arrived at the outskirts of the village.

This time we took the main trail into the village, hoping to be seen and taken to the chief. We carried gifts of Spanish coins, jewelry, and knives, and had not gone far when we were surrounded by eight or nine braves, several with guns. We tried in the language of the First People, in Spanish and signs, to tell them we came in peace and wished to see Chief Brave Eagle. They spoke in their tongue and gestured and prodded us toward their village where they herded us into the gathering house. Several old men sat on benches which surrounded the room. Our captors spoke to one old man, who nodded his head, leaving. The others looked us over curiously. We could not have made too impressive a sight, wet and wrinkled as we were.

We waited for perhaps an hour before the chief and his Spanish woman entered the gathering house. Today they were not dressed so splendidly as they had been on the other occasion I had seen them, but they were still a striking couple. He wore tan pants and brown leather boots in the white man's style, but his chest was bare except for the thick, curly hair that covered it. Around his neck was a heavy gold chain of the kind the Spanish used both as jewelry and money. Each link could be removed and spent, and different links had different values.

His thick black hair curled loosely around his strong, handsome face, which held no discernible expression.

She walked behind him today. Her shift was of turquoise and came to just below her knees. A belt of silver links cinched her tiny waist. Her feet were encased in beaded white doeskin moccasins. A thick braid of lustrous black hair hung over one shoulder. Wide silver bracelets adorned both wrists. Her lovely neck was encircled by a thin silver chain from which hung a single large baroque pearl. She held her head down, and I thought I glimpsed a tear in one lovely blue eye.

Leaping Cat stood in front of us, facing the other chief. Despite his drowned appearance, he stood straight, tall, and proud. He said, "I come in peace, as your brother." Brave Eagle's response was unintelligible to us.

Leaping Cat signaled me forward. As I stepped beside him, I repeated what he had said in Spanish.

The Spanish woman lifted her face and translated my words in a monotone.

Brave Eagle spoke, she translated. He had said, "I have learned when others come in peace, they usually are weaker than I, and they have a favor to ask. Who are you, and what do you want?"

"I am Leaping Cat, chief of the First People. This is my beloved niece, Flamingo. She is also our shaman. Here is my son, Water Gift, husband of Flamingo. The other is Squint Eyes. Our people used to live and hunt in this whole area. The Spanish called us Calusa. Now our numbers are small. Many have been killed by the white man or his diseases. Others have been taken away by the white man. The last of us except for my small band left sixteen winters past for other islands far away.

"We seek to live in peace with you. We do not want to fight, or to leave. We do not want to be slaves. We do not want our small band to be killed. We want to be your brothers. We have brought gifts for you."

We brought forth the gold doubloons, silver pieces of eight, jewelry, and steel knives as the woman translated and held them out to him.

He reached out and took the gifts as one of the old men came forward with a basket to hold them. Then I heard him say her name for the first time. It was Maria.

"Come, let us sit over here," he said, and he led us to the benches.

We talked for a long while, Maria translating into Spanish, and I into the language of the First People, then the reverse.

Brave Eagle wanted to know where our village was, exactly how many we were, how I had come to be among the People, and how we had come to know of his village. Leaping Cat answered all his questions honestly. We were completely at his mercy. The future of the First People was at his mercy.

Leaping Cat asked one question. "Why does Maria cry?"

"There is a sickness among our people. Nine have died. As many more are sick. One is her son, Esteban. Our shaman has not been able to help him. If your shaman, Flamingo, can save Esteban, we will discuss becoming brothers."

When this had been translated, Flamingo said, "Take me to the child."

Chief Brave Eagle said Flamingo and I should follow Maria and him. I would have to help translate. We were led to the chief's chickee. Inside lay Esteban. An old woman who had been attending him was sent away. Flamingo knelt by the boy, placing the back of her hand against his forehead. "He is burning hot, and he is in the sleep from which he cannot awake," she said.

"The others who died and those who are still sick had the fever and the sleeping sickness, also. Esteban cried that his head hurt. Then he began to vomit violently. He went to sleep and we cannot awaken him," Maria said, tears streaming down her face.

Flamingo asked for water. Then she put some herbal potion in the child's mouth for the fever. When the water was brought, she put something from her pouch in it and began to bathe the child. After a while, the woman who had been tending him returned. The chief spoke to her, then told us we would stay with Maria, the child and the old lady. I had the feeling the old lady was to report everything to him. Was it that he didn't trust us, or Maria?

Chief Brave Eagle left us.

Flamingo told me to tell Maria that she, too, was a mother, and she would do everything she could for the child. She had been told of this sleeping sickness by the shaman who had instructed her. He had taught her how to treat it, but inevitably it killed some of those stricken, usually the very old and the very young. Esteban seemed a healthy little boy, otherwise. She would do all she could for him.

Flamingo forced the unconscious boy to eat watered-down sofkee and to drink water. She removed all the child's clothing and covers. She continuously bathed him and ordered smudge fires to keep the mosquitoes away. She used herbs and barks to try to break his fever. The child just lay there, but after a week he was still alive.

The tribe's shamans had come to observe. Flamingo told them how to treat the other victims. At the end of a week, five of the nine were still alive. And those who had succumbed were as Flamingo had said—the very old and infants.

During this time I made several attempts to talk to Maria about herself. Only she and I spoke Spanish. But she would only raise her unhappy eyes to me and shake her head as if forbidden to speak to me of herself.

Brave Eagle visited several times daily, but he did not bring Leaping Cat or Squint Eyes. Nor was I allowed to leave the boy's chickee.

Finally, after ten days, Esteban opened his eyes and said, "Mama." Maria made no effort to contain her joy.

We stayed with them for another week. By then he was up and about, and eating constantly. Three of the others had recovered, another had died, and one remained unconscious. We were finally allowed free reign of the village, but because of language differences we had difficulty conversing with the inhabitants. Mostly, I was curious to know Maria's story. How did a Spanish beauty who seemed to be well born, maybe even of royal blood, happen to become the wife of an Indian chief? I felt Maria and I had a lot in common, even though I was neither well born nor of royal blood. I sensed some tragedy in her past and even felt she was not here entirely of her free will.

I had been told that these Indians had previously lived in the American colonies to the north. They had been driven from one place to another, harassed, and many of their number killed; had taken in Negroes, free and slave, further angering Americans; then led by Brave Eagle into Florida where they had raided across the border, stealing cattle and horses. When it got too hot for them near the border, they had come here to form this village. That was only a few moons ago. They had scouted the area before deciding this was the place they wanted to be.

One day when Flamingo was checking on Esteban, and Brave Eagle was with them, I visited the trading post which had been established since our scouting mission. Trader Jim extended his hand in friendship, a wide smile on his lips. He was astonished when I said, "Hello. I'm Rafael Reyes. The People call me Water Gift."

"You speak English? Come inside, man. I'm Jim Stokes, Trader Jim. If Brave Eagle knew you spoke English, I doubt he'd let you come here alone."

"Why? Do I know something he doesn't want me to tell? Or do you know something I'm not supposed to know? I have gotten the feeling he didn't want me to talk to Maria."

"I'm not sure. But he's already questioned me about whether I knew Spanish or the language of your tribe. I don't know either. But I just got the feeling he didn't want us to communicate.

"Rafael Reyes, eh? I knew you weren't an Indian. How'd you come to be Water Gift? Don't answer if it's too personal," he said.

"It's a long story. Let's just say I'm a Minorcan who's a long way from home."

"Did you come from that New Smyrna colony that Dr. Turnbull ran?"

"Yes. What do you mean, ran? Does someone else run it now?"

"Well, I get the news with my supplies. Just last week I learned your people left New Smyrna and went to St. Augustine. They are now under the protection of Governor Tonyn. Turnbull is in London complaining about Tonyn, and he doesn't know it yet.

"Seems those poor folks had been starved and mistreated and then enslaved when their indentures were over. But the colony's through now. Guess Turnbull is ruined," the trader said.

"That's the best news I've had in years. You say East Florida has a new governor? It was Grant last time I was in St. Augustine."

"You have been in the woods for a while. Tonyn's been governor since '74."

Just then an Indian entered the door, and Trader Jim pretended to be trying to understand what I wanted to buy.

The Indian tried to help. I finally left, shaking my head as if in exasperation.

Next day I again visited the trader. I waited until he was alone. This time I asked about Brave Eagle and Maria.

"Brave Eagle's a secretive sort. He's flamboyant, but he doesn't want much known about him and Maria. Wants to remain mysterious. But there's something strange about them. The other Indians both love and fear him. He's a half breed, you know. His mother was an Indian. His father was French, or maybe it's Spanish or Italian. No one's sure.

"Don't know anything about Maria and the boy 'cept the boy's not Brave Eagle's son. He's not Indian. The Indians won't tell anything about her. Just, 'Chief Brave Eagle's woman.' Maybe they don't know anything more.

"All I know is Brave Eagle grew up with the Indians. His father took him away when he was sixteen or seventeen. When he rejoined his tribe about three years ago, he had Maria and the boy with him. He was a hotshot troublemaker. Got the Indians stirred up against the whites. When it got too hot for them in American territory, they crossed the border. When it got too hot there, they came here.

"Maria dotes on the boy. Seems she wants him to become a gentleman. He wants to be like the Indian kids. Understandably. They're the only kids he knows. Appears Brave Eagle uses the boy to keep Maria in check. Maria's a beauty, isn't she?" Not waiting for an answer, he continued, "The chief won't let Maria come to the post without him coming with her I think he's afraid we might find some way to communicate, or maybe she'll try to slip a letter out or something."

If he had given me a chance to answer, I would have agreed that Maria was a beauty, but I would have added I felt sorry for her, and I didn't know why.

Trader Jim and I became friends during the time Brave Eagle kept us in his village. Then in September, the trader told me the proper month, Brave Eagle summoned Leaping Cat, Flamingo, and me into the gathering house, along with his council. The peace pipe was lit, and we all smoked it. We were now brothers and would live together in peace.

We could finally return to our village. Leaping Cat was satisfied the People would continue to live undisturbed as before. But I had a very uneasy feeling.

That night as Flamingo prepared for bed, she complained of a headache. I felt her forehead. It was very hot. She began to take the potions and herbs she had used for Esteban. She had exhausted herself, staying beside the boy day and night, not only for his and Maria's sake, but for the sakes of our own children and those of our whole village. She had told me she had to save Esteban, else she didn't believe Brave Eagle would leave us in peace.

I found Maria and told her I feared Flamingo had the sleeping sickness. She herself brought a shaman to attend Flamingo. By morning Flamingo had sunk into a deep sleep from which we could not awaken her. She lasted only a week. Maria stayed with her until the end, as did I.

I couldn't believe Flamingo was gone. She had been so alive, so good at healing others. She had been my teacher, my friend, my sweet lover. How could she be dead? How could I go on without her? Then I remembered our children. They were now motherless. They had only me. I had no choice. I had to go on.

The canoe trip back to our village was a blur to me. It took forever, yet it was over before I knew it. We had been gone from our village for two moons. We returned to a village of ashes. Everything had been burned to the ground.

We found the bodies of our old people and the men, except for the pirate, Jean. No sign of the women and children could be found. The state of the bodies, the size of the weeds that had grown in our village and gardens and the ashes of the chickees told us this must have happened soon after we left for Brave Eagle's village. Any clues the perpetrators of this heinous crime might have left had been obliterated by nature and the passing of time.

Everything of value had been taken, even the silver and gold ornaments and jewelry from the bodies of the dead. But most devastating of all, the future of our tribe had been stolen with the kidnaping of our women and children.

We were horrified and totally desolate. Leaping Cat turned from a strong, brave, youthful-seeming leader into a useless old man before my eyes. I was numb. From the rubble of one burned chickee to the other, to the burned gathering house, to the burned fields and canoes and dugouts we ran. We knelt, I in my prayers and they in theirs, over each body.

We buried the dead sitting, their heads resting on their knees, hands wrapped around them. They were turned to face the east, the rising sun. We built a fire and chanted prayers of mourning all night.

After several days we left the village site to search the surrounding islands for our women and children. Maybe at least some of them had gotten away and were hiding on another key. For several months we searched the many islands that dotted the waters. We found not one, nor any sign that anyone had been on any other key.

We returned to the burned village. Broken men, Leaping Cat and Squint Eyes decided to return to Brave Eagle's village to live. I bade them a tearful farewell. For once, none of us tried to keep the way we were feeling from showing on our faces. I doubt we could have. Each of us had lost everything.

Leaping Cat and Squint Eyes took one canoe and left me the other . These were all that were left of our village; they would have been gone, too, had they not been with us.

I do not know how long I stayed on the island. I did not try to keep track of time. It no longer mattered. Nothing mattered. I talked to the ghost of Flamingo and all the others. My wife was dead. My children were lost to me. Except Leaping Cat, there was no one I loved, no one who loved me. Except—except—and then that dimpled face, Caty's face, appeared before me once again. That angelic face. I still had a wife. Maybe we had a child. Maybe they were in St. Augustine still.

My days and nights were jumbled. Winter came and went. Reality left me for long periods. Then one day I relived my life in the village of the First People. I remembered Flamingo's dream that I should hide the Spanish treasure. She had been right. Everyone else's share, including that kept in the gathering house for ceremonies and gifts, had been stolen. I still had my share buried under my chickee, which had been built on the site of the one that had been burned.

I began to dig. When I had uncovered the treasure, I realized I was quite rich. The feeling was hollow. What good are riches when all you would share them with are gone? Here I sat in the middle of nowhere with a fortune in Spanish gold, silver, and jewels with no one to spend it on. I threw back my head and laughed at the irony of it all. It was not a pretty sound.

Then I saw the diary. I reread it from beginning to end. I reread Caty's parting love letter to me.

> *Dearest Rafael,*
>
> *I cannot remember a time when I did not love you with my whole heart, my whole soul, my whole body, and my whole mind. I cannot imagine a time when I would not. You are my whole world, my life.*
>
> *We will wait for you, our baby and me. We will wait for your return to St. Augustine, no matter how long it takes.*
>
> *My prayers and my love are with you always, my darling.*
>
> *Yours forever,*
> *Caty*

It had been more than nine years since Caty had written that letter. Was she still waiting for me? Could she still love me? I had to know.

I decided to put my life since I had left her in writing. I made a pen from the feather of a heron and the black dye of ashes and water we used for body paint in place of ink. Then I began to write. The more I wrote, the more my mind cleared. When I had finally put it all down on the blank pages in Caty's diary, I was ready to decide what I should do.

Who had my children? Had they been kidnapped by pirates? Slavers? Other Indians? Were they alive? Were they still in Florida? In the northern colonies the trader had told me had revolted to become the American states? Across the Atlantic Ocean? Across the Gulf? Were they slaves?

I knew I could never find peace until I knew the answers to all these questions, until I did all I could to find and free my beloved Little Conch and Fawn, Juan and Margarita.

What about Caty and the child I had never seen? Were they alive? Were they still waiting for me in St. Augustine? I had to know that, too.

So, I decided to go to St. Augustine. The more I thought of it, the more I ached for Caty. I knew if there was any balm, any healing at all for me, I would find it in her arms.

Filling a pouch with gold coins, I reburied the rest near the center of the island in a hammock, just so many paces west of a certain distinguishing tree. Wanting to leave no trace of my existence here, I burned the chickee I had been occupying. The coins I carried would be enough to carry out the plan that was starting to form in my mind. For, after I had found Caty and our child, I meant to find the twins.

I paddled until my arms ached. The sun guided me through the grassy water. Thank God it was not so rainy this trip, or I would never have found my way to the other side of the great swamp. Squint Eyes had taught me how to find the little channels. Once across the swamp, I carried my lightweight skin canoe across land between creeks. When I reached Lake Mayaimi, called Okeechobee by the Seminoles, their word for big water, I stayed near the eastern shore. Then I followed a river north-northeast to a chain of lakes, the top of which joined the great river which flows north, the St. Johns.

Shortly after arriving on the river, I met some peddlers on a raft laden with goods. I asked them where I was. They told me I was about forty-five miles from Picolata. When I reached Picolata, I would find a wagon trail that would lead east to St. Augustine. From the peddlers I bought some supplies, including a pair of trousers. I didn't want to walk into town in a loin cloth. On the other hand, my search for my children called for me to continue my Indian identity.

When I arrived in the old town, I asked a little Minorcan boy to deliver a package to the Adams house on St. George Street. The pouch contained that part of Caty's diary she had written before I boarded the ill-fated ship to New Smyrna.

Part Three

I

Held fast in strong arms, I felt I was home at last. I opened my eyes to look into those of my darling. Rafael had returned from the dead. My head was spinning. Maybe, instead of Rafael returning to life, I had joined him in death.

Then Rafael bent his head and pressed his lips to mine. His kisses were tender and sweet. Then he set me back on my feet, and we kissed with wild abandon. We couldn't get enough of each other. Alive or dead, it didn't matter. We were together again at last.

Finally my senses returned. Reluctantly, I tore my lips from his and pushed him back to look at him. Yes, it was Rafael, but a far different Rafael than the one I had known so long ago. This Rafael was an Indian, a savage. We had not yet spoken a word. Nor did he seem inclined to. For even now he was pulling me back into his arms, drowning me in passionate, delicious kisses. I tried to break away, to ask him where he had been and a thousand other questions, but his lips would not leave mine. His arms would not let me go. And then I forgot the questions, no longer cared what the answers were. It was enough that we were here in each other's arms—that we could savor now.

I remember thinking I must be in heaven. Then Rafael spoke at last. "Caty, my darling, I love you. All these years I've loved you. Even when I had no memory of anything, your face appeared before me. And you waited for me, just as you said you would. Just as you wrote in the diary.

"I've so much to tell you. We've lost so many years. I'll make it all up to you. Oh, Caty, tell me you love me. I've longed to hear you say it for ages."

"I never stopped loving you, Rafael. I never forgot you. But they told me you were dead. Drowned in the hurricane on your way back to New Smyrna. The captain's log—you were hit in the head by a broken mast—swept overboard by a wave. They said you were gone—lost to me forever," I wept.

Rafael held me while I cried uncontrollably as all those terrible, wrenching emotions once again washed over me. "I know, my darling. It's all right. It's true the ship wrecked in a hurricane. I washed ashore in the keys. I couldn't remember anything. But I kept seeing your face. Some Indians adopted me into their tribe. I've been with them until . . ." His face took on a tortured look, and he stopped abruptly.

Then he said, "What about you, Caty? You thought I was dead. Yet you stayed here, still waiting for me? And our baby—do we have a child?"

Suddenly the present was returning, and I didn't want it to. "We have a daughter. Her name is Ana Marie. She is eight years old. After your death—I mean, after I thought you were dead, she is all that kept me going. Then Sarah died, and I lost control again."

Rafael held me while I cried my heart out, for I knew I had to tell him. When I could talk again, I said, "Rafael, I married Joseph Adams six years ago. I didn't know . . . Oh, God! I thought you were dead. We, Joseph and I . . . we're going to have a baby. God help us all, what are we going to do?"

We clung to each other, neither saying anything.

Then, still holding me, Rafael said, "Caty, please believe I love you and always have, and I always will. But my memory was gone for almost two years. The only memory I had of my past was an apparition of a beautiful face, your face. I didn't know whose face it was, only that it belonged to an angel who had kept me from drowning.

"An Indian girl nursed me back to health. Her uncle adopted me. We were married by Indian law. We had twins, a boy and a girl. Only after they were born was I given back my diary. When I read it, my memory returned."

I tried to pull myself from his embrace, but he would not let me go. I felt betrayed. Rafael had married someone else. He had other children. Oh, I was so mixed up, so confused. Then Rafael removed something from a pouch at his waist. He said, "Here is the rest of your diary. I have written about my life among the Indians in it. I want you to have it. I want you to know everything. For now, I just want to say that my Indian wife, Flamingo, died. She was a brave and good person. I think you would have liked her.

"My children have been stolen. I don't know by whom or why. I only know I won't stop until I find them. I came here first to find you and our child. I didn't know if you'd be here. I had no idea what I'd find, but I hoped and dreamed that we would be together as a family," he said.

My heart ached for him. I tried to imagine what I would feel if Ana was suddenly snatched from me. The thought was too horrible. My mind totally rejected it, but my poor Rafael could not reject the thought. He lived with the reality.

Then he asked, "Caty, are you happy with Joseph? Is he a good husband and a good father? I have to ask. I have to know."

"Rafael, he is the best. I don't understand this. I don't know how it can be. And I doubt if you can understand, but please try. I love you, Rafael, and I never stopped. But I love Joseph, too. It would not have happened if I had not been sure you were dead. But it did happen, and he has been the best of fathers to Ana. They worship each other. She knows he is not her real father. She calls him Papa Joe.

"Oh, Rafael. I don't know what to do. I'm going to have his child, his only child. He's wanted one for so long. How can I leave him now? What must I do? I have two husbands, and I love them both."

"My God, Caty. Don't ask me. I don't know. I only know you're my wife and I want you. I don't want to do anything to hurt you or that good man, but I have to be a father to Ana, don't you see?" he pleaded. The pain in his eyes was as great as that I felt.

"I can provide for you and Ana," he said, as he tried to press several gold doubloons into my hand.

"It's not that, Rafael. It's not money. You must know that could not keep us apart. Yes, Joseph has plenty of money. He sees we have the best of everything. Rafael, it's not for the money that I can't leave him. Can't you see? Please try to understand. I just can't leave Joseph. And he mustn't know you're alive. I'm so sorry. I have to think. But that is what I believe is best for now," I said. "But what about Ana? I want to see her, meet her," he pleaded.

"Oh, Rafael, please don't insist on meeting her just yet. How can I keep this from Joseph if Ana has met her father? Besides, look at you. Ana knows her father is Rafael, a Minorcan, not an Indian.

"Why are you still pretending to be an Indian, anyway? You nearly frightened me to death when I saw you coming toward me. But then I saw your eyes . . ."

"I told you. I'm going to search for my Indian children. My plan is first to search all the Indian villages in the Floridas. I'll visit all of them on this continent, if I have to. I won't stop searching for them until I find them or satisfy myself they aren't there. It will be best if I go among them as one of them, I think," he said.

"Even if you don't want Ana to know I'm her father yet, I still have to see her. Can't you understand that, Caty? My God, she's my child, too. I've always loved her, even before she was born. I've always wanted to know about her, to know her. I have to see her."

I was silent for a while, thinking of the brief period we were together after I told him we were going to have a baby. Thinking of what he did to see that Ana and I were safe, and of how he had suffered. Then I said, "Tomorrow is market day. Josie, Ana, and I always spend Wednesday afternoons in the market shopping. You can see her there. But you mustn't approach her. She's frightened of Indians."

Rafael took me back in his arms. For a long time he just held me, neither of us speaking. My mind was spinning, as I'm sure his was. In spite of all the confusion his return had created, I felt so much comfort, so much hope just knowing he was alive—in being held in his arms again. Then reality crashed down around me. I knew he must remain dead to me, to my family. Still, the thought of leaving his embrace was unbearable.

I don't know how long he rocked me in his arms, each of us locked in our separate thoughts. When I finally withdrew, tears were running from both our eyes.

"I don't know what we're going to do, Caty. Having found you, I don't feel I can ever let you go again. We've lost nearly ten years of our lives that we should have spent together. You were a seventeen-year-old girl when we were torn apart. Now you're twenty-five, a woman, and I'm thirty-one, no longer a boy. We have a daughter. We're a family, yet we can't be a family, because you're married to Joseph." Placing his hand on my stomach, he continued, "And you're going to have another child, his child. Oh, Caty, my heart just screams at the thought of you living with another man as his wife, having another man's child . . . and yet, I had another wife. I have two other children. That must be hard for you, too. But, Caty,

I couldn't be a father to them, either. Indian customs are strange compared to ours. Will I ever be a father to any of my children?

"My instinct is to grab you and Ana and run. We love each other. We shouldn't be parted again. But then there's my children and, of course, Joseph. He did his best for us when we left New Smyrna. He has taken care of you and Ana. We owe him so much.

"I have to find my children. They are only seven. I can't stand the thought of them being alone among strangers. They may not even be together. Are they slaves? Are they treated well? Have they been adopted into another tribe? They have always been well-taken care of and loved. They must wonder where Flamingo and I are. They don't even know their mother died.

"Caty, it's all so complicated. I couldn't take you and Ana with me while I search for them. It might not be safe for you. The living conditions would be miserable. No, it wouldn't work. I have to look for them, Caty."

"It's all right, Rafael. Go find your children. I understand, and you must understand that Ana and I could not go with you anyway. You and I are no longer children, as you said. The lives of others are totally dependent on what we decide, what we do. We cannot live for our desires. In this new world we came to, we have never been able to. First there were our indentures to that tyrant, Turnbull. Then there was our unborn child to be considered. And then I thought you were dead. You were injured and lost your memory. We both made new lives for ourselves. Now there's Joseph and Ana and your children to be considered. We mustn't allow our love for each other to harm those who need and depend on us. Oh, my darling, it's much too late for our desires."

"I need you, Caty," he groaned, as he pulled me into his arms again. "Don't say it's too late. It's never too late. I'll never give up on us. For now, we have to part again. But you and I . . . Caty, I have visions of our growing old together. Let's hang onto that, Caty. It's all we've got."

Suddenly I realized it was no longer raining. The sun was bright and it was slipping down in the sky. We had been here for hours. Ana would wonder where I was.

"I have to go, Rafael. We will be in the plaza to do our shopping about ten in the morning. Please don't speak to us. I'm so sorry, but it has to be this way."

He pulled me to him for one last kiss. Then he checked to see if anyone was about before he allowed me to leave. Tears blurred my vision, and I had felt them on his cheeks, also.

That night I read what he had written about his life with the Indians by lamplight. In some ways he had suffered more than I had. Poor Rafael. He had lost Flamingo. His children were God knows where. He could not be Ana's father. He could not have me. I spent the night wrestling with a variety of thoughts and feelings. Foremost of them was, *I am married to two men at the same time, and I can't bear to give up either.* Yet, I knew I could not have them both.

I felt such joy in the fact that Rafael was alive. But that knowledge could cause as much confusion in the lives of Joseph and Ana as it was already causing in mine, maybe even as much as his reported death had caused me. I could not let that happen to dear Joseph. But, oh, I wanted to shout to the world, *Rafael is not dead! He is alive! He is here in St. Augustine!*

I had to stick with my resolve to protect Joseph from the knowledge that Rafael lived. But the thought returned again and again, *Oh, but it's so unfair to Rafael. And to me.*

Ana, Josie, and I were approaching the plaza. I became aware that Josie was talking to me, but I had no idea what she was saying. My mind was on Rafael and yesterday, on seeing him again today.

She said, "Caty, what on earth is wrong with you? Are you sick? Ana and I have chattered ever since I got to your house this morning, and you haven't said a word. And there are circles under your eyes. Did you even sleep last night?"

"I'm not sick. I've been thinking."

"So I noticed. Want to tell us what about? Or is it some deep, dark secret?"

"I can't, Josie. I can't."

"Now you're really upsetting me. And you've got my curiosity aroused. You and I have talked about everything since I came to St. Augustine. Everything. We have no secrets. What could be on your mind that you can't tell me? I won't let this go, Caty. You can't keep it from me," she said.

Now Ana was concerned. "Are you all right, mama? You haven't been yourself since you came back from wherever you went yesterday."

"I'm all right, baby. Don't worry about me. I'm fine." I shot Josefina a warning look. But I knew she was right. I would have to tell her. She would never leave me alone until I did. And I desperately needed to discuss it with someone. I could trust Josie with my secret.

We visited the various stalls in the market, looking over the offerings of vegetables, fruits, and fish, most of it supplied by Turnbull's ex-colonists. There were meat and fur brought in by the Indians; tobacco, indigo, and rice from the English plantations, as well as some beef and chickens. The wives of the English soldiers paid for their purchases with cloth, beads, and army knives. Minorcan women bartered with fish, fresh or dried vegetables and fruit, or items woven of palm fronds or pine needles. I was one of the few who had English coins with which to shop. My mind was not on any of it. Then I felt Ana tug at my sleeve. When I turned to her, she said, "Mama, why is that Indian staring at us?"

I turned to see Rafael leaning against an oak tree. Today he was dressed as the local Indians. He wore European pants and a bright shirt. The long side of his hair had been cut to match the shorter, which had not been shaved since he left the Indian village to come to St. Augustine. It was all just long enough to curl up on the ends around the length of cloth that was wound about his head turban style. He was eating an orange and pretended not to be interested in us.

Josie saw him, too. When their eyes met, Rafael turned away. Josie gripped my arm. I turned to her and realized to my horror that she had recognized him. I hadn't thought she would, since she had been a child of twelve when she last saw him. And then he had been a handsome young man of Minorca. Now he was a scar-faced Indian, although still handsome in a rugged way. "No, Josie, please," I begged in a whisper. "We'll talk later."

Turning to Ana, I said, "It's all right, Ana. He's gone now. Let's finish our shopping and go home."

Josie was as silent on the way back as I had been on the way to market. Ana spoke occasionally of this or that. I tried to respond intelligently. When we arrived at our home, I sent Ana to the kitchen to help Mandy put up the fruit and vegetables and told her to practice her handwriting and numbers while I helped Josie get her purchases home.

Neither Josie nor I trusted ourselves to speak before we reached Thomas and Josie's farm outside St. Augustine. She held open the whitewashed picket gate. I stepped into her clean and neatly raked sand yard. A sidewalk of coquina stones quarried from the pits on Anastasia Island led to the steps. Large hydrangeas laden with blue blossoms flanked each side of the steps. We climbed to the porch, went through the house and out the breezeway to her kitchen. Silently we put away the fruit, vegetables, and other things Josie had purchased.

I guess she was thinking of questions to ask, and I was lost in thoughts of what I could say to her as she put on water, made tea, and we returned to the porch to drink it with biscuits Josie had made yesterday. We sat on the east-facing porch to catch the afternoon breeze off the ocean. As I lifted the cup of tea to my mouth, Josie said, "That was no Indian in the market, Caty. Was it who I think it was?"

"Yes, Josie. Rafael is alive. I met him yesterday in the old mission. When the hurricane hit, his head was injured, and his leg was broken in several places. Did you notice he limps? He was washed overboard and nearly drowned. Then he washed ashore in the keys near an Indian village. He couldn't remember who he was, couldn't remember anything. An Indian girl nursed him back to health. They fell in love, were married by Indian custom, and had twins, a girl and a boy. Then his memory returned. To make a long story short, his wife died and his children were kidnapped. He came back for Ana and me."

"Oh, my God, Caty. What are you going to do?" she asked.

"What can I do, Josie? As I see it, I don't have a choice. I'll stay with Joseph. I don't want him to know Rafael is back, or even that he's alive. It would cause him too much pain. I don't know what he might do if he knew. He's so good. His conscience would not rest if he thought he had something that belonged to another, particularly a wife.

"Rafael was in the market today to see Ana. I didn't have any idea you would recognize him. It's been nearly ten years since you saw him, and then you were just a child. He looks so different now. I barely recognized him myself."

"Now I know why you were so preoccupied today. How can you talk so calmly about it?" How did you persuade Rafael not to tell Ana who he was? How did you get him to agree to go away and not to tell Joseph? Do you still love Rafael? Oh, Caty, don't cry. I'm sorry. It's just that I've got a hundred questions. But I won't ask anymore if you don't want me to," she said.

"It's all right, Josie. I need to tell someone. Yes, I love him. I'll always love him. But part of my life died when I thought he'd drowned. I'm married to Joseph now, and I love him, too. And we are going to have a baby. I know it must be hard to understand that I can love two men at once. I never would have believed it possible. But it is. And I do. I can't help it. I can't change it. But mine and Rafael's lives together have been over since 1769. Would you have me finish my life with Joseph, too? Oh, Josie, don't make it any harder for me than it already is. Whether I'm right or wrong, I've made my decision. I don't know how I could decide otherwise. Besides, Rafael plans to search for his twins as an Indian. Ana and I would only be in his way.

"Promise me you won't tell anyone. Not even Thomas. Don't tell anyone that Rafael came back, that he's alive," I begged.

"Don't worry, Caty. You know I won't. I'm glad I know. You'll need someone to talk to. I'll always be ready to listen when you need me," she said.

"Thanks, Josie. It's so hard. So hard to know what's right. I've tried to live a good life. I'm not feeling sorry for myself, but I went through hell when I thought Rafael had died. Then I fell in love with Joseph. Just when things have never been better between us, and we're going to have the baby we want so badly, I find that Rafael isn't dead after all, and my love for him is very much alive. I've got two husbands. What about that, Josie? What am I supposed to do about that? What would Father Camps say? What is the teaching of the church on that? Am I really even married to Joseph?

"I can't go to Father Camps about it. If my marriage to Joseph is no longer recognized by the church, the baby I carry is illegitimate. And I don't believe there are grounds for annulling my marriage to Rafael. I don't know what my status is with the church. I don't know if even the church could straighten this out. And if Father Camps had to have the Vatican's help, it would take years. I don't dare go to the church with this. As long as everyone thinks Rafael is dead,

both my children will be considered legitimate. As long as
he is thought to be dead, maybe I can keep any of this from
causing Joseph pain. But I'm no actress. It's going to be so
hard to carry on as though Rafael hadn't literally returned
from the dead. I'll need all the help you can give me."

"I hadn't even thought of that. This keeps getting more
complicated. Caty, you mustn't blame yourself. Don't let this
make you sick, for your sake and the baby's. You say you've
made your decision. Try to be happy with it. I know you and I
can't forget Rafael isn't dead. But we must pretend he is in
the presence of others. But when you need a shoulder to cry
on or an ear to listen, remember, I'm here."

I wept and she held me. "I don't know how I'll do what I
have to do. I must try to push Rafael's return out of my mind
just as I eventually pushed thoughts of his death from it. Pray
for me, Josie. I'm not sure I even have the right to pray anymore. As long as I do nothing to have one of my marriages
annulled, I am a bigamist, a terrible sinner. I want to be a
good Catholic, Josie. I have always tried to be. I love the church.
But I can't be responsible for what might happen if Joseph
learns that Rafael is alive. If I can keep this from him, at least
his life won't be disrupted again. He went through so much
pain when Sarah was sick and when she died. He might not
be able to take the thought of possibly losing me, too. And
Joseph is forty-six now. He's no longer young. I have to protect him. If I'm wrong, if God holds this against me, I'll have
to suffer the consequences. At least He will know I am not
selfish, that I thought of someone besides myself. At least I
think this is the least selfish thing to do."

"You mustn't stop praying, Caty. You need His guidance
now more than ever. Don't feel you're not a good Catholic.
You are the kindest, least selfish person I have ever known.
Your conscience is alive and well. Of course I'll pray for you.
And Rafael, Joseph, Ana, and the baby, too. God only knows
what any of us would do under the circumstances. Who knows

what's right or wrong, or even if there is a right or wrong
thing to do? I'm sure your conscience is guiding you, as it
always has. The best thing you can do is follow its dictates,"
Josie said.

II

The fear of an invasion lay heavy on the minds of the residents of St. Augustine. Late in the summer two thousand British reinforcements came to town led by General Provest. There had been no invasion attempt on the part of the Americans since March when about three thousand men had crossed the St. Marys to Fort Tonyn. They had moved south all the way to Alligator Creek Bridge on the Nassau River before being repelled. Evidently, Governor Tonyn had asked for the reinforcement in order to be prepared in the event of another invasion attempt. Or maybe he planned a retaliatory attack. At any rate, the citizens of St. Augustine were mentally prepared for war with the Americans.

By November, I was six months pregnant. I could no longer hide my girth under voluminous skirts. Ana was delighted with the prospect of a little brother or sister. She loved to lay her hand on my stomach to feel the movements of the baby. We shared delight in its growth and eagerly looked forward to its birth. Ana was nearly nine. It had been a long time between babies. Neither thoughts of an invasion nor thoughts of Rafael could dim my happiness at the prospect of having another child.

I was able to go whole days without thinking of my dilemma concerning Rafael's return. I felt I was again behaving as I had before that fateful day when I had looked into the face of an Indian and saw the eyes of my beloved Rafael.

Then one market day while Josie and Ana were looking over some woven baskets and I was selecting some oranges, I looked up into those eyes once again.

He spoke low, "Tomorrow at ten. Same place." Then he was gone.

I didn't have a chance to refuse. I didn't know if I could have anyway. And I knew without a doubt that I'd be in the old mission at ten the next morning.

I told Josie before she left to return home. I guess she had made up her mind not to oppose whatever I decided in this matter, because she didn't try to persuade me not to go. She just hugged me and said, "Be careful, Caty."

After she left, I wondered what Rafael could want and whether there was anything left to say that hadn't already been said.

When I stepped inside the mission the next morning, I felt a little angry. Rafael came forward and reached to take me into his arms.

"No, Rafael. We've been through all this before. I won't change my mind. Don't you know how hard you're making things by coming back again and demanding I meet you?" Part of my anger was directed at myself, because I knew that once he touched me, once I was in his arms, it would be so easy for me to forget decisions I had already made.

He was stronger than I, and he wouldn't allow me to stop him. Once his lips met mine, my resolve turned to jelly. After a kiss that was long and passionate, he led me to an old bench along the dilapidated wall and helped me to sit. Then he said, "Now, Caty, you listen to me. It seems to me you are the one who is making it hard on me. I'm allowing this charade of yours to proceed. As far as Joseph and Ana are concerned, I'll play dead. But I'm not going to let you forget I'm alive. I'm not going to let you forget your love for me, either. I need it too much."

He placed a huge, rough hand gently on my swollen stomach.

"No!" I said protectively.

"I'm not going to hurt your baby or you, Caty. You can't think I'm some sort of monster. It's just when I saw you in the market yesterday, now obviously pregnant, I thought I'd never seen you look so beautiful. I wasn't around when you were this far along with Ana. I just want to share in this pregnancy."

The baby jumped inside me. Then Rafael knelt at my feet and did a touching thing. He placed a hand on each side of my stomach and laid his head to rest on it. "I could love this child, you know. Your child. I could be a father to it."

I looked down at his head, uncovered today. My hands of their own volition went to his hair. I didn't know what to say. I loved him so much. I hurt for him. But what he was implying could never be. This was Joseph's child. It could not be Rafael's. I could not take Joseph's child from him.

"I can't help it, Caty. I can't stay away from you. I love you." He kissed me again.

He had not found his children. Nor had he any leads. He had found a local Indian to accompany him to the Indian settlements and to teach him the Seminole language. They had returned to St. Augustine for his companion to visit his family and for him to see Ana and me. He told me he had been very careful that Ana and Josie did not see him this time.

I told him Josie knew, that she had recognized him. I begged him not to come again.

He replied, "You must know I'd never force myself on you, Caty. As much as I desire you, I love you too much for that. But I *will* see you when I can. You and Ana are all I have now. I need to at least see you, talk to you, hold you."

A few minutes later he asked, "When is the baby due?"

"In February," I answered.

"When will Joseph return?"

"He left in May. He is due back between March and May. It depends on how long his business takes and how favorable the winds are. Why do you ask?"

"He should not have left you alone when you are expecting a baby. He should be here when your time comes."

"He had already left when I learned I was pregnant. I wrote him several times, but sometimes my letters never catch up with him. Anyway, I won't be alone. I have Mandy, and Josie will be with me."

He said no more about it. He left the next day to continue his search for his children.

One day we saw General Provest leading his troops out of St. Augustine to the north. Rumors flew that Fast Florida was entering the war against the Americans. Some of our Minorcan boys had joined the East Florida Rangers under the command of Daniel McGirt. We all prayed for their safety.

As I neared the time for the birth of the baby, I began to feel bad. My feet and legs were swollen. I was weak, had no energy, unlike when I was pregnant with Ana. Dr. Johnson said I should stay off my feet as much as possible, lest I miscarry. I could not lose this baby who meant so much to Joseph and me.

Josie suggested Ana and I should stay with her until after the baby came. She had an extra bedroom. Since her father had completely recuperated from the starvation and ill treatment in Mosquito, he and Thomas did nearly all the farm work. She would love having our company.

As I was fearful for the baby, I agreed. Thomas came for us in his carriage. Mandy would stay to manage things at home.

I found it hard to sit about while someone else did all the work. I felt guilty. Finally, Josie brought me her mending. "I hate sewing. You can sit by the fire and do these for me," she said. After the patching was done, she brought me the quilt pieces she had so painstakingly cut to just the right pattern. I began to piece them together for her.

Thomas and Uncle Gaspar ate breakfast and left the house before daylight. As I felt more tired with each passing day, I did not wake until after they had gone. Never in my life had I slept late in the morning before now, except during that awful period when Dr. Johnson kept me drugged after I had first believed Rafael dead. Nor did I stay up late, either. I was in bed shortly after supper.

I had little time to think about Rafael, because my waking hours were spent with Josefina and Ana. There was never a moment when we weren't chatting about something while they went about their daily tasks, and I pieced together the quilt. My nights were spent in exhausted sleep. So only in my dreams did Rafael come. The dreams came nightly. Troubled, jumbled dreams that occasionally woke me, shaking, weeping, desolate.

Christmas came and went. Ana and I missed Christmas at home with Joseph. Then came New Years'. Shortly after the new year, Uncle Gaspar told Ana about the two new calves that had just been born. The next afternoon after lunch she begged to go with him and Thomas to see them. She was so enchanted by them as well as the baby pigs. She began going with the men every afternoon. Thomas assured me she was a big help to them.

I had begun to take an afternoon nap. One day when I awoke from my nap, Josie said, "Caty, I don't know how to say this, so I'll just blurt it out. Rafael is working for Thomas."

"What? How? Does Thomas know who he is?"

"No, Thomas things he's a mestizo, a half breed. He just appeared at the barn yesterday and asked Thomas for work in exchange for sleeping in the loft and meals which he will take in the barn. Thomas told me last night that he had hired a man. But I didn't see him until after lunch when he came to the kitchen door for his food. He calls himself Water Gift. When he saw the look on my face when I carried his plate to him, he put his finger to his lips, winked, took the plate, and walked away."

"Why do you think he came? He won't try to take Ana, will he?" she asked.

My heart was racing: *Why indeed.* Then I thought I knew why. "No, he wouldn't do that. But maybe he just wants to know her. He's terribly disturbed about the loss of his other children. And about my marriage to Joseph. He doesn't like the idea of not being able to claim Ana as his daughter, not being able to know her. He says he can't be a father to any of his children. But Ana's afraid of Indians. I guess she'll meet him this afternoon. I wonder how she'll react to him."

"I imagine Ana will tell us all about him and the way she feels about him when we have supper," she said.

I was quiet for a while, thinking about this new development. Then I said, "Josie, maybe it's not so bad. I know Rafael would never hurt Ana or me. And she is his daughter. He won't tell her he's her father as long as I ask him not to. He promised me. But I can understand his desire to know her. I doubt he'll stay long, unless he's found his other children. Next time you see him alone, ask him if he has."

At supper all Ana could talk about was the Indian Thomas had hired. He spoke English. He knew just about *everything.* She had asked him to teach her to shoot a bow. He was going to get her a puppy. "Mama, he's the Indian who was staring at us in the market that day. You, know, the one with the scar on his face. I was scared of him then. But when I asked him why he had stared at me, he said because I was just about the prettiest little girl he'd ever seen, and he couldn't take his eyes off me. He told me he was sorry he had scared me."

Thomas said, "He's a hard worker. He really knows a lot about animals and farming. He doesn't talk much about himself or where he came from, but he's not one of our local Indians. He's not pure Indian, either. You can look at him and tell that. And he speaks English with an accent similar to yours, and Josie's."

I hoped Thomas didn't dwell on that. I didn't want him to learn Water Gift had the same accent as we did because he had learned to speak English in Minorca like us. I knew his knowledge about animals and agriculture had not been learned from Indians, either. That was also learned back home long ago.

But in a way I was glad that Ana and her father were getting to know each other. It saddened me that it couldn't be as father and daughter, but it just couldn't. Not now. Maybe not ever.

When Josie asked Rafael in private if he had found his twins or learned anything about their whereabouts, he said no. He told her he wanted to talk to me and would come by the first opportunity he had.

A few days later I awoke from my nap when Josie came into my room. "Caty, Rafael is here. He wants to talk to you alone. Do you want to see him?"

"I'll see him, Josie. You don't know him. If I refused, he'd come right in here to see me. Tell him I'll be out in a few minutes," I said. I poured water from the pitcher into the basin and splashed my face, combed my hair, and pinched my colorless cheeks. I looked at my swollen body in the mirror. I didn't want him to see me this way. But, I knew if I didn't go out of my room soon, he'd come in.

When I entered the living room, Josie said, "I'll be in the kitchen if you need me, Caty. Would you like tea?"

I looked at Rafael. He said he didn't care for tea. Neither

did I. Rafael barely waited for her to leave us before he crossed the room. His arms were around me in an instant, and he was kissing my hair. "Caty, I've been so worried about you. Are you all right?" he asked, leading me to the sofa.

"I'm not doing so well, Rafael, but the doctor says I just need to stay off my feet as much as possible and get plenty of rest. That's why I'm here with Josie."

Rafael looked at my swollen ankles, my pale face. He pulled me back into his arms, and I sensed he was afraid for me.

Gently I pulled away. "Rafael, you don't need to worry about me. I'm going to be all right. I'm eating well and getting plenty of rest and sleep. Josie won't let me do anything but sew to keep my hands busy.

"How did you know we were here? Why are you here?" I asked.

"When you weren't in the market Wednesday, I had a boy go to your door and say his mother hadn't seen you lately, and she was concerned about you. Mandy told him you weren't feeling well and were staying with the Andrews.

"I know the baby is due soon. I wanted to be here when it comes, and I know Joseph won't be. I'm glad you're with Josie and Thomas, but I am still worried about you. I had to see you. For once, I want to be here if you need me.

"I didn't know our daughter was such a tomboy and spent so much time helping the men with their chores. But it's giving me an opportunity to get to know her, too. She's really special, Caty. You are doing a wonderful job with her. And she does love Joseph. She talks constantly of Papa Joe' I'm glad he's so good to her and she is so well adjusted, but I can't help wanting to be her Papa."

"Rafael, Uncle Gaspar might recognize you."

"I worried about that at first. I didn't know the old man was here until it was too late. But I never knew him well, and his memory doesn't seem too good. Neither does his eyesight.

But if he recognizes me, I'll just tell him the truth, and that you don't want anyone to know He loves you, Caty. I think he'd do as you ask."

He added, "But right now, it's you I'm concerned about. How often do you see the doctor?"

"He comes once a week. He says I'm holding my own. Don't worry, Josie's taking good care of me," I told him.

We talked for a while of this and that. Then he said, "By the way, Caty, have you heard that General Provest's troops have pushed their way through the Americans into Savannah to prevent more raids on St. Augustine? At least you can rest on that score."

I didn't see Rafael again for the next couple of weeks, but Josie said he asked about me every time he came to get a meal.

A young Minorcan couple, Rosa and Andre Falany, had married a year ago. Saturday, January 28, there was to be a barn raising for them, followed by a potluck supper and dancing. We were all invited. I, of course, could not go.

Josie said, "I'll stay with you, Caty."

I knew she really wanted to go. It would be so much fun. She loved parties and people. The baby wasn't due for weeks. I urged her to go, that I'd be fine.

So early Saturday morning they all left for the barn raising. When I awoke about 7:30, I was alone. I arose, bathed, dressed, and went to the kitchen for breakfast. It felt good to do for myself again. I was more hungry than usual. I scrambled eggs and made toast which I smeared with Josie's good butter and jam. I drank a glass of milk. I hadn't felt so good in days.

After breakfast I opened the back door to see a beautiful sunny, brisk day. I hadn't been out of the house since Thomas had brought me here. I thought, *A morning walk in the yard will do me good.* My ankles were hardly swollen at all, so I wrapped a crocheted shawl around my shoulders and went outside. The cold air felt refreshing. The puppy Rafael had given Ana ran to greet me, yipping and wagging his tail. Fluffy, the name Ana had chosen for him, and I had covered the yard several times when a slight pain started in my back. Then it traveled around to my stomach, causing it to harden and tighten. I waited until it passed before starting for the porch steps.

When I got back into the house, I sat on the sofa and thought about what I should do. My labor was starting, and I was all alone. All the neighbors had gone to the barn raising, too. Even had someone been home, the nearest neighbor was at least a half-mile away. The barn raising was about three miles north of us. I was thinking how foolish I had been to insist that Josie go and leave me here alone—of how foolish I had been to walk around in the yard—when the next pain started. It had been about ten minutes from the first, and the pains were still slight.

Should I try to go to the barn and hitch up the carriage to go home where Mandy could fetch the doctor? Then I remembered: *The carriage isn't here. Thomas drove the family to the barn raising in it.*

Rafael, I thought. *Maybe he's at the barn.* But Thomas had said he had given Water Gift the day off.

Stay calm. Think. The pains aren't bad yet. They aren't real close. Maybe if I lie still they'll stop. But if the baby comes and I'm alone, I need to have things ready, I thought. So slowly and carefully between pains I gathered clean blankets and towels. I hung a kettle of water over the fire in the fireplace. I stoked the fire. I put fresh linens on the bed. By then the pains were harder, but no closer. I climbed into bed to wait. By noon the pains were seven minutes apart. They were hard enough to cause tears to slip from my eyes. A few minutes after noon, Fluffy began to bark by the kitchen. A minute or so later he was still barking, but now he was at the front of the house. Someone was walking across the porch calling, "Caty!"

I got out of bed and started to the door. Halfway across the living room an enormous pain ripped through me. I groaned loudly and sank down on the couch.

The door burst open and Rafael ran toward me. "Caty, what's wrong? I saw you coming through the window. Then I heard you moan and saw you half fall into the sofa. Is it the baby?"

I nodded, but couldn't talk until the pain passed. Then I said, "What are you doing here? Thomas said he gave you the day off."

"He did. But I stayed, because I didn't think you should be alone. I came to check on you."

I told him what was happening. In between pains he carried me gently back to my bed.

"Please get Dr. Johnson and Mandy," I said.

"I can't leave you alone," he said.

"Can you deliver my baby?" The color drained from his face.

"Hurry, Rafael," I said as another pain began.

He had started for the door, but as I moaned, he turned back to me, a look of indecision on his face. He returned to the bed and in an effort to soothe me, I suppose. He attempted to hold me.

"No!" I screamed. "Don't touch me! I hurt too bad! If you want to help me, get the doctor! Oh, God, please hurry, Rafael!" I pleaded.

It could not have been more than an hour and a half when Rafael returned with the doctor and Mandy. He had put Mandy on the horse with him, the horse he had bought and learned to ride since coming to St. Augustine. However, it seemed the pains had been tearing me apart for an eternity. They were now two minutes apart. One barely ceased when another began. I had thrown off the covers. Sweat covered my body. I could not control the shaking of my knees. I was in agony, sure that neither the baby nor I would live.

Dr. Johnson and Mandy washed their hands in the basin. While he examined me, Mandy heated a blanket and towels and filled the basin with clean hot water from the kettle. I glimpsed Rafael standing half hidden just inside the bedroom door, watching with a look of shock, pain, and sympathy on his face. I wanted him to leave, not to see me this way, but I hurt too badly to talk.

Dr. Johnson could not hide his concern. "The baby isn't turned just right. And the umbilical cord is around its neck," he told Mandy.

I could no longer hold back. I had to push. Finally, I heard the doctor say, "The head is out. But I can't get the cord loose. If she doesn't push it out quick . . ."

Mandy said, "I've seen this before, Doctor. That baby got to come now," and to my horror, she threw her body with all its weight across my abdomen.

I screamed, and I guess I blacked out, because when I came to Dr. Johnson was holding my baby upside down and spanking him across his bottom. The baby gave a lusty yell, and the doctor said, "You have a son, Mrs. Adams. He seems healthy, though a little small. I don't mind telling you, it was pretty scary there for a while, though."

Behind him I saw Rafael come forward. He had a look of tender wonder on his face. I didn't know if it was for this child, or because he had just witnessed the miracle of the birth of a human life. At any rate, his absorption in what had just happened was short lived, because Mandy noticed he was in the room. She turned on him in a rage, "What you doing in here, Indian? You get out of here. Ain't no man but the doctor supposed to be in the birthin' room. Git!" She pushed him out and closed the door.

Mandy turned to me, "I'm sorry, Mis' Caty 'bout jumpin' on you like that. But that poor baby was turnin' purple. You wasn't able to push him out fast enough. I had to help you or that cord would of caused somethin' bad to happen to him."

Dr. Johnson said, "That was fast thinking on your part, Mandy. The cord was cutting off oxygen to the baby's brain. It could have caused retardation or other problems. It might even have caused his death. But, I believe he was freed in time."

And so I owed my healthy son to Joseph's slave, Mandy, and to Rafael for being there to get the doctor and Mandy when my time came.

I named my baby Joseph Adams, Jr. As soon as Dr. Johnson and Mandy finished with me, I fell into a deep sleep. I awoke sometime in the night to hear the baby crying and to see Josie standing by my bed with him in her arms.

While I nursed him, studying each perfect little part of his body, Josefina told me how sorry she was that she had not been here when I needed her. She had looked in on me before she left for the barn raising. As I had been so soundly asleep, she didn't wake me.

"It's all right, Josie. I felt great when I awoke in the morning, and everything turned out fine. Don't worry," I said.

"Rafael didn't come to tell us until around ten o'clock. He said he wouldn't leave until the doctor finished and was ready to go. He had to know how you and the baby were before he would leave."

"How did he explain finding me?"

"He said he decided to go to town about noon. When he was passing the house, he heard the puppy barking and scratching at the front door like something was wrong. So he tied his horse and went to the door. He heard you moaning. When he looked through the window you were on the sofa in labor. He said you sent him to get the doctor and Mandy. That's what happened, isn't it?"

"Yes," I said, not feeling it was necessary to go into more detail. "Did Mandy recognize him?"

"I guess not. She's still talking about 'that Indian stand-ing in the bedroom with his mouth hanging open whilst Mis' Caty was having her baby.' She didn't notice him there until after little Joseph's birth. Then, she said, he hung around on the porch 'like he was that baby's father' until the doctor left when she thought he'd have enough sense to 'go fetch Mis' Josie.'"

"Josie, if he hadn't come along when he did . . . I saw him standing there while I was having the baby. I didn't think he should be there, either. But I hurt too bad to talk. You should have seen the look of wonder on his face when he saw my son. It was like he was seeing his own child being born. Oh, Josie, what a mess our lives are," I said.

"Let me put the baby back in his cradle, Caty. You go back to sleep and stop worrying. You need sleep, now. It's not good for you or little Joseph for you to fuss about things. And Mandy told me about what a tough delivery you had. Oh, Caty, I should never have left you alone."

"Well, I thank God Rafael come along when he did. And I thank Him that Mandy knew enough to help us, or things might not have turned out so well," I said.

I think I fell asleep before Josie left the room. Having a baby is the most exhausting thing imaginable. But sleep didn't stop the thoughts that plagued me. Thoughts of Joseph, Rafael, Ana, and the baby, all pulling me in different directions, tearing me to pieces. That was what was happening to me emotionally; I was being torn to pieces by my love for—my marriage to two men. That and all the imaginable consequences.

When the baby was two weeks old, I was nursing him on the sofa one afternoon when Josie announced that Rafael had come to see me. Before I could remove the baby from my breast, he stepped into the room on her heels. Josie left us, and he sat across the room seeming content to watch me with my child.

After a while, he said, "I'm leaving in the morning, Caty. I have to resume my search for the twins. I came to say good-bye. I've already told Thomas. I'll be gone a long time. I don't know for sure how long. I'm satisfied the twins are not living among the Florida Indians. I'm going into the northern colonies and Spanish Louisiana to look for them. The revolution is causing the Indians to keep streaming into Florida. The rebel Americans hate them. But I won't let a revolution or any other danger keep me from trying to find my children."

"I'll be praying for you, Rafael. And for your children. I hope you find them well, and soon."

"Ana tells me you and the little one are doing well, and that you'll be returning to town in two weeks," he said.

"Yes, we are going home. We are doing fine. Rafael, I haven't had a chance to thank you. We are so fortunate you happened by when you did."

"Happened along, Caty? I didn't just happen by. The reason I came here, the reason I asked Thomas for a job, was to be here when the baby came. Joseph wasn't going to be here. You told me that. But he was here for you when Ana was born when I couldn't be. I guess I felt I owed him, but I wanted to be here for you, too, Caty. And, well, I guess I wanted to be here for me. I planned it so I would be here for this one's birth.

"I was so frightened for you, Caty. And for the baby. Things weren't going well. I could have lost you. Oh, God, Caty, I was so scared. And there was nothing I could do. I didn't know what to do. But Mandy knew. I thought she had gone crazy when she jumped on you like that. But she pushed the baby out. And then, when I saw that new life, when I knew you were both alive and seemingly well, I can't explain the way I felt. It was like I'd seen a miracle, been part of a miracle. I've never experienced anything like it before," he said. Now he was kneeling beside me. His arms were around me and my child, and there was that look of pure wonder on his face.

"May I hold him?" He reached for my son. Looking into his sleeping face, he asked, "Does he look like Ana did?"

"Sort of. But where Joseph's hair is light, Ana's was black. And Joseph's eyes are blue, like his father's."

"But, he looks like you, Caty. I see dimples when he moves his mouth. And Ana looks like you, too. They are both beautiful."

Still holding him, Rafael said, "When I heard you were going to be here alone all day and half the night, I couldn't believe it. You hadn't been doing well. You looked really sick the last time I had seen you. That's why I didn't go to town that day. I came by because I wanted to check on you." He hugged my baby to him, then laid him in his cradle. Sitting by me on the sofa, he took my hands in his. "Caty, I don't know what is going to happen to us. But I know I love you, and I always will. Nothing can change that. I'll never give up on us having a life together some day, some way. I won't give up on it." He pulled me to him and held me close. In a few minutes he lifted my chin and kissed me tenderly. "This is good-bye, then, for now. Take care of yourself and the children. And, Caty, say it just once more, please, so I can carry it with me in my heart. Tell me you love me."

I couldn't hold back the tears. "You know I do, Rafael. God help me, I can no easier stop than I can stop breathing. Oh, it's so hard to let you go. But I have to, can't you see?" I pleaded as I clung to him.

He kissed me once more, and we released each other with reluctance. "Pray for me, Caty. And pray that I'll find my children, that they are alive and well." And he was gone again.

In late April of 1779, Joseph returned from England. I had just settled the baby for his afternoon nap and was in the kitchen with Ana and Mandy. We heard him call, "Caty! Ana!" as his footsteps came in our direction.

"Papa Joe's back!" Ana exclaimed joyfully, running toward him. I was on her heels.

Joseph hugged her to him, but looked over her shoulder for me. He held out an arm, and the three of us stood there, hugging each other tight.

"I've missed my two girls," he said. Then he released us,

and holding me at arm's length, he looked me up and down. "I received a letter, Caty, and left as soon as I could. Caty?" He seemed almost scared to ask more.

"You have a son, Joseph, Jr. He was born January 28. He's three months old, has blond hair and blue eyes like you. I just put him down for a nap.

Ana said, "He can already roll over both ways! He holds his little hands up and turns them this way and that just to watch them. When I pick him up, he laughs."

"Well, let's go up and see him. I'll try not to wake him," said Joseph.

When Joseph looked down at his son, his face held a look of tenderness and happiness I had never seen on it before. I lifted the sleeping baby and placed him in his father's arms for the first time. Then I led him to the rocking chair. When he sat, I knelt beside the chair, my hand on Joseph's arm as we shared the joy that was our son.

Ana looked at the three of us, and seeing with a wisdom beyond a mere nine years said, "I wish I could paint a picture of the three of you just like this."

Our son smiled and cuddled up to his father. Joseph's smile could not have spread any farther across his face than it did at that moment. He bent his head to kiss his son. Then he put an arm around me and pulled me to him for a kiss. "Caty, you have made me happier than I have ever been. Now my life is complete. I have a beautiful wife and daughter and a wonderful son. We are all healthy. What more could a man ask?"

When we were alone in our room at last, Joseph swept me into his arms. "I've missed you so. Thoughts of you have driven me to distraction. I could barely keep my mind on business. I hated leaving you. Your letter made me so happy, but didn't reach me in time for me to be here for the baby's birth, even though I left the next day." He held me tighter. "I love you so much. I don't believe I could go on without you."

"I love you, too, Joseph. And I've missed you, too." And it was true. But his words about not being able to go on without me confirmed my own thoughts, and I knew I could never leave him for Rafael.

He swept me up in his arms and carried me to our bed. It was so wonderful to have him back, to be in his arms again. It had been so long—so long. Our reunion was wildly, sensually passionate. It was only after that thoughts of Rafael entered my mind to torture and confuse me. I tried to push them out. I told them they had no place in my mind. That I had made my choice. But they refused to leave. Throughout the night they tortured me.

Joseph was beside himself with joy. I had never seen him so happy and proud. He even seemed to grow younger, his step more lively. He planned his days around his son's waking hours. He wanted to be with little Joseph every minute the child was awake. He was truly possessed by this child, our son.

If I was lost in my own terrible thoughts, distracted as I never had been before, if there were slightly dark circles under my eyes after sleepless nights, Joseph didn't notice. Or if he did, he must have thought they had to do with my being a mother again, perhaps with recuperating or waking nightly to feed and change little Joseph.

I truly loved Joseph, but that didn't prevent me from occasionally being overcome with a feeling of guilt. I don't know if it was because I was married to both he and Rafael, or because I was happy with Joseph while Rafael was all alone. I tried to convince myself I could not be responsible for the happiness of either, but particularly for Rafael's. At any rate, I was becoming a little more successful at pushing unwanted and unbidden thoughts of Rafael from my mind. Still, those times that I couldn't were filled with longing for him and what might have been.

Joseph had been surprised to find St. Augustine had

filled with so many loyalists fleeing the American colonies. The revolt was growing more ferocious. He said rumor in England was rampant that England might also soon be at war with Spain. Spanish troops were as close to Florida as Louisiana and Cuba. Rumors in St. Augustine continued to claim the rebellious Americans would send troops into East and West Florida.

St. Augustine held a Negro population left over from the Spanish occupation. Slaves who had escaped to Florida and became Catholic had been given land by the Spanish who had made them into militia units. They even had a fort called Fort Mosa. Around the fort a community developed where Negroes, Mulattos, Zambos, and Mestizos lived. Not all had left with the Spanish. It was constantly growing because Governor Tonyn's policies encouraged runaway slaves and free Negroes to come to Florida and become British citizens.

This community north of St. Augustine was frequently raided by Yuchee Indians from Georgia who captured the inhabitants and sold them in South Carolina as slaves. It continued to irritate the American rebels whose slaves still sought Fort Mosa and the vicinity as a haven.

In an effort to defend St. Augustine and the surrounding area from attack by rebels from the north, Lieutenant Governor John Moultrie had built four galleys he called Thunderers to patrol the waters of the St. Johns and the inlets at St. Augustine and Mosquito. These ships were made of heavy metal and drew very little water to prevent them getting stuck on the sand bars that had been the bane of so many invading or unknowledgeable craft.

Many of the refugees coming into town were extremely poor, down and out. Many were sick. The large influx of new settlers caused many shortages. The price of food and clothing had escalated beyond reason.

St. Marks Fort, which the Spanish had named Castillo de

San Marcos, was being used as a prison to hold French, American, and Spanish seamen from ships captured by the English. And in June Spain did declare war on England, as had been rumored. Governor Galvez of Louisiana began capturing British settlements on the Mississippi River for Spain.

Governor Tonyn had promised protection to loyalists who were being prosecuted. Now they were coming in droves: rich, poor, white, slave, free blacks, men of every trade. Bands of Indians came and went. English troops further swelled the population. Housing was not available.

My Minorcan friends and relatives were kept busy, as food supplies were no longer allowed to come in from the north. We were under blockade by the Americans. Minorcan farmers, hunters, and fishermen supplied fresh meat, fish, and vegetables. Since we had come before, our people were already farming the best pieces of ground on the outskirts of the city. For once in this new world that had held so much promise and delivered so much suffering, we were no longer at the bottom of the heap. There were finally opportunities for my people, and they were grasping them. They were naturally hunters, fishermen, and farmers, and had learned Florida's growing conditions. Now they were needed.

Minorcan fishermen particularly profited. Many already owned ships, a few owned fleets. The Indians did not bring as much fish to market as they did game.

Then in October, Governor Galvez took Natchez, the last British settlement on the Mississippi. When the news reached St. Augustine, Governor Tonyn and the British loyalists, including Joseph, were beside themselves. They were sure an invasion of West Florida was close.

In March their fears increased when Galvez, with Spanish reinforcements from Cuba, took the fort at Mobile, a principle British settlement in West Florida. We were celebrating our pre Lenten festival when the news arrived. Actually, it

mattered little to most of my people, who associated
themselves more with Spanish culture and language than
with British.

Every morning Joseph went to the plaza to read the official notices as well as the criticisms of the government posted
on the corner outside Paine's Store. In May 1780, the news
began with the English capture of Charleston. They already
held Savannah, so now Joseph, along with the rest of us, began to feel the Americans would not attack us.

The latest refugees from the north brought the dreaded
smallpox into St. Augustine. Joseph, the children, and I lined
up with much of the population to be inoculated against the
deadly and disfiguring disease.

Joseph was becoming increasingly concerned about the
future of Florida. One evening after the children were in
bed, he told me he felt certain Florida would not remain
British. He felt the British would give up all America. He
knew Spain wanted the Floridas back, and he was sure America
wanted them, too.

"I feel now is the time to make our move, Caty. Otherwise,
we may lose everything. We have to make some decisions.
I've been giving a lot of thought to returning to England.
Would that suit you, Caty?" he asked.

I felt the chill of panic. "No, Joseph. Please don't make
me go there. I want to remain here among my people. I have
nothing in common with your people. You have become Catholic and seem to like both my people and our customs. You
have a mutual love and understanding of each other. I don't
want to leave; I want to raise my children here in the ways of
my people."

"I was sure you would feel that way. Well, then, I'm going
to try to sell the business. There have been several offers for
it from loyalists who would run the American blockades. We
have never been busier with all the lumber, tar, turpentine,
and other naval stores that are leaving Florida now. But when

England relinquishes Florida, as I'm sure she will, either we will be under Spanish rule or American. If the Americans get Florida, all the loyalists here will probably flee. There won't be anyone left but your people, the Indians, and perhaps some Negroes. There will be no business, no buyers. I will be ruined.

"Should Spain get East Florida, I feel it will only be temporary. These Americans seem to have their minds set on having the whole continent. They speak of 'manifest destiny' as though they believe God means for them to have it all. And, again, if Spain has it even for a little while, all those who wish to stay will have to profess Catholicism. Just as it is not right for a nation to reject Catholics and Catholicism, neither is it right to force it on the people. This will cause many, who might otherwise wish to stay, to abandon their properties and leave. Whether Florida falls to America or Spain, I see no business and no buyers, at least for a while after. And that could bankrupt me.

"When I find a buyer, I will invest some of the money in Spanish ventures in Havana, but most in American business. What with blockades and all, there's no shipping business now, except for smugglers and blockade runners. I've been approached by some of them, already. Yes, Caty, America will be the future of the Floridas, I am sure. But my investments must be secret. If word should get out, I could be considered a traitor.

"Like you, Caty, I like it here. And when this is all settled, when Florida finally becomes American, there will be many opportunities," he said.

III

The festival of St. Elana was in progress. As part of the festival, we married women held nine night Novenas to St. Elana, each night in a different home. St. Elana was one of our favorite saints. She was the mother of Constantine who discovered the cross of Christ's crucifixion.

After the Novenas, we held posey dances. Those who wished to vote for the king and queen of the dance gave a donation in their choice's names the night of the first dance. Whoever received the most donations was elected. We danced and feasted half the night. On the night of the second dance, the queen chose a new king for the following night. She made her choice by presenting him with two bouquets of Spanish pinks, and he chose his queen by giving one of them to her. The new king paid for the next night's party. New selections were made each night until the final dance. Each dance was held in a different home where there was a young, unmarried woman. It was all great fun, and a continuation of the culture we had been accustomed to back in Minorca.

Before the dances, we had prepared a step like altar

covered with flowers and lit with candles as part of the celebration which preceded the most solemn time in the church calendar: Lent, the time of fasting and preparation for the celebration of the resurrection of Christ.

Toward the end of the solemn forty days of Lent, on Good Friday, one of our fishermen dressed as St. Peter. Christ had taught Peter and his apostles to be fishers-of-men. In this game honoring that teaching, our fisher-of-men carried his cast net through town. Little boys teased him as we watched. He cast his nets in attempts to catch the children. When he caught one, we all applauded. The children loved it, and the adults laughed indulgently.

On the eve of Easter, the young men performed the Fromajaridis Serenade until midnight. Groups of them serenaded each home, playing guitars and singing a song to the Virgin Mary, assuring her of her Son's resurrection. Then they asked for gifts of food—cakes, eggs, cheese pastries. We dropped these goodies into a bag carried by one of the young men.

Easter morning began with Mass. Following Mass, Josie and her family came home with us where we put the finishing touches on our Easter dinner, the main dish being one of Thomas's wild turkeys.

After dinner Josie announced she had something important to share with us. Thomas stood with his arm around her, smiling proudly while she said, "We're going to have a baby."

We all rushed forward to congratulate them. "When, Josie, when is the baby due?" I asked.

"It's due in October. I'm so excited. And we want you and Joseph to be godparents. There. I asked you before you could jump the gun like I did with little Joseph."

Little Joe, as Ana had dubbed her brother, was now sixteen months old. He toddled after his sister everywhere she went. They adored each other, and she was a great help to me with him. Joseph already took him to the docks once a week.

I had become mostly successful at putting thoughts of Rafael from my mind by now, and I only had an occasional dream that wrenched my heart and soul and mind. It seemed that each time I got this close to gaining control, something happened to set me back.

Market days had become family outings for Joseph, the children, and me. These were times when Joseph could show off his son to the whole town. It was on a market day when we were strolling between the stalls that Ana grabbed my arm and said excitedly, "Mama, I saw Water Gift!" She turned and pointed, saying, "Look!"

Joseph and I both looked just in time to see him get lost in the crowd. Ana tugged at my arm, "Come on, Mama. Let's find him. I guess he didn't see us."

I tried to pull back, not knowing what to say, not wanting to call Joseph's attention to the color I could feel rising in my cheeks. I didn't know what to do.

Joseph, with Little Joe in one arm, grabbed my other arm as Ana still tugged me toward where Rafael had been. "Whoa, girls," he said. "Who did you say you saw, Ana? It sounded like you said 'Water Gift.'"

"That's right, Papa Joe. He's an Indian. We first saw him here. Then, before Little Joe was born, when Mama wasn't well and we were staying at the farm with Josie and Thomas, he came to the farm and asked Thomas for a job. He's the one who got the doctor for Mama when the baby was coming."

Trying to gain control of both my composure and the situation, I said, "Ana! We don't discuss such matters in public.

"I don't see the Indian now. Either he didn't see us, or he didn't want to be seen for some reason. At any rate, I don't see him now. Let's finish our shopping."

I could feel Joseph's eyes on me, but I couldn't force myself to look at his face. We continued our shopping, but Ana twisted this way and that in search of Rafael, while I tried very hard to keep from doing the same.

That night after we had retired to our room, Joseph turned me to him. He said, "Caty, do you want to tell me about this Indian? I saw him watching you and Ana before she saw him. The way he looked at you worried me. And frankly, he didn't look Indian to me." I could feel the color again rise to my checks. I didn't know what Joseph suspected. I said, "Thomas said he's half French or Spanish. Why don't you talk to Thomas? He's the one who hired him. Ana saw him in the market the first time and was scared, because he was looking at her. You know how she used to be about Indians. Then when Thomas hired him, she took a liking to him. He taught her things about farming, animals, and how to shoot the bow. He gave her Fluffy."

"What's Fluffy?" he asked.

"Oh, that's right. You never saw Fluffy. He was a fuzzy white puppy. Water Gift gave him to Ana when we were at the farm. But just after we came back home, he got out of the yard somehow and was run over by a military wagon. Ana was upset for weeks."

"What was Ana talking about when she said he got the doctor when you had our son?"

"Well, Thomas, Josie, Ana, and Uncle Gaspar had all gone to the Falany's barn raising . . ."

"What?" he interrupted. "They left you alone?"

"I urged them to go, Joseph. The baby wasn't due for a couple of weeks. I knew how much they wanted to go. Anyway," I continued, "Thomas had given the Indian the day off. When I started having pains early in the morning, I thought I was alone at the farm. I got everything ready in case I had to have the baby alone. Then the pains got bad and I guess I was moaning, because Fluffy was barking, and someone was knocking at the door. I was glad someone had come. But when I started to the door, a pain hit me. I fell onto the sofa. He was looking in the window and saw me fall. He burst through the door.

"I asked him to go get Mandy and the doctor. He did. When they came back, he wouldn't leave until the doctor came out and told him we were fine. Then he went to get Josie and them from the barn raising.

"Oh, yes. He has twins, a girl and a boy, who were stolen from his village somewhere in South Florida. He's trying to find them."

"Poor fellow. Well, I'm grateful for what he did for you. But there's something about him that bothers me. I can't seem to . . .

"Come to bed, Joseph," I said, pulling at his clothing. "I'll help you forget that Indian." I pulled my nightgown over my head and climbed into bed. I silenced all his talk and thoughts of Water Gift, at least for the night. But there was no respite from my thoughts for me.

The next day Josie came by. She brought a jar of her homemade preserves to us. But why she really came was to tell me Rafael had been to see her. He had told her about Ana spotting him in the market. He wanted her to tell me he was sorry if he had caused a problem. He just had to see us, to be sure we were all right. He was leaving again to continue his search.

I suppose to most of my fellow Minorcans I was well off, even spoiled. Few were fortunate enough to own slaves. And though we only had Mandy, a house slave who seemed like part of the family, she did many of the chores.

Our community rose early and most attended morning Mass daily. Most of the women had to go home and heat leftover ash cakes and cassina tea on the coals for breakfast. Mandy had our breakfasts ready for us when we returned.

Most did not have the luxury of beds, or even separate

rooms to sleep in. They had to roll up their sleeping mats to get them out of the way. On a typical day we hung our blankets out to air, swept and dusted the house, and we scrubbed the floors weekly if we were fortunate enough not to have dirt floors as some houses did.

We weeded and swept our yards, because we did a lot of our work outside. Snakes and rats could hide in weeds. We grew our table vegetables and fruits, and had to tend these gardens. Some women who lived on farms even helped with the farm chores. We soaked clothes to be washed overnight, then washed them in wooden troughs, scrubbing them on metal washboards until our knuckles bled. Some women who didn't have clotheslines hung their clothes on bushes to dry. Some of the really poor who had no wells took their clothes to the creek to wash. The rest of us had to draw our water from the well with buckets attached to ropes.

We made our soap from ashes, our candles from lard. Produce from the garden that couldn't be used fresh was strung and hung to dry, as datil peppers and green beans, to be used later in soups or stews. We made fruit preserves. We dried corn in the corn crib to grind into hominy and meal.

Those who had cows had to milk them and made cheese and butter.

We made sausage, cured hams and bacon, and smoked and salted down the fish and game which we could not use fresh.

We gathered and brought in firewood, collected nuts, picked wild berries in season, and gathered oysters from the marsh. We tended the beehives and did the shopping.

We cared for our children.

Most of us ate our largest meal at noon, with the men coming in from the fields or other work to eat. After cleaning up, we did afternoon chores such as whitewashing our homes or weaving baskets, mats, or other things, or patching, darning and making clothing.

Supper was usually light. Most of our women and children went to bed early, tired from their daily work, while many of the men spent the evenings in local taverns.

Here, I was fortunate, too. Joseph rarely visited a tavern, although several of my countrymen owned taverns. One at the northern end of town was frequented by British soldiers from the fort, as was another near the barracks in the south of town. Minorcans rarely fraternized with the soldiers. Most of the taverns were in the Minorcan quarter, in the homes of the owners. Usually customers were relatives and friends. There was also a Minorcan tavern on the bay front which fishermen and dock workers used.

My people were close knit. We lived together in the same section of town. This, however, was because after the rebellion in New Smyrna, they settled where Governor Tonyn told them to. Joseph's home just happened to be on the fringe of the new Minorcan section.

Besides living close together, we were all Catholic. The Greeks among us, having no Orthodox minister, attended Mass with us. The English detested our faith. Most of us spoke Catalan, a Spanish dialect, although Rafael and I had also learned English back in Minorca. (Papa had arranged for an English teacher for some of the children in our village, since the English owned Minorca.) Most neither read nor wrote. Rafael and I were also fortunate that we had learned to do both. Most married others within our group. Josie and I were notable exceptions. So were our husbands, both of whom were broad minded and had embraced our religion. They were beloved additions to our community and a bridge between the cultures.

It was June, the beginning of the festival season for our people. This began with St. John's Eve, the Fiesta of San Juan, on June 23. Midsummer's Eve, another name for it, was celebrated by masked parades and balls. During the day we promenaded through the streets, women dressed as ancient chivalry riding decorated horses, and men dressed as ladies of ancient times. Although Joseph enjoyed it all and participated in much of it, he could not be persuaded to dress as a lady.

We made altars throughout town and decorated them with draperies and flowers. A silver statue of Jesus sat on each altar amid a hundred lit candles. To each man who visited an altar, the woman who attended it presented a bouquet of flowers.

Good food was abundant. The British joined in the fun and dances which were held in the streets to the sounds of guitars and castanets.

Romance flourished in our section, too, and was subject to the customs we practiced before we came to this new place. On many nights the sounds of a young man playing his guitar and serenading the young lady of his affections wafted on the air past the open windows of her neighbors.

Life in the Minorcan quarter so much resembled that which we had lived in Minorca that at times it seemed only the rocky cliffs, the caves, and the goats were absent.

St. Augustine was at this time bustling with activity. Loyalists continued to come. Farmers, hunters, and fishermen, mostly from our quarter, were hard pressed to feed them. Stonemasons and carpenters, many of them also Minorcan, worked daylight to dark renovating old buildings and building new. Little housing was available for the swelling population.

Sixty-three American rebels were captured in Carolina and sent to be jailed in St. Marks. Governor Tonyn asked them to pledge that they wouldn't escape and he would give them freedom of the town. Many had friends and relatives among the English in the colony. All pledged so except one, Christopher Gadsden, who was kept in the fort. Three of the prisoners were said to be signers of the American Declaration of Independence.

Lieutenant Governor Moultrie's brother, Alexander, was one of the prisoners who was released. He went to live at his brother's plantation, Bella Vista.

The whole town was concerned with what was happening in the colonies to the north and trying to contend with the massive in surge of people fleeing those parts.

And then in October, Josie came to stay with us until the birth of her baby. Her labor, unlike mine, had been easy. She gave birth to a beautiful baby boy, Thomas Gaspar Andrews, named for her husband and her father.

Shortly thereafter, Joseph's solicitors found a buyer for his business. He sold all except for the boat he had christened *Ana*.

Across the Matanzas River from St. Augustine there lived two men, Luciana Herrerra and his friend, Jessie Fish, who were among the few who had stayed over from the Spanish occupation of Florida. They were suspected of spying for Spain. Joseph liked them both, nonetheless. It was to them that Joseph went to help him with investing money in Havana. He didn't want to put all of it in either Spanish or American interests, gambling that should something happen to the economy of one, the other would survive. However, he felt that the future of this whole continent would rest with one or both, and that England could not long hold its interest in the area. Since we had decided this would remain our home in any event, and the British crown was still indebted to him, he decided English interests were not a good investment.

He gave his trusted solicitor the task of investing the rest of his money in American endeavors, but not in the war effort against England. Neither were Herrerra and Fish to invest in Spain's war efforts.

In February of 1781, Governor Tonyn finally allowed East Florida to elect an assembly. By then the American prisoners had been paroled and allowed to return home.

The council, led by Lt. Governor Moultrie, and the commons under Speaker William Brown, met on March 27, 1781. A form of democracy had come to East Florida, probably prompted by fear that what was happening in the north might infect the colonists here if they did not feel they were represented in their government. The East Florida government, though, was strictly a loyalist government.

One morning when Joseph returned from reading the messages posted at Paine's Corner, he was very distressed. He told me the Spanish had taken Pensacola. He felt sure the end of England's hold on Florida was near.

In October, the town was buzzing with the news that Lord Cornwallis had surrendered his army of seven thousand men to the American forces under General George Washington. St. Augustine was under attack warnings.

Then Joseph was contacted by his friend Luciana Herrerra. Governor Tonyn had troops looking to arrest him for spying for Spain. He was fleeing to Havana. Jesse Fish would be able to contact him. If he needed to contact Joseph concerning his investments, he would do so through Mr. Fish.

As far as the English were concerned in this new world, things were going very badly in a hurry. Joseph was visibly shaken. He seemed pulled in two directions. On the one hand he was an Englishman. He did not want to give up his citizenship to the land of his birth. On the other, he loved Florida. But above all else, he loved his family. And I would not—could not—go to England. After being separated from my people and our customs once, I could never be again. I loved my people, our culture and religion. Except for Joseph, Sarah, and Thomas, most of the English I had met were alien and unfriendly to us. They acted as though we were beneath them. I didn't want this for my children. And now that my people were here, I loved this city. Secretly, I felt St. Augustine without the British government would be an even lovelier place. But I thought I understood Joseph's feelings, and I suffered for him.

As the situation became more tense for his country on this continent, his health began to fail. He became thinner, distracted, and less amiable than he had been.

Then news came that Francisco Sanchez, a holdover from the Spanish period, had helped some Spanish soldiers who shipwrecked off St. Augustine in stormy weather. Already suspected by Governor Tonyn because he was Spanish, this act that both Joseph and I felt was a perfectly natural thing for him to do, further heightened Tonyn's suspicion of the man. Tonyn no longer considered him a subject of the English king and refused to protect his property from raiders and squatters. This refusal to protect him and some other property owners added to the disorder already rampant in the colony.

In May of 1782, when the British Commander Sir Guy Carlton ordered Savannah and St. Augustine evacuated, a member of the council came to tell Joseph. After the man had left, while Joseph was telling me what had happened, his hand flew to his head. His eyes took on a glazed, pained expression. He looked as though he would fall.

"What's wrong? Let me help you to the sofa," I said in alarm.

"My head. It hurts terribly," he said.

I called for Mandy to bring a cool, wet cloth which I placed on his forehead.

"I'll send for the doctor," I said.

"No, no, just let me lie here for a moment. I'll be all right," he insisted.

I sat by his side, sponging his face. He did not appear to be getting better. Within an hour I knew he was not going to get all right without help. His speech became slurred. Saliva ran from the right corner of his lips, and tears streamed unchecked from his right eye. I sent Mandy to get the doctor.

By the time he arrived, Joseph's mouth was pulled down grotesquely on the right side, and he could not move his right arm or leg. I was terrified.

Dr. Johnson said Joseph was suffering from apoplexy. He didn't know if it would get worse. If it did, he might not survive. At any rate, he might not ever walk or talk again.

Ana and I were devastated. Little Joe, now almost three and a half, couldn't understand why his father wouldn't get up and play with him.

Of course, we could not evacuate. Josie and Thomas came to take the children with them. Ana refused to go. And Joseph's eyes followed little Joe as though they couldn't get enough of him. Ana begged that he not be taken away, because Papa Joe loved him so. She promised to take care of him, and he would be no trouble to Mandy and me. At twelve, Ana was a mature and caring young lady.

Able neither to talk nor move the right side of his body, Joseph became angry and frustrated. Only when Ana and his son were near him did he try to control these emotions.

Then, miraculously, he began to speak again. At first it was only a word or two. Within a week he was making sentences. At night I lay close to him in bed and begged him not to leave me. "I love you so much, Joseph. I need you. The children need you. You have to get well. We'll go to England if it will make you happy," I said. Suddenly I realized Joseph was even more important to me than I had imagined. He was even more important to me than being with my people. For the first time I fully realized how much Joseph loved me. He loved me enough to give up his country for me. Could I do less if it might help him return to good health?

"No, Caty. We won't go to England. You have been through so much, my darling. I couldn't separate you from your people again. And I know how much your religion means to you. You wouldn't be happy in England. If you were not happy, how could I be? You and the children are my happiness. Besides, Caty, what if we got to England, and I did not survive? Even if I do, I'm fifty years old. You're only thirty. While most of my life is behind me, most of yours is before you. I'll be gone long before you. I have had a most happy life. I have known the love of two wonderful women and two precious children. No, Caty. I thank you for your thoughtfulness, but we will stay here."

Fortunately, there had been no invasion. Joseph continued to improve. In August we heard Sir Carlton had changed his order. East Florida was now to be a haven for loyalist refugees fleeing Savannah and Charleston. Even larger numbers of people poured in quickly. White, Negro, many sick and without a penny to their names. Within a year more than seven thousand new refugees came. There were now more than seventeen thousand people in East Florida.

The new refugees, in keeping with the English tradition, were provided land, tools, and rations. New towns sprang up. Many of the people had to live in palmetto huts like those we had built at New Smyrna.

In March of 1783, Joseph, now walking with the aid of a cane, insisted we attend the first performance of the St. Augustine Theater. It was a benefit to assist needy refugees.

We now had a newspaper in town, the *East Florida Gazette.*

In June, the news again turned bad for Joseph and his fellow Englishmen. Governor Tonyn had been notified that East Florida had been returned to Spain.

When Senor Sanchez heard the news, he left immediately for Cuba to meet with the governor appointee, Vincent Manuel de Zespedes. He told Zespedes he had lived in Florida since the first Spanish period and would stay as a loyal Spaniard when England left. He wanted to sell his beef to the new governor for the Spanish soldiers and others who would be coming to East Florida with the governor.

When Sanchez returned to his home, he found that seven hundred whites, Negroes, and Indians had camped there and he was missing four hundred cattle. Governor Tonyn refused to help him get his cattle back or to apprehend the guilty. Senor Sanchez had no choice but to become friendly with the bandit, Daniel McGirt, former leader of the North East Florida Rangers, in an effort to get his property back and prevent further raids on his property and cattle.

Joseph was greatly disturbed by the news that Spain had regained Florida, even though it had been expected. He was also upset by the lawlessness that he expected to get even worse during the changeover from England to Spain. Still in fragile health, he suffered another attack of apoplexy. He did not last the night.

I went through the necessary motions of helping to wash and dress Joseph's body in his best shirt and suit as though in a trance. We laid him out in the living room. Around his body we placed eight large silver candles. Their glow cast a flickering light over the paleness of his features. My people came in a steady stream, bringing dishes of all kinds of food. Father Camps led the rosary over his body. The house and yard overflowed with people, mostly from the Minorcan quarter, but many English, also. They told stories about the good things my husband had done for them or someone they knew. They ate. They stayed into the wee hours of morning.

The next morning pallbearers carried his body into the church of St. Peter at the head of a large procession of weeping mourners. After Father Camps said the funeral Mass, my beloved Joseph was buried in the Catholic cemetery named Tolomato, just west of town.

During the whole process it was as though I were floating somewhere above it all, watching my body do the things expected of it. It was almost as if I were watching it all happening to someone else. Afterward, I collapsed. Dr. Johnson ordered me to bed and prescribed some potion that kept me asleep for the better part of a week. During that time my mind drifted backward and forward. At times I was not sure who I had lost, Joseph or Rafael. I relived the time when I believed Rafael had died in a hurricane. Somehow that became mixed up with Joseph's death. Then I believed them both gone. I wanted to die, too. I prayed for death.

Occasionally I would be comforted by the small, warm body of Little Joseph snuggling in my arms, wiping away my tears. He would say, "Don't cry, Mama. Papa will come back. He won't leave us." At other times, he ,too, would be crying, saying, "Where's my Papa? I want my Papa."

Gradually the drug wore off, and I was forced to return to the world of reality. Oh, the pain was so great! There was my personal grief and the grief of my children to deal with. There are great joys in this life, but most earthly joy is so brief and fleeting, while the grief goes on and on and seems to penetrate so much deeper. To be felt with so much more intensity. Again I thought of the sweet release death must bring—relief from all earth's pain and suffering. But there could be no such relief for me. There was Ana and Little Joe. They needed me now more than ever.

And so the process repeated itself. The numbness, the withdrawal from all but the necessities. The starkness of emotions. There were only my children and me, this horrible pain, and the oh so real memories in the little world in which I lived. But the world outside did not stop for my grief. The American Revolution was over, however East Florida was in a transition period in which chaos reigned. Those who had raided both sides of the Florida-Georgia border during the war were being led by Daniel McGirt in raids on both rebel and loyalist plantations. They stole cattle, kidnapped those who used the roads, and ambushed the British troops who tried to stop them. They were said to have their hideouts in Diego Plains near the ocean northeast of St. Augustine.

Then, thankfully, a plot by some British soldiers that

could have been disastrous had been uncovered and prevented. The soldiers claimed death was preferable to discharge from the army. They wanted to burn the barracks and loot and destroy St. Augustine, capture St. Marks Fort, arm the Negroes, and kill all the whites who didn't want to keep East Florida for themselves.

Somehow I made it to May of 1784. Nearly a year had passed since Joseph's death, a year of torment inside my own heart and mind as well as to the territory of East Florida. I was beginning to learn to live with the loss of Joseph. The children were nearly back to normal. Children can adapt in a year to things which may take an adult a decade or more to accept. Things hit them severely, but they have a resiliency that is much quicker than ours. They had accepted Joseph's death, and although they missed and would never forget him, life went on.

Those who had lived in East Florida had to decide whether to stay and publicly profess belief in Catholicism or leave Florida. That was no problem for me, since my choice had been made long ago, and I had always been Catholic. Those who planned to leave had to apply for space on ships that would carry them away from Florida.

It was during all this confusion that I was forced to realize that fourteen-year-old Ana was no longer a child. I was in my room one evening when I heard a guitar and a young man's voice singing a love song to the object of his affection. Suddenly I realized the serenade was coming from beneath Ana's window.

I went to her door. It was open. The lamp was on, and one of Joseph's books lay open on her bed. But she was standing against the wall by the window, peeking through the curtain at the serenader. Abruptly she turned her back to the wall and giggled. Then she saw me. Blushing, she put her finger to her lips, motioning me to be quiet and to come over beside her to see her admirer.

Peeking carefully between the curtain and the window frame, I could see him in the light of a full moon. He was tall, broad shouldered, and his black hair formed a cap of loose curls on his head. His eyes were blue. I recognized him as the son of Marcus Generini, a Greek who had been a Turnbull colonist, and Elana Triay, a Minorcan woman. He was about twenty years old. He had quite a reputation with the young ladies, and now he was turning his eyes on Ana, who had secretly had a crush on him since she was twelve. I felt a pang of fear. But I didn't know if it was fear for Ana's virtue, fear that her heart might be broken, or fear that Ana was no longer my little girl, fear that I might lose her to this handsome young rascal.

I tossed and turned during the night, a new problem added to my list. But when I slept, I did not have the tortured dreams of Joseph's death, of Rafael's loss, or even of losing Ana to young Marcus Generini. I dreamed of long ago in Minorca when a dark-eyed, dark-haired boy with a dimpled chin played his guitar and sang beneath my window. I was once again thirteen, full of hope and love and fairytale dreams of a future filled with only good things. A future with the then seventeen-year-old young man who sang beneath my window. And that young man shared all these good dreams.

When I awoke, I felt a warmth and feeling of comfort I had not felt in a long while. I remembered the dreams in every detail. It was wonderful. I knew Ana was beginning to experience a similar dream. I hoped and prayed that her dreams would follow a happier pattern than mine, one uninterrupted by death, rumors of death, horrible hunger, poverty, and loss of all freedom. I prayed for a future in which reality even surpassed her dreams.

But that dream set me to thinking again of Rafael. And now that Joseph was gone, there was no reason for us to be apart. "Rafael is alive. I am alive. We love each other. He can claim his daughter now. He can claim me as his wife. But where is he? Why doesn't he come for us?" I thought.

I began to take more interest in life, in the way I looked. The children noticed the difference in me. So did Josie and Thomas.

In fact, one evening when Josie, Thomas and Tommy came by to visit, Thomas said, "Caty, I think you're ready now for this," and he placed a sealed envelope in my hand.

As I turned it over, I saw it had my name on the front in Joseph's handwriting. "What is this?" I asked.

"It's a letter Joseph wrote to you after he began to recuperate from his first attack. He told me in the event of his death, I should give it to you when I thought you were ready. Caty, Joseph and I talked about events discussed in the letter. He told me all of it. I haven't told anyone else. If you feel you need to talk about it with me, I'm available anytime."

I put the envelope aside until after they left, but I could not put it out of my mind. After their departure, I picked it up and stared at this message from beyond the grave. When I finally got the courage to open it, I read:

> *My Darling Caty,*
>
> *When you read this, I will have gone to my just rewards. But I want you to know, my dearest, how wonderful my life has been with you. I only hope your have been as happy with me.*
>
> *You are loving, kind, and generous. You have graced my life with your beauty and intelligence. You have been all any man could hope for in a wife and mother. You gave me the one thing I wanted more than all else, except you, and that I had despaired of ever having: my precious and wonderful son. And you allowed me to be a father to your lovely daughter, Ana. She is as my own.*
>
> *Please do not have any regrets about anything*

you imagine you might have done differently. Don't look back. Go forward with your life.

And now, my darling, I must tell you that I know your secret. I know that Rafael is alive. I can only imagine what joy and pain, what suffering of the heart and mind you have had since you found out. And yet, you never allowed your own suffering to interfere with our relationship.

You see, the day we saw Rafael, also known as Water Gift, in the market, I had seen him watching you before Ana saw him. There was something about him that was so familiar. Thoughts of him continued to bother me, and I tried to discuss him with you that night. The next morning when I was going to see Thomas, I saw him leaving the farm. I called to him. When he saw it was me, he started to kick his horse into a run. In that moment I knew. I shouted, "Rafael!" He reigned in his horse and allowed me to approach him.

We talked for a long time. He told me about his loss of memory, his life among the Indians, and about coming back to find you married to me. He told me about your dilemma with your conscience because of being married to both of us; that if we were not truly married, our beloved son Joseph might be considered illegitimate. And he told me you had chosen me. But, he said he still loves you.

He said he had come to work for Thomas because he wanted to be near you when you had our child, since I was gone. He also wanted to get to know Ana. He was in the market that day to see you both, to be sure you were all right.

He told me you didn't want me to know he had not died, because you didn't want to distress me or to cause me to insist that we annul our marriage so you could return to him. You must have had the notion that I was some kind of selfless saint. Well, Caty, I have to confess, I am not. I couldn't even tell you that I knew about Rafael. I was afraid if you knew I knew, I would lose you to him.

My Caty, please forgive me for being less than you imagined. Did I love you too much to give you up, or not enough to do so? I have wrestled with that question so many times. I never found the answer. I only know I love you and I was much too selfish to let you go.

I thank God you chose to stay with me. I could not have blamed you had you decided your place was with Rafael. But I would not have wanted to live without you.

I fear that you may feel the same, now that I am gone. But, my darling, you must not. Now Rafael can claim his rightful place as your husband. You are not alone. You have Ana and Little Joseph. Someday Rafael will find his other children or decide his search is futile. When that happens, he will come back to you.

Once you told me that no one could ever take Sarah's place in my heart, nor Rafael's in yours. you said something about each love having a place of its own in a heart. So just as my loving Sarah didn't take anything away from my love for you, it must be the same concerning your love for Rafael and me. Caty, that love for Rafael must still be there sleeping, just waiting for Rafael to come back to awaken it.

Have no regrets concerning me, my darling. Time will help you to live with my passing, as it did when you thought Rafael had died. And Rafael will return, I am sure, when you are ready.

Tell my children, both of them, I love them dearly,

and that my love will be with you all even now that
I no longer am.

     Good-bye, my darling Caty.

               Your adoring husband,
                   Joseph

Tears streamed down my face. My throat ached with choking pain. My darling Joseph had known that Rafael was alive. He must have lived with the uncertainty of whether I would change my mind and choose Rafael—the uncertainty of whether I stayed with him out of love or pity. I had wanted so badly to shield him from all the doubt and pain of knowing about Rafael. But he had found out anyway. He never let on that he knew.

Then I felt a pang of anger. Anger at Joseph for not telling me he knew. Anger at myself for not telling Joseph that night after we saw Rafael in the market. Anger that neither of us trusted the other enough to talk about the situation we found ourselves in, a situation that was no one's fault. Anger for all the suffering we both had gone through that might have been alleviated by talking about it. And anger at what poor Rafael had gone through, was still going through, because of my decision.

As my thoughts turned to Rafael, another emotion hit me: fear. Fear that Rafael had found someone else. Fear that he no longer cared for me. Fear that he may never come back. And worst of all, fear that he, too, might be dead.

And I was struck by a thought: how uncertain is the world in which we live. We don't know anything about the future for certain. We aren't even sure what the next second will bring. Yesterday is gone forever. It cannot be changed by any human. There is only now. Only this second.

So, I decided I would try to live for now. I would continue to have my hopes, my dreams for the future. I would still pray about it. I would try to remember only the good about yesterday. I knew unless I accepted this, I might as well have died with Joseph.

Governor Zespedes and five hundred Spanish troops arrived in St. Augustine on June 27. Also in the entourage were two priests. The Spanish flag began to fly over the fort for the second time.

On July 12, 1784, it seemed the whole town assembled in the plaza to see Governor Tonyn turn the city of St. Augustine over to the new Spanish governor. Then we all followed the formal delegation to the fort, where in another ceremony, Governor Zespedes was given charge of it. There was feasting and dancing, bright Spanish colors, and gaiety. The festivities were enjoyed by Spanish, Minorcans, Indians, Negroes, the foreigners among us, and even many of the English. Ana and Joseph were delighted. My son informed me he wanted to be a Spanish soldier on a white horse when he grew up.

The next day many of my people presented the new governor a memorial congratulating him on his safe arrival and on the Spanish possession of East Florida. It told him that we felt ourselves to be natural-born subjects of Spain and we were happy to be once again under the command of the Spanish, as Minorca had been previous to English rule. We offered our service and promised love and obedience.

On July 14, while the town was still celebrating the Spanish takeover, South Carolina and Georgia loyalists raided the home of Governor Tonyn's friend, Sam Farley, stealing a number of slaves. Daniel McGirt, who had been under arrest in the fort, had bribed guards to resume his raids.

Governor Zespedes sought to remove the raiders from Florida by offering those in trouble with the English a passport out of the territory. Or, they could become Spanish subjects.

McGirt accepted the Spanish offer in an effort to buy time and protection from Governor Tonyn, who was authorized to stay to protect British citizens. But, McGirt continued to terrorize travelers and residents with his stealing and kidnaping.

Governor Tonyn was extremely upset that most of my people did not agree to leave St. Augustine with the English. But we had never felt English. We had always been one with the Spanish.

Although most of the English liked Governor Zespedes and found him honest and fair, Governor Tonyn quarreled with him constantly.

British home, business, and plantation owners found the prices of their properties had fallen to about one-tenth of what they had cost. I could see how right Joseph had been in his predictions when he had decided to sell his business a few years back. Since all the British but a handful were leaving, and all the Americans who would not become Catholic had to also abandon their properties, the market was loaded with real estate, but there were very few buyers. Properties could be had for near nothing if a person had the cash. Thomas and Josie were looking into purchasing a plantation on the St. Johns.

As much as I would have liked to have a country estate, a woman alone with children had best stay in St. Augustine where she could be protected by the Spanish military.

A tent city on the St. Mary's River became the temporary home of the rich and poor, free and slave alike, who waited for space on vessels to take them to the Bahamas or other colonies still held by the British. Raids of these settlements for slaves and property were common.

The departure deadline for the English had been March

19, 1785. It passed with many still in the territory and was extended to July 19.

Much to my delight, in May, Governor Zespedes and Father Hassett set up school to teach the Minorcan boys. Father Traconis was to teach. But Father Camps and my fellow Minorcans were upset because the new priests, now three, could not speak the Minorcan dialect. Father Camps was ill. He had not been home for eleven years. He wanted to retire and go back to Minorca. But he would not leave us to priests whom most of us could not even talk to.

Meanwhile, a large new Catholic church had already been begun by the Spanish. It was to hold five hundred faithful. My people were so happy they would finally have a church. They gave whatever they had to help—corn, chickens, lime, lumber. It was scheduled to be finished in a couple of years and would face the plaza on its southern side.

Times were extremely hard in St. Augustine. Spain wasn't sending money to pay troops or officials. Everything was being bought on credit by the government. Most people were living on small amounts of salt meat and flour plus a little fresh beef supplied by Senor Sanchez. Although Minorcan farmers and fishermen filled the market with produce, no one had money to buy. A few Minorcans were even forced to leave, because they could no longer make a living, but most stayed.

Finally, in mid-November, Governor Tonyn and the last of his colleagues left Florida.

Luciana Herrerra was back in town. Governor Zespedes appointed him to be in charge of Indian affairs in East Florida.

Once again Minorcans were the largest group in or near the old town.

Then, one afternoon toward the last of November, there

was a knock on the door. I opened it to find an old and weary-looking Father Camps standing there. His face was very grave. "I have discovered what really happened to your first husband," he announced.

Part Four

I

Rafael docked the *Captain's Revenge* at the St. Marys wharf. Leaving Juan and Leaping Cat in charge, he bought a horse and saddle and followed the King's Road to St. Augustine. As he approached the Andrews farm north of town, he decided to stop in and find out what the current situation was before he looked Caty up.

Thomas, Josie, their son and Josie's father were just sitting down to lunch when he knocked on the door. They invited him to join them. He was surprised to learn Thomas already knew Water Gift and Rafael were the same. Josie sent Thomas, Jr. out to play and returned to hear Rafael tell his story as though lost in reverie:

When I left Caty at the mission that first time, I was assaulted by a variety of emotions. I loved her. That could neither be denied nor changed. Nor could I refuse to respect her decision to stay with Joseph. On the darker Side, I was jealous. Joseph had it all. My wife, my child, and a life I envied. He had what I wanted—what by all rights should be mine.

There was anger and hatred for Turnbull because of the

broken promises and ill treatment that had forced us to leave New Smyrna, and at his insistence that I return. Had he kept his promises, Caty, Ana, and I would never have been separated. I also felt a terrible hatred toward those who had raided my village, killing the people I had learned to love and stealing my children.

I was frustrated. I wanted my family all together. I ached for Caty both emotionally and physically. Knowing she felt the same made it all the more frustrating that it couldn't be—not then, maybe never. I had fought the urge to do what a man and his wife, who love each other, normally and rightfully do when they are alone and in the grip of passion. Even at the time I felt I could have continued with very little protest—and that not heartfelt, from Caty. On the other hand, I could not help but think of the future. I love Caty. I didn't want to cause her any more suffering. I knew that after our passion was spent, she would find it hard to live with herself. Her huge conscience would feel she had betrayed Joseph even while she carried his child. I loved her too much to increase her suffering.

Too, there was the frustration of not being able to claim Ana as mine, not being able to be her father.

I felt so bruised and battered by conflicting emotions—love, hate, anger, and a deep sense of responsibility toward Caty, Ana, Margarita, Juan, and yes, even Joseph. And also to my conscience which I could not escape. I felt cheated. Cheated out of my wife and all three of my children. And the confusing part was, I didn't know on whose shoulders to place the blame.

I knew, however, the first thing I must concentrate on was finding the twins. I could not waste time feeling sorry for myself. Whatever was to happen, I had to make it happen. I would find whoever was responsible for taking them. When I did, I planned to exact a terrible revenge.

Caty and I had arranged for me to see Ana in the market.

When I finally saw my daughter, I knew I would have recognized her anywhere. She looked exactly like Caty. When she saw me, she was afraid. I suppose a scar-face savage who stares at children would be frightening to most people. I longed to go to her, to tell her I, not Joseph, am her father. If it hadn't been for the fright in her eyes, I might have done just that, in spite of my promise. But then, I heard a gasp. Josie had seen and recognized me. So that was all I had—just a brief glimpse of the child Caty and I had sacrificed our chances of being together for when we left New Smyrna. I had never doubted she would be worth it, even had I truly drowned in that hurricane.

When I left the market, I followed some local Indians to their village on the outskirts of town. They put me up in the house reserved for guests. One man seemed particularly friendly, a young man about my age. He was called Tony, having been baptized Antonio by a priest during the Spanish reign in Florida. Tony spoke both of the Seminole dialects; I offered him employment as a guide and interpreter. He accepted. A few days later he said good-bye to his pretty young wife and baby to lead me to the first Indian village I would visit.

We left St. Augustine and headed west to Picolata where we crossed the St. Johns River on the ferry. We camped for the night at the Poopoa Fort on the banks of the river. The next day we continued west into land such as I had never seen in Florida. I had thought the whole territory flat, but here there were rolling hills and, in the valleys, ponds and lakes. This part of Florida was supposed to be reserved for the Indians. Whites traveled west of the St. Johns River at their own risk.

The hilly country contained tall pine forests, sandy live oak hammocks, scrub oak, cactus and sandhill pines. The ground was treacherous to the feet of the horses, because here, there, and everywhere were the holes of gopher tortoises. The hills continued to grow in height and size until we reached what is called the "backbone" of Florida. As we continued on, the hills decreased in size, and we reached a flat plain of grass, palmetto, and short shrubs. Then we again entered forest from which we emerged on the vast flat, grassy area Tony called the Alachua Plains.

"We are in the lands of the Alachua Indians," he said. "Their chief is called Se-Pe-Coffee. His village is Cuscowilla on the lake of the same name. The cattle and horses that roam the plains of Alachua belong to his people. That is why the British have another name for him; they call him Chief Cow Keeper."

We passed many small villages of this tribe. Four days out of St. Augustine we rode into the town of Cuscowilla. I was surprised at how different the Alachua villages were from the Calusa village where I had lived on an island south of Florida's coast. It was even different from the Seminole village of Brave Eagle west of the Big Water.

There were no palm-thatched chickees here. These Indians households contained at least two buildings, both much larger than chickees, to a family. One, the winter house, contained two rooms—the kitchen and bedroom. This is used in cold and wet weather. The other is some distance away and contains a second story. Its upstairs porch is the summer bedroom. The house itself is used to store food and other belongings. When the weather is hot, cooking is done in the yard. There were also some separate granaries and warehouses.

The walls and roofs of the houses were of cypress bark over wooden posts and frames. Each collection of buildings stood in the center of a square, clean-swept yard surrounded by a low earthen wall.

Cuscowilla had about thirty such homes and a meeting house. The lake was a few hundred feet downhill from the village. It had a sandy beach, and one end grew orange, magnolia, live oak, and palm trees. Tall pines were sparsely scattered between the village and the lake. It was pretty and clean.

Each home had a garden which grew corn, tobacco, and beans. A couple of miles away at the edge of the Alachua Savannah, the community garden grew most of their vegetables and potatoes. We had passed it on our way into the town and had seen children and elders chasing away crows. Some of the boys killed squirrel and small game that came to raid the garden with their bows and arrows. Tony said the men took turns guarding the garden from deer, bear, and raccoons at night.

We had followed a creek into town and were welcomed by some young Indians who led us to the chief's house. It stood on the highest ridge and was larger than the others. As we dismounted, our horses were led away to food and water. The chief and several elders shook our arms in the Indian salutation. The chief led us to the meeting house where Chief Se-Pe-Coffee passed his pipe around for us to smoke with him.

After we had smoked, a large bowl of liquid was served from a wooden dipper passed from the chief to each in turn until we had all drunk from it.

The chief asked in the Muscogee dialect what had brought us to Cuscowilla. I told him about my village in the keys, that while I was away it had been raided by unknown persons, the men and old people killed, and the women and young stolen. I asked if he knew anything that would help me find my children. I thought they might have been taken by Indians or pirates and sold as slaves. Tony translated.

The chief asked, "How did you, a white, come to be in the Calusa village?"

"I was shipwrecked and washed ashore. When I recovered from my injuries, I was adopted by Chief Leaping Cat and named Water Gift. His niece became my wife," I explained.

Chief Se-Pe-Coffee had an unusual presence. Even seated, I noted he was tall, his shoulders were wide, arms and legs muscular and his hips narrow. His face was leathered and wrinkled, belying the youthful-appearing body. The man had to be well past sixty. His dark eyes, however, held a lively sparkle above a long, narrow nose. His head was shaved except for a strip in the middle which stood up a couple of inches high. A loose braid of still mostly black hair hung from the back of his head. Tony had told me the Alachua were formerly called Oconee, part of the Lower Creek Nation who wore their hair in this fashion. The chief wore a breech cloth and was tattooed around both thighs, his upper arms, and neck from his chest to his back in zig zag patterns and banded designs. Around his neck he wore a silver chain with a tiny silver crucifix.

"Tell us about the village you speak of near the Big Water. We do not know of it. The one you were visiting when your village was raided," Chief Se-Pe-Coffee said.

I told him all I knew of it and added, "Perhaps you do not know of it because it has been there such a short time, less than two years, I think."

"They did not get there by land. They could not have passed through here without my knowing it," he said.

"We have many slaves among our people. We raid the Americans in Georgia and Alabama who steal our land and property and kill many of us. There are no twins among our slaves. You may mingle freely with my people and search among our slaves as you wish. You will not find any of your people here. I'm sorry. I cannot help you," the chief told me.

Among Se-Pe-Coffee's slaves were many Yamasee captives. They were treated almost as members of the families who owned them. Many had been taken in marriage by the Alachua Indians. Their children were free members of the tribe. Even the children of slaves who married each other were free. But nowhere in this village was there a member of my former tribe, nor any information about them.

While we were in the town, other visitors arrived, a band of about one hundred East Florida Rangers led by Colonel Thomas Brown. They were white and Negro, English and cracker. Instead of uniforms they wore hunting shirts, breeches, and leggings. They were here to plan a raid with the Alachua into American territory where they would plunder, burn crops, steal cattle and horses, and take slaves, both Negro and Indian. The cattle they would divide between the chief and the British in St. Augustine to replace those previously stolen by Americans on similar raids into Florida.

After the meeting a huge feast was held. During the festivities I was engaged in conversation by one of the rangers. Having noticed that Colonel Brown's head had no hair, only skin that was scarred and shiny, I asked the young ranger why his leader was friendly with Indians when one had scalped him.

"Oh, no. That wasn't done by Indians. The colonel was a royalist living in Georgia. He was caught by American rebels. They tarred, feathered, and scalped him up in Augusta. He went to St. Augustine after and asked the governor to give him some rangers to lead, so we could retaliate and get revenge," he said. "The Americans have been raiding into Florida, so Governor Tonyn was happy to have Colonel Brown to help and to get cattle to feed the British, what with blockades, raids, and all."

The Indians had prepared barbecued and stewed beef, vegetables from their gardens, and cornmeal cakes with honey in honor of the rangers. After supper there was music and dancing. I saw some of the young, unmarried Alachua girls and some of the town's prostitutes, the only women who painted themselves, giggling and eyeing some of the rangers. I watched as first one and then another approached rangers and drifted off with them. My guide, Tony, was also alert to what was happening. "Time for us to return to the guest house and go to bed," he said. "If one of those girls favors you, and you refuse, she could make trouble for you. I have a wife. I am a Christian. If you are interested, you can stay."

"No," I said. "I have enough problems." I had not told him about Caty and Ana. He only knew about Flamingo and the twins.

Early the next morning, having satisfied myself that I would not find my children here, we left to visit the other Alachua Indian villages that were scattered in the vicinity. This, too, proved futile. We found no one in any of these villages who had been a member of my little tribe, nor any information about them.

So we headed for Tallahassoc on the Suwanee River. Tony told me this was another main town of the Seminoles. Seminole was the name given by the Spanish to the various upper and lower Creek Indians that had run away from the Americans into Florida, he explained. But the Indians called themselves the People of the Peninsula. Their villages were scattered in much of East and West Florida.

The area of the Tallahassoc is gently rolling hills and wet savannas, occasional lakes, rivers and ponds called sink holes, as well as forests of stately pines. Springs in the area flow water, cold and clear, into lakes and the Suwanee River. We frequently saw wild game as well as herds of Seminole horses. The Indians here sometimes used dogs to keep the horses together. In the town there was a trading post. The town itself sat on a bluff about twenty-five feet tall on the east bank of the river. It held about thirty homes similar to those in chief Se-Pe-Coffee's town.

The Tallahassoc villagers built cypress longboats very much like those of the First People in which to hunt and trade. The chief was called the White King. I gathered this meant he was the king of the "peaceful" village, since I had learned white was the Indian symbol of peace, red that of war.

The chief was of middle age and medium height. He seemed on the one hand to be a dignified and royal ruler; his friendly smile and the wrinkles it caused at the corners of his eyes showed him to be kindly, also.

I told him why I had come to his village. He was sympathetic. Like Chief Se-Pe-Coffee, he assured me he had never raided my village in the keys, nor even visited it, although he said his men followed the Suwanee into the gulf and hunted down the west coast of Florida as well as some of the keys. They also took their dugouts to the Bahama Islands and Cuba to trade. In fact, we drank coffee with sugar and smoked tobacco which I was told had come from Cuba. They also got liquor there. For these they bartered honey, deer hides, fur, beeswax, bear oil, and dried fish. I also learned the Spanish traded at St. Marks and other ports on the Gulf.

The White King, too, gave me permission to roam his village in order to satisfy myself that none of my people were there. So far I had found only friendly Indians, and at each village had been honored with a feast. This village was no exception.

In the village Tony and I saw captives, but again, I recognized none. And as always they were well treated.

Among the inhabitants of the village I saw several people, both men and women, whose ears were missing. I asked Tony why their ears had been cut off. He said, "Among these Indians, when someone commits adultery and is caught, the punishment is to crop the ears of the guilty. Those without ears are forever disgraced. Everyone can see who they are and know their crime."

That evening we were summoned to the public square by the sound of drums and the tempting smell of broiled meat. Only the chief, shamans, warriors, Tony, and I feasted in the square. After we had eaten, the rest of the food was divided between the villagers, who carried it to their homes as was their custom when there were visitors. Then the chief invited us to accompany him to the council house.

Inside the chief and elders sat on one bench, warriors on another at their right. The bench on the left was reserved for visitors, and we were motioned to it.

We smoked Cuban tobacco from the chief's pipe as it was passed to us. Then we drank weak white drink that did not make us sick, but was rather like that used by whites in Florida and called Cassiene tea.

Next we returned to the square where there was music and dancing all night. The music was made on drums of stretched animal skins, some drums containing water, dried gourds made into rattles and flutes from reeds. Several Indians sang songs of love.

Tony and I left the dance and retired before the dancing was over. The melancholy air of the soft music filled the guest house with its sound. My memory returned to St. Augustine—to Caty. I could now understand some of the Muscogee language and the songs of love that drifted on the breeze stirred my emotions. I tossed and turned. I thought of what could not be. I remembered a sweet time in a little sand-bottom stream so long ago. Caty and I had frolicked in the water and then made sweet, passionate love. I wanted her so much. My need was both immediate and forever. How could I continue to stay in the same world with her and allow her to live with another man? So the night passed in agonizing thoughts that tortured me mentally and physically. When sleep finally claimed me, I dreamed I had led an Indian raid on St. Augustine. We killed Joseph Adams and captured his family. I awoke covered with sweat, my heart pounding wildly in my chest, in terror and loathing for what I had done in my dream.

We visited other Seminole villages, but the result was always the same. We were treated with kindness, but found no one nor any clue to aid in my search.

We returned to St. Augustine briefly. Tony visited his family. I saw Caty and Ana in the market. I told Caty to meet me in the old mission where we had met before. When she arrived she was angry at first. I knew I was disrupting her life. I'm sure one part of her wished I would disappear again, that she felt my return complicated her life beyond reason. But I had to see her, to hold her. And perhaps it was perverse, but I wanted to stay in her thoughts, as she was in mine. I couldn't give up the hope that someday she'd be mine again. I didn't want her to forget how it felt to be in my arms. I knew I held a magnetism for her. She melted when I touched her. I wanted to remind her of that, not by anything I said, because she had already won that battle, but by holding her in my arms, kissing her, causing her to want more—just as I did. Oh, yes, she had that power over me, too. It was a thing of its own, besides the love and concern we felt for each other. Yet, it was a part of that, too. All that we had was too overwhelming, too wonderful, to just give it up.

We left the old town to continue our search among the Indians. This trip we were headed for the Yuchee Indian town on the Chatahoochee River. We again passed through the Tallahassoc territory and stopped to visit our friends. We were told a very important visitor was present. His name was Alexander McGillivray, a partner in the trading firm of Panton-Leslie. But his importance stemmed from more than that.

When I met McGillivray, I was surprised to see he was an Indian. He was twenty-one years old, a tall man with black eyes, bronze skin, high cheekbones, and a beakish nose. He wore a red turban around his head and long, dangling ear-rings fell from his earlobes. Around his neck were beads and a silver gorget. The red jacket of the British military hung comfortably from his shoulders. I was intrigued by this man and his conflicting name, face, and apparel. When we talked, he turned the conversation to me. He seemed genuinely interested and sympathetic when he heard my story.

McGillivray was staying in quarters belong to the trading company and invited me to visit him there. After he had asked all the questions he wanted of me, and I had answered, apparently to his satisfaction, I asked some of him.

"You speak English and Muscogee equally well. You look Indian, yet your name is McGillivray. You seem well educated in both the English and the Indian sense. You have me completely confused. Would you mind telling me about yourself?"

He laughed and said, "My father was a Scotch trader. My mother's father was a Frenchman. I was schooled in Charleston by a cousin, Reverend Farquhar McGillivray. When my education was done, I returned to my mother's tribe, the Oconee. She was of the Wind Clan, so through my inheritance I am a chief.

"I consider myself Indian. You know, of course, that Indians inherit from their mothers. My only Indian grandparent was my mother's mother," he said.

"My wife, Flamingo, was of the Wind Clan. She was a shaman. Her Uncle, brother of her mother, was chief. My daughter was to be a shaman, also, and my son, chief," I said.

"How did you come to be involved with Panton Leslie, if you don't mind telling me? You seem to have bridged both worlds better than anyone I've yet heard of," I said.

"William Panton is Scottish, as is my father. Both are loyalists. My father's estates were taken by the Americans. He returned to Scotland. When Panton approached me to become part of his trading concern, it was to our mutual benefit. We neither like the Americans. They take Indian property. They take British property. If they complete their design to oust Britain from the American colonies and the Floridas, Panton Leslie could be replaced by American traders. And there may not be any Indians left in either place.

"Panton needs me if he wants the Indian trade. No matter who finally ends up with Florida, if there are Indians here, I can secure their trade for him. The Indians need Panton, too. He helps us by getting British protection for our lands. He sells us guns and ammunition to protect ourselves. The British need me to enlist the help of my people. They have made me commissary to the Creeks. All presents and arms to my people come through me. I am a colonel in the British army. I bring the British forty-five thousand Indian allies.

"I have one ambition. I love my Creek Nation. I want what is best for my people. To achieve security and help for Creeks and other tribes, I will be as sly as they are," he said.

I liked McGillivray from the start. He was leaving Tallahassoc in a few days for Pensacola. He would be passing through the Yuchee village and asked us to accompany him that far.

We traveled together for six or seven days on the way to the Chatahoochie River, following the old Spanish trail that connects St. Augustine, capitol of East Florida, with Pensacola, capitol of West Florida. McGillivray and his party of seven braves were well provisioned. Two of his party caught fresh fish or killed game daily for us. We arrived on the Chatahoochie River bank to be met by members of the Yuchee tribe, who were expecting McGillivray's party. They carried us and our belongings across the river to their town.

Here I saw a completely different village than any I had seen yet. It was also the largest. The well-built houses were red clay plastered over a wooden frame with cypress shingle roofs. More than a thousand people lived here. Their language was similar to the Calusa language of the First People. McGillivray said it was the Sioux tongue. These Indians were not of the Creek Nation. Although they were not exactly friends, they had joined with the Creeks to promote the general welfare of Indians in their struggle with the whites.

The Yuchees did not look like Indians at all. They were

tall, handsome people with fair skin and blue eyes. They called themselves Children of the Sun. They had other towns in Tennessee, South Carolina, Georgia, and West Florida.

McGillivray himself seemed well liked by the Yuchee and was received as royalty by the villagers. When he was invited into the council house by the chief, he insisted that I accompany him. Even before he discussed his business with the chief, he told him my unfortunate story. But I was not to find my children in this village, either.

The next day, after yet another night of feasting, we said our good-byes to the Yuchee people and to my new friend, Alexander McGillivray. He invited me to visit him in Pensacola where he would be staying at Panton-Leslie's head-quarters for West Florida for some time. He promised to use his power to find out anything that might help me to find my children.

Then Tony and I, in a canoe borrowed from the Yuchees, headed up the Appalachicola River to the Indian town of Appalachicola. It was built on a high bank. Tony told me Appalachicola is to the Creek Confederacy like St. Augustine is to East Florida, a capitol city. It is also a safe place where there is always peace, and Indians cannot be harmed or punished there.

Here I didn't find my children, nor did I learn anything to help me. But I learned the town was a sanctuary and about a mile away there had been another town by the same name in the past that had been abandoned about twenty-five years previous. The Indians believed it haunted, because they had once burned all the white traders to the area in a house in that town. Tony showed the old town to me. There were mounds here such as those I had seen on one of the keys which used to be a great and ancient city. The mounds formed terraces. The river sometimes flooded parts of it.

The inhabitants separated and formed several villages, one being the new Appalachicola town. Others built villages farther down the river, some on the gulf coast. The next town, Coweta, is called the bloody town. In Coweta death sentences and punishments are carried out. This is also where parties assemble for war against common enemies. These two are the leading towns of Lower Creek peoples.

Disappointed and heartsick at not yet having learned anything of help in finding my children, we returned to the Yuchee town to trade their canoe for our horses and turned again toward St. Augustine. It was nearing time for Caty to have her baby. I intended to be there when the baby came.

I waited in the market square all day, but saw neither Caty nor Ana. I walked down St. George Street to her house. I stood on the street near her gate trying to decide whether I should knock at her door, knowing she would not want me to do so. A neighborhood boy came out of a nearby house and skipped past me. He, too, was Minorcan, so I spoke to him in my native tongue. I gave him a coin to knock on Caty's door and inquire about her, saying that his mother had sent him. I learned Caty was at the farm of Thomas and Josefina Andrews.

A man farther down the street gave me directions to the Andrews farm. Instead of going to the house, I went into the fields in search of Andrews, whom I had never met. When I found him, he was with Caty's Uncle Gaspar. The old man showed no signs of recognizing me. I asked in English if Andrews would let me work for him in exchange for a place to sleep and meals. To my surprise, he hired me.

A few days later I went to see Caty. I was alarmed to find her pale, weak, and with swollen limbs and a puffy face. Her condition frightened me.

The day the baby came, everyone had gone off to a barn raising, leaving Caty all alone. If I hadn't been there, I can't bear to think of what might have happened to Caty and her child. Thank God I was there, and I got the doctor and Mandy there in time.

I was in the room when the child was born. Mandy saved the baby's life, I am convinced, when she used her weight to force the baby to leave Caty's womb. The cord was wrapped around the child's neck and was holding him back. He was turning blue.

When I saw that child emerge from Caty's body, saw that new life take his first breath, I cannot describe the emotions I felt. It was as though I had witnessed a miracle. I suppose that is what birth is, after all: a miracle. I felt the most over- whelming feeling of tenderness toward that new, tiny, help- less being. And toward my Caty, who, just as the Bible says, had gone down "into the valley of the shadow of death" to give life to him.

Then Mandy saw me. In a fit of indignance, she chased me from the room. When I next saw Caty, she was nursing the baby. What a beautiful picture they made! And I wanted them both to be my family, along with Ana.

I spent most of each afternoon at the Andrews farm with Ana. She had become so dear to me. She was no longer afraid, and we so enjoyed each other's company. I found her beauti- ful and intelligent. She was kind and self-sufficient. No one would ever push her around. She was strong, eager to help, and capable.

Oh, how I wanted to tell her I am her father! It nearly broke my heart when it was time to tell her good-bye.

I didn't leave until I was sure Caty had regained her health. I hoped and prayed she would change her mind. That she would again be my wife. I could have loved the baby as my own. But she still could not bring herself to hurt Joseph, although I am sure she loved me. But, then, I know it is possible to love two spouses at the same time. I had loved Flamingo and Caty. I would never understand how it could happen, but I knew it could. I could not force Caty to come back to me.

So once again I left my beloved in what, so far, had been a vain and futile attempt to find Flamingo's and my children.

I visited the Alabama Indians whose village is in the fork of the Tallapoose and Coosa Rivers where they join the Alabama. They spoke the same language, and their village was similar to Creek villages.

I visited the Choctaw. The men of this tribe let their hair grow long and hang free. The men also had flattened heads. They reformed the heads of boy babies by using a hinged board attached to the baby's board to press the forehead. They thought this made a man more attractive.

I visited the Micosuki, the Apalache, the Yamasees. I found nothing that would help me find my children.

When I returned to St. Augustine, I was feeling extremely low. I had visited Indian villages for nearly a year and had searched for a year before that in the islands and keys south of Florida. I still had no clue.

Then I saw Caty and Ana in the plaza. Joseph and the baby were with them. Ana recognized me. Joseph saw me. I fled.

Later that day Tony told me he had heard Alexander McGillivray was in town. He was said to be staying at the inn on St. Francis Street across from the barracks.

When I arrived at the inn I was greeted by the proprietress, an English woman named Mary Hudson. She was an elderly lady of perhaps sixty. I inquired if Mr. McGillivray was presently staying here, and she led me through the house and out into a beautifully landscaped yard where McGillivray sat on a bench near the kitchen. He looked up from the papers he was reading. Upon recognizing me, his face broke into a broad smile, and he arose to grip my arms in greeting.

"I am so glad to see you," he said. "I had no idea you would be in St. Augustine. However, I have not forgotten you and your quest. I have come across some information that might be of help to you. Remember the Indian chief, Brave Eagle?"

"You mean the chief of the Seminole tribe on the Big Water? Yes, of course. How could I forget him?" I asked.

"Well, he is not a Seminole, for starters. He is the son of a chief's sister of the Tunica tribe. His father was a Spanish trader. His village was on the west bank of the Mississippi River not far from the gulf. He was educated by Catholic priests in Cuba. When he returned to his villages he led the Tunicas in raids on English boats traveling the Mississippi. Then he became involved with taking and selling Indians he captured from neighboring tribes.

"When his uncle died, he was to inherit the chiefdom. Among his tribe the chief is the absolute ruler, the king, you know? He could not wait for the chief to die to have that kind of power, so the tribe eventually split. He left with about half of the villagers. It is believed he was also joined by members of other tribes. The Tunica were great friends with the French, but he associated with evil elements in that society—pirates and the like.

"At any rate, no one seemed to know where Brave Eagle led his faction of Tunicas. But you have found him," McGillivray said.

"Do you think, then, that Brave Eagle has the answer to what happened to my village? My children?" I asked.

"Have you found any other leads?"

"No."

"Then I think you would be wise to pursue this one."

"What about the Spanish girl, Maria, Brave Eagle's consort?"

"I believe she may be the widowed daughter of a nobleman, an official of Spanish Mexico. She and her small son were aboard a ship bound for Cuba. It was last seen in the Florida Strait and never arrived in Cuba. It is widely believed the ship was looted by pirates and either destroyed or stolen," he said. "The woman on board the ship was named Maria de la Rosa."

It all fit together. She had to be the Maria I had met. The Indian, Brave Eagle, must have been the half-Spanish Tunica.

I felt a new surge of hope. I would return to the village where Flamingo had nursed Maria's son through the sleeping sickness. I did not know if Maria was with him because she chose to be, but she owed her son's life to Flamingo. The least she could do was to help me find Flamingo's children.

The next morning I went to the farm to see Josefina. I told her what had happened in the plaza and asked her to tell Caty I was sorry if it caused her a problem. I wanted her to tell Caty I loved her, and I didn't know when I would be back, but I would return as soon as I could.

As I was leaving the Andrews place, a man on horseback was heading for it. He called to me, and I recognized Joseph. I turned my horse and spurred him in an attempt to leave before we came face to face. But I was too late. Joseph called, "Rafael!" He had already recognized me.

I drew back the reins to halt my horse. There was nothing to do but face him. I must admit I felt a flood of relief wash over me. I would no longer have to live a lie to spare him.

We talked for perhaps an hour. He had seen me in the plaza even before Ana had. He had noticed me watching Caty and Ana. He thought there was something familiar about me. But when he had tried to discuss me with Caty, she would change the subject. I had been on his mind, and when he saw me on the horse, and I had tried to run, he suddenly knew who I was.

I had no choice but to tell him the whole story. But I, no more than Caty, hadn't the courage to tell him Caty still loved me. Nor would Caty have wanted me to. But she was right about him. He seemed to age before my eyes. It appeared as though I had lain the weight of the world on his shoulders. I felt a sudden kinship with him. However, he felt Caty should not know that we had met, that he knew I was alive and well. When he asked me if I still loved Caty, I could not lie. I could never lie about that. Even if I had, I felt sure he could look at me and tell I was being untruthful. So I said, "I will love Caty until my dying day, and then from beyond the grave."

He nodded and lowered his head to look at the ground. He pushed at the sand with the toe of his boot. I saw a tear escape the corner of his eye and fall unchecked down his cheek. There was nothing more to say, so I mounted my horse and started to ride off. Without raising his head, Joseph said, "I, too, will love her always. I promise you, Rafael, to take the best of care of her and of Ana. You are a better man than I. Feeling as we both do, I could never give her up—I wouldn't want to live without either of them. I will no doubt feel guilt. But surely life without her would be so much more painful.

"Thank you, Rafael. Thank you for—how can I put into words all that I have to thank you for? I suppose I mean thank you for my family. Thank you for allowing me to continue the life I am leading. I will pray for you. And for your children," he said.

I turned away. I could say nothing. I felt as though my emotions were choking me. I spurred my horse viciously and left Joseph standing there, unable to raise his head and look me in the eye. I did not know how to respond to a man who had just thanked me for giving my family to him.

I rode until my horse was lathered. Then I dismounted by a creek, watered and tethered him. I sat beneath an oak and thought about Caty. About Ana. I don't know how long I sat there while waves of despair washed over me. Then I remembered my meeting with McGillivray. I had to push all else from my mind and concentrate on finding my children. That had to come first. I would deal with everything else after I had found them. Now I had to plan what I must do next.

It was nearly dark when I finally had a vague plan in my head. I first had to see McGillivray once more. He had told me he was meeting Mr. Leslie at Leslie-Panton's St. August-ine trading post this evening. I headed there and found him just preparing to leave. I told him I needed to hire a half-dozen

Indians from the Suwanee River village. Would he somehow help me to get some who were trustworthy and brave? He again proved to be an invaluable aid and friend.

"I will give you a peace pipe. You can show it to any Indians you meet. Tell them Alexander McGillivray gave it to you, because you are my friend and I wish you to be treated well. It will guarantee you safe passage and any help you need will be given to you," he said.

I could never thank him enough. But I needed one more thing. I needed a Kentucky long rifle and ammunition. He arranged for me to buy one right then from Mr. Leslie.

The next morning Tony and I left St. Augustine to go to Tallahassoc. We were warmly greeted on our arrival. When we met with the White King again, I told him McGillivray had sent me to him. He was impressed and most eager to help when I showed him the pipe the leader of the Creek Confederacy had given me. I told him I needed six strong, trustworthy men who knew the west coast of Florida and the keys and islands beyond. I also need a longboat and provisions. I would pay.

We were in the village a week before we had the necessary provisions and men to start my mission. During that time I was in a very agitated state. Now that I finally had a lead, I was anxious to move on it. Finally the White King called me to his home. Already there, six other Indians sat on the upstairs porch of the summer house with him, enjoying a gentle breeze and smoking tobacco rolled up in some sort of leaf.

When I had climbed the ladder to the porch, I was immediately given some of the same to smoke.

The White King said, "Your longboat and provisions are ready. These are your men. (He motioned to each one and called his name) Long Arrow, Brown Bear, Red Bird, Crazy Fox, Alligator Teeth, and Bent Knife. They are at your command. They have made many trips down the coast and to the islands beyond, and are loyal, brave, good hunters and fishermen."

The men ranged in age from about eighteen to forty-five. The youngest, Brown Bear, was tall and muscular with wide-set eyes, a long, aquiline nose, generous mouth, and a strong chin. In contrast, Alligator Teeth was small and wiry with a sharp face, close-set eyes, a nose bent slightly to one side, and teeth that were irregular and protruding. He was in his mid-thirties. The oldest, Bent Knife, was also tall, a powerfully built man with a ragged scar on his left cheek and shoulder. His face was round, his nose large and wide.

Crazy Fox and Red Bird were brothers, both in their middle twenties. They were of medium height. Crazy Fox was slim and Red Bird chunky. Their faces strongly resembled each other, each having thick eyebrows, beakish noses, and cleft chins.

But Long Arrow was the one whose appearance was exceptional. He was perhaps thirty. He had the same intelligent, dark eyes, wide cheekbones, and high-standing strip of hair down the middle of his head which was shaved on both sides as the other Indians'. However, he stood a good foot taller than any of them. He had to be over seven feet in height. His shoulders were the widest, his upper arm muscles the largest I had ever seen. When he stood, he crossed his arms on his chest and gazed down at everyone from deep-set eyes under what appeared to be a single lowered eyebrow that went from over the outer edge of the left eye to over the outer edge of the right in an unbroken line. He looked as if he could lift any one of us and snap us in two in a split second.

Observing my scrutiny of the man he had assigned me, the White King said, "Long Arrow will be the next chief. His mother is my sister. You would do well to appoint him your second in command. The men respect him. He has proven himself to be a leader among men as well as excelling in battle, hunting, fishing, rowing, and navigation. He speaks

the Tunica language. The others have all pledged their loyalty to him. Because I have said so, he will be loyal to you."

"It is done as you say, Mico," I said. Mico is the Seminole
word for leader. I had now learned their language passably
well.

I turned to Long Arrow. "As well as my second, you will
be my navigator. We will leave early in the morning," I said.

II

The cypress dugout was about twenty-five feet long and had been well provisioned. We took our places in it, Long Arrow in the bow and I immediately behind him. Tony, then the other Creeks, were behind me. We were eight in all. Lifting our paddles we began our journey down the Suwanee a short way, then into the gulf where we followed the west coast of Florida. We would search for the entrance to a river leading to the Big Water and the village of the Tunica chief, Brave Eagle.

I had known nothing of Indians before arriving in New Smyrna. I had rarely seen an Indian while there. Those in the area were referred to as Seminole. In St. Augustine the Indians had been Seminole, too. But the Indians I had lived with, the First People, were definitely not the same as any others I had seen. However, Chief Brave Eagle's people had appeared to me to be the same as the Seminole. I had apparently been wrong.

I had since visited villages of Yamasee, Yuchee, Apalache, Micosuki, Choctaw, Alachua, and Alabama. Except for Tony, the Indians under my command were from the village of

Tallahassoc, and were Lower Creeks. Most of the others were sub tribes of either the Upper or Lower Creeks. To make things more confusing, it seemed all of those who settled in Florida were lumped together under the one name by the English, meaning runaway—Seminole.

The first day we traveled down the Suwanee into the Gulf Sea, then south to an island where a small village of Indians related to the Tallahassoc villagers lived. We were well received, and after spending the night, we resumed our travel down the coast to another village tucked into a bay on the banks of a river which flowed crystal water into the gulf. The water was home to scores of playful seacows that we were careful not to startle. Should one come up under or jump on the canoe, its great size and weight could cause a catastrophe.

The Indians of this village were also friends to the Tallahassoc, and one of our group, Bent Knife, had a sister here who was married to a villager.

On the third day we camped in a tiny cove with a white, sandy beach. Tony and Red Bird speared fish which we barbecued for supper. We had seen no sign of human activity here other than where Long Arrow showed me he had made previous overnight camps.

We were all tired from our third day of constant rowing and fell into a deep sleep after supper. Sometime during the night we were awakened by a loud crash. Our campfire had died away. The night was moonless, pitch black. We could feel the vibration of heavy footsteps better than we could hear their thud on the soft sand. But as we could see nothing, we didn't know what to do, where to go.

Suddenly someone yelled, "Run! We are not alone! Into the trees, quick!"

We were unable to see. Having been awakened from a sound sleep, we were disoriented, our directions uncertain. We ran into each other. Some ran into the surf. Someone ran into it. "It" was large, furry, and smelled extremely familiar. It also ran, confused by the pandemonium. It knocked Tony, Red Bird and Alligator Teeth down in its haste and confusion. Panic reigned. Finally, someone found the trees, yelling, "Over here!"

We all ran in that direction, tripping and falling in our fear and haste. I found the trunk of a tree and began to climb into its outstretched limbs. Too late, I learned I was in the same tree with it. We both vacated the tree at the same time. By the grace of God, I did not land on it, nor it on me. I heard it running through the leaves and then crashing through the palmettos for several minutes before the sounds faded into the distance.

Long Arrow said, "It's gone now. We can go back to camp, if we can find it. We'll light a new fire, and this time we will post a guard to keep the fire going and watch for intruders."

"What was it? It smelled familiar. We ended up in the same tree," I said.

"When we light the fire, I'm sure you will find bear tracks. It was probably after our food," Long Arrow said.

Sure enough, a bear had been in our camp. It had eaten the remains of the fish we'd had for supper. We had turned the dugout over on top of our supplies, and the noise which had awakened us was probably the bear throwing it off our provisions. Luckily, we had scared him off before he had eaten our food supply or done further damage.

Crazy Fox was appointed to be on guard until dawn, just a few hours away. I slept nervously the rest of the night, my Kentucky long rifle by my side.

In the light of day the events of the night seemed funny, and many jokes were made about it as we prepared breakfast, ate, and broke up camp. We resumed our journey. Late in the day we entered a passage between the peninsula and a barrier island. We stayed the night on the island, posting a guard to be changed every two hours.

On day five we entered a huge bay and traveled northeast across it to an Indian village on the Hillsborough River. The chief of this village greeted us warmly. He invited us into his home to smoke the pipe with him. He was interested to know what had brought us to his village.

I told him I was searching for a river from the gulf that went into the lake called Big Water.

"You want to go to Okeechobee? There is a tribe there that is jealous of that area. It is dangerous," he said.

"Do you know Chief Brave Eagle?" I asked.

"I know of him. Small bands of his braves have driven our people out of the bay of Caloosahatchee. The Caloosahatchee River flows from the Okeechobee. We have seen pirate ships come and go there. That is not a good place," he said.

A sudden feeling of elation flowed through me. At last I was sure I was on the right track. I told the chief about my village and what had happened. I said, "I have to go there. I must find out if he had anything to do with taking my children and killing my people. He is the only clue I have."

He replenished our supplies and had a feast prepared for our supper. He told us we were about four days from Caloosahatchee. It would be a wide river past another large bay named Charlotte by the Spanish.

Long Arrow was familiar with Charlotte Harbor and the Bay of Caloosahatchee, but had never gone into the river.

Four days later, we arrived at the mouth of the Caloosahatchee River. We spent part of the night on an island in the bay. Several hours before daylight we entered the river. Under cover of darkness we paddled into it. At dawn we pulled the canoe into the bushes, swept away our tracks with shrubs, and hid the boat. Brown Bear and Alligator Teeth went in search of game. Long Arrow and I scouted the area.

At midday we cooked and ate four rabbits the hunters had gotten and settled down for a nap. After dark we would continue to follow the river.

Just before dark, Tony, who had been on guard, awakened me. I could hear voices coming from the river. I went to the bank and hid in the trees. A brig was coming from the bay. After it had passed, I went back to wake the others. We ate cornmeal cakes and pemmican, put the dugout back into the water, erased our tracks, and paddled down river after the brig. Several hours later we came upon it at anchor. All was quiet aboard. Several dugout canoes were tied to the ship, but the Indians who owned them must have been sleeping aboard with the pirates. We paddled quietly past the ship. The river narrowed suddenly here. This, then, was the port used by the pirates. We continued down the river until just before dawn, when we again hid our dugout and made camp onshore.

After daylight we could see a well-worn path ran along the northern bank of the river. Fortunately, we had chosen the south bank for our camp.

That night we again manned the dugout after dark to continue our journey to the village. A couple of hours before daylight the river widened into a lake, and I heard a dog bark in the distance. I remembered the village was near this lake which was much smaller than the Okeechobee. We hid the canoe, and Long Arrow and I headed in the direction of the barking dog.

We were soon on the edge of the village. We gave it wide berth as we skirted it. We passed the garden and the horse corral. Presently we were behind the house of Brave Eagle. We lay on our bellies and slithered as close as we dared. The chief had replaced his open chickee with a thatched house on stilts, as had many of the other villagers. His was larger than any other and stood farther apart.

Shortly after daylight Chief Brave Eagle and little Esteban emerged and met some other Indians. They went to the corral, mounted, and left the village headed in the direction of the river. I sent Long Arrow to follow them until he found out where they were going and when they'd be back.

Within a little over an hour, Long Arrow returned. He said, "They left the village at a slow pace. It was easy to keep up on foot. They followed the path on the north shore. I heard them say they were going to the port to unload the pirate ship and bring the cargo here. They took covered wagons. The wagons should return here in the afternoon of the third day from now."

Maria emerged from her house. She was impeccably groomed. Her fair skin gleamed and her lustrous black hair hung down her back in one long, thick braid tied with a blue ribbon. She wore a blue tunic of soft cotton that left her slender arms bare. Gold bracelets twined snakelike around her arms above the elbows. Nestled between the swell of her creamy breasts was a gold cross suspended from a wide, flat, gold chain. On her feet were blue sandals studded with golden beads.

Long Arrow gasped at her beauty. I realized I had also drawn in a breath I had forgotten to release. She was without a doubt the most exquisite woman I had ever seen.

Immediately two women appeared to escort her to the meeting house at the end of the square. A chair, the only one I had ever seen in an Indian village, was brought forth from the meeting house and placed where she directed. Then a loom, not the primitive kind used by Indians, but of European design, was set before her, as well as baskets of brightly colored thread. She began to weave.

I whispered to Long Arrow, "Let's go."

So mesmerized was he by Maria's beauty that he did not hear me. I took hold of his arm, and he turned his head toward me as though he had forgotten I was even there.

"Let's go," I repeated. We searched the west side of the village, following a trail well worn with horses hooves and wagon ruts. It went to the Okeechobee. Scattered near the inlet where the river and the lake met were several chickees and a large thatched warehouse. In the water were two huge rafts. Wagon ruts ran down a sloping incline to the edge of the water. I realized that wagons were loaded onto or off of the rafts here. But why? All of this had been built since my earlier visits.

By the time we returned to the village, it was dusk. We hid in the woods behind Brave Eagle and Maria's house. Her chair and loom were no longer there, nor could I see her from my vantage point. But shortly after dark the two women accompanied her back to her house. One went in ahead of her, then came back out and nodded at Maria. She then went inside.

We waited until the village was asleep for the night. Knowing that Maria was alone, I sneaked into her home. By now the moon was full, and a moonbeam fell across the bed where Maria lay, her body covered by a light blanket. She slept face down, her hair a black mass fanned out around her head. Her left arm was stretched straight down by her side above the blanket; the right, out at the shoulder, elbow bent and her hand lost under the fan of hair.

I stepped across the room and slid one hand under her hair to cover her mouth, my other around her waist to pull her back against me. As I did so, moonlight flashed on the blade of a knife she held in her right hand.

"Drop it, Maria," I whispered in Spanish. She attempted to stab me, but found it impossible because of the way I held her. "Maria, it's Water Gift. Remember me? My wife Flamingo saved your son. I'm not here to hurt you. I need your help. After I left here, I returned to our village to find it had been destroyed, everyone killed or taken away. My children are missing. I know about Brave Eagle's involvement with pirates. I think he knows what happened to my twins. Maybe you do, too. Can you tell me anything to help me find them?"

She went limp, dropped the knife on the bed, nodding almost imperceptibly.

"I'm going to uncover your mouth, Maria. Don't scream. I don't want to hurt you."

She nodded again. I removed my hand from her mouth but kept my other arm around her waist from behind her. She twisted in my arm and put hers around my neck. Her cheek pressed against mine. It was wet with tears. The blanket fell to the floor, and I realized with a mixture of alarm and unbidden arousal, she had been sleeping naked in the Indian custom.

"I'm so sorry about Flamingo. I liked her very much. She was good to me," she said. "She gave me back my son. And I'm sorry your children are missing. If I can help you, of course, I will. I owe that to you." She pulled back from me and stood full in the moonlight. The creamy beauty of her perfectly formed body took my breath away. I forgot everything but her standing there before me. Then, ever so slowly and gracefully, she reached for her blanket, swept it up and around her body, sarong like, in one motion.

Even while I felt a deep regret that she had covered her beautiful body, I fought the desire that was consuming me. I did not love this woman, but from the very first time I had seen her, she had held my fascination. Her beauty was unbelievable. It seemed to paralyze me. Not only me—it had the same effect on Little Bear when we first visited here. The trader also had been taken by her, as had been Long Arrow. No doubt, so were Brave Eagle and all the red-blooded men in the village.

No, I didn't love her. I didn't even know her. But I desired her. As I stood here alone with her in the middle of the night, I was face to face with a purely sexual feeling for a woman I didn't know. I had never been in such a situation. I thought briefly of Caty back in St. Augustine. My conscience struggled with the feelings Maria stirred up and my love for Caty. But Caty was married to Joseph. Who would know, anyway? Then my conscience reminded me, *I would know*. But I was here, this was now. Suddenly Maria threw her arms around my neck and clung to me. She was weeping. "God, help me," I moaned.

She pulled me down to sit beside her on the bed. Her arms were around my neck, one of mine still around her waist. I was losing control. Then she began to speak.

"Water Gift, I hate it here. I have come to hate Brave Eagle. I hate living like an Indian. Take me away from here. Promise me if I help you, you will take my son and me away," she said as she lifted her lovely face so that her lips were a few scant inches from my own.

I told myself to forget every part of my body except my ears. To listen, not feel. "Tell me everything, Maria," I said. The words sounded unnatural, strained, and were said with supreme effort. But suddenly I knew if I bowed to temptation I would pay, and not only in the hereafter. The price could be not ever finding my children or having Caty again.

As she continued, I willed myself to concentrate on her words, not the body that pressed so close to me, as we sat alone together on the edge of her bed.

"I was brought here against my will. I am a widow. I was on a ship from Mexico bound for Cuba. Our ship was attacked by pirates. They spoke French, and among them was a man who also spoke Spanish. He appeared to be in command. He was called The Eagle by the French, and Brave Eagle by the Indians. When I was found hiding among the cargo with Esteban, I was taken to him. I knew by the look in his eyes that I would be his, that I would have no choice in the matter. It had been the same with my husband. He was much older than me, you see, a friend of my father. He was of royal blood and very rich. He looked at me the same way. When my father gave me to him in marriage I was fifteen. He was fifty-eight. Men had been looking at me like that since I was twelve. But, at least, I remember thinking, this man is young and handsome and he seems nice. Little did I know.

"I know my father had no choice. His fortune was gone, and my husband made a large settlement with him in exchange for having me as his wife. It is done this way often among the upper classes.

"Anyway, Brave Eagle took my arm and spoke soothingly to me. I held my little boy by the hand. He promised no harm would come to us and had us put up in his cabin aboard the ship. There were other women and children also, who had been taken aboard the pirate ship, but I never saw any of them again."

She had said Brave Eagle spoke Spanish. "If Brave Eagle speaks Spanish, why did you and I have to interpret when I was here before?" I asked.

"Because he did not want you to know he could understand you. He trusts no one. Not even me," she said bitterly.

I had taken my arm from around her, and she now sat twisting her hands together, her head down. "I got the idea that he didn't trust you. But when he wasn't around, you wouldn't talk, either."

"I was afraid. He uses my son as a pawn. Esteban adores him."

"You are Maria de la Rosa, aren't you?"

Surprise showed on her face. "How did you know my name?"

"I have been searching for my children among the Indians. I thought they may have been taken in an Indian raid and were slaves of the raiding tribe, or maybe even adopted into it. I think I was right about that much, only I never thought the raider was Brave Eagle. Anyway, I became friends with the leader of the Creek Indian Confederacy, Alexander McGillivray. He found out that Brave Eagle is a Tunica whose village was on the Mississippi. He learned, also, that he had become involved in piracy and disappeared from the Mississippi area along with a large group of followers. Shortly thereafter, the ship you were on disappeared. I had told McGillivray about Brave Eagle having a Spanish wife with a son, so when he learned who Brave Eagle was, his reputation, and that you were aboard the missing ship, he thought Brave Eagle's consort might be Maria de la Rosa.

"But, what of my children, Maria? What of my village, my wife's people? What do you know of what happened to them?"

She began to weep aloud. "When you came here, we had not been here long. Brave Eagle had only one of his two ships left. But your chief brought gold coins to him. He knew there must be more back in your village. He planned to kill you all, but when we learned Flamingo was a witch doctor, I thought she might be able to help my son. In spite of everything, I believe Brave Eagle is fond of him, even though he uses him to make me do as he likes. I have no doubt he is capable of harming him if I displease him, though. Anyway, had Esteban died, Brave Eagle would have lost his power over me.

"He promised me, as he did you, if Flamingo saved him he would let you and your party go; but he told me he would keep you here until his pirates had gone to your village and returned. They were to take your gold and other things of value, including those who could be sold as slaves," she said.

I found myself gripping her by the shoulders, shaking her. "You said they took people to sell. They returned here. Do you mean they brought people from my village to this place while I was here? My children were here even before we left? Are they still here? Tell me, Maria! Where are my children?"

"Yes, they were here. Well, not here, exactly, but on the ship on the Caloosahatchee at the pirate base. But I don't know where they are now."

I still held her shoulders in a vicious grip. "You mean, Maria, while my children's mother was saving your child's life, your husband's pirates were killing, looting, and taking her people as slaves? That you knew about it and did not warn us? That my children were brought here, and we were held so we wouldn't suspect who did it? How could you be so ungrateful? So callous and cruel? Why didn't you warn us?" I had never wanted to hit a woman before. I wanted to now. As much as I had wanted her before, I now loathed her. No, I hated her even more. It took all of my power to keep from hitting her.

"I'm so sorry! Please believe me! I wanted to tell you, but I was scared of Brave Eagle. Scared of what he'd do to my son. Scared of what he'd do to me. I felt so guilty. Oh, Water Gift." She tried to press herself against me, but I flung her away. She sat huddled in a corner of the bed, her feet drawn up, arms held before her as though to ward off a blow.

"I want to hit you," I said. "But I have never yet hit a woman. I've never met one like you before, either. You are despicable," I said.

"Water Gift, I'm really sorry. You don't know. You don't understand. I'm so scared. My life is hell. Please help me. Take me away from here," she begged.

"What about Leaping Cat and Squint Eyes? They came here after we had searched the keys for survivors. Are they here?"

There were several minutes of silence. Then she said, "Did you have a French pirate named Jean in your village?"

"Yes, but what's that to do with Leaping Cat and Squint Eyes?"

"It has everything to do with them. Jean was a pirate aboard Brave Eagle's ship before we came here. When your village was raided, he was freed and brought back here. He helped kill some of your villagers and bring others back. He chose those to be sold as slaves. He told where the treasures were kept and helped to get them. When your chief and your friend arrived, he asked Brave Eagle to give them to him to be his slaves."

"No!" I groaned. *How terrible for both of them,* I thought.

Particularly for brave and proud Leaping Cat. He was so despondent when we parted. And now this.

"Where are they now? Do they sail with him? Are they still alive? Are they treated well?" I asked. I had not seen slaves mistreated in any other Indian village. But the man who "owned" my friends may only have had revenge in mind. And he was a pirate, not an Indian.

"He took them to the ship he now commands. I know nothing else of them," she said.

"You said Brave Eagle had only one ship when he first came here. How many does he have now?"

"He had two, but one disappeared. No one knew what had happened to it until . . ."

"Until my village was raided and the pirate Jean was found there," I finished.

"Yes. Why did you attack and burn that ship?" she asked.

"Because we were less than forty people. We had no weapons against the pirates' guns. We feared for our lives when that ship anchored off our neighboring key. We felt our only choice was to get them first. We could not allow anyone to escape for fear they would return," I said.

"Well, when Brave Eagle saw the gold coins Leaping Cat brought on his first visit here, he knew there must be a lot more in your village. He wanted it to buy more ships so he could enlarge his piracy operation. Your villagers financed his business. He has six ships prowling the Gulf, Caribbean, Florida Strait, and the south Atlantic coast of Florida, now."

"So, they bring the booty into the port on the Caloosahatchee. Brave Eagle brings it here on wagons. Does the trader ship it out through the trading company?"

"Brave Eagle decides what he wants for himself. He has this thing about fancy clothes and jewelry for himself, Esteban, and me. He parades us around the village in outfits that are ridiculous for an uncivilized village in the middle of nowhere."

A vision of Maria as I had first seen her flashed across my

mind. She had been walking through the village with her son and Brave Eagle, and she had been wearing a beautiful and formal white wedding gown.

"Go on. What about the rest of the pirated goods?" I asked.

"He allows the ships' captains a certain amount of the take. Sometimes crew members are rewarded with something that catches their fancy if they have particularly pleased Brave Eagle or their captain. But mostly they are paid a share after the goods are sold. The stuff is brought here and Trader Jim buys what merchandise he thinks he can sell here in the village. The rest is taken by wagon to the Okeechobee where it is rafted across the lake to a river on the other side. From there it is taken by wagon along the bank to a port on the east coast at the mouth of that river. English, French, Spanish, and American ships come to buy the contraband. Some is resold in British, Spanish, and American colonies to the north."

"So, it comes in pirated on the west coast and is bought without question on the east. Don't the buyers know it's stolen goods?"

"I guess they don't care. They save time and money by getting it there instead of having to go across the ocean to China, Spain, or some other faraway place for it," she said.

"You have to get us away from here. Brave Eagle would kill us if he knew I had told you all this," she pleaded. Moonlight shone on a face contorted in fear and anguish. I fought back the twinges of pity I felt at the sight, remembering instead that she had kept silent about my children and their fate, even while my wife was saving her child.

We had talked until the early hours of morning. "I have to go before people begin to wake. I will see you again before Brave Eagle returns," I said. "Meanwhile, try to think of anything that could help me find my twins."

Before she could answer, I was out the door. I found

Long Arrow alert and on guard when I returned to where I had left him. We moved away from the village and returned to our camp. For breakfast we ate corn cakes and pemmican, not daring to build a fire. I told him what I had learned. By then it was dawn. We slept through the daylight hours.

I wanted to find and free Leaping Cat and Squint Eyes. I prayed they knew something Maria did not, or had not, told me. As for Maria, my hatred had turned more to pity, as I began to think about her situation. I suppose she could not have done things much differently without endangering her own child. If she could have, she was too scared for Esteban's safety to say anything. What a terrible thing for a beautiful young woman such as Maria, or for any woman for that matter, to have been sold by her own father into marriage in order to save his property. Then for her to fall into the hands of a savage like Brave Eagle. I do not call the man savage because he was half Indian. I considered him a savage no matter his race. For an exquisite woman such as Maria to never have known the wonders of marriage with someone who truly loved her seemed a travesty. Suddenly, I knew I could not leave her here, either. When I left, she and her boy would go with us. But I would beware of her charms. I could not let my attraction—nay, my lust—further sully her, nor come between me and my genuine love for Caty. She well knew her power over men. She had told me so. And she had learned to use that power to her advantage. It evidently did not work with Brave Eagle, a man who seemed to have no conscience or genuine feelings for any but himself. But, I knew it was there, that it did affect men. She had tried to use it on me. But, could I blame her? It was all she had in life except her son. Her life, her dealings with men, had taught her to believe her beauty was the only thing of value she possessed. She knew it could drive men wild; that men wanted to possess her beauty, her body. So far they had done it to their own advantage. But given the opportunity, she meant to use it to hers. Maybe understanding this would help me to keep my own head, prevent me from becoming her pawn. At any rate, I could not leave her to the nonexistent mercy of her consort. Even realizing the danger she represented to me, I could not do it.

That night I hid outside the trader's house until after the village was asleep. Then I slipped into it and called his name. He woke immediately and jumped from his bed.

"It's all right. I won't harm you. I am Rafael Reyes, Water Gift to the Indians. Remember me? I was here about two years ago with my wife, the Indian witch doctor, Flamingo."

"What the hell are you doing here, man? They'll kill you if they catch you," he said.

"Why are you still here? You must know what's going on."

"I didn't know when I first came. By the time I learned, the only way to stay alive was to stay here. They can't let me leave here, man. I know too much."

"Can I trust you?"

"As long as we don't get caught together, and you promise not to involve me in whatever you're doing here. You may think I'm a coward, but I sure ain't stupid. I know what Brave Eagle will do to a man who crosses him."

"All right. I just want information. I already know about the pirate port on the Caloosahatchee and the trading port on the east coast. I know Brave Eagle is a Tunica King. I know Maria is the widowed daughter of a Spanish official from Mexico, that her ship was attacked by pirates and she and her son were kidnaped. I know Brave Eagle's pirates attacked my village while my wife was here caring for Maria's son. Captives from my village were brought to the Caloosahatchee port. My adopted father, the chief of our village and my friend, Squint Eyes, are captives on a pirate ship. What else can you tell me?"

"Damn, man! Seems like you know it all already. Who told you all that?"

"Never mind that. Maybe it's best you don't know. Do you know if Leaping Cat and Squint Eyes are alive? Are they still slaves of Jean, the pirate captain? Which is his ship?"

"Jean's ship is called the *Captain's Revenge*. He named it that because he got it through his revenge on your village. It is in port now. I don't know about the slaves, though."

"Do you know where my children are? They are twins, Fighting Conch and Fawn. They would be nine years old now."

"No, I don't. Some of the children taken are cabin boys. The rest were sold as slaves. But none are in this village. I am sure of that," he said.

"If I could get you away from here, would you go?" I asked.

"Do you think you could?" I could hear a thread of hope in his voice.

"I have a plan. I have men. Do you know anything about sailing the craft used here?"

"As a matter of fact, I used to captain an American brig. Why do you ask?"

"I need a captain. By the way, how long will the *Captain's Revenge* stay in port?"

"A week to ten days. They'll unload her, bring some Indian women on board, party a few days, load provisions and leave. Why?"

"Because the *Captain's Revenge* will be your ship. We'll leave as soon as it's provisioned. Be ready to go when I come for you."

"But, how . . ."

"That's for me to worry about. No more questions. Are you with me?"

"That I am."

"Expect me to come for you about this time of night, when the village is asleep. Travel light."

"Wait. What about Maria and her boy? They don't belong here. Can we take them, too?"

"What do you know about Maria?"

"She's unhappy. She doesn't love Brave Eagle. She's not here because she wants to be. He parades her around the village like she's his queen, but she's really his slave, his play pretty."

"How do you know all this, my friend? Did she tell you?"

"She didn't have to. I see what's going on. Besides, we have very little chance to talk. Two women accompany her everywhere. Both are kinswomen of Brave Eagle. But they don't know Spanish. I don't speak much of it, but I found a Spanish-English dictionary among the pirate booty just after I arrived. I studied it. She has said things to me, but she warned me not to reply. She definitely wants someone to know her problems. She even slipped me a few notes, and I've put answers in the goods she purchased. She'd leave if she could. I don't want to leave her here."

I realized then that he had fallen under her spell. I felt a pang of pity for them both. But I didn't want to discuss any more of my plan than was necessary with him. I just told him I would have to think about it and see if it could be arranged.

When I left him, Long Arrow and I returned to where we had left our men. I told them my plan. They were to be alert to what was happening. When they spotted the wagons bearing provisions going to the ship, they would know we would be along soon after.

The next night I returned to Maria's house to tell her as much of my plan as she needed to know. When the village had gone to sleep, I entered her door. She was fully clothed and sitting on her bed waiting for me.

"Thank God you've come tonight. He should be back tomorrow night, unless he decides to stay aboard for the partying. I was afraid you wouldn't come back," she said.

"Are you saying Brave Eagle might not return tomorrow?"

She lowered her eyes, twisting a fold of her skirt nervously in her fingers. "Sometimes they have captives aboard the ship. If there are young women, Brave Eagle has his choice. If one catches his eye, he will stay on board with her, sometimes until the provisions are loaded and the ship is ready to sail. If he does stay, he will send Esteban back with the pirated goods," she explained. I could see the hurt and shame she felt when she admitted his infidelity.

"It will make it easier to get you away from here if he stays, but I would not wish that he would force his attention on some unwilling female," I said.

"Nor I. But, from what I have seen here in the village, and even from my own experience, I don't think he has often to resort to force. He can be very charming. He can make a girl believe she is the only one in the world. He can stir up desires and emotions most men only dream they could," she said. Moonlight sparkled on a tear, tracing a path down her cheek.

"You loved him very much once, didn't you?" I asked, feeling pity again for this beautiful, unhappy woman who had been so used.

"That was a long time ago. When I first met him, he swept me off my feet. I thought I had finally found what I had been searching for all my life. But it didn't last long. We had not been here two months the first time he stayed aboard for a party. When he returned three days late, I was worried, scared, and angry. That's when I found out tears bored him, clinging to him gained his contempt, and anger toward him put him in a rage. He told me every detail of what had happened. I didn't want to hear it. It was sick, shameful, and degrading.

"But he would never willingly let me go. I am his possession. Also, he has this thing about royalty and beauty. His wife must be of royal blood, and the most beautiful of women. He would only replace me if he found someone with more claim to royalty than me, someone prettier and younger. And then he would not divorce me. According to their laws, he can have other wives.

"I was afraid you would not come, because I know you must hate me. I'm so glad you did. Please forgive me. Please let me leave with you. You are the only chance I have to get away from here, from Brave Eagle. The only chance I have to live a real life."

"Be ready to leave the night of the day the provisions leave the village for the ship. Bring only what you have to have. You and Esteban must wait in the edge of the woods back there for me. If Brave Eagle is here, I don't know how you'll manage. But you will have to take care of that part yourself."

"But . . . he would never leave the house that night. He will have a hangover, and want only to sleep, if he returns. He is a light sleeper. If we tried to sneak out, he would wake up." Her voice held a hint of panic.

"What about the boy? Will he give you a problem?"

"I can handle my son. But Brave Eagle . . ."

"Maybe you won't have to worry about him. Maybe he won't come home. But just in case, go to the shaman and tell him you are having trouble sleeping. Get him to give you a sleeping potion. Then double the amount you are supposed to take and give it to Brave Eagle in something he eats or drinks before bed. And don't forget, be back in the woods the night of the day the provisions leave. Dress comfortably. Take only what is necessary for a couple of changes of clothing for each of you. Food will be provided courtesy of Brave Eagle."

"How are we leaving? Where are we going?"

"Does it matter as long as you get away from him? You will have to trust me. The less you know, the less you can tell. I'll see you then." And I left her standing there in the doorway, torn between her desire to leave and her fear of what my plan was and whether it would work.

Two mornings later we saw the wagon laden with provisions leave the village bound for the pirate port. After dark that night I went first to meet Trader Jim. He had a light pack slung over his shoulder and was waiting for my arrival. "Let's go get Maria and the boy. They're supposed to be waiting for us in the woods behind their place."

"All right! I was afraid you were going to leave her. But how is she going to get away from Brave Eagle?"

"She was to get a sleeping potion from the witch doctor for herself, but slip it to him in a double dose. Quiet now, and follow me."

We slipped around the outside edge of the village to where I was to meet her. She was hidden behind a tree watching for me. She whistled like a bird and stepped out when she saw me.

"Where's the boy?" I asked.

"He's here, asleep. I will carry him if you will carry our things." She held out a leather pouch with a shoulder strap. Just then the trader stepped forward.

"I'll get the boy," he said.

Maria said, "Jim! You are going with us! I'm so glad!"

"Quiet! Let's go." I reached for her bag. I led them back to the river where my men waited with the dugout. We climbed in and paddled noiselessly away from the village. When we were far enough away that I was sure it was safe to talk, I said in a low voice, "Did you have any trouble getting Brave Eagle to take the potion?"

"He didn't come home. He's still at the ship. I gave half a dose to Esteban, though. That's why he's sleeping," she said.

"But, why?"

"I tried to talk to him about leaving here, but he didn't want to leave. He loves his friends. He loves the hunting and fishing. He's happy here. I could see he was upset, so I dropped the subject. Since Brave Eagle had not returned,

I decided it would be best to give him the sleeping potion so he would not oppose me or make any noise," she said.

"Yes, you were right. It's probably best all around. Perhaps you should keep him asleep until we've left the port. Much will happen that it is best for a child not to see," I said.

"Now it's time to tell you my plan. The wagon has a full fourteen hour lead on us, but we will travel faster in this dugout than the provisions can go by wagon. We should arrive at the port before they finish loading the provisions aboard. After dark when the Indians have left the ship to return to the village, we will board and take it over. We will leave here in it. After we get away from here, I'll tell you the rest," I said.

III

We paddled all night and half the next day, pulling the dugout ashore to hide it just before the last bend of the river before the pirate port. We could hear the sounds of voices drifting toward us from the ship.

Long Arrow and I led the other men through the woods to the place where the river suddenly widened. We left Maria and her son near the dugout. The pirate ship stood on the opposite shore. Trader Jim had learned the ship would not leave until early the next morning, so we would make our move during the night. I gave each his order, posted a guard to watch the ship and trail. The rest of us returned to sleep near the dugout until dark.

Maria was upset that we were going to wait until after dark.

"I'm sure men were sent to look for us as soon as they learned we were missing this morning. What if they find us?"

"I thought of that, Maria. I figure when they found you, Esteban, and the trader gone, they'd think you ran off together. I had Alligator Teeth and Bent Knife leave a trail for them. It led to the Okeechobee. They even stole a canoe, took it out into the lake, and sunk it. When they find the trail, and the boat missing, they will think you left by canoe on the Okeechobee. Their search will start there."

"What if they send someone to the boat to tell Brave Eagle we are missing? They might find us. They might . . ."

"Don't worry, Maria. Do you think they will want to tell Brave Eagle you are missing? I believe the whole village fears him. They will want to try to find you and bring you back before he learns you are gone. I'm sure there is a massive search on for you now. I really believe they will concentrate on the trail we left and the Okeechobee and its tributaries. But I left Brown Bear on guard. If anyone comes, they will surely come by water since that is the fastest way. He will wake us, and we will do whatever we have to in that event. Now, try to sleep and keep the boy asleep with that potion. That way he can't give us away."

At dark I awoke everyone except Esteban. We ate pemmican, dried fruit, and corn cakes. I told my men we were going aboard. I had sent two ahead to take care of the Indian watch posted on the other shore, and they had already returned. I gave orders no captives held by the pirates were to be hurt. They were to be especially careful not to harm Leaping Cat and Squint Eyes and any children if they were there. I wanted Brave Eagle alive, and the pirate, Jean, was mine. I would go directly to Brave Eagle's cabin when we boarded. Maria would stay here with her sleeping child.

The guards had seen no one approach the brig during the night. Clouds now covered the moon, and the night was dark except for occasional flashes of lightning over the gulf. We put the dugout in the water, and the six Creek Indians, Tony, the trader, and I paddled softly toward the *Captain's Revenge*. Lanterns glowed here and there on deck, and the sounds of last-night-in-port partying carried over the water.

As we drew near the boat, we found the anchor line. It was slack, falling nearly straight from the deck. After tying

288 LATRELL E. MICKLER

our dugout to it, we shimmied up it one at a time. We carried clubs and knives tucked in our belts, and Trader Jim had supplied himself and me with pistols. Long Arrow led the way, and I was behind him.

When Long Arrow's head was high enough to see on deck, he scanned it for how many people were there and where. Then he lowered his head to tell me what he had seen.

"There is a pile of rope and some kegs just on deck. We can hide behind them. There are seven men. Three of them are with women. They are sprawled against the cabin wall. One man walks on the far end of the deck. Three are over there, drinking and throwing dice by that lantern," he said.

I assigned a target to each man. When they had taken care of those on deck, one would hold the women together, another would guard the passage to below and take care of anyone who tried to come on deck, and the other Indians would go below, taking care not to kill women, children, or other captives. Trader Jim and I would take care of those in the cabin.

Jim flattened himself against the wall by the door, his pistol cocked and ready. I threw open the door and entered the cabin.

Brave Eagle leapt from the bunk where he had been lying with a young girl not more that fourteen. She screamed in terror as he came at me with his knife. By now, the trader was inside the cabin against the wall by the door, waiting to take anyone who entered.

A sudden burst of wind and wave threw Brave Eagle off balance, his knife missing its mark by inches. The sour smell of his alcohol-drenched breath nearly gagged me. I lifted my club and crashed it down on the hand holding the knife. He howled in pain, his patrician face slack from the effects of the whiskey he had drunk, his eyes filled with rage. He lifted a large, muscular arm and slammed his fist into my stomach, knocking the breath out of me. Then I was on the floor, he astride my belly. His fist was lifted to punch me in the face. The door was suddenly thrown open, and a man burst in, a sword raised above his head. A pistol shot rang out as the trader fired. The pirate, Jean, landed across my face just as Brave Eagle slammed his list down. The blow hit the pirate, knocking him off me. The ship lurched again as my fist connected with Brave Eagle's nose. He fell sideways, blood spurting across my shirt. I twisted from beneath him.

Voices, screams, and thuds came from below deck. The battle was raging between the pirates and my Indians. Jean was getting to his feet, clutching a flesh wound to his shoulder from the trader's pistol. The trader was on him in a flash. "I'll try to take him live like you said. But, I ain't gonna let the dirty scoundrel kill me!" he bellowed.

I realized my strength was no match for that of Brave Eagle. Only the fact that he was drunk had gotten me this far. I either had to kill him with my pistol or knock him unconscious with my club. I needed him alive. I thought he could tell me where my children were. We struggled and rolled around the small cabin, two sets of men tangled together in what could be mortal combat. His hand, large and strong, circled my wrist and held me fast.

The girl sat huddled in terror in a corner of the bed, her eyes wide, teeth chattering. Then Leaping Cat suddenly appeared. He held a club. He lifted it and brought it down on Brave Eagle's head. The chief collapsed, half on me. Leaping Cat brought the club down again before I could stop him. "No!" I yelled. "Don't kill him! We need his help to find the children!"

Leaping Cat seemed not to hear. His eyes were glazed over with hatred. He lifted the club again. "No, Leaping Cat! No! It's me, Water Gift. If you kill him we can't find the twins!"

Slowly he lowered the club. "Water Gift, it is you," he said, as he grabbed my hands and pulled me to my feet. I had rarely seen him show his feelings as he had this night.

Then he turned to the two men struggling on the floor just as Trader Jim knocked the pirate unconscious.

"Tie them up so they can't get loose. I'm going below," I said, leaving the cabin.

When it was all over, we had eleven dead pirates, three wounded who had surrendered and pleaded for their lives, Brave Eagle, and Jean. Both of them were severely wounded. There were three Indian prostitutes that had been on deck plying their trade when we arrived. The girl in the cabin had been taken from an English ship the pirates had plundered. Her father with whom she had been traveling had been killed. Her mother was in New York. Below deck we found my friend, Squint Eyes, and a boy from our former village, sixteen-year-old Dark Feather, who had been serving as a cabin boy.

My men suffered only minor wounds. The element of surprise had been such that the unsuspecting drunken pirates had not had much chance against us.

While the rest of the men brought the bodies on deck to be buried later at sea and put things back in order, Long Arrow, Trader Jim, and I put down a ladder, descended to our longboat, and returned to shore for Maria and Esteban. By now the storm had reached us. It was pouring rain, and lightning struck frequently and with instantaneous loud claps of thunder.

When we reached shore near where we had left them, Long Arrow stayed with the boat. "Maria, it's all right. We've come for you," I called.

She rose from where she had hidden herself and the boy under some palmetto fans in the edge of a large palmetto patch. A flash of lightning revealed us to her. She saw the trader standing there, his clothes bloody. "You're hurt!" she cried and threw herself in his arms.

I went to lift the sleeping child while he assured her the blood did not belong to him.

"We can go as far as the gulf tonight," the new captain of the *Captain's Revenge* said. "But we cannot go into the gulf until we can see. The water is too shallow and the coral heads too numerous and treacherous."

"Well, lets go that far, then. We need to put as much space as we can between us and the village. We'll drop anchor there until daybreak. Do you think you can handle this brig?" I asked.

"I'm sure of it. It will feel good to have a ship again, too," Captain Jim said. From here on the trader would be called by his new title.

They had taken Brave Eagle and the pirate captain below and done what they could for the wounds. I put Maria, the boy, and the English girl, Prudence, in the cabin. Then we set sail in the stiff breeze that was the aftermath of the summer storm. As we sailed, I told Maria that Brave Eagle was badly hurt, having been hit in the head several times with a club. She nodded, but said nothing. I asked her if she wanted to see him. A tear escaped her eye, but she said, "No," in a voice that was barely audible.

Then she looked at the scared young girl who sat huddled now on the floor across the cabin. "He was with her, wasn't he?" she asked.

"Yes. But I can't believe she was a willing partner. She's little more than a child. She was traveling with her father. The pirates killed him when they boarded the ship they were on."

Maria just turned her face away from the girl and said no more.

Prudence sensed we were discussing her. She said timidly, "Who is she? What did she say about me?" For Maria had spoken in Spanish and the girl only understood English.

"Her name is Maria. The boy is her son. She, too, was kidnapped from a ship. Brave Eagle fancied her, also. He made her his wife."

"Oh!" the girl gasped. "Oh, she must hate me! But, I could not stop him. I tried. At first I really tried. But he was very insistent. And he's so persuasive. So handsome. And I was afraid if I didn't do what he wanted, he would give me to the others. He said he'd protect me. And then, he was so kind and gentle with me. I really liked him, and I quit trying. All I cared about was him. But I didn't know he was married. Oh, I wish I had died with my Papa!"

"No, Prudence. She doesn't hate you. She knows about him, about his vices. I'm sure she'll understand when the shock wears off. You mustn't wish yourself dead. You're very young. We'll get you back to your mother as soon as we can. But, first we have other things to do. You calm down. No one is going to hurt you or mistreat you again."

I found Leaping Cat on deck, helping with the sails. I was happy to see that he had regained his spirits and seemed nearer his old self. I asked him, "Do you know where the twins are?"

"I know where Fighting Conch is. He is cabin boy on Brave Eagle's original ship, *Eagle's Claw*. There is a cabin boy of my people on each ship. But, I haven't been allowed to talk to any of them except Dark Feather, who is here. I don't know where Fawn is," he said.

At last I knew where my son was! I felt great joy and relief at learning he was not only alive, but near. I would concentrate on finding him. Maybe along the way I'd learn where Fawn was, too. But I cursed myself for not coming here with Leaping Cat and Squint Eyes after we had searched the islands near our village for them. Maybe the three of us together could have found both of the children and gotten them away from here then.

"I have been looking for them ever since we parted. I won't give up until I have them both back. All of these except Tony are Lower Creek Indians from a village in West Florida called Tallahassoc. They are here to help me. Tony is from a village on the edge of St. Augustine. You remember the trader, Jim, the new captain of this ship? And Maria," I asked.

He nodded.

I continued, "Maria wants to get away from Brave Eagle and back to her own people. He has mistreated her. As for Jim, he, too, wanted to leave the village. The three pirates who surrendered—do you think they will be any help to us? I plan to find the other five brigs owned by Brave Eagle. We will take back my son and any other of the First People we find aboard."

"Put me in charge of the three who surrendered. They know how to rig the sails, and one is a good carpenter. He can make repairs to the ship. They know how to treat the hull to prevent worms from eating away the wood. They are able seamen and navigators as well as pirates," he said.

I saw Squint Eyes just then. He was in the bow of the ship wrestling with a large coil of rope. Excusing myself, I went to him. When he saw me, he dropped the rope. His eyes lit with pleasure at the sight of me. I clapped him on the shoulder. "Old friend, it's good to see you again."

"It's even better to see you," he said in his sober voice. "How did you know we were here? Why did you come back to this place? We thought you had forgotten us."

"I could never forget you. My search for the twins led me back here. I'll tell you all about it later. We'll have plenty of time to reminisce," I said.

At dawn we entered the gulf. Leaping Cat suggested we sail south to Marco Island. He said Brave Eagle's ships had a base there where they all stopped before returning home. It was there that they careened their ships to protect them from wood-boring mollusks that ate away the outer layer of planking.

The pirates would beach their ship, unload it, and mount their guns, one pointed to protect the entrance to the passage between Marco Island and the coast of Florida and another to protect them from the gulf to the west. Then they'd scrape the bottom of the ship, patch it, and smear it with tallow and pitch. According to Leaping Cat, the only ship of worm-resisting cedar that Brave Eagle had was the one we were on, the *Captain's Revenge*. The other ships had to be careened every three months. Therefore, each brig must return here at approximately three-month intervals or risk sinking due to the damage caused by the tiny boring creatures.

"We can find a cove near Marco Island and watch for the other ships to come," he said.

This made more sense than searching the vast seas for them. This way I could not miss them, and they could not return to the Caloosahatchee to find that Brave Eagle had disappeared, as had his wife, her son and the trader—all at the same time the *Captain's Revenge* had left. They would suspect nothing.

We chose a bay northeast of the island. Two men were sent in one of the landing boats to the island where they would watch for approaching sails. Another sentry was posted on a point of the mainland shore to receive the signal, either smoke or the flash of sun on a mirror, that would tell us a ship was coming.

We set up a camp of sorts in the trees off from a sandy beach. Maria took control of the women, telling the three from her village they would not be harmed and would be allowed to return to the village only if they were cooperative. Having been in awe of her since Brave Eagle had brought her amongst them, it was natural for them to obey her. Prudence was another matter. She was sullen and spoke only English. Maria had ignored her until now. Prudence was torn between the guilt she felt concerning what she and Brave Eagle had done and the jealousy she could not help feeling for the beautiful Maria.

Maria's son, Esteban, had awakened to find himself and

his mother on the *Captain's Revenge*. He could barely remember the voyage from which they had been kidnaped. To a young boy raised in an Indian village, being aboard a pirate ship was high adventure. He was full of questions about how he got here, why, and where he was going. He also asked about Brave Eagle. Maria handled his questions somehow. It may have been true that he adored Brave Eagle as Maria said, but the great affection between mother and child was definitely evident. So was the resilience of youth, and it gave me hope for my own children.

I went below to see the captives. Brave Eagle had regained consciousness. He was chained to his bunk and under guard. His face had suffered the most damage. His eyes resembled those of a raccoon, so black were the circles around them. His nose was broken, and there were several gashes about his face and head. One hand, the one I had smashed with the club, was horribly swollen, and he needed to be bathed, shaved, and his wounds tended.

"Brave Eagle, I am Water Gift. Do you remember me?"

"You're the bastard that took my ship," he said.

"Before that. I came here with my wife, Flamingo. Your village had an outbreak of the sleeping sickness."

Recognition dawned in his eyes.

"I have come back to find my children and the others who were stolen from my village. I have searched for them since I returned there and found only death and destruction. Then I learned about you and your love of piracy. It all added up. Aboard this ship I found my two old friends, Leaping Cat and Squint Eyes. Also, the cabin boy, Dark Feather, is one of us. I have learned that my son, Fighting Conch, is also a cabin boy aboard one of your vessels. But where are the women and girls? Fighting Conch had a twin sister, Fawn. What happened to her?" Brave Eagle had lain impassively in his bunk staring at the ceiling while I had spoken. Suddenly, he turned his face toward me and spat in mine.

Angry, disgusted, and filled with hatred toward him, I reached down and tweaked his broken and misplaced nose until he screamed in pain.

"Now, shall we start over? By the way, Maria is here. And the boy."

I saw in his eyes a flicker of something. But, he smothered it immediately,

"Eleven of your men died when we took this ship, in addition to the guard you posted on shore. The other three sailors have joined us. Now we lay in wait for your other ships. I will destroy your whole pirating operation. I will destroy you if you do not tell me where my daughter is," I said.

He turned his head away from me. In a rage I grabbed his nose once more and used it to turn his head toward me. "You will look at me when I talk to you," I said.

"Go to hell," he replied.

Realizing I was getting nowhere with him, I turned to the pirate, Jean, who had been a captive in my village at the time of the raid. He, too, was chained to his bunk. "Where are the women and children of the First People?" I asked.

Taking his cue from Brave Eagle, he just stared at me. I'd had enough. I had not come this far to let Brave Eagle have the upper hand. I suddenly remembered a terrified, vomiting Jean at a corn festival several years ago. I turned to Alligator Teeth who had accompanied me below. "Send out the hunters. Tomorrow we will have a great feast. We will sacrifice this one to the spirits, so that they will look kindly on our mission. He will be burned at the stake during the festivities." I spoke in the language of the Calusa. Neither Brave Eagle nor Alligator Teeth understood a word I said. But Jean was too terrified to realize they didn't.

"No!" he screamed. "I will tell you what I know. Please! Oh, God, no! Don't do it. I'll tell you!"

Brave Eagle gave him a look that chilled even me to the

bone. "Shut up! I'll eat your heart myself if you tell him anything!"

"Get me away from him! I'll talk! Kill him instead!"

I had Alligator Teeth bring Jean on deck so we could talk away from Brave Eagle.

The chief screamed threats and curses at him in Spanish, French, and Tunica. We left him shouting. Jean was terrified. His face was covered with beads of sweat, his complexion a sickly pallor. He was afraid of Brave Eagle, afraid of me. But for now, I was in command, and he knew it.

On deck I found a comfortable seat for him on a coil of rope. I called for Leaping Cat to join us. After all, he was chief of the First People, and his wife and grandchildren were among the missing. "Now tell us what happened to our women and children," I said.

"Do you promise to protect me from Brave Eagle? That man is crazy, capable of anything. Will you take me somewhere safe and leave me unharmed?"

"I make one promise to you, Jean. If you don't tell us what we want to know, you will burn at the stake until you are dead, a sacrifice to the spirits who guide the First People."

He shivered, a look of wild terror on his face. How I hated this cowardly pirate who had turned butcher against the people of my village, and who, I was sure, would do the same for any victor to save his own miserable hide. But he held the key to finding Fawn and the others. I had to control my hatred.

"When we sailed into port, Brave Eagle was sent for. The women and children were with us. All the females who had reached puberty were brought on deck to be shared among us after Brave Eagle had his choice," he began.

"What of my wife, Little Wren?" Leaping Cat broke in.

Jean averted his eyes and hesitated a second. Leaping Cat pulled his knife, placing it at Jean's throat. Jean screamed, looking to me for protection.

"Leaping Cat, please. Put it away. He will tell us all he knows. If you kill him we will not learn where to find any of them," I reasoned.

Reluctantly, he did as I asked and put the knife back in his belt. For the first time I saw on his face a look of hatred.

"Continue," I told Jean. "What happened to Leaping Cat's wife, my adoptive mother?"

"Rather than submit, she grabbed a knife from one of the men, ran to the edge of the deck, and shoved the knife into her stomach before she threw herself into the river," he said, looking nervously from Leaping Cat to me.

Tears rolled down Leaping Cat's cheeks and suddenly he appeared to be a very old man. I could see it took great control for him to prevent himself from killing Jean immediately. "I'm sorry, Leaping Cat. She was a brave and good woman. Her death was a tribute to that goodness and her love for you," I said.

"She died an honorable death. She lived an honorable life," he said, gaining control of himself. "What of the others?"

"Each captain chose a cabin boy. Then we took the women, girls, and other young boys by boat across the Okeechobee to the port where Brave Eagle sells goods and prisoners. An American slave ship bought them all."

"The ship's name? Do you know it, or that of its captain?" I asked.

"No, but we later heard the ship was set on by French pirates from Guadeloupe in the leeward islands. The captain of that ship was Robert Marchant," he said. "That is all I know of them."

Although I questioned him for a long time, I was convinced he could tell me no more. Leaping Cat was also sure we had learned all he could tell us. Before I could stop him, he leaped upon the pirate and slit his throat. I stood there in horror, and he said, "I have avenged Little Wren."

There was nothing I could do. It was done. I could not help but think the man had an easier death than he deserved. It had been quick and humane and occurred so suddenly, he was probably not aware of what had happened.

Then Leaping Cat scooped up the body and carried it below deck. I followed and watched as he went to the bunk of Brave Eagle and dumped the body on top of the chief as he lay in his bed. Then Leaping Cat turned and walked out without a word.

But Brave Eagle knew, as I did, that this was not so much a warning as a promise of things to come.

We waited for perhaps a fortnight until the sails of not one, but two ships appeared on the horizon. I did not think we had enough men to take them both. I decided we would watch and wait until both had been unloaded and turned upside down for repairs. On the third night my spies told me all was ready. We sailed the *Captain's Revenge* into the harbor of Marco Island in the dark of night when all were asleep in the palm-thatched huts that made up the camp. The fight was neither bloody nor long. Those pirates who would not surrender and join us were few and were killed in the fight. Neither ship was the *Eagle's Claw*, so my son was not among them. There were, however, a twelve and a fourteen-year-old, both cabin boys, who were from my former village. They were delighted to be free and to be in the company of Leaping Cat, Squint Eyes, Dark Feather, and myself. We had now freed five of the First People.

The pirates who had surrendered finished careening the ships. Even though they professed to join us, we had taken their weapons away and kept them under careful observation. The ships had not been repaired and returned to the water a full day when the third ship appeared. It came on, seeing its sister ships, suspecting nothing. We waited until everyone had come ashore, the Indians, Captain Jim, Maria and the woman and boy, and I out of sight. Then my men surrounded them. They all surrendered. By now I was getting nervous. I had no stomach for killing, but we were greatly outnumbered by our prisoners. Although they swore allegiance to us, I didn't trust them. We had forty-five such pirates versus eleven of my men, four teenage, Esteban and the women. I could not be sure about the three Tunica prostitutes, either, although Maria vouched for them.

I called the cabin boys together and asked them to tell me who were the worst of the pirates. Then I decided we would take these men, a dozen in all, and make examples of them. I hoped this would not only keep the others in line, but rid them of their gruesome leaders. We held a trial for each, with witnesses against them. I was surprised to see many of their former shipmates testified to the cruelty of these men. They were each found guilty, and each was carried to a separate small island in the area known as ten thousand islands. There each was marooned with a bottle of water, a bottle of powder, a pistol and shot.

Now there were thirty-three of the former pirates and fifteen men and boys, plus the women. That some could be trusted, I had no doubt. And there were among them several boys between the ages of fifteen and nineteen.

Captain Jim and I drew up a set of rules to be followed and assigned the men I trusted most, a couple from each ship, to police the others. I promised them that those who followed me in truth would be allowed to keep all the booty they had in their holds at the time they had entered Marco Island, minus provisions we would need. I also promised them two of the four ships we now held. They in turn had to promise to remain friendly with us and to turn to legal means to make a living with the help of the ships they would be given. If they kept their bargain, they could also have the other two ships after my mission had been accomplished.

Before we saw the sails of the fourth ship, I ordered all but the *Captain's Revenge* be hidden in the bay where we had waited, and that they be stripped of their sails and the sails placed below deck on the *Captain's Revenge*. I now felt sure we were fairly safe.

Maria decided she wanted to see Brave Eagle. Both Captain Jim and I tried to dissuade her. She said she had to face him. By now the cuts were angry purple scars, the bruises reduced to yellow stains on his skin. The bone in his nose had begun to knit. His guard told me Brave Eagle himself, in a supreme command of his own will, had taken hold of the lopsided nose and put it back in place. It appeared that except for some scars, he would still be a handsome man.

Maria had gone below and sent the guard out. I followed and, unbeknownst to her, stood just outside the open door.

"So, you've finally come," he said. "Come over here and sit by me," he commanded her.

"No. I'll stand. Where did it go wrong between us?" she asked.

"Maria, what do you mean? You know I love you. I always have. You are my beautiful queen."

"No, Brave Eagle. I'm not your queen. I never was. I was more like your slave. You liked to show me off. Your beautiful possession, but love? No. I believed that once. It seems so very long ago. When we first met, you were so charming, so sweet to me. Even though you had kidnaped Esteban and me, you were kind to us. You didn't force me to do anything. Before we had come into your port on the Caloosahatchee, I was in love with you. You had been kinder and more tender than any man I had met. And I loved you so much. I believed I had found someone who loved me, too. Not just someone who wanted to possess my body. But, then we had not been married long when you began to sleep with other women. You drank too much. You hit me. Still, I could not stop loving you. Worst of all, you used my son as a weapon against me. You threatened to harm him if I did not do as you liked."

I could hear her sobbing . I heard his chains rattle as he

reached out to take hold of her. She stepped back, didn't allow him to touch her.

"Maria, I do love you. Those other women, they meant nothing to me. It was always you I loved."

"The girl, Prudence. You told her the same things you told me. She told me so. You told her how beautiful she is. How much you loved her. That you would make her your wife. That I am getting old. Im just twenty-five, Brave Eagle. She is only fourteen years old, a mere child."

"If I said those things to her, I must have been drunk. I only love you, Maria. Come here. Let me show you how much I love you."

"You can't charm me anymore. It's over between us. That's what I came here to tell you."

"It's not over. It will never be over. You will never get away from me. You belong to me. If I can't have you, I will fix you where no one will want you." He lurched at her, pulling the chains that bound him to their limits.

Maria screamed. From somewhere in the folds of her clothing she pulled a pistol, loaded and cocked. She shot him in the chest before I could shout, "No, Maria!"

He fell back on the bunk, a look of shock in his eyes. His dying words were, "You're mine, Maria. You've killed me, but even in death you're mine. You'll never get over me. Never forget . . . ."

She tossed the pistol to the floor while I stood frozen in the doorway. She seemed unaware of my presence. "You can't hurt me anymore. You can't threaten Esteban ever again. You're dead now, and I don't have to be afraid of you anymore," she said in a voice calm and cool as she turned to leave.

"Maria . . .," I started.

"I did what I had to do," she said, and pushed past me. She seemed more sure of herself and more in control that I had ever seen her. In that moment my pity for and hatred of the beautiful Maria was gone. She had regained control of her son's and her own lives. And she had killed the man I hated more than any other—the sinister, sneaky slime who had ravaged Flamingo's people while she was helping his. I suppose we both felt a great weight lift from us.

The *Eagle's Claw* came limping in. Her sails were torn and sooty; great holes punctured her hull. When she drew near, someone aboard her yelled, "Send boats to pull us ashore! There are only five of us left alive!"

About ten of us boarded the craft, while others attached lines and pulled her ashore with powerful arms bent to the oars of the smaller boats.

I asked for the captain. "Dead," they said. I told them I was taking command of the ship and asked if they wanted to join me or fight. After they realized I had control of the island and the other ships, they opted to join me. Then I saw him. He was propped against a keg, blood running from a gash in his forehead. "Fighting Conch! Are you all right?" I was beside him in an instant, checking the wound, stanching the flow of blood with my shirt.

He looked into my face, recognition dawning in his eyes. "Water Gift, my father. Where have you been?" he asked.

I hugged him to me. "Thank God you are alive," I said. I remembered Flamingo's death, and felt the smile fade from my face.

"My mother. Is she here?" he asked, as though he read my mind.

"No, I will tell you about her later. Now I have to take care of that wound." I removed the shirt I had been holding tightly to his head. The wound did not appear life threatening. I tore the shirt into strips and tied a bandage around his head.

"I had a dream," he said. "My mother came to see me. In the dream she told me good-bye," he said. "It's true, then. Flamingo is dead." It was not a question. It was a fact he had already accepted. I held him to me.

"Yes," I said. "She died of the sleeping sickness. We were

ready to come home to the village when she fell ill. I'm so sorry. She loved you and your sister so much."

"My sister. Where is she? Have you found her?"

"I haven't found her yet. I have been looking for you both since I returned to find the village destroyed. I have found three other boys besides you, Leaping Cat, and Squint Eyes. I will wait here for the last of Brave Eagle's brigs to come in. I have been told the cabin boy is one of us. Then I will look elsewhere for Fawn."

"There is no need to wait. That ship was with us. We came upon a Spanish merchant ship and raced in for the attack. The *Dark Dance* shot across her bow. The *Eagle's Claw* hit her broadsides, winging the rigging. Then a man-of-war that had been shadowing her out of sight came about and attacked us. The last we saw of *Dark Dance*, it was afire and sinking. Our own sails had been set ablaze, and men were attempting to douse the flames when we took a cannon ball through the bow. We ran for it, but they kept firing. Shrapnel was raining down on us. They chased us for some ways, killing most of the men and nearly sinking us. Then they noticed the merchant ship was also on fire. They turned back to help her, and we got away," he said.

There was no longer any need to stay here. We had one badly wounded ship and four in good shape. There were barely enough men to handle three. I gave the pirates two of the ships, and except for enough to provision the *Captain's Revenge*, all of the pirated goods that had been aboard them. We parted friends, and I felt reasonably sure they would keep their part of the bargain and not attack us. After they had gone, we took the other two ships, one at a time, into creeks along the coast, took down the sails and stored them below decks, and hid the ships as best we could with limbs and foliage. We removed the cannons, adding two more on deck the *Captain's Revenge* and storing the other two below.

Now I had to find the Leeward Islands and Robert

Marchant. But first, I kept my promise to the three Tunica women. We took them back to the entrance to the Caloosahatchee and gave them rations to eat on the walk back to Brave Eagle's village. We told them to tell their people what had happened to Brave Eagle and his pirate band. We hoped from here on they would be peaceful and treat others as they would like to be treated. The women had become friends and great admirers of Maria. They stood crying and waving as we sailed away, leaving them on the shore.

IV

At night I lay in my bunk and thought how good life was aboard the *Captain's Revenge* reunited with my son. I felt I had a new chance to be his father, a father in practice instead of just the husband of his mother as Indian fathers are, and I liked it. His head was healing nicely and we were together constantly.

I had abandoned my Indian identity. There was no longer a need for it. Maria cut my hair in a fashionable style, and I asked everyone to call me by my real name, Rafael. I discussed it with my son, and he didn't mind my calling him Juan from now on, either.

Mindful that this time of year was the hurricane season, I told Captain Jim to get us through the Florida Strait and head back up the keys until we found the island of the ruined village of the People where I had lived with Flamingo. We would stay there until November when the storm season was over.

One night while we were on the island, after all the others were asleep, I awoke Juan. We slipped to the site where I had buried the Spanish treasure, dug it up, and hid it aboard ship in a secret compartment Leaping Cat had shown me in the ship's hold.

Although the season brought several tropical storms and northeasters, no hurricanes came to the keys. In late November when the danger of hurricanes was over, we left, our next stop Tortuga Island. Here we bought provisions at outrageous prices from stores owned by pirates. We sailed past Hispaniola, Puerto Rico, and the Virgin islands, finally reaching the Leeward Islands.

These islands are the top half of a group forming a crescent in the Atlantic. The bottom half of this string of islands is called the Windward Islands. Guadeloupe is at the bottom of the Leeward Islands. It is shaped sort of like a butterfly, with its main port, Pointe-a-Pitre being between the wings at the bottom. It was here we came in search of Captain Marchant.

I ordered the Indians to stay aboard, along with Maria and her son. The rest of us went ashore. We learned in the nearest tavern that Captain Marchant was not in port.

One of the former pirates who had joined us was something of an artist. Since Juan and Fawn were twins and looked very much alike when I had last seen her, I asked him to draw a picture of a female version of Juan. I took it to all the taverns and stores in the town, offering a reward for information that led to my finding her.

We stayed at Pointe-a-Pitre for about ten days, and were reprovisioning the ship to leave port, having had no leads as to Fawn's ever having been here. Then I heard a commotion on deck and ran up to see Brown Bear about to throw a lad I didn't remember ever seeing off the ship. The boy was speaking in French, but I understood enough to know he was trying to tell them he had news of the girl in the picture.

"Let him go and send Henri, the artist, to me," I said. I led the boy, who was perhaps seventeen, to a crate and motioned for him to sit. When Henri came, I told him I needed him to help me understand, for Henri spoke Spanish as well as French.

The boy's name was Robert. He said, "The girl in the picture—I think I know her. But she was never here. I was a cabin boy on Captain Marchant's ship. He took her, along with others, in a raid on a slaver. The girl I remember was a brave little girl, and she knew a lot about healing. I was kind to her. One day she noticed I had sores on my arms and legs. She carried a pouch on a rawhide thong around her neck and under her shirt. She got some powder from it and put it on my sores. She did that every day for three days. The sores began to heal and finally went away. When I told Captain Marchant, he allowed her freedom of the ship and access to the ship's medicine. She was just a child, but she treated all the ill with amazing success.

"Then about six months ago, we were on Barbados. Captain Marchant was drunk and gambling with the captain of another ship. The other captain had heard of Fawn's healing abilities and wanted her for his ship. He won her in a game of chance. Things were not the same after she left. I hid when the captain took the ship out of port last month. I would like to join your crew and help you find her," he said.

"What was the captain's name, the one who won Fawn?" I asked.

"Captain Jones of the *Racing Moon*," he said.

"Welcome aboard, Robert. Get your things and say your good-byes. We leave as soon as you return."

"I have no one here. I have nothing. Let us go," he said.

So we left Pointe-a-Pitre, Guadeloupe, bound for Barbados to the south-southeast. We arrived a few days later to learn the *Racing Moon* had left port for parts unknown.

There was a sinking feeling in my chest. I had been searching for such a long time. Every time I had a good lead, I followed it up, only to find I was too late. However, I had no choice but to continue on. I couldn't bear the thought of just sitting in Barbados and waiting for the *Racing Moon* to return to her home port. I learned she usually returned about every three months to be careened. I would search for her in the meanwhile, returning here at the expected time of her arrival if I had not found her.

We sailed around in the Caribbean between the Leeward and Windward Islands on the east, New Granada to the south, and Puerto Rico to the north, before returning to Barbados, having seen no sign of the *Racing Moon*. Nor did it return when expected. While I waited, anxious and fearful, news of Captain Jones's ship arrived. It had attempted to take a merchant ship north of Puerto Rico. Spanish men-of-war guarding the merchant ship sank the *Racing Moon*. It was believed all hands went down with it.

I was in shock. I had searched for so long. I had been so close. Now Fawn was dead. Not even Juan could comfort me. *Flamingo, dead. Fawn, dead. Ana and Caty lost to me. Why? What had I done to deserve such losses? There will be no solace for me,* I thought.

After a time of wallowing in pity, I decided I should take Maria to Havana where she could reunite with her people. Fighting a deep depression, I paid little attention to what went on around me as we sailed across the Caribbean. I was truly shocked one evening late when I entered the captain's cabin without knocking, thinking to have a few drinks of rum with him before retiring to my bed. For there on the bunk sat Captain Jim with his arms locked around Maria. So absorbed were they with each other, they didn't even know I had opened the door. I retreated and closed the door as quietly as I could.

"So," I thought, "that's how things are." Then I remembered things I had seen that didn't register, because I had been so wrapped up in my own plans, and then in my grief and pain. Things like the way Maria's eyes followed the captain everywhere; the way their eyes fairly smoldered when they locked and held; the way he never moved close to her without putting a hand on her shoulder or waist or arm, however briefly; the way they sat together when possible and spent so much time talking to each other. They were in love. Then I wondered if I would lose my captain when I reached Cuba.

By now I had learned all I needed to know about sailing the ship. My crew was well trained and congenial. I knew we could manage. I would talk to Jim tomorrow.

I returned to my bunk, and for the first time since I had learned of the sinking of the *Racing Moon*, my mind turned to other things. High on the list was love—my love—my Caty. She came to me once again in my dreams. She was sweet and beautiful as ever. And unlike when I had last seen her, she did not hold back the passion she felt for me.

Jim and Maria planned to be married as soon as arrangements could be made. They asked me to stay in Cuba to be their best man. I paid Jim for his services and gave him a handsome sum as a wedding gift. I arranged for a tailor to make suits for Juan and myself.

Even after the wedding, I was in no rush to leave. Then, suddenly, one day it hit me: I, too, had once been believed dead. But I lived. No one knew for sure that Fawn had died. I would visit every island in the Caribbean. I would show my drawing at every tavern. Perhaps I would find her yet.

I could tell Captain Jim nor Maria thought I would find Margarita. But I guess the forbidding look on my face kept them from trying to dissuade me.

The *Captain's Revenge* sailed out as soon as I could provision her. We sailed first to New Providence in the Bahamas, then on to Tortuga and Port de Paix, Leogain, Petit-Grove, and Santo Domingo, Hispaniola. We left Hispaniola for Puerto Rico, then onto St. Thomas and St. Croix in the Virgin Islands. We made our way down the Leeward and Windward Islands and Barbados, stopping at every port. No one recognized the drawing of Fawn.

We sailed on to Trinidad, Margarita, Caracas, and the

islands of the lesser Antilles. From there we went to Gibraltar and Raracaibo, then on to Rio de la Hacha, Santa Maria, Cartegena and Tolu. We crossed the Gulf of Darien and stopped at Portobello. We were all suffering from scurvy. I had been pushing the men too hard and they were grumbling. We spent a pleasant three months ashore, eating plenty of fresh fruits and vegetables. But all the while I fought the anxiety to resume the search, to find my daughter.

We left Portobello healthier, and I promised the men we would slow our pace, spending more time in port. Our next stop was Providence Island, then Santiago de la Vega, Jamaica. We arrived back in Cuba, at Santiaga, in July 1784. I decided to stay here until the hurricane season had passed.

All this time I had found nothing to encourage me in my search. One evening in early October, I entered a local tavern, one that I had frequented since arriving here, to find a different girl serving tables. She was neater and cleaner than those I had previously seen here. I learned she was the tavern keeper's daughter. When she approached my table, I saw on her finger a ring. I grabbed her hand to look at it. The emeralds, sapphires, rubies, and diamonds formed a bright and beautiful peacock.

"Where did you get this?" I demanded.

She jerked her hand away and put it under her apron. "It is mine," she said defensively.

"But where did you get it? My son has one like it," I said, and thrust Juan's hand toward her.

She looked at Juan's ring and then his face. A look of confusion entered her eyes, and she started to back away.

"No! Don't leave, please. We won't hurt you. Please! You know Fawn, don't you?" And I pulled the paper with her likeness on it from my pocket and held it out to her. ""I am her father. I have been searching for her. I gave her that ring when she was a little girl. Please help me find her," I begged.

"I cannot talk to you now. If you will wait, we close at midnight. I'll talk to you then."

Juan and I were so excited, we couldn't eat. The hours dragged by until midnight when the girl came back to our table. Her name was Lucia.

"Where is Fawn?" I asked.

"I cannot tell you that, because I do not know. She came here about three years ago. She had been aboard a pirate ship that was sunk when it tried to attack a merchant ship. She and a few survivors were picked up by a man-of-war that was escorting the merchant ship. The captain took her to his home to help his wife. Their home is in the next street.

"Fawn worked all day helping the woman, Mrs. Estavez, and then the woman hired her out to my father here at night. Mrs. Estavez came to collect her pay. Fawn told me she didn't mind the work, but the woman was cruel to her, beating her frequently.

"We became friends. She told me about her village and how the pirates came killing, destroying, and kidnaping. She told me about you and her brother and Flamingo, her beautiful mother.

"One night when she came to work, her eye was black and swollen, and she was limping. She said she was going to run away. She had a place in mind, but she wouldn't tell me where. She said I was her only friend, and she wanted me to have her ring. She gave it to me, honest," Lucia said.

I believed her. I questioned her some more, but was convinced she had told me all she knew. She said Fawn would not tell her where she was going for fear the Estavezes would somehow make her tell them.

Fawn is alive! At least I knew that. *But, where is she?* We searched the whole village, even going so far as to peek into windows at night. I showed her picture at every door. Although some people remembered her, none had seen her since she ran away from the Estavez house.

As for Mrs. Estavez, I visited her, too. She denied that she had ever been cruel to Fawn. She said she had treated her as one of her own, had even taken her to church on Sunday and had her baptized, made into a Christian. Then she said, "The ungrateful little wretch ran off, probably with some sailor she met at that tavern where I got her a good-paying job." She did not say that she was the one who collected that pay.

I had picked up my daughter's trail again and just as quickly lost it.

We left Santiago in December. I stopped at Havana to visit Jim, Maria, and Esteban. Maria was happily awaiting the birth of a child. They were delighted to learn that Fawn had not gone down with the pirate ship.

I decided I would search for one more year. If I didn't, by then, have a trail to follow, I would return to St. Augustine, to Caty and Ana, at least for a while. I ached to be with them, too. I prayed they would be there, safe and alive. As for Joseph— well, I'd cross that bridge when I came to it.

Hurricane season was over for another year. I had spent this one in Campeche, Mexico. I had not found Fawn nor any hint that I was on her trail. I was tired and feeling far older than my thirty-eight years. I had despaired, after searching all these years, of ever finding her. She and Juan were now fourteen. I wanted Juan to have an education. And Caty— Lord, how I wanted and needed her and our child, Ana.

I left Campeche and headed for the Florida Strait. I felt I was finally going home—home to my people—home to my Caty.

What would I find in St. Augustine? I didn't know. But I couldn't let myself think that I wouldn't find Caty and Ana there. They had to be there. They had to want me as I wanted them.

Conclusion

Father Camps' face was grave. "I have discovered what happened to your first husband, Rafael Reyes," he said. He walked past me into the room. Turning, he said, "Come, my child," he beckoned to a girl of perhaps fifteen years who was with him.

She was beautiful, tall and graceful, with long, straight black hair falling to her waist. Her skin was slightly darker than my Ana's, her eyes as black and slightly slanted. There was a cleft in the middle of a chin that looked so familiar. Her clothes were neat, clean, of Spanish cut, and very reserved. I knew before Father Camps said so that she was Rafael's daughter.

"What we have to tell you will come as a tremendous shock, Caterina." He led me to the sofa, for I was shaking, and no doubt he feared I could not make it on my own. He helped me to sit, then sat beside me. He motioned the girl to a chair.

"This is Margarita. It is her story, so I'll let her tell it. But, I must tell you," he said kindly, "I have no reason to doubt her."

The girl began, "I was born and raised in a small village of the First People on an island in the Florida Keys. My mother was of the People. Her name was Flamingo. My father was from a place called Minorca. He was shipwrecked, washed ashore, and adopted by my great-uncle. He had no memory of his past. He married my mother.

"After my brother and I were born—we are twins—his memory returned. I remember when I was very small he used to call me Margarita, even though my Indian name is Fawn. His name before he came to our village was Rafael, but among The First People, he was Water Gift, a gift of the sea.

"One day Water Gift, Flamingo, my uncle, Chief Leaping Cat, and another man left on a mission of importance to all of us. While they were gone, pirates came. They killed many people and kidnaped women and children. I was sold to a slaver. His ship was attacked, and I was again stolen, this time by the captain of the attacking ship. He lost me while gambling with another ship's captain. Then the new captain's ship was sunk by a Spanish man-of-war while he was trying to rob a merchant ship. I was taken to Santiago, Cuba, where the man left me with his wife.

"Mrs. Estavez treated me cruelly. I cleaned, cooked, and cared for her children all day. She had me work in a tavern at night, and she kept my pay. I was only ten when I came to her. I hated it worse there than I had at sea. One day after a terrible beating, I ran away.

"The priest of Santiago had been kind to me. I had been baptized by him. I went to him for help. He arranged to send me, along with a priest who was passing through, to Havana by ship. There I was taken to a convent where I lived with the nuns and studied medicine.

"My mother had been an Indian medicine woman. She had taught me about herbs, medicine, and healing. I, too, was to be a medicine woman. Now, I am a nurse. I have finished my training. The nuns wanted me to be one of them, but I did not feel the call.

"My father had talked of St. Augustine. I asked Mother Superior to help me to get here. I thought I might find my father. She asked the bishop of Cuba to arrange passage for me, and he did.

"When I arrived today, I immediately looked up Father Camps. But, he says my father is not here, and that he was thought dead since the shipwreck seventeen years ago.

"Did Father Camps tell you who I am? What my connection to Rafael is?" I asked.

"He only said there was someone I should meet. But when you opened the door, he said he had found your first husband. Did he mean my father?"

"Margarita, my husband and I were married and expecting a child when he was shipwrecked. When I received word the ship had broken up and sunk in a hurricane, I did not believe he was dead. I would not believe it. Then someone found the captain's log. It said he had been injured on the head and leg and swept overboard. There was no doubt he had drowned.

"Our child was born, a daughter. Her name is Ana. Later I married a wonderful man named Joseph Adams. We had a son, Joseph Jr. My second husband died," I said.

"My father, Water Gift—he always had a slight limp. And on his forehead from eye to hairline there was a scar. It happened in the hurricane. They were the same, your husband and my father, weren't they?" she asked, a look of wonder on her face. "I was not sure—it had been so long ago I heard him say his other name, Rafael Reyes. So long since I had heard 'Minorcan' and 'St. Augustine.' The clues were so little. But it was all I had to go on.

"I didn't want to spend all my life in a convent. The nuns were very good to me. They cared for me and taught me. I could not have made it without them. I am grateful to them for all they did. I believe in the Catholic faith they taught me. But I did not feel the call to be one of them. So, I had no other hope, no other place that I might go to find someone I am related to" she said.

Rising, I went to her and knelt beside her. I hugged her to me, tears filling my eyes and spilling down my cheeks. "Welcome, Margarita. I am so happy you are alive and well and that Father Camps has brought you to me. You will stay here with my daughter, Ana, and me, won't you? Wait, don't answer yet."

I turned to Father Camps. "I have a confession, Father. But first, I want Ana to hear, too. Please excuse me while I get her from the garden."

I returned with Ana, having told her she was going to meet her half-sister. After introducing them, I told the three of them the secret I had kept for seven years.

When I had finished, we were all in tears. "Father," I said, "forgive me. I did the best I could. I really didn't know what was right or wrong. And I loved them both so very much."

"My child, come to me in the confessional, and if there was sin, I will absolve you of it. I do not know how I could have helped you earlier, if you had come to me. I did not have an answer for all the questions you pose. I might have had to contact Rome. It could have taken years to get an opinion. You are a good, strong, brave woman, and you have struggled with this alone for so long. I believe you did your best to protect Joseph and your children. As for Rafael, he had this quest for his other children. He, too, has been brave and strong through it all. He could not have been a husband to you and a father to Ana and still be gone to search for them.

"Where is he now? Is he still looking for Margarita and her brother?" he asked.

"I don't know where he is, or if he is still alive. But, if he lives, I know he is still searching. I saw him last in May of 1780, more than five years ago."

Margarita asked, "What of my mother? You speak of my father and his being married to Mrs. Adams, but he had another wife, Flamingo. As an Indian, he could have two wives. As a Christian, he could have but one."

" I had forgotten her," said the priest, turning to me, his face questioning.

I put my arms around Margarita. "I am so sorry to have to tell you this. Your mother died of the sleeping sickness before Rafael returned to your village. Rafael told me she had saved the son of a chief's wife and some other villagers who were stricken with it. Weakened from nursing them day and night, she herself became ill and died. Your father said she was a good and courageous woman, and he loved her very much."

Ana and Margarita became fast friends. Margarita began her nursing career at the Spanish military hospital. Ana and her beau, Marc Generini, were making plans for a wedding in the spring. And I had a new spring in my step. My heart was no longer heavy with the guilt I had carried for so long.

All was finally right between my beloved church and me again. I said many prayers of thanks to the Virgin Mary for helping me through all these years of confusion and grief. Only one thing was lacking in my life now. It had been lacking for seventeen years. Rafael. My need for him was a living, growing thing, and there was no longer a reason to deny it.

I prayed that he was alive and well with even more fervor, and that he would soon return to his family. Each morning, Ana, Margarita, and I lit candles in church for his safe and soon return.

Christmas and New Years passed. Our home had become a lively gathering place for Ana, Margarita, Joseph, and their friends. One evening in late January Margarita had to work the evening shift at the hospital. Ana and Joseph were visiting the home of Ana's betrothed, Marc. I found myself alone except for Mandy, who was finishing something in the kitchen.

I decided to curl up in bed with a book, something I had not done in a long while.

I was lost in the pages of an exciting novel, when a hand appeared and took the book away. A startled cry escaped my lips before strong arms encircled me and warm lips covered mine. Rafael had returned!

When he lifted his head from mine, I said, "Oh, Rafael, I have so much to tell you . . ."

"And I have so much to tell you. But, not now," he said. "I've waited seventeen years for this night. I can't wait anymore. I won't." And his lips again covered mine.

What followed was so wonderful, so long in coming and so very much worth all the waiting. My love, my Rafael, had returned to fill at last a place in my heart that had always been only for him.

THE END

Author's Note

The story of Dr. Andrew Turnbull's colony, New Smyrna, named after the birthplace of his wife in Greece, is a matter of history. The mistreatment of the colonists is well documented. Visitors to St. Augustine can see a statue honoring the colonists, whose descendants represent the largest number of families to continuously reside in the area, on the west side of the Cathedral facing St. George Street. It depicts Father Pedro Campos (Peter Camps) and a family of Minorcans, and was created by the sculptor Josep Viladomat. Many names on the statue are still prominent in St. Augustine and St. Johns County.

William Bartram, a naturalist who traveled Florida and chronicled the vegetation, animals, and people of the period, described the Indians and their villages. Although the Calusa (the First People in my story) were presumed to have left with the Spanish a few years previous, some historians acknowledge a few may have remained hidden in the Everglades (Grassy Water) region.

Although the uprising in the Minorcan colony that appears early in this book, and the fate that befell the leaders, actually happened, I have taken the liberty of having it occur one year later than it really did.

Some historic characters inhabit the pages of this book, but their interaction with fictional characters is also purely fictional.

Pirating and smuggling was a part of the history of the period, as was the sinking of ships on Florida's reef. Hurricanes, too, made regular visits to the area. And as for snow, although it is extremely rare, December of 1989 saw it fall over much of Florida, and it didn't melt for several days. It is not impossible to believe snow could have on rare occasions fallen two hundred years ago in the area.

I would like to thank my husband Yulee for his patience and encouragement in this endeavor and in everything I do. A special thanks to my daughter, Cathy, who taught me to use a computer, and whose computer expertise solved most of the computing crises I experienced while typing my manuscript into the computer. Thanks also to the rest of my family who are always supportive of me. I also wish to thank Mary Sue Keoppel, Professor of Communications and Journalism at Florida Community College at Jacksonville, for reading one of my first drafts of *Indigo*, and her critique and kind encouragement.

I would be remiss if I did not mention some authors whose works have been invaluable to me in writing *Indigo*. I have already mentioned William Bartam, without whose work I would not have been able to describe the Indians or villages that Rafael visited in his search for his lost children. Also extremely important was the first book I found about the Minorcan colony and my Minorcan ancestors, E. P. Panagopoulos's *New Smyrna, An Eighteenth Century Greek Odyssey*. Jane Quinn's *Minorcans in Florida* and Patricia C. Griffen's *Mullet on the Beach* were also helpful. I turned to Charlton W. Tebeau's *A History of Florida* for information and confirmation of the history of the era. *America's Fascinating Indian*

Heritage from Reader's Digest Books increased my understanding of Indian customs. *Pirates,* by David Mitchell, was essential in developing that part of *Indigo* dealing with pirates and pirating. Thanks to all of them, I found the information I needed to blend fiction with the history and environment of eighteenth-century Florida.

Latrell E. Mickler

Jacksonville, October 2000